I0614404

Once Upon a Snowy Moon

by

Cheyenne Meadows

Once Upon a Snowy Moon

Cover Art by *Debbie Taylor*

The Wild Rose Press, Inc.
PO Box 708
Adams Basin, NY 14410-0708
Visit us at www.thewildrosepress.com

Publishing History
First Black Rose Edition, 2018
Print ISBN 978-1-5092-2413-5
Digital ISBN 978-1-5092-2414-2

Published in the United States of America

Dedication

For my sister, Teresa,
who always believes in me
and encourages me to persevere.
Your support and encouragement is amazing.
I couldn't continue to weave stories without you.
Thank you from the bottom of my heart.

Chapter 1

Men suck.

Tara cut one more scathing glare to the guy who was supposed to be her blind date for the evening, spun around, and ran smack into a solid wall of a man wearing a dark suit. A fleeting scent of subtle cologne waved through the air, adding to the overall picture of a built guy with expensive taste. Attractive and wealthy normally caught a woman's eye. Not hers and certainly not right now. Especially since she just happened to greatly dislike the opposite sex as a whole. "Oh, excuse me."

He steadied her and offered up a crooked smile, his blue eyes catching her attention. "No worries." His grin faded. "Are you all right? You seem distracted."

She nodded, all too eager to leave the establishment and the source of her latest debacle. "Yes, thanks for asking. My date just sank like the Titanic so I might as well get going. Nothing worth hanging around here for now." Pushing past the guy, she hurried to the parking lot and her waiting car.

Tara opened the door, tossed her purse to the passenger seat with a huff, then plopped down. A quick jerk settled the seat belt over her before she clicked it into place. "I swear. What's the point of going out on dates when they all end up being creeps? I can find those on my own. Already have. Like a legion of

1

them." She shoved the key into the ignition and cranked the engine as a shiver rolled through her. Her long coat didn't curb the frigid wind, not when she started out wearing a frilly blouse, slacks, and flats. Unfortunately, the car's heater would take a bit to warm up but at least she had shelter from the mess outside.

Snow came down hard, with large flakes landing on her windshield, nearly obscuring the view until she clicked the wiper blades. The defrost on high helped to melt them as they landed, only to be shoved away as liquid with each swipe of the blade. January in Minnesota never was for the faint of heart.

"The perfect ending to a crappy day." She'd been excited about the upcoming event. Sort of. After the fiasco of the last three, things had to be better. Or so she thought. Too bad this guy took one look at her, and a flicker of disappointment and disgust covered his face. He greeted her, drew her toward the bar, then he changed direction and struck up a conversation with a skinny beauty perched on a nearby seat when Tara excused herself to go to the bathroom. By the time she returned, he ignored her and seemed planted on the bar stool, entranced with the lithe redhead next to him.

Tara took the hint.

Loneliness had followed her around like a dark cloud day in and day out for the past few months. She saw all her friends happily tie the knot and move forward with their lives to other parts of the country with equal parts sadness and envy. It left Tara the remaining single woman out of the large group of good friends from Wells dorm at State College.

She wanted what they had. Happiness. Love. A companion for a lifetime of adventure. Someone to come home to every night and to hold her as they slept. *Is that asking too much?*

Tara pushed her hair away from her face and sighed wearily. "How many rejections can a girl take before she recognizes the outright truth?"

Deep down, she knew the answer. She'd had enough.

Slipping the car into gear, she carefully eased out of the parking lot and onto the snow-covered street. While the snow wasn't deep yet, the blustery conditions made visibility difficult. She leaned forward, kept her eyes on the road, and said a quick prayer to get her home safe and sound. With the weekend upon her, she had a little over a day to dig out before having to worry about traveling again. *Once I reach home.*

"Face it, Tara. You couldn't find a good man if he jumped out in the middle of the road and you hit him with the car." With the endless snow and white out conditions, she probably could do just that. Cautiously, Tara drove at a snail's pace, keeping her eyes locked on the way in front of her the whole time.

Nearly home, she turned off the highway and onto a much smaller road. A dark colored blur appeared out of nowhere. Tara slammed on the brakes and fishtailed to a halt.

Thud.

Oh, my God. Fear sent icy tendrils around Tara's heart. She clutched her chest as her pulse raced and breathing became difficult. Knowing what she had to do, Tara opened the door, pulled the coat around her, and stepped out while sending up another small prayer. A few steps to the driver's side tire found a large lump lying in front of her car and nearly in the middle of the road. The bright snow and car headlights illuminated the area enough for her to make out more details. A tail. Muzzle. Dirty, mud-encrusted fur.

A dog. And a big one at that. Sadness and horror drove her feet forward until she knelt at the animal's side. Covered in mud, muck, and a layer of frozen precipitation, the dog didn't move. Still, she had to be sure. Hesitantly, she placed one hand directly in front of his nose and the other on his side and waited. Seconds passed. Just when the first tear fell, she detected a breath. "Oh, thank goodness."

Glancing around, she realized her predicament. Well away from a main road and the nearest vet, she had no one to help. Her cell phone never picked up a signal in this area, and the lack of traffic during a blizzard pretty much ensured she was on her own. Her gaze dropped to the injured animal once more.

His eyes opened and he whined.

Her heart broke, prodding her into action. Tara shucked her coat, spread it out on the snow nearby, then very gently turned the dog from side to side in order to get the material under him. While he didn't protest or try to bite, she watched him with a keen eye, knowing that any injured animal was dangerous. While she didn't detect any broken bones, that didn't mean he didn't have internal injuries or a concussion. She couldn't know for sure until they visited the vet. *Which won't be tonight with all the offices closed.* The nearest emergency clinic in Rockford was over an hour away. On another evening, she'd gladly go there. Tonight, with the roads worsening every minute, she knew she couldn't make it.

If he's too hurt to survive, at least he'd know

warmth, food, and love before he goes. Her eyes welled up once more.

Ignoring the flood of tears, she focused on the present need—getting him off the road.

"Okay, puppy. Here's the deal. I'm going to use the coat like a sled, pull you to the back seat of the car, and lift you in. Please, please don't bite me." The possibility of rabies flashed through her mind. If he became aggressive, she didn't have many options. No muzzle. No tranquilizer. She had to rely on her gut instinct and his placid demeanor. Hopefully, it would be enough.

She stood up and started tugging, relieved when the coat slid easily on the quickly rising layer of snow. As soon as she opened the back door, she gathered up her courage, wrapped the coat around the dog, and whispered to him as she lifted.

"Dang, you're heavy." She awkwardly held him around the middle, trying to aim his long legs into the open door without banging him around in the process. Two tries later, she managed to settle him inside without a single fuss from him. Thankfully, although the lack of fight worried her all the same. "Such a good puppy." She scrambled to shut the back door and plop down into the driver's seat on the slippery surface. "Let's go home. I know it's not much, but it's better than here."

****

How do I get myself into these messes?

Max stared into the brunette's green eyes filled with compassion and caring. She'd been kind enough to stop and pick him up out of the road. Not everyone would have done so. On his last leg, he'd resigned himself to succumbing to the elements as all hope vanished with the brutal storm. Then the woman appeared, lugged him into her car, and took him to her house.

Now, she kneeled next to the porcelain bath tub, busily bathing him while he soaked in the shoulder high water. Her rolled up sleeves didn't protect her from getting wet but, instead, said something about her. She wasn't afraid to get dirty. Considering all the muck and grime now coloring the water, he'd been a walking glob of ick. And she'd be carrying half of it by the time they finished. She'd already emptied the tub and refilled it with clean, hot water twice. Yet, she hadn't hesitated a moment, just lifted him up out of the car and carried him straight to the tub. Her smudged dark green blouse told of her determination and concern. She made him the priority. The thought amazed him.

"Poor baby. You've been on your own for a while and not doing so well at it."

If the bath didn't feel so good he would have protested. *Who the hell am I kidding?* She hit the nail on the head. Thus, the reason she found him collapsed on the rural road, in the snow, nearly frozen to death. Meals were few and far between in the frozen tundra of a Minnesota winter. Hunger gnawed at him day and night. Even when he managed to catch something, it was always small and never satisfied him completely. Add in the cold, the caked mud on his fur, and the lack of shelter, and he was on the edge.

"That's okay. Your luck just changed. You found a home. With me." She rubbed the cloth over his head. The scent of the baby shampoo she'd dug out from a cabinet tickled his nose. "We'll be best friends." She smiled at him and scrubbed over his chest.

Best friends? Oh, goody.

She dropped her hand down to rub over his stomach than back between his legs.

He jerked as she wiped over tender areas. *Whoa. Hey lady, that's my dick you're scrubbing. It's attached, too.* No sooner had he breathed a sigh of relief when she moved onward than she lifted his tail and rubbed all around his rear. He winced in embarrassment. If that wasn't degrading enough, she edged her hand lower and washed his balls with the soapy rag.

"Oh, you're still a boy. I mean, an intact boy. We'll have to make a visit to the vet soon to get that fixed."

Oh, hell, no. Try to neuter me and I will *kill you in your sleep.* He eyed her warily, thrilled when she seemed satisfied with the cleanliness of his junk and sought out new parts. If he had the strength, he'd jump out of the tub and make a dash for freedom through the front door. As it was, he could only stand there on shaky legs and tolerate her fussing.

"First of all, I need to come up with a good name for you. Let's see." She studied him a second before commencing with the washing. "How about Bingo?"

Really? Bingo? Do I look like a yappy, bouncing Jack Russell terrier to you? He met her gaze with annoyance.

"No? Well, how about Fred?"

As in Flintstone? He wanted to beat his head against the walls of the tub. Before he could, she pulled the plug to let the dirty water out and plucked the shower wand from its holder and used it to rinse him off. The heated water warmed him from the outside in while soothing his itchy skin and body aches.

"Fido?"

He sneezed.

She laughed, the sound easy on his ears. "I take that's a no. Hmm. This is harder than I thought."

For a long time she focused on her task, going quiet in the process. "Oh, look at you. So pretty. All white. I never even thought that would be the color when I picked you up. Definitely a looker." She continued rinsing. "Considering this revelation, how about I call you Cotton?"

How about not? Still, it was better than the other ideas she'd had so far. Marginally.

"Such a good boy. Not even trying to bite."

He stared at her vexed. *Yeah. Yank on my dick again and all bets are off.*

"I wonder what kind of dog you are. Husky? Malamute? Heinz 57?"

Dog? He was tempted to snort. *At this rate, she'll be tossing me doggie cookies and trying to teach me to play fetch. Again, why me?*

Because I screwed up, that's why.

"It doesn't matter. I like you just the way you are. Long legs, big boned, stocky, pointy-nosed, bunny ears, and all." She grabbed up a nearby towel and started rubbing it over his face. "Besides, dogs are so much better than men. Loyal. Unconditional love. Snuggle buddies."

Max nearly choked on his own spit. *Unconditional love? Bunny ears? Snuggle buddies? Where does she come up with this crap?*

He caught a glimpse of himself in the standing mirror in the corner. Considering he stood on four legs and was presently covered in thick fur, her idea, however far off the mark, made sense. Dogs could be all those things. However, he wasn't a dog. Not even close. Sure, he shared some common DNA, but enough of the wild side ran through his veins to make him less of a lap puppy and more of the big bad wolf. A hybrid at that—if you considered a subspecies cross between an artic wolf and an eastern timber wolf a hybrid. Only wolf researchers and the Throwback Pack seemed to note the difference or even care. More importantly, he was part wolf and part man. That made him a wolf shifter.

One that obviously sucks at living solely in my wild form.

"Out you go. We'll get you dried off. While you hang out in the living room, I'll see about getting you some hot food." The woman picked him up with one arm around his chest, the other bracketing in his hind legs, and hefted him out of the tub despite his size.

He'd give her credit for strength.

Once again, he studied her. Her kind green eyes reflected hope and sympathy. The flawless complexion and deep brunette hair that was presently pulled back into a ponytail, accentuating her round face. All those traits spoke of beauty, intelligence, and kindness—something he'd never seen in the same package.

Hell, he'd never seen anything remotely resembling empathy in any of the pack females. The rare human woman he'd crossed paths before didn't sell him on the idea of the fairer sex possessing the ability to love or even capable of anything more than their own agendas.

So far, this lady seemed to be the exception to the

rule but only time would tell.

A few minutes later, she tossed the damp towel into a nearby hamper and made her way into a nearby room.

Max followed along hesitantly, fatigue limiting his number of steps. Pain radiated up and down his right shoulder, testament of being bumped by the car. Thankfully she'd been going so slowly or she would have squashed him in the road. *At least it would have been quick rather than this death by starvation and freezing.*

His inner beast growled in annoyance at the thought.

Yeah, yeah. I know. Over the past several months, he'd been on his own. Pain had pretty much been his only friend in one version or another. Wounds, injuries, and hunger became everyday obstacles to be dealt with. He hadn't given up yet, but it was damn close.

With nowhere to go and fearing being caught by his relentless pursuers, Max simply kept moving around, searching for a new place to stay, but always coming up empty handed. He had no phone, no money, and no identification. Add in the lack of clothes and he was pretty much screwed as a human. In his wolf form, he managed. Sort of. Even then he'd been quickly failing as a lone wolf trying to make it entirely on his own.

He ignored the pain, taking comfort in the fact that it would probably disappear when he shifted. Although, when that might happen, he didn't have a clue. With the weakened state of his body, he didn't have the strength to pull off the feat. Not yet, anyway. Time and food would remedy that fairly quickly, though. He'd try as soon as he could. Weakness would lead to his downfall and he wasn't ready to call it quits yet.

He watched as she pulled a package out of the fridge, placed it on the counter, filled a pan of water, then set it on the stove. After turning on the burner, she added the meat, and placed a lid on top. Another pan followed in the same way.

The clothes outlined a body that reminded him of a real woman. No skinny runway model, yet not obese, either. Just healthy without hints of diet obsessions that some ladies fixated on these days. He found her shape pleasing to the eye nearly as much as her rounded face and compassionate eyes. Dark brunette hair had been pulled back and cinched with a fancy emerald green barrette. Hanging free, he knew it would hit her mid-back and hold a natural curl that added to a sense of mischief and playfulness that he'd glimpsed on her face for a scant second.

The scent of raw meat set his stomach to growling with immense hunger. He hadn't eaten for three days and couldn't wait much longer to get something into his gut. That or he'd collapse, this time for good.

"I know you're starved. I figured boiled chicken might be better on your stomach than something else. But, that will take a bit to cook. So, let's find you a snack." She returned to the fridge, opened the door, and searched.

Yes. Oh, heavens yes. He waited impatiently for her to come up with something. Anything. At this point, he'd eat cardboard if he had to.

"Aha." She pulled out a container, placed what appeared to be a couple of hamburger patties on a plate, covered them with a napkin, then put them in the microwave. The machine kicked on as Max counted down the seconds.

A peppy beep launched Max's feet into gear. Just as she set the plate on the floor, he drew in the intoxicating aroma of food and wasted no time in digging in. He scarfed both pieces down and licked up the juices remaining on the platter.

The woman lowered a plastic bowl filled with water next to him. "Here you go. Fresh water."

With his immediate needs satisfied, he lapped up water as if the streams were drying up. Nothing had ever tasted as good with the exception of the hamburger.

She patted his head. "Good boy. That should tide you over until the chicken is done. I don't want to give you too much too soon and risk you vomiting."

Yeah, not my idea of a good time, either.

"We should take care of business then." She looked around then disappeared down the hall once more.

Business? Surely she didn't mean what he thought she meant.

She emerged a second later with a bright pink belt in hand.

Yeah, she did. He blew out a resigned breath.

She took a narrow leather belt, slipped it through the metal clasp, and placed the resulting loop over his head. "This will work. I don't have any dog supplies, so we'll just make due for now." Two paces took her to the front door. "Let's go outside and potty, then we'll settle in and wait for dinner to get done."

Max followed along dutifully, though with a decided lack of enthusiasm. *If the bath wasn't humiliating enough, now I get the honor of peeing three*

12

*feet from her and at the end of a leash. The good times
keep on coming.*

The biting wind and pelting snow along with his
still damp fur encouraged him to find a spot and
quickly. Not picky, he hobbled over to a nearby large
rock, hiked his leg, and did his business. *Thank God I
don't have to do anything more. Talk about mortifying.*
He finished and hurried back.

If Jacques were here, he'd be laughing his ass off.

Jacques. His best friend in the world. Hell, his only
friend. Who might or might not have succumbed to his
injuries. Max longed to know how he'd fared, but had
no way of finding out. Living as a wild wolf limited his
options as did his lack of money and opposable thumbs.

Tara let them back inside the house and locked the
door behind them. "Dinner should be done very soon. I
know you're more than ready."

No kidding. He found a rug near the heating vent
and plopped down. The air warmed him as well as
assisted in blow drying his coat. A win-win situation in
his book. At least for now.

Taking the opportunity to check out his
surroundings, he noted the kitchen and living room
shared one large space without any apparent dividers. A
couch and a recliner along with one end table served as
the sole furniture in both rooms. A small television sat
on a stand in the corner. The size of the screen was
enough to make a far-sighted person squint severely in
order to see a show. Several area rugs of different
designs but in the same basic colors covered most of
floor. Laminate in deep redwood peeked out where the
rugs didn't quite meet. A short hallway led to the
bathroom while a single bedroom sat right across from

it. One more doorway at the end of the hall probably contained a utility room or a second bedroom or perhaps even a storage area.

Small but cozy. While nowhere near a mansion, the house appeared clean and tidy. Respect for the lady grew. She might not be able to afford much but apparently cared for and took pride in what she possessed.

His nose told him she lived alone. No other smells mingled with hers, either human or animal. Just the lemony odor of dusting spray and the tantalizing aroma of dinner mingled with her individual scent. The combination wasn't off-putting.

Maybe, just maybe, this can be a safe place. For a few days, nothing more.

He ran through his options and decided he had no choice but to accept the woman's offers. He truly was at the end of his rope.

"Here you go." She placed another glass dish in front of him along with the same water bowl as before. The pieces of chicken had been torn apart, making them more nibble sized. He didn't care. Too hungry to mince details, he dug in, savoring the flavor of the first full-sized, hot meal in seemingly forever. The blandness didn't bother him a bit. Food was food and he was too hungry to be picky.

As he filled his stomach, he kept an eye out for his new roommate. She disappeared for a couple of minutes only to emerge from the hallway carrying an armload of blankets with a pillow perched on top. She placed all of them on the floor and arranged them into a fluffy pallet. "I don't have one of those fancy dog beds, but I thought this might do."

He licked more pieces of meat from the plate and chewed, his attention divided between her and the rapidly emptying plate.

"I wouldn't mind you sleeping in my bed, but I'm afraid you'd hurt yourself trying to jump down, especially since I'm still not sure what injuries you might already have. So, better safe than sorry."

The idea of sharing her bed intrigued him until he recalled his present animal form. *She sees you as a pet, not a man, dumbass.* Besides, he'd had enough problems with the fairer sex to last him a few lifetimes.

"I'm going to take a shower. Promise to be back soon." She caressed his head with a gentle hand. "Rest, Cotton. Heal. And don't worry. You've found your forever home." With a quick smile, she strode back the way she'd come.

Max watched her go before settling on the blankets, finding both warmth and comfort. He carefully stretched out, laid his head on the pillow, and sighed. After weeks on the run, he'd finally found a safe place to spend the night.

Worries evaporated as he closed his eyes and fell into an exhausted sleep.

Chapter 2

The tantalizing aroma of food woke Max the next morning. He sniffed the air and his mouth began to water. Standing up, he turned in order to spy the woman flitting about in the quaint kitchen, fixing breakfast, dressed in loose light gray sweat pants and a matching top. White socks covered her feet and a scrunchie held her hair back away from her face.

Tara. Tara Livingston. The name fit.

He'd woken in the middle of the night, discovered that she'd covered him with a soft throw, and had went to her bedroom for the night. Her consideration touched him as well as increased his curiosity about the woman who'd clobbered him with her car, then carried him home and treated him like a loved one. With night having long since fallen and the soft sounds of Tara snoozing away, he decided to do a little snooping— after quickly shifting to human form. The transition pretty much healed his wounds but also sapped his energy. Still, his inquisitiveness demanded he check things out while having the freedom to do so. A quick glance at a couple of bills on the small kitchen table told him her name. No other details came forth except for the fact that she appeared to be single, far from wealthy, and worked a regular job. Doing what, he didn't have a clue. Relegating himself that time will tell, he'd returned to his beast form, plopped back down on the comfortable bed of blankets, and soon fell back asleep.

Until now. When the delicious scent of hot food made his stomach rumble.

She chose that moment to turn around. A quick smile appeared on her lips. "Good morning, Cotton. I trust you slept well?"

Would it be asking too much for her to forget that ridiculous name in her sleep and come up with something better? Like Savage or Death or something equally powerful.

Obviously so. Damn it, anyway.

He considered her query. Indeed, he'd slept well. Too well. He hadn't heard her rouse from bed, emerge from the hallway, enter the kitchen, or even gather the items to prepare for their meal. The realization proved concerning especially since his survival depended on his being aware and observant. *Many more slip ups like this and I'll be dead before the next full moon.* He shook his head and forgave himself just this once. After all, he'd known nothing would bother him while he stayed with her. A warm place to sleep along with the first decent food in ages made him lazy. And damn reluctant to turn down future offers of pampering by hitting the road once again.

"I fixed all kinds of goodies for you. Sausage, eggs, and bacon." She glanced over her shoulder and back again. "Pancakes too, although I'm not so sure if they're good for you."

He just about snorted. Anything and everything would be perfect and highly digestible. As long as she didn't get to the store for some nasty dog food. Or worse, insist on taking him to the vet. A check-up would be useless. Vaccinations wouldn't agree with his system. Neutering proved just too horrific to think about. Which meant he had to convince her to bypass the veterinary clinic.

"I've got a big ham in the freezer I can fix for lunch. You can have the bone to chew on." She turned back to the skillet on the stove and poked at the sausages.

Bone? I can have the bone? He groaned to himself. *Give me the whole fucking ham, lady. I'm hungry.*

An idea sparked. She'd probably return to work in a day or two. She mentioned a freezer. Surely she wouldn't mind if he helped himself to whatever was in there. The plan solidified and improved his mood greatly.

Testing out his injured shoulder, he took a few steps, then trotted into the kitchen to sit at Tara's side. For the first time in forever, pain no longer existed. Just lingering fatigue and hunger. A definite improvement. Hope resurged along with the knowledge that a few days of doing nothing but eating and resting would do the trick of getting him up to par once again. More than that. Back up to his old self. Stronger than since he'd left the pack, and struck out on his own.

Leaving, shit. More like being driven out and barely escaping alive. The resulting wounds took weeks to mend despite the advantages of carrying shifter DNA with genetic programming to heal rapidly.

Tara plucked a platter from the counter and started loading it with links of sausage. Bacon waited on the other end while a separate plate contained a heap of pancakes.

Max's stomach growled again. He thumped his tail

and stared up at her with a pleading expression, knowing she'd give in.

"Hungry, huh?"

Ya think? He added a small whine to punctuate the previous non-verbal request.

She dabbed the meat with a paper towel, then set the offering on the floor.

He stared at her for a moment, a bit confused. *Surely, she didn't fix all that just for me?*

"Go on. Eat up. That's yours. A couple of pancakes will be more than enough for me." She smiled and patted him on the head.

Not about to wait for a second invitation, he dug in, forcing himself to chew rather than gobble down the delicious food in huge mouthfuls. He'd never tasted anything so good. The slight spicy flavor of the meat only added to the deliciousness. Greedily, he crunched the bacon, devouring every slice before finishing off the last of the sausage.

Finished and appeased for the moment, he peered up at Tara again, finding her watching him with a warm smile. "You might eat me out of house and home but I'm not about to give you up." She gathered up the pancakes, carried them to the table, and sat down. A couple of condiments awaited as well as a full glass of milk.

Max would have loved to drink down the cool liquid but wasn't dumb enough to try to stand up on his hind legs, place his front paws on the table, and dip his tongue inside. Tara had been more than accommodating, downright generous, in fact. His continued stay at her house revolved around him minding his manners. At least for right now. Once she returned to work and left him to his own devices, he'd finally have some freedom to do whatever he liked. Including supping some of the delicious looking milk.

"I wonder where you came from. Lost? Dumped? Did you get frightened and run away? Have a good home at one time and lost it? Or perhaps, a bad home that treated you cruelly?" She stuck a fork full in her mouth as she maintained eye contact with him.

You wouldn't believe the story if I told you, lady. Max sat quietly and watched her eat. He craved to share the rest of her meal but refused to press the issue. Besides, better to take smaller amounts more frequently than try to stuff himself like a glutton at Thanksgiving. Strength and stamina would return if only given some time and patience. With the frozen tundra outside and the comfortable accommodations inside, he wasn't ready to take off. *Yet.*

His bladder tingled in warning. Needing to make her understand, he swiveled his head and stared at the front door.

She reached out and ran her fingers over the top of his head. "You seem smart. Definitely well-behaved. Probably even housebroken. A definite plus." She dipped another bite into syrup then placed it in her mouth and chewed.

Yeah, and if you wait too much longer, I'm going to prove you wrong and soil your floor. He trotted to the front door and whined.

"Oh. You need to go potty." She jumped out of the chair and hurried over.

Potty? Oh, my god. What am I? Three?

As soon as she unlocked the front door and held it open, he darted outside, shivering when the thick snow coated his legs and brushed against his stomach. As part arctic wolf, he should have been right at home in the harsh conditions. Hell, his other half, an eastern timber wolf, normally dealt well with the ravages of winter. Those days were long past that he played in the white fluff and braved the wind to do its worst. At least the snow had stopped, but the stiff breeze cut right through his tattered coat and to the hide beneath, sending a shiver coursing through him. He kept his tail down and hurriedly found a spot away from her prying eyes in order to do his duty. Bad enough to have to pee on a leash last night. No way would he poop that way. Better to just find a partial clearing, do his business, then be done with it. Max dug his nails into the ground, made some scratching motions, and darted back. A single bark had the door opening with Tara shaking her head as soon as he stepped inside.

"Stay right here. Can't have you running around the house covered in snow like that." She hastened to the bathroom then returned a few seconds later with a large towel.

Max signed in resignation as she dried his belly then each foot in turn. Sure, he could have protested the treatment but didn't think she'd be thrilled if he made the couch soggy with wet feet. So, he stood still for a bit, then wiggled away.

"Much better." She scratched behind his ears. "You're such a good boy, the way you listen to me. Just like you actually understand what I'm saying."

Uh, huh.

"Let me look you over. I can scrape the driveway and get you to the emergency vet if needed." She ran her hands over his body, thorough, yet gentle, paying particular attention to his hips, shoulders, and legs. Much like the bath from last night, she handled him with gentleness, yet didn't miss a single spot.

"Anything sore?"

Like I'm going to answer? He would have rolled his eyes if he could have. Instead, he stood impatiently for her to finish the inspection.

She took his right front paw in hand and checked out the pads, spreading them to peer in between each one before lightly squeezing. Seemingly satisfied, she moved on to the next one.

By the time she rubbed her hand down the middle of his belly, he'd lost patience. Not because he tired of her hands on his body, but because she moved ever so close to his cock, which had decided it liked the full body massage and responded accordingly.

Well, shit. Just what I need, a hard-on. Like that is going to be easy to hide.

He arched his back and wiggled out of her reach.

A frown appeared on her face. "Hold still. If you're injured, I need to know."

Oh, you'll know all right. Keep petting me like this and you'll find more than you bargained for.

Her hands returned to where she left off, brushing against his shaft.

Max sucked in air and squirmed.

"Does that hurt?" She palpated lightly all along his stomach.

Hurt? No. Make me horny as hell? Yes.

He stared directly at her, relieved when she seemed appeased and moved on to his hind legs.

"It might not be a bad idea to have you checked out after all."

Oh, hell, no. Not like a vet worth his salt would miss the fact that he wasn't a dog at all. Thinking fast, Max darted to the kitchen, grabbed the hot pad from the counter top, then ran back to her. Once there, he dropped it directly in front of her.

She glanced down, picked it up, then smiled. "You want to play fetch?"

Not really, damn it. But if he didn't get her mind off the vet and onto cooking, he'd be in trouble.

She tossed the mitt back into the kitchen.

Dutifully, Max trotted over to retrieve it. *Just call me a fucking Labrador.* He picked it up with his mouth and returned. Only this time, he held onto it.

"Let me have it." She lightly tugged on it.

He spat it out.

"Good boy." She smiled and scratched under his chin before tossing it once again. "Go get it."

He looked at her, then the mitt, then back to her. With a lift of his head, he jumped up on the couch and settled in.

"Guess fetch isn't your favorite game." Tara stood up.

No kidding.

She smiled at him with amusement. He found the expression beautiful, playful, and endearing. "Maybe you really are okay after all. You're eating, drinking, pooping, peeing, and dancing around. Surely, if you were hurt, that wouldn't be the case."

Bingo.

"I know you still need to be checked out, but if we can wait a few days, that would be so much better." She frowned slightly. "I don't want to put you at risk, but rent on the shop is due tomorrow. Things are tight, especially at this time of year."

He heard the sadness and worry in her voice, causing a flinch of pain in the vicinity of his heart.

Mentally, he shook his head. *I'm leaving. Soon.* The promise sounded weak to his own ears.

She shrugged, then put on a forced smile that didn't reach her eyes. "Since you're not up for more fetch, I'll see about a few chores." She disappeared down the hall.

Warmth from inside took a few minutes to replace the chill of outside. With a full belly, he stretched out and watched her move around the house. First, she carried a load of clothes from one room to another. Seconds later, he heard the washer kick on. Task finished, she returned to the kitchen, took a ham out of the freezer, wrapped it in foil, then put it in the oven.

Max enjoyed the way she went about the household tasks with grace and pep. No complaining or dramatic sighs. Just an efficient and almost cheerful attitude toward the whole thing. A new experience for him.

His gaze landed on Tara once more. She was different. Kind. Caring. So far, she proved to be the polar opposite of the pack's females. He'd bet his next meal that not a single one of them would stop after hitting a wolf with her car, shifter or not, pack him up, then take him home as a pet. Granted, he wasn't a dog and the whole idea of being a pet rankled him somewhat, but still, her heart was in the right place.

Yet, after all he'd been through, he couldn't help but wonder when the other shoe would drop. Life wasn't easy and nothing was free. What price he'd pay for her salvation, he had yet to determine.

She returned to the freezer and stared inside. "Hmm. I wonder what else to throw together. I hate to come home and cook after work. Better to just have it already made, stick it in the oven, and call it a meal."

The fact she talked to herself didn't surprise Max in the least. He actually liked the sound, both soothing and quiet, as if she'd kept herself company all the time. Considering what little he knew about her, he believed that to be the truth.

In the next thirty minutes, she cut vegetables into hunks and placed them into a large cooking pot. After adding in some spices, she put the lid on top, and washed her hands. "That should do it." Walking over, she peered out the front window. "Might as well make a dent in that." She retreated to her room then returned covered by a heavy coat and carrying some boots. After slipping them on, she pulled on a pair of mittens, and went outside.

Intrigued, Max jumped down from the couch and walked over to the window to look out. He saw Tara shoveling a trail in the snow. A grouping of trees to the side of the house marked the line between a woody area and civilization in the form of Tara's small house. The gravel driveway lent itself toward a more rural feel while a paved road picked up at the end. Where he was didn't register. Nothing more specific than northern Minnesota came to mind. Just another spot on a map, cold and filled with snow. The details really didn't matter. Not when he had no home, no destination, and no one waiting for his arrival.

The thought plummeted his spirit that much further.

Movement caught his eye. Tara veered off the

driveway and to the left, sending snow flying with every shovelful. The trail she made started at the door and made its way to the edge of the trees where he'd chosen to use the facilities. The realization that she was making him an easier path stunned him. No one had ever made anything easier for him. Not in the pack and not since. Yet, this woman braved the cold in order to keep him from having to step into deep snow.

His heart kicked against his ribs and a little bit of guilt washed over him. He shouldn't be so cranky. After all, she'd just rolled out the red carpet for him, fixed him delicious food, and cared enough to bathe him. Not a bad situation—if he were truly a dog. He wasn't, and despite her kindness and vow to keep him, he knew this was temporary. His pack wouldn't stop trying to hunt him down, not after he stood toe to toe with Garrison and lost while disobeying a direct order. He also didn't have the luxury of shacking up with her. Even if he wanted to.

In an impossible quandary, Max simply sat down and watched her work.

If only things were different. But, they weren't. *Wish in one hand and spit in the other and see which filled up faster.* His father's favorite saying ran through Max's head. Life was hard. Period.

He'd lost track of time when she'd finished shoveling snow, came inside, and took a shower. What he did notice was when she wandered back into the kitchen with only an off-white towel wrapped around her. She bent over, peered into the oven, and just about flashed Max in the process. A hint of vanilla scent carried to him—from her soap or her shampoo, he wasn't sure—but he liked it.

He liked something else, too. A whole lot of something else.

He stared at her, unable to tear his eyes away. Even with her hair down and still dripping and devoid of any makeup, Tara radiated beauty. He found himself wanting to lick up the drops of water as they made little meandering paths southward from her shoulders and over the rise of her upper breasts before soaking into the towel. The knotted towel between her breasts drew his attention to them, teased, and made him wonder what would happen if it gave way, leaving her bare for his viewing pleasure. His cock stood up and took notice, inspired by the scene in front of him and the imaginary one in his head.

Just great. Not like that image will go away anytime soon.

Reluctantly, he turned away, forcing himself to look out the window rather than at the woman who seemed to instill life back into his recently dormant libido. He ignored the throbbing of his dick and actually breathed a sigh of relief when she retraced her steps and disappeared from his view.

At this rate, he'd be jacking off as soon as she went to sleep. *Yeah, right. A little hard to do without opposable thumbs.*

He eyed the couch pillows with newfound interest.

Oh, hell no.

The fact he even considered humping the cushions was downright pitiful. Besides, he was fairly certain Tara would severely frown upon him creaming over them, too.

With a soft snort of disgust, Max rested his head on his paws. Just pondering the possibility of jacking off on pillows was a new low for him. Really low. A sure sign that he had lost his mind somewhere in his travels.

The sooner I heal up and get out of here the better. Because he knew for a fact that if he stuck around long enough, Tara would grow on him. Her sweetness would become addictive and he'd never leave. In doing so, he'd bring danger to her. *If* she could accept the fact that he was a shifter instead of her beloved pet to begin with.

And that was a major *if* since shifters kept their existence a huge secret. No one wanted lynch mobs and hunters on their doorstep day and night, fearing being captured or shot just because of what they were. No matter the species or pack, the first rule of shifter-hood was to keep your mouth closed and never change forms in front of a human. The consequences were too scary to even consider. Even worse than the possibility of those tailing him showing up at the doorstep.

Tara returned wearing light blue sweats. Her damp hair had been pulled back into a ponytail. She smiled, then took the seat next to him, drawing his head onto her lap.

Too surprised to protest, he simply let her have her way.

She began to lightly stroke his fur, first his head, then down his neck and shoulders. Each caress gentle and sweet. "Such soft fur. Not sure if it's you or the baby shampoo, but we'll happily take it."

He relaxed completely, thoroughly enjoying her attention. Comfort. That's what came to mind as he lay there soaking up everything she had to give—from the words to the petting. He'd never been treated like this before. Cared for and about. The few times he'd bedded a pack female, she'd immediately kicked him out when she was done, through with him once their needs were sated. No one bothered to offer him a meal or a simple hug. He couldn't recall the last time anyone touched him with kindness. Until now.

Cherishing the moment, he blew out a breath, closed his eyes, and fell asleep.

****

Tara peered down at Cotton, easily read the begging in his eyes, and noticed the wagging tail. Instantly, she gave in. How could she say no to the hungry beast? "Okay. Okay. It's still hot, though." She used the fork to pry off a large hunk of ham from the bone. After cutting it into smaller pieces, she placed them on a separate plate, then placed it on the floor in front of Cotton. "Here you go."

He didn't hesitate. Instead, he dug in, eating every single bite before licking the plate clean.

His ravenous appetite didn't surprise her. Considering his thinness, nearly to the point of being gaunt, and the lack of luster in his coat, Tara knew Cotton must have been on his own for a while. Certainly, he wasn't doing well and couldn't continue. No matter. She was keeping him. Never would he ever be hungry again. Not if she had anything to say about it.

Since that was the case, she had to make some plans to stop by the pet store. Dogs needed all kinds of things, everything from a collar to a food bowl. *Might as well jot those down while I'm thinking of it.*

She stepped around Cotton, made her way to a drawer, and pulled out scrap paper and a pen. With the necessary tools in hand, she returned to her seat, forked a piece of ham, and dropped it in her mouth. As she chewed, she started to make out a list. "Let's see. I know we'll need a food and water bowl. Dog food too."

Out of the corner of her eye, she caught Cotton lifting his head and leveling her a serious stare. She could almost see the disapproval in his expression. "I know. You like people food better. But, I'm sure it's not good for you. Dog food is supposed to have all the nutrients you need."

Cotton scrunched his nose.

She grinned at his reaction. More than once she'd swear he understood her every word. Dogs were smart and picked up all kinds of things from their owners. Emotions such as panic attacks from post-traumatic stress disorder, low blood sugars, even pending seizures. She knew because she'd watched a documentary on how dogs helped people with certain needs. Cotton might have had a hard time, but he wasn't dumb. Not by any means.

"A collar and a leash, definitely." She wrote those down on the list and glanced around the room. "Since you've taken over the couch and I don't mind sharing my bed, I doubt you need a special dog bed of your own." She took another bite as she contemplated what else she might require as a new pet owner.

Cotton whined, sat down, and stared at his empty plate.

She picked up on his wants immediately. "Okay. Okay." Standing, she returned to the stove where she cut off another large hunk from the meat. After slicing it, she grabbed Cotton's plate, filled it again, then set it in front of him. He smiled a toothy grin, wagged his tail, and dug in.

"I know. You're making up for a few lost meals."

She plopped down once more. "A trip to the vet is a must. Checkup with shots."

She glimpsed him lift his head and pin his ears.

She blinked, then grinned at his reaction. Not the least bit afraid, she simply offered up a shrug. "I can't help it. It's the law. No shots, no getting to come with me to work. Besides, what if you bit someone? I don't want you put down for fear you have rabies."

Cotton made a grumbling noise.

She could have sworn he timed that sound on purpose. The thought made her grin.

Loneliness had been with her for so long, she didn't realize how much it consumed her life. Now that she had Cotton, she had someone to talk to, someone who seemed willing to listen and understand. It made for a nice change. "No worries. We'll get you squared away. I'm not going to let anything happen to you. You're mine now."

Cotton finished eating, appraised her with a tilt of his head, then nudged her hand. She scratched behind his ears. "We're going to make a great team. I just know it."

He stepped back, sat down, and watched her.

She took the last bite of her dinner, then carried the dishes to the sink. A couple minutes later, she dumped the scraps of ham onto Cotton's plate, and stashed the leftovers in the fridge. While the sink filled with hot water, she added detergent and the dirty dishes. Taking a gander over her shoulder, she noted that Cotton had finished, leaving nothing behind. She added his plate to the rest of the dishes, busily washing them by hand.

Cotton stretched out on the kitchen rug and studied her.

She smiled at him as she worked. "This is nice. Kind of like I had envisioned with the man of my dreams. I'd wash. He'd dry. We'd chat and tease. Finish the dishes, then head to the couch for some snuggling before bedtime." She sighed. "Since those perfect men are obviously already snatched up, I guess I should let that dream go."

Cotton looked at her as if mildly interested.

"That's okay. I'm tired of searching for Prince Charming. All I find are toads anyway. Better to just throw in the towel and embrace dog ownership."

Her career might be barely on track, but her social life still stunk. Men entering the store didn't seem to see her as girlfriend material. Blind dates became one catastrophe after another. Finally, she placed all her hopes into the online dating site, taking advantage of a free sign up weekend. "And look how wonderful that worked out." *Guess you get what you pay for.* She snorted to herself.

The facts were just that—facts. She was fast approaching the age of demarcation, which she called the ripe old age of thirty-three. Before that age, women were attractive to all men, they had their lives in front of them, and the energy and ability to go wherever necessary to follow their dreams. After that, in Tara's opinion, women were established and held responsibilities. No haring off after dreams, dropping everything, and taking a leap of faith. Jobs and a mortgage payment tied people down and put a big shackle around their ankles. Not to mention her advancing years put her in another dating category, one with less potential and fewer quality possibilities. As shown by her dismal luck thus far.

Men and society as a whole valued youth. Unfortunately, she was quickly leaving that portion of life behind while watching it fade away in her rear-view mirror. Rapidly.

"Spinsterhood isn't so bad. I just have to adopt a dozen cats, put in numerous flower beds, and take up quilting." She thought a moment about that idea before shrugging. "It's doable." Then, she spied Cotton once more. "Okay. Maybe forget the cats. A dog will fill the void just fine. You won't hog the covers or drop your clothes on the floor for me to pick up and wash. You won't scratch your balls while drinking beer and watching sports on television." She pursed her lips before chuckling. "You probably lick yourself. That's all right. Much better than a man any day."

Cotton arched his eyebrows, then returned to staring off in space, as if her conversation bored him.

She rinsed the dishes, then placed them in a plastic rack to dry. Wiping her hands, she reached over to pat Cotton's head. "Let me grab a brush and see what we can do with that fur of yours."

Cotton padded along after her. He didn't make any sounds despite the laminate flooring. She recalled his nails were short as if he'd worn them down by long hours of running, climbing, or digging.

She entered the bathroom, dug through a drawer, and finally pulled out the particular brush she was looking for. The bristles were plastic and spaced fairly wide, allowing for her to get down deeper. Tool in hand, she patted her leg and called Cotton to follow her.

By the time she sat down on the living area rug, he'd caught up. "Ready for a spa day?" She smiled at the quizzical look on his face. "If you're good and let me brush you, I'll give you a massage."

Whether he understood or not, she couldn't say, but he lay down in front of her, angling so his back was closest to her.

"Very good." She ran the brush through his coarse hair, gently tugging it through, making sure to not pull or scrape his hide. Stroke after stroke, she went over him, removing loose hair and tangles. The simple act soothed her, providing an excellent stress reducer as well. "Who knew brushing a dog could be so relaxing?" She kept up the motions, in no hurry. "Oh, yeah. I'm thinking dog ownership is the way to go. No mean dates that forget I exist when they lay eyes on a strange woman sitting at the bar. No more disapproving looks, no more creeps that just think I'm out for a slap and a tickle. No more jerks that are looking for a sugar momma and dump me the moment they realize I'm not made of money." She lifted Cotton's front leg and started to work on his underbelly. "I don't have to be someone I'm not with you. Can tell you anything. It's…refreshing." She chuckled. "Heck, I guess you wouldn't even hide if you saw me first thing in the morning with bed head hair and smelly breath."

He sighed heavily.

"Yeah, maybe you're right. Maybe that would be a little scary for you."

She found herself rattling on, just talking to Cotton as if he were an old friend she hadn't seen in forever, pouring out her thoughts while he took them all in. Satisfied, she put aside the brush and started to lightly work on the strong muscles under Cotton's hide. From shoulders to back and hips, she pressed and rubbed.

Cotton eased under her hands, going into a doggie

stupor, at least that's what she considered the totally lax state. He closed his eyes, stretched out on his side, and didn't budge, not even when she finally regained her feet, arched her back to work out the kinks, then made her way down the hall to change the laundry around.

Tomorrow would be another long day at work. Her quaint little book store didn't bring in much business but she needed to be open. Locked doors meant no sales, and goodness knew she needed the money. Unless income started to pick up at the second-hand bookstore, she'd have to close. Her lease ended next month. Right now, she wasn't so sure she could renew it.

The truth pressed her shoulders down and weakened her resolve.

At least I'm not alone. She had Cotton now. Something told her fate had a part in putting him in her path.

The small hope cheered her.

Chapter 3

"Look, Cotton. I hate to leave you alone for so long, but I don't have much choice. I have to work and don't want to take a chance on taking you with me. Not yet. You've been through a rough time, and I don't want to stress you out by exposing you to all kinds of people today."

Max blinked at her. She wore an emerald green sweater that brought out her eyes and a pair of jeans. Sneakers finished the outfit. *Wherever she works must allow for casual day every day.* Not for the first time, he wondered what she did. Certainly nothing that would rake in the dough and the lack of a uniform narrowed down the options further. Still, he drew a blank.

She patted his head and smiled before retracing her steps.

He'd been more than eager for this morning to come. She'd leave and he'd have the full run of the house. *Great, if only she'd hit the road.*

"I know it's a long time to hold your bladder, so I'm going to put this newspaper down on the kitchen floor." She bent over and spread it out.

He fixated on her heart shaped butt rather than the improvised bathroom area.

"Pay attention." She snapped her fingers.

He lifted his gaze back to her face.

"Use the papers, please. I really don't want to clean

up pee from the area rugs."

As if. He barely refrained from rolling his eyes. If she would hurry up and leave, he'd be able to use the real bathroom, in human form. No chance of accidents in the least.

She walked over, squatted down, and rubbed his shoulders with both hands. "I'll be home as soon as I can." With a quick kiss to his head, she gathered her purse off the table, and headed out the door.

Through the window Max watched her leave, the car easing its way down the driveway, leaving tracks in the snow.

Doesn't she know that a car in this kind of weather is pretty much useless? He shook his head and fought back the sudden and surprising urge to talk some sense into her. Hard to do when he possessed fangs and four feet.

She needed a four-wheel drive. A truck or an SUV. Something taller that wouldn't bog down in the snow. And, northern Minnesota had snow. Tons of it. More than enough to warrant purchasing a larger vehicle able to handle storms and piles of the white, fluffy stuff.

At least the sun shone brightly in the sky. He had no clue as to the temperature, but the dripping of water from the roof to the ground in front of him told him it was enough to melt some of the snowpack. Perhaps much of the mess would be gone before she had to start on the trek back home again.

With nothing else to do, he turned around and appraised the house, noticing a few more details this time. The area rugs were worn in a few places, telling of either age or constant use. The lack of a dishwasher. The old couch with material that didn't quite match the décor of the rest of the room. Everything spelled out a couple of facts—Tara didn't have much wealth. If she did, she hid it well. Secondly, she made things last. He'd warrant she'd gotten the furniture already used. Same with the rugs. Whether she purchased them at a second-hand shop or they came with the house, he couldn't say. Just that nothing was flashy or recently made, but everything was well cared for.

He appreciated that fact. Especially since some of the snootiest pack females would have screamed in disgust at having to not only step into such a place, but upon seeing the lack of first class, brand new furnishings. He really hated those women. So much so that when one of the higher-ranking bitches picked him as a fuck buddy and potential pairing, he flatly refused, choosing a death sentence rather than hook up with the biggest witch in the world. She didn't care about him. Just his size, his family name, and his looks. And the power that came with being the sole beta to the current alpha.

Bet she changed her mind now. Max snorted to himself. Nothing like Tara. Not in the least.

He glanced once more at the empty driveway, sighed, then summoned his human form. The change always hurt for a second, as bones snapped and reformed, muscles lengthened and tightened, his body molding into that of a human. Having achieved his goal, he looked around the house from a new angle, higher and with more depth perception. That didn't matter, not as much as his opposable thumbs did.

Without hesitation, he made his way to the freezer, pulled out a large casserole that Tara made the evening before, shut the lid, and returned to the kitchen. The small twinge of guilt reminded him that he had nothing to give her in return. No money, no gifts, no chores that could repay her for the meal. He brushed the sentiment aside as he had no choice. Food became a necessity. Several good meals under his belt allowed him to continue on in his journey. Lacking them, he wouldn't be able to regain his strength before setting out once more.

I'll play fetch a couple more times. Maybe that will even the deck.

He shook his head at the thought. *Pretty damn pitiful, but that's all I've got.*

With nothing else to offer, Max went about his task. A quick push of a button turned the oven on after he removed the lid and placed the dish inside. He had no idea how long it would take, but settled on a lower temperature and perhaps a longer time. After all, he didn't need to cook the casserole any more, just get it hot. While definitely hungry, he was no longer starving, so he could be patient. His nose would tell him when to remove the dish. A benefit of his shifter genetics.

Task complete, he made a beeline for the bathroom. After such a long time on the run, he couldn't wait to experience the luxury of a long, hot soak in the tub. He might end up wrinkled as a raisin but he didn't care. The welcome indulgence would be so worth it.

An hour later, he reluctantly stepped from the tub. "Brrr." He shivered and wrapped the damp bath towel around his hips. After soaking for so long, the house felt more than chilly, driving him in search of something…anything to wear.

He felt like he was snooping, and, in truth, he was.

Since he had no clothing, having left those behind months ago, he lacked the basic wardrobe. Hell, he lacked any wardrobe. He doubted Tara had anything that would fit him but decided to check anyway.

Her unique scent, like a patch of summer wildflowers mixed with a hint of vanilla, permeated the bedroom. He drew it in, deciding it matched her perfectly. Pretty. Soft. Bright. All the things he wasn't.

Goose bumps popped up on his arms, spurring him to get moving. He walked around the queen-sized bed, freshly made, with a colorful quilt on top. A dresser sat to one side, a little scratched up and missing one handle. Cozy. The word came to mind as he raked the area with his gaze. Functional and clean soon followed. Nothing fancy or new, certainly. Just a quiet place where the basics fulfilled their obligatory uses.

Spying a closet door on the opposite wall, Max strode over, opened it, and peered inside. He found clothes neatly hung up and two pairs of dress shoes on the floor—one white, the other black. Both carried scuffs but lacked heels. Simple. Rudimentary. He pushed hangers aside, searching for anything large enough to serve as a shirt. Finally, he came across a robe. Though still too small to cover him completely, at least it would provide a little protection against the chill inside the house.

Sure, he could return to wolf form and be toasty in his natural fur coat, but after months of pretty much living as a canine, he reveled in the chance to stand upright and enjoy a few niceties that being human afforded him.

He tugged the robe from the hanger, slipped it on, and rolled his eyes when it lacked about eight inches to meet in the front. The arms were snug and the sleeves barely reached his elbows. Glancing down, he decided that wearing the silly thing would be more embarrassing and annoying than simply running around in the buff. *And freezing my ass off in the process.*

After returning the robe to where he found it and closing the closet door, he backtracked down the hallway until he found another door. He opened it and blew out a breath in relief. "Much better." A few neatly folded blankets occupied two of the shelves. An extra quilt took the top one, while bed linens were relegated to the bottom. While not exactly what he was searching for, at least he could wrap himself in a blanket. *Better than nothing.*

He had blankets on the couch from where she'd made him a nest, but he didn't want to disturb those. They made for a grand bed—for his wolf form. Since she'd been kind enough to make such a place, he didn't have the heart to tear it apart unless he absolutely had to.

The scent of chicken casserole became too tempting to ignore. He pulled a thick blanket from the closet, shut the door, wrapped it around himself, then made his way back to the kitchen. One peek inside the oven told the story. The bubbling of the juices declared the entrée hot enough to enjoy.

Max turned off the oven, found some mitts, then plucked the meal out and set it on the empty burners. Steam warmed his hands, and the delicious aroma made his stomach growl with hunger. He recalled where Tara kept the plates and utensils, snared what he needed, and then grabbed a glass. He pulled the milk from the fridge and poured until the glass was halfway full, wishing he could be more generous.

As it was, he had to be careful. Too many items disappearing or seeming out of place might clue her in that something wasn't as it seemed. He doubted she knew about shifters so the likelihood that she would make the connection hovered around slim. Yet, she might believe someone had broken into her house. The resulting fear would be a punishment she certainly didn't deserve.

He glanced at the newspapers in the floor. No way was he going to pee on them, not when he had a perfectly good bathroom steps away. Instead, he made a mental note to get a glass of water and pour some on it. He'd just have to wash all the dishes by hand, put them back where he found them, and hide the fact that he will have eaten an entire casserole from her freezer.

It'll be fine. I just have to be careful. He made a mental note to wash all the dishes and return everything, including his blanket, just as he found them. "Just for as long as I'm here. A few days. No more."

He carried his plate over to the stove, filled it with casserole, then took a seat at the table. Eating heartily, he considered the woman who made such a delicious dish and where she might be at the moment.

****

Tara glanced up as the small bell on the door rang cheerfully. She recognized her visitor instantly and plastered a wan smile on her face. "Hello, Nora." In all reality, the woman wasn't a horrible person, just a business woman who happened to own half the block and make a living off the high rent she charged all the small businesses who tried to eke out a living. As far as Tara knew, Nora never worked a day in her life. She'd married a much older, wealthy man way back when, inheriting his entire fortune when he passed a couple of years ago. Judging by the stern expression always on Nora's face, the woman hadn't enjoyed a particularly happy life.

Of average height, Nora always dressed to the max. Her body, probably once vibrant with curves, now tended toward skinny. Her breasts were perky as ever, making Tara believe they were fake, just like Nora's nose, her nails, the brilliant blonde hair color, and the brittle smile Nora tried out once in a blue moon. The sharp angles of Nora's cheeks made her appear all the more severe. Maybe once it drew attention of a positive kind. Now, Tara could only say the woman appeared a little scary.

"Tara." Nora glanced around. "Kind of slow today."

"It's a Monday." Tara shrugged it off as if it was to be expected. The truth happened to be that every day had mirrored lackluster Mondays. Since the economy soured, customers visited less and less. Tara thought the lapse would help as she sold second hand books at reasonable prices, but the optimistic thought didn't pan out. Instead, she'd taken a hit. A big one at that. "I have your rent money right here." She hit a button on the cash register, waited for the drawer to open, then handed over the check.

Nora tucked it away inside her purse. "I don't know why I bother with all this." Nora waved her hand. "Joseph kept up with all the rent payments, the taxes, the leases. Personally, it's a huge bother."

Tara nodded slightly in acknowledgement. She'd rented the space just after Joseph had died and never met the man.

"I wish I could find someone to buy this blighted area and take it off my hands." Nora turned to leave.

Tara bristled and bit her tongue, refusing to invite Nora into more of a conversation. No need to. After all, Nora said pretty much the same thing every month. She had a chauffeur drive her around, entered each business, collected the money, then climbed back into the vehicle. Honestly, Tara didn't know why Nora didn't just have one of her helpers pick up the funds. Nora wouldn't have to deal with it and the renters most certainly would appreciate seeing less from the thin lady with abundant frown lines.

"That day can't come too soon." With those parting words, Nora pushed through the door.

Tara watched Nora enter the upscale, brand spanking new SUV, and be whisked away by the driver, presumably to torment another of the vendors in the small strip mall in the old section of town.

Her spirit sank along with her shoulders. She scrubbed her face, and wracked her brain for the hundredth time to figure out a way to bring back her customers and to return her business to the level of thriving that it once enjoyed. "I can't fix the economy. And nothing else has worked." She'd tried sales, banners, even spending precious money on ads in the paper. All for naught. A few loyal customers trickled in but even they spoke of the hard times that had settled on Pointer's Gap. Layoffs were happening, people were packing up and moving elsewhere to find work, and those remaining tightened the belt a little more each month. Just like she did.

The bell rang once more.

Tara glanced up to find Rose, a sweet elderly lady who always had a smile for anyone. Sage advice as well whether a person wanted to hear it or not. "Hi, Rose. Surprised to see you out in the snow today." Rose had swung by pretty much every day the store was open. Tara had found a grandmotherly quality to Rose that she relied on as well as found endearing. Though Rose didn't purchase a stack of books, Tara adored her for the company and companionship which outweighed any sale.

Rose made her way to the front counter, using her cane for balance with each step. Her large, black leather purse swung from her elbow with every step. The slightly bent over stance told of her age, most likely over ninety, though she didn't look a day over seventy in Tara's opinion. "Oh, pshaw. This isn't anything. There was that year a while back, before you were probably born, that snow was so high, a person couldn't see anything but white for miles all the way around. Oh, maybe a top of a tree here and there, a rooftop if you were lucky." Rose sat in one of the old recliners that Tara positioned next to side tables and lamps in an effort to produce a mood of lazy reading.

Tara hurried to the coffee pot, poured a cup for Rose, then carried it to her. "I'm glad you stopped by, don't get me wrong, I just don't want you falling or getting frostbite in order to come here and keep me company in the afternoons."

Rose accepted the drink and took a sip. She lowered the cup to rest on her thigh. "It does an old lady good to get out of that house now and again. Those walls close in if I stay at home too many days in a row." Rose took another swallow then stared at Tara. "You've got that worried look again."

As hard as Tara tried to mask her emotions, Rose always saw right through her.

"Would it have anything to do with that snippy, good-for-nothing Nora that just left?"

Tara shook her head. "Nora is just…well, Nora. Picking up her rent payment as always." She spared a look at the door, then took a seat next to Rose. "She's barely civil to anyone."

"That's surely the truth, child." Rose ran her finger over the rim of the cup.

The short silver hair spoke of Rose's age but the intelligent blue eyes hadn't dimmed in the least. Rose didn't miss a thing and had more intuition than anyone else Tara had ever met. The woman had guts as well, broaching subjects and crossing lines when she saw fit. Meek and mild wasn't Rose. She had no problem stepping in to say her three cents and had a definite knack for picking apart other people's arguments. Tara had yet to see Rose lose a debate, be it in hair color, fashion, or a frank differing of opinion on politics.

Rose loved swing music, had flown fighter planes over the ocean during the last World War, and proudly showed off the tattoo of her military insignia to anyone that cared to look. Pushing well into the geriatric category, Rose had lived a full life, to her own admission, and still kicked butt. Though in her own way and with a little less strength but just as much enthusiasm.

Tara only hoped she'd age like Rose and be able to do half the things she'd done.

"Might as well tell me what's bugging you, miss. You know I'll drag it out of you eventually." The gleam in Rose's blue eyes promised it.

Tara sighed. "Okay. Okay." She didn't want to discuss the bleak sales, so she went with option two—her personal life. "I had another date lined up. He took one look at me, scanned the room, then made a beeline for the bar to chat up another woman."

Rose *tsked*. "Men are blind. Dense, too." She took another sip. "That silly online dating isn't for you, Tara."

Tara nodded. "I know. I canceled my enrollment this morning. I'm happier alone." *It's not like I can afford it anyway.* She lifted her head with a semblance of pride she didn't really feel.

"Don't get me wrong, dear. Men are wonderful creatures, but you have to find the right one. He'll make all the insanity worth it."

"I'll take your word for it." Tara brushed a lock of hair behind her ear. "Right now, I have other things to focus on." She thought of Cotton and smiled. "I found a stray dog Saturday night. Named him Cotton."

"Oh?"

"He's big and beautiful. Well, more so after his bath. Poor guy was filthy. Probably been on his own for a while. Very hungry, too. I swear he's going to eat me out of house and home but I don't really mind. He's sweet and very smart." Tara realized she'd been rambling along and closed her mouth.

Rose chuckled. "You might not have found a man but it sure sounds like you've found yourself a pet."

"Yep. He's been through rough times, that's for sure. But he's found a home—with me." *He's the only bright spot in my life right now.*

Rose took another drink, staring at Tara over the

top of her cup. "Maybe you've found what you've been searching for after all."

"A dog?" Tara grinned. "Let's see. Loyal. Obedient. Protective. Good snuggler. Yep, I think I have." She really had no clue on where Cotton fell on most of that list, but she'd take any and all of the above.

She didn't need a man. She had a dog instead.

"You should bring him with you one day. I'd love to meet this new man in your life." Rose grinned.

"He hasn't had his shots yet. I don't want to get in trouble if he gets upset and tries to nip someone." Tara clasped her hands on her lap. She'd love to bring Cotton here, to keep him with her all day, but was worried about how he could accept the changes. It'd only been a little over a day after all.

"It sounds like he's smart. Bring him with you. If he can't handle the customers, then you'll know to leave him at home. But I have a feeling he'll do just fine."

Tara peered over at Rose. "How do you know these things?"

"A woman's intuition, dear. A woman's intuition."

Those words carried Tara through the rest of her day. She closed up shop at six, swung by the store, and hurried home, eager to see how Cotton had fared on his own. She'd envisioned messes, torn up furniture, and pillow stuffing strewn all over the house. To her surprise, she found none of the above, only Cotton curled up on the couch, watching her as she entered the living room from the garage, carrying a large bag of dog food, which she deposited in the kitchen. "I brought dog food."

Cotton simply stared at her as if in disapproval.

She didn't take it personally. After all, she'd left him home alone all day long. He was bound to be a trifle upset.

"Wow. You're such a good boy." She walked over and petted him, then glanced back to the kitchen to find the papers just as she'd left them with only a little wet spot in the center. "Very good boy." Proud and delighted, she scratched his chin and pressed a kiss to the top of his head. "Need to go outside?"

When he wagged his tail, she gestured toward the door. "Let's go, then I'll fix us some dinner."

She let Cotton out, keeping an eye on him as he sniffed around, presumably searching for the perfect spot. Since the sun came out and temperatures rose above the freezing mark, some of the snow had melted away, leaving bare places where she could glimpse the ground underneath. The change made it easier for Cotton to get around and less snow that he'd carry back inside. A win-win for both of them.

As soon as he finished, he trotted back over. She had him stand just inside the door in order to wipe his paws with a nearby towel she'd left just for that purpose the night before. Task done, she ran her hand over his head and gushed over him. "You're so smart. I can't believe anyone wouldn't want you."

He peered up at her with those brown eyes filled with intelligence.

She smiled in return. "Right. Let me get something on to eat." She made her way to the kitchen, pulled some hamburger meat out of the fridge, and put it into a pan. Pasta followed in another pan filled with water. "How does goulash sound?"

Cotton tilted his head and thumped his tail.

"I take that for a vote of approval." As she worked, she couldn't help but talk to him, a new habit that eased her soul. "I'm thinking about taking you to work with me tomorrow or the next day. Just to see how it goes."

He stared at her, his tail no longer moving.

"I hate leaving you alone all day long by yourself. Yes, you were wonderful, but that's a long time to go without being able to go outside. I'm pretty sure you ate up what I gave you right after I left, so you've been starving all day long."

Cotton stretched out on the floor and rested his head on his front legs.

"At work, I can take you out more often and you'll have food all day long. I'll just bring the dog food with us."

She swore he frowned, if a dog could make such an expression.

Chapter 4

I went from being the top beta under Jacques to becoming this woman's pet poodle. Max scowled as Tara grasped the end of the leash attached to his collar and tugged.

"Come on, Cotton. Let's go."

His inner wolf protested.

I know. Shit, I know.

With a grumble, Max jumped out of the car, and walked beside her to the back door of the store.

He'd been dreading this since she'd told him of her plans, much preferring to stay at her house all day, enjoy more luxuries that he'd been without for way too long. Two whole days he had the run of the house and stuffed himself with her delicious food, soaked in the tub, and did little more than be a lazy bum. Now, he had to look forward to wearing the itchy collar, playing nice with customers that wanted to pet him, and subsisting on damn dry dog food. *Let's not forget the indignity of having to pee at the end of a leash in public. Goody for me.*

Already cranky, he couldn't bring himself to even act the part of a happy companion.

She let them in, then locked the door behind her. After clicking the lights on, she made her way to the front, unlocked that door, flipped the Closed sign around, and returned to open the register. She pulled a leather bank container from her purse, unzipped it, and placed money and change inside the register.

Max scanned the room, finding it filled with bookshelves along two walls with more in the middle, reminding him of a library—albeit a small one. A long table stood in the front window with books stacked on top of it while a handful of chairs waited for people to come in, grab a book, and take a load off. A coffee machine perched by itself on a smaller table to the side, complete with Styrofoam cups, and all the extras anyone would want to add to their java.

Even as he watched, Tara wandered over, opened the top, put in a new filter and a large packet of coffee, and hit the start button.

Never one to care for the brew, he still enjoyed the aroma.

Speaking of scents, everything smelled old with more than a hint of moth balls. Faded deep green carpet ran the length of the floor, appearing left over from the '60s. Well-worn and bare in a few spots, it at least kept the floor a smidgen warmer than other products. The cement walls didn't offer much insulation and added a chill to the already cold air. Tara had tried to liven them up with posters and banners but couldn't quite pull off the trick. The small business appeared deflated and tired despite her best efforts.

He gave her credit for gumption and fortitude. Perhaps stubbornness in order to keep her dream alive. But, she needed a new venue, one that didn't remind a person of better times gone by.

The morning crept by, with Tara dusting, rearranging, and answering two sole phone calls. Three customers came in, each spending less than ten dollars each. Cotton watched them from the security of the back room, not feeling up to being social in the least.

He spent most of his time simply listening to Tara go about her day and understanding that her business was suffering a slow death. She didn't have much and certainly the money she brought in thus far wouldn't do more than buy a meal, perhaps two. He saw the sadness and resignation in her eyes, heard it in her voice. He ached for her impending loss.

By the afternoon, he was bored to tears and hungry. The dog food sat untouched, even though he'd lapped up some water, tasted the chlorine, and sneered at the chemical tang. After that, he simply plopped down on a blanket Tara thoughtfully brought along and opted to sleep the rest of the lackluster day away.

The chiming of the bell announced another customer. Max, tucked safely in the back ignored the new arrival, until an aroma caught his attention. Instantly, he sat up, then walked forward, peeking around the doorway to catch a glimpse of the person he easily identified as another wolf shifter.

Shock struck as he spied an elderly, silver-haired lady slowly making her way to the interior of the store. Her body appeared frail but the spirit in her eyes couldn't be denied.

"Rose. I'm so happy to see you."

The older woman smiled at Tara, even as her gaze landed on Max. "You said you were bringing in the new pet today. I couldn't wait to meet him."

"Yes, I did. He's pretty shy, though." Tara rounded the corner. "Come on, Cotton. I have a friend for you to meet." She grasped his collar and led him to stand before Rose. "Rose, this is Cotton. Cotton, this is my great friend, Rose."

The shifter inside the woman was undeniable. Max scented not only that she was a wolf but also that she carried power. Most likely a matriarch at that. For such an older lady to hold that position said something about her fortitude and inner strength.

"My, aren't you a pretty...dog." Rose grinned down at him, the twinkle in her eye telling him she fully understood what he was.

Max groaned to himself at this latest mess he'd gotten his paws into.

The phone rang.

Tara released Cotton's collar. "I need to get that." She glanced worriedly at Max.

"Go ahead, dear. I'm just going to sit down. Cotton can keep me company, can't you boy?"

Max wagged his tail in agreement for Tara's sake and walked slowly by the woman's side, escorting her to the plush chairs along the far wall.

Tara went the other direction, picked up the phone, and started chatting.

Rose sat down, put her cane on the arm of the chair, and appraised him critically. "Now, what are you about?" She voiced the question in a whisper.

Cotton whined softly, trying to communicate the basics to the lady.

"You better not be taking advantage of sweet Tara." Sternness coated Rose's voice along with a definite threat.

Max shook his head. Technically, he was using Tara as a much-needed pit stop in order to gain strength and rest before resuming his goalless journey. Those reasons were genuine and made the situation necessary in his opinion. He'd gladly pay her back if he could. That took many things he didn't currently have and weren't likely to obtain any time soon.

"Let me guess. A lone wolf?" Rose tapped her chin, then ran her hands through Max's thick coat. "Got some scars there. I'd say you tangled with the wrong wolf and lost your pack in the process."

He nodded. After all, what could he really say in his present form? He sat in front of the woman and met her gaze readily.

"Sorry about that." Tara came over and took the other seat. She reached for Max and scratched him behind the ears. "Looks like you two are getting along well."

"Yes. He's a good boy. I can see that for myself."

"I still need to get him to the vet. Don't want him to nip anyone and then have to be put down because he hasn't had his rabies shot." Tara frowned as her eyebrows furrowed with obvious worry.

"Why don't you take him to my family vet? He's really good with Cotton's kind," Rose offered.

Tara looked at Rose. "I can't afford much. Business isn't what it used to be." She whispered the last words as if they hurt to admit them aloud.

Max rested his head on her knee, wanting to offer some comfort. She'd done so much for him and he hated to see her upset. He might be a wolf shifter and a hard-assed one at that but he still felt. Deep down, he had a heart, scarred and broken, but a heart.

"Oh, he's very reasonable," Rose assured, turning her attention back to Max. "Why don't I give him a call?"

"Well, okay."

Rose pulled out her phone. "Yes, let me speak to Damian." A few seconds passed by. "Hello, Damian. Rose here. I have a friend that needs to bring her pet to see you. Uh, huh. Yes. He's needing his shots so he can stay with her at the bookstore. Yes, that's right. Okay. I'll send her right over. And thanks." Rose disconnected the call. "He can see you right now. Just over on Timberline Road, at the junction of Harris Street."

Tara's mouth dropped open before she shook her head. "I can't leave the store, Rose. Sure, I might not get any customers in the time I'm gone, but I can't afford to miss any either."

"I'll watch the store for you."

Hope crossed Tara's face, tempered with guilt. "I hate for you to do that."

Rose waved her hand. "I think I can handle it. The prices are marked, the coffee is hot. No problem at all."

Max watched as a slow, relieved smile appeared on Tara's face. "Are you sure?"

"Yes."

"Thank you. I owe you so much."

Yeah, me too. Sarcasm dripped from the thought. Max eyed Rose warily, noting the wicked smile on her lips. While she might have done him a favor, his gut told him she was getting a little payback in at his expense.

"Go on, you two. Damian is waiting."

Max dragged his feet, having a good inkling what Damian was and intended. Tara's firm grasp on his collar and strong pull left him little choice but to play along. That or make a break for it now and be back on his own. Not quite ready to leave his cozy spot in her house and the intriguing woman who took him in, he swallowed his pride and let her lead him to the latest humiliating event in his recent life.

Thirty minutes later, Max's sullen mood turned to one of irritable grumpiness as the veterinarian, Damian, examined him. It was all Max could do to keep from growling at the man as he cajoled his inner wolf into allowing the guy to check him over without going off the deep end. One glance told Max that Damian realized Max's annoyance and didn't intend to back off in the least. Damian's obvious wicked sense of humor had emerged and Max knew Damian would have a ball with this situation.

Max clung to his failing patience with a steely resolve. The same one that got him through the months of living off the land after escaping the death sentence Garrison handed out.

"I don't think I hit him hard with the car, but he was hurt. I'm sure of it. Couldn't get up. I had to carry him inside the house, too." Tara stood next to Max who sat on the exam table filled with aggravation at this latest insult by another male shifter, no less.

Damian listening to his heart and lungs was tolerable, but when the guy started getting handsy in his exam, Max bared his teeth.

"I know I have to get his shots and get him neutered too. To be honest, my budget is a little tight but whatever he needs I'll pay for." Tara sighed as she stroked Max's side.

Max leaned into her touch, enjoying the caress even as Damian checked out his paws. The woman had a talent, being able to quell his anger with a few caresses and softly spoken words. In short, she eased him and gave him peace. Something he'd never had before. Unfortunately, with another shifter so close, Max found himself on protective overdrive. He didn't want Damian near her any more than he wanted Damian feeling him up like a champion Chihuahua at a dog show.

Damian patted him on the head. "He's a sturdy one. Kind of skinny." Damian grinned slightly. "Don't worry about the neutering right now. He needs some recovery time before you should consider that. Save it for later." Damian smirked.

Max leveled a less than amused look at the vet. *Next time you try to fondle my balls, you'll be checking to make sure yours are still there.*

"I'll give him his shots, though. Chelsea, why don't you take Tara to the desk and get her rabies tag on for her?" Damian removed the collar and handed it over to her assistant.

Tara lightly rested her hand on Max's shoulder. "It's okay. I should stay with him. He's a little tense with all the new things happening to him."

Damian smiled warmly at her. "I've got this. Chelsea will get you settled up."

Tara hesitated. "If it's all the same to you, I'll stay."

That's my girl.

"Going to hold his paw?" Damian asked as he prepared a syringe. Chelsea left the room with the collar, presumably to attach the rabies tag to it.

"Something like that." Tara chuckled as she rubbed Max's neck. "I've only had him a few days but I'm pretty partial to him."

"Love at first sight, huh?"

Tara nodded. "Yeah, you could say that. It's like

58

I've had him forever. He's sweet and a great listener. Makes me smile, too, even if he doesn't seem to care for fetch very much."

"A dog that doesn't like to play fetch?"

I will bite, you jackass.

Damian met Max's eyes and smiled.

Oh, he's enjoying this way too much.

"Maybe you should get him a squeaky toy instead. Some dogs love those."

Maybe a little nip. Just one. What would it hurt? It's not like he wouldn't heal.

Damian bumped Max's rear leg with his hand, but no sting of a needle followed. Max realized he'd been spared the vaccinations that would invariably make him sick.

Sicker than a proverbial dog. He mentally shook his head, but let up on his grumpiness with Damian. The guy had done him a favor, after all.

Max always repaid those. He glanced at Tara and cringed. Or tried.

"He hasn't been eating the new dog food I got him, either." Tara rubbed Max's head.

"No appetite?" Damian asked.

"Oh, his appetite has been excellent—for people food. He's been scarfing down hamburger, ham, eggs, and sausage. I gave him dog food and he won't touch it." Worry carried in Tara's voice.

A twinge of guilt washed over Max. He'd been hungry enough to eat anything. Then she'd spent money on dog food and he couldn't bear to hardly look at it, let alone give it a try. The tasty dishes she'd made and tucked away in the freezer served him well along with the fresh stuff she'd prepared, keeping his belly happy despite today's lack of intake.

"Doesn't care for the dog food, huh?" Damian rubbed his chin. "Imagine that."

Max lowered his head and pulled back his lips to flash his fangs. As strong a warning as he could give without growling.

Damian arched an eyebrow.

Of course, you're going to be a bastard, aren't you? If Damian sentenced him to dry, unpalatable dog food, Max wouldn't be responsible for his actions.

Damian patted Max on the head once more. "Perhaps you should stick with the table food. I suspect he's been living off scraps for a while now."

"What about all the salt and stuff that's not supposed to be good for dogs?" Tara gripped Max's fur lightly in her hand.

"It's fine. He can handle a lot of calories and everything else right now. Get him fattened up a bit."

Okay. Maybe I won't have to bite you after all. Max smiled at Damian, a toothy one, but a smile just the same.

Damian tilted his head in acknowledgement. "We can give him a bath if you'd like."

Tara shook her head. "Thanks, but I can do that myself. He didn't seem to mind too much before, so we'll just make due."

Max turned his head to peer over at Tara. *Yeah, we'll make due just fine. As long as you keep your hands off my dick.*

"Here you go, Tara. I attached the rabies tag to his collar. All legal now." Chelsea returned, handing over the leather collar.

"Thanks." Tara started to put it on, only for

Damian to lend an assist.

"I've got it." He kept it fairly loose, which Max greatly appreciated. Damian eyed him critically for a long moment. "I think you're good to go."

"If you're ready?" Chelsea led the way to the front.

Max hopped down, paused at the end of the exam table, and contemplated hiking his leg to pee on the thing. A sharp yank from Tara and a disapproving frown changed his mind.

She took him in to the front room where Chelsea waited.

"It'll be five dollars."

Tara blinked at her. "Surely, it's more than that?"

"Friends and family discount, compliments of Dr. Kendall," Chelsea explained.

"I really appreciate it but know his time is worth more than that." Tara pulled out two bills. One she gave to Chelsea, the other she dropped in a jar labeled for the humane society.

Again, Max witnessed her generosity. She didn't have the money to spare, yet was willing to give everything she had to take care of him. Not only that, she donated to charity.

The more time he spent with Tara, the more he liked about her—the sinfully sexy woman who ran around in her bath towel as well as the caring individual who put his needs before her own.

Unable to resist, he licked her hand.

She smiled lovingly down at him. "You're a blessing, Cotton. My blessing."

The words embraced his soul.

Right after, pessimism reared its ugly head in the form of harsh reality. *And probably your worst nightmare.*

He sighed wearily, rubbed his head against her leg, and debated how to get out of this predicament without hurting her feelings. His too, if he were to be completely honest.

No answer came readily.

Chapter 5

"Obviously you haven't told her yet."

Max glanced up at Rose, finding censure in her gaze. He lowered his head a little sheepishly.

"You know the longer you continue on with the ruse, the worse you're going to break her heart."

Yeah, he knew it. He also couldn't seem to simply take off again, leaving her behind. He'd considered it a dozen times, just going out and not returning, but each time he saw Tara's smile as she patiently waited for him to finish his business and he caved.

No other reason existed for him to stay, except he couldn't bear the thought of her tears. Those alone had the power to leash him to her side. Ironic since they'd never swayed him before with the pack females. A few of them had a talent in that department. They cried at the drop of a hat in a manipulative attempt to gain what they sought. He'd been played a fool once, then wizened up. Now, he found the thought of Tara grieving unacceptable. She'd never broken down in the days since he'd shown up, though he watched as her business dried up. The stress and strain showed on her face and in her eyes, yet every time she looked at him, love shined through.

He struggled with guilt and an inability to take the plunge in showing his true self. She'd be furious, hurt. Maybe even scared. More than embarrassed when she realized all the secrets she'd whispered to him every night. The trials and tribulations of her failed social life, the challenges of keeping the doors of her bookstore open despite the downturn in sales. The loneliness she felt after her grandparents who raised her passed away, leaving her the house she presently lived in. He'd listened to her bare her heart because that's all he could do. A nudge here, a lick of her hand there, that's all he could provide in his current state. But, she acted like every effort was a treasure. She praised him often, brushed him every evening, and made sure he had plenty of rich, full dinners to eat. That alone probably busted her budget.

Another wave of culpability washed over him.

If only...

"I don't know who you're running from, but it's time to take a stand." Rose continued to speak softly to him while Tara worked in the back room.

Yeah. Been there, done that, just about lost my life in the process.

"Besides, you're among friends," she added with a small smile.

He blinked at her, doubtful. In his experience, friends were rare and other packs weren't interested in the rogues of another, stereotyping them as problem wolves best left to their own devices.

Rose *tsked*. "I know you're not cruel, nor lacking in intelligence or bravery. Tara adores you in this form. What makes you think she'll reject you as a man?"

Cotton glanced over at Tara as she picked up the ringing phone, and sighed. He feared her reaction when she discovered his secret. Not the banishment from the pack, but the simple fact of his genetics. For a society who didn't know about the existence of such a species as shifters, their reactions could run the entire gamut, including Tara's.

The thought of her love-filled eyes turning to hate and fear knotted his gut.

I'm such a fucking coward.

He grumbled to himself, his inner wolf joining in the chastisement. He'd taken advantage of Tara's generosity for almost two weeks. Plenty of time to rest, heal, and eat his belly full every day. Back at full strength, he no longer possessed a reason to stay— besides the fact he couldn't just walk away.

Time to man up. One way or the other.

"Take an old woman's advice. Give Tara a chance to accept you as a man. You might be surprised on how well it works out."

Max glanced back to Rose, seeing the small smile playing on her lips as well as hearing the not so subtle hint in her voice. She had matchmaker written all over her. Whether her pack listened or not didn't really matter. He was unlikely to meet any of them, especially if he took off for the hills in the opposite direction.

"Sorry about that." Tara walked over with a grin. She bent over and rubbed Max's head. "You two look chummy."

"He's a sweet boy. I can see why you love him." Rose folded her hands onto her lap.

"He filled a void in my life that I never knew I had," Tara admitted.

Rose appraised her. "What about a man?"

Yeah, what about that? Max remained still, waiting to hear Tara's answer.

Tara shrugged. "I'm through searching for one. If

one comes along that is outstanding, then I'll consider it. Otherwise, I'm done fishing. Too many tadpoles and small fry for my taste."

"Hmm. Maybe you're fishing in the wrong pond." Rose tapped her chin. "I might know of some single men. Just tell me what you're looking for."

Tara held up her hand. "Thanks, but no thanks. I've had my fill of blind dates."

"How are you going to meet your knight in shining armor if you don't try?" Rose asked.

"I don't need a knight. I have Cotton." Tara gave him a quick hug and kissed the top of his head.

Max's heart buoyed even as another wave of guilt washed through him. He'd kept up the charade long enough. Time to make a decision and stick with it.

Rose left shortly afterward, shooting him one final glance as she departed. Max didn't miss the meaning behind it. No way could he. The matriarch sent him a clear message—buck up or else.

Tara sighed, walked over, and flipped the sign around to say Closed. She turned the lock, then made her way back to the register.

Max watched her pull out the cash, count it, then put it in a bank bag, the small stack of bills less than impressive.

Max enjoyed watching Tara at work, the gliding movements, the genuine smiles for her customers, the peace and quiet at the store. Only too quiet as the lack of sales cut into Tara's happiness. He read it easily on her face when she tallied the cash register each night. Sadness replaced her contentment and pulled at Max's heart. Certainly he didn't know the dismal numbers, but understood that her business was slowly dying. How much longer she could sustain, he didn't have a clue. But, something had to give at some point.

He mentally shook his head, banishing the concerns. They weren't his worries—he had plenty more of his own. Survival. Being hunted. Not knowing Jacques's fate. That alone made Max antsy. He needed to find out what befell his one and only friend. To ensure that he'd delivered the former alpha to help in time. The fear that he didn't ate at him.

Maybe it's time to go see for myself.

"It's been a slow week, Cotton." Worry coated her voice. "Time to start facing the facts and work on Plan B."

He didn't bother to get up from his blanket where he rested on his stomach, his chin on his forelegs. Instead, he watched her carefully.

Yeah, I'm on Plan B myself.

She'd have more money if she hadn't spent a chunk on him, everything from the vet, to food and supplies, to the prepared meals he'd gulped down when left alone at her house for a couple of days. Little could she afford those things but she'd not uttered a single complaint about the purchases.

Guilt rode him harder than before.

He'd wracked his brain all day trying to find solutions to his problems, coming up short. He'd eyed her cell phone and wondered how he could shift to human form, borrow it, make a call to Becky to check on Jacques, and wipe the evidence without Tara finding out. He had the ability but lacked opportunity. Even at night while she slept, she could easily wake when hearing a man's voice or hear a door opening. Although, that gave him the only chance he could see.

With the lack of a landline phone, he had very little choice. Even her laptop computer she kept on a small desk in her bedroom, charging every night, giving him no chance to send a quick email, either.

Or I could just take off like before.

His stomach clenched at the thought of returning to that kind of life—living off the land, enduring the brutal cold of a Minnesota winter. Starvation.

He'd barely gotten his strength back as it was, but he had to face the facts. Staying wasn't an option. He'd already hung around way too long.

Time to get my head out of my ass and grow a pair of balls. Either find a way to check on Jacques and resume his human form for long periods of time, or go back to living a wolf's life. He couldn't continue to stay in limbo like he did now. Tara deserved better—a man that could stand by her side, support her business, and give her the love she merited.

And that's not me.

Lowering her burden gained importance. He'd just have to suck it up, steal some clothes from a donation container, and make his way back to Florida. No fancy jet this time. Until he could replace his identification cards, he didn't have access to any funds. All that took time, connections, and technology he didn't have access to.

Yet.

"Come on, Cotton. Time to go home."

Home. The word fit in regards to her house. The peaceful evenings after dinner where Tara dug out the brush and pampered him. The petting. The kind words—all for her dog.

His spirit sank as he realized the pipe dream had

come to an end.

He'd taken enough from her and couldn't bear to do it any longer. He was one piss poor excuse of a man for his actions. What began as desperation had turned to sheer laziness. To continue to take advantage of her generosity would only double his sin.

No, the time had come to leave.

Max scanned the store for the last time, knowing he'd carry fond memories of it, then followed Tara to her car. He settled into the passenger seat as was his usual. This time, however, he watched Tara instead of the road. Memorizing her face—something that would have to be enough to carry him through the rest of his life, however short that might be.

He debated his decision a dozen times before sticking with his original plan. Take off through the trees, keep running until dark, find some clothes, then make his way to Becky's pack. If Garrison's thugs caught up with him along the way, so be it.

"We're home." Tara opened the passenger door.

Just do it already.

Dutifully, he jumped out of the car, making a final decision in the process. He sprinted for the woods, not daring to look back. He hit the tree line, then slowed his pace slightly to accommodate the rough terrain. Bushes, trees, and large rocks littered his path. Each one, he navigated around, picking his way deeper into the woods, heading generally southeast.

The stiff wind blew through his coat, cold and damp. Snow remained, covering his feet and lower legs as he traveled. Thankfully, his animal form had been created for just such weather, though he knew the moisture on his feet would be hell later.

Been there, done that. Almost got ran over by a car in the process.

"Cotton. Wait!" Tara's voice carried to him.

He tuned her out, pressing hard to put some distance between them, his heart cracking in the process.

Even his wolf whined at him.

We're doing this for her, jackass.

The inner growl disagreed.

Max ignored his beast's displeasure, focusing on his trek.

"Cotton?"

The sounds of leaves crunching under feet caught his attention. Tara. Following him. Calling to him. His breath caught.

Still he pressed onward, telling himself that once he was far enough away, he'd no longer hear her. Then, it would get easier.

The calls continued, echoing through the trees. Each one faded slightly as he put more distance between himself and Tara.

"Cotton, please. Please come back."

The soul-wrenching tone of the words halted him nearly in midstride.

"Please Cotton. Come to me. Please."

He'd expected frustration, even anger, not the pleading and tearful begging that knifed through his determination.

He drew in air, peered at the rolling hills in front of him, and waited a second. Two. Three.

"Cotton?"

His feet refused to move as Tara's voice carried to him once more.

Well, hell. Max spun around, picked up speed to a lope, and followed the sound of her voice back to her location.

She stood next to a tree, her hand resting on the trunk for support, as her gaze searched all around. Red marks marred her beautiful complexion on her face, testament to the hike through the rough terrain in her quest to find him.

Pausing, Max watched her for a long moment, noted the worry on her face, the tears building in her eyes. A lump formed in his throat.

He'd been wrong. It was too late to run. To do so now would break Tara's heart. He knew for certain she'd put up posters, take to social media, and do everything possible to find her dog. She loved Cotton that much.

He thought of Jacques. How he'd fretted over his friend's condition with no way of checking on him. It bothered him, the not knowing.

Just as the loss of Cotton would eat at Tara day in and day out.

With a resigned sigh, Max sprang from his hiding place behind a thick bush, bounded over a small thicket, and trotted up to Tara.

Tara beamed as she dropped to her knees down and opened her arms wide, then drew him into a hug, holding him snug. "Oh, thank God you came back." She sniffed, wiped the tears off her face, and petted him enthusiastically. "Such a good boy. I'm so proud of you."

A shiver coursed through her body extending to Tara's hands presently buried in his fur. He noted the color to her cheeks and the lack of a heavy coat to ward off the chill.

The facts added up in his head. She'd freeze to death in an attempt to follow him.

"I bet those rabbits are fun to chase, though." Her voice became nearly breathless and a little ragged with the chattering of her teeth.

Not really.

"Let's go inside. Get out of this cold, and I'll make us something hot to eat."

He peered back toward the woods, saw the freedom it represented, then turned back to Tara. She stood up, brushed the leaf litter from her jeans, and walked a few steps. The darkened hue of the material told him the wet snow soaked through, added to the frigid conditions she'd endured all for him.

She walked a few steps, then patted her thigh. "Come on, boy."

Without further hesitation, he followed.

****

An hour and one bath later, Max walked into the living room, flopped down on the couch, and waited for his coat to dry. The warmth felt good as did the soft blankets that made up his bed.

He'd sulked the entire time, frustrated with himself for not sprinting off, starting the next leg of his journey. Then, he'd take a glance at Tara's face and berate himself for putting her through such anxiety.

At least her gentle hands washing over his body provided a little distraction, although an uncomfortable one. He hated that he responded to her but couldn't seem to help himself. Just like he couldn't leave her behind earlier.

He heard the water running in the bathroom and

imagined Tara rinsing the tub after his bath and drawing hot water for her own. She'd been cold but had seen to him first. As many times as he'd glimpsed her caring nature, it still surprised him.

Her cell phone resting on the corner of the kitchen table caught his attention. *Jacques.* Maybe, finally, he could make that call. Find out if Jacques had survived Garrison's coup. Becky, Jacques's sister would know. After all, he'd left Jacques with her and her pack in Florida weeks ago.

The memory returned in a flashback. Jacques. Fighting for his life. Max trying to get him to safety in the dark of night.

Max ducked under a branch, careful to avoid crunching any dead leaves littering the forest floor or brushing against the various limbs from trees and bushes. The metallic stench of blood served as his guide along with the obvious trail of crimson. All signs pointed to an injured animal dragging itself over the land. It had been easy to follow. Too easy.

All typical forest sounds abruptly ceased at the eruption of violence as if nature itself hid and held her breath in anticipation of the outcome. Even the wind died down, remaining still several minutes after the completion of the brutal battle. The air nearly crackled with electricity. Still did. Eerie and enough to make the hairs on the back of his neck stand on end.

Max opened up his senses and allowed the light from the full moon to show the way. Step after slow step, he tracked his target, always keeping an eye out for others. He came alone and in secret. His life depended on it.

A glimpse of black fur caught his eye. He studied

the area for a second longer. A small bit of relief followed as he realized he'd finally located the exact animal he'd been searching for curled up under a thick canopy of a recently budded out small tree.

Max kept his voice low as he spoke to the injured wolf. "It's Max." He approached cautiously, carefully paying attention to what his nose, ears, and eyes told him, not only to detect life in the wolf, but also to be aware of anyone sneaking up on him. To approach the beast was dangerous enough. If others viewed his actions, his life went from threatened to downright endangered.

The wolf didn't move. Not a single whimper, motion, or ear flick. That concerned him. When he kneeled down and saw the damage done to the wolf's body up close, anger and fear rushed to the fore. He'd seen the violent battle, had an inkling of the injuries Jacques must have suffered before he'd collapsed from loss of blood and a brutal throat bite that pretty much suffocated the air out of Jacques's lungs. He'd been left for dead by the prick Garrison.

A lump formed in Max's throat. Never had he expected to find his alpha, no matter that he'd just lost the savage battle to a usurper, lying on the chilly earth in such a state. Barely breathing. Broken. On the verge of death.

Gravely, Max reached out, putting his hand in front of the animal's nose. Air barely brushed his fingers as the wolf struggled to breathe. Shit. This is bad. Really bad.

Max glanced around, knowing what he had to do, but needing a foolproof plan. Jacques's only chance lay in Max getting him to a safe house and now.

Somewhere that could care for him in such critical condition as well as ensure his safety through utmost secrecy. Quickly, he ran possible places through his mind, finally deciding on a single one. Far away, but distance would be their friend. If only he could reach it in time.

Max shook his head, dispelling the grisly images. He blinked and focused on the cell phone once again. Overpowering need prompted him to give it a try. He had to find out about his friend. Little else mattered.

He considered how long Tara would soak and opted to take a chance. Stealthily, he jumped down, hurried over to the table, and quickly changed forms. Once he stood on two legs, he grabbed the phone, strode to the garage door, then quietly let himself out. There, he began dialing as soon as he obtained a signal, making his way to the far corner in order to cut down on the echoes.

The phone rang and rang. Each one tested his patience all the more.

The fourth one, it rolled over to voice mail.

With a muffled curse, Max clicked off the call. He dared not leave a message and risk Becky calling back on Tara's phone. He'd risked enough just trying to make contact. More irritable than before, he made his way back to the kitchen, replaced the cell phone in the exact same position he'd found it, and morphed back into his wolf form.

Annoyed and bored, he decided to go check on Tara.

Not like I can easily pick up the television remote and thumb through channels. He rolled his eyes at the lack of abilities in this form. Tasks he'd once taken for granted.

Max peeked around the corner and into the bathroom, where Tara had left the door wide open. He found her submerged, chest deep in the water as she reclined against the back of the tub. In between the soapy bubbles, he caught a glimpse of her bare body. The top of her cleavage rose above the water line, though the lack of suds allowed him a perfect view of her modest but pretty breasts, each one topped with a rose-hued nipple. A flat stomach widened into flaring hips, then down to toned thighs and shapely calves. As he studied the vision before him, he noticed her gaze focused on him.

"Was I taking too long and you thought you'd check to make sure I didn't drown?" she asked warmly and followed with a smile.

Not really. I just decided a little sexual torture would make for a nice change.

Her scent called to him. The mixture of soap, shampoo, and even the detergent emanating from her discarded work clothes in a nearby hamper drew his attention. A tantalizing vanilla. Too delicious and alluring to ignore. He could sniff the wonderful aroma all day long and never get enough. The same with her touches, her smiles, the sweet way she spoke to him. Magical. That's how he described her sweet affection.

Spying her naked only added to the mixture, igniting his libido into a demanding hunger. He'd been too long without sex, but that wasn't the issue. Tara, in her infinite goodness, sparked his desires like no other. Which sucked considering this wasn't the time or the place for pending romance. Hunted men didn't reap such luxury.

I have to leave. Tomorrow. Just take off.

Yeah right. See how well that turned out already. He snorted at himself.

"You look so serious, Cotton. Like you're really worried about me." She sat up, reached a hand over the edge of the tub, and rubbed his chin. "Everything is okay. I promise."

Oh, how he wished she had the power to make such a vow.

"You'll get frown lines if you don't smile," she teased. "It's a proven fact."

Like that's a threat.

He nuzzled her hand, unable to keep his gaze off her exposed breasts. The soap suds framed both, while adding a peekaboo enticement. Small, but perky, they held his attention while shooting a healthy dose of lust into his already hardening cock.

At this rate, I'll be humping those damn pillows.

He forced himself to meet her eyes, saw the happiness there, and his decision to leave wavered all the more.

You got yourself in one hell of a pickle this time, bro.

"Guess I should get out of the tub and see about dinner, huh?" She pulled the plug to let the water out, then stood up, leaving her glistening body on display for Max.

He stared, unable to look away, taking in every inch of Tara's beauty, deciding this view was even better than when she soaked in the tub. That might have been more erotic, but her totally exposed flesh jacked up his hunger in a major way.

She grabbed her towel and used it on her hair. Her

breasts jiggled with the motion, drawing his attention to the pebbled peaks that he so craved tasting.

Lust ran free causing his cock to ache. He exerted his iron control to keep from changing right then and there, just to get a brief touch of her lips on his. As it was, the days she'd left him while she went to work, he'd jacked off in the shower. The release only appeased him for a short period of time, until she came home, then he found himself in the same boat—wanting her. Needing her. Wishing she was his for the taking.

Tara wiped down the rest of her body, tossed the towel into the hamper, then headed toward the bedroom.

Max didn't follow. He couldn't. Not without presenting himself more torture than he could bear. That was the same reason he chose to make his bed on the couch every night. To sleep next to her would prove too much of a lure. Better to hang out by himself rather than take a chance on shifting in his sleep, and have her waking up screaming in panic.

He made his way back to the couch. His safe zone. Well away from the temptation of a beautiful woman, a lady that he wanted for his own, standing in all her naked glory before getting dressed.

Tara emerged a few minutes later, wearing loose sweats. She stopped at the large standalone freezer, opened the lid, and bent over to reach deep inside, giving Max a perfect view of her ass. The sweats pulled snug, outlining her heart-shaped rear. His body responded all the more.

Damn it. Why couldn't she be an ogre? He'd have no problem leaving a mean person. But, combine her compassion with a nicely curved figure and he was a goner.

And if she didn't do something pretty quick, he'd be taking advantage of his wolf form to lick his own fucking cock.

"I thought I had a casserole in here somewhere." She stood up and brushed her hair out of her face. But, I can't seem to find it anywhere." She eyed Cotton. "I'd accuse you of eating it, but that's just not possible."

He looked up at her innocently.

She shook her head. "I must be getting forgetful. Too much on my mind lately." She pulled a white wrapped package out before closing the lid on the freezer, patted Max's head, and returned to the kitchen. "I'll just put the chicken breasts on to bake. They won't take too long since they're fresh. I'll prepare this pot roast for the slow cooker tomorrow morning and we'll eat it for dinner."

After making her way back to the kitchen, she busied herself at the sink. "I need to go to the store and soon. We're going through a lot of meat. Expensive and another hit on the budget." She peered over at him. "It's okay though. I'll figure out a way. I always do."

He sighed, the heavy weight of fault nearly squashing him. He couldn't even look at her any longer, knowing he bore much responsibility for her hardship.

She finished in the kitchen, slid the chicken into the oven, then wandered over to sit on the couch beside him. Languidly, she ran her hand over his head and down his back. "I'm so lucky. You make my life complete." She played with one of his ears. "Times might be hard but you make everything better. Give me hope. A reason to be happy and appreciate the small stuff. Thank you."

Her words hit him deep.

Even though he wanted her for more than a pet owner, he couldn't keep himself from edging closer in order to lay his head on her lap and soak up the rapt attention. Affection. Adoration. Love. He'd never really known those emotions. Until now.

For a person that had so little to give, she never acted like he'd been a burden—just the opposite. She smiled often, worked hard, and seemed determined to make the world a brighter place. In his former life, such a sweet woman would have been beaten down by some of the more jealous and aggressive pack females and/or taken advantage of by the men searching for a quick hook up. Her charitable personality would have suffered greatly at their hands. For the Throwback Pack didn't believe in anything but ruthless domination and rigid rules. Jacques tried to tamp that down, but to no avail in the end. Yet, Max wasn't naïve. He'd seen the same attitudes in the human population. Greed. Indifference. Hate.

Except for Tara and the little town she called home.

Face the facts, Max. You don't want to leave any more than you want to return to that hellhole called a pack. Perhaps they could eke out a life here. Just the two of them. Leaning on one another during the difficult times, celebrating the good ones. She made him smile and laugh, more so than he ever recalled doing. He craved her touch, found himself listening to her voice just for the soothing quality, and worrying about her safety, her happiness.

Everything boiled down to one thing—all he had to offer was trouble.

While he'd protect her with his life, he wouldn't be strong enough to best two or three shifters at a time. Granted, he'd traveled over a thousand miles on foot in the past few months but no distance would be good enough if Garrison wanted him. And, knowing the bastard, he wouldn't give up until Max's wolf hide was cured and hung on the wall of his lodge. Max could deal with his own demise but the idea that Garrison came across Tara concerned him. If Garrison linked the two of them together, he'd make her suffer greatly before killing her.

I can't let that happen.

Taking off would protect her, but he couldn't handle her tears. He didn't have much need for emotions, but she'd plucked his heart strings with her calls. He'd rather get his paw stuck in a trap than put her through that again.

But, how else can I ensure her safety and shield her when I'm a hunted man?

Chapter 6

"*Aiding and abetting an enemy is an offense punishable by death,*" *Garrison bit out.*

"*Big words.*" *Max taunted him, tired of the pissing contest. He sidestepped, putting his back to the hallway. In order to buy himself a few precious seconds, he needed to get a head start. Simply rushing out the front door didn't give him that ability. But, locking them out of the bedroom and exiting through the window would.*

"*I'm going to rip you apart just like I did Jacques, you mixed breed piece of shit. You'll beg for mercy before I'm done.*"

"*Go fuck yourself.*" *Max leapt into his bedroom, slammed the door shut, put the wooden bar down to keep it shut, and locked the door. He yanked the window open, shifted, shook his clothes loose, and jumped out in less than two seconds. He sprinted toward the woods, only for a large wolf to ram him from the side.*

Max toppled and rolled. When he came to his feet, he faced Garrison, in his wolf form. The gray and brown ticks of his coat were unforgettable as well as the cruelty in his eyes. Max snarled, his hackles up, as he stared at Garrison head on.

His wolf clamored for control. Max let him have it, relying on centuries of instincts to aid in this bid for survival.

Garrison pounced.

Max evaded him, managing to clamp onto Garrison's foot in the process. He clamped down hard and twisted.

Garrison yelped, curled around, and raked his nails over Max's side, leaving furrows of blood in his wake.

Adrenaline kept Max moving. The instinct to survive strong. He withstood crushing bites, poundings, and scratches. Garrison clamped down on Max's rear thigh, tearing into muscle all the way to the bone. Max managed to break loose and bit in return, but he was no match for Garrison in sheer strength. Hurt, bleeding, and rapidly losing energy, Max focused on an escape route. He'd found nooks and hiding places over his lifetime in the pack as well as a handful of areas that no one could follow his scent, not even the best tracker in the pack.

I just have to get there.

Steeling himself against the pain, Max dove forward, snapping his jaws onto Garrison's cheek. He yanked, ripping the flesh away.

Garrison went down. His second in command, Conley, took a flank position next to the alpha, but didn't actively pursue Max.

Max wasn't about to look a gift horse in the mouth. He turned and darted for the woods. Tagart nipped at his heels, but couldn't get close enough to do more damage. Three bounds later, Max hit the creek, crossed it, and set his sights on the far north range of pack lands. If he could reach there, he had a chance.

Max jerked awake with a start. For a second he was back there, running for his life. His breath sawed and his heart pounded.

Then familiar scents caught his attention. He glanced around the room, finding the cottage undisturbed.

He sat up, scrubbed his face, and shoved the awful memory to the recesses of his mind. Not that it stayed there long. Every so often, that same dream haunted him. Reminding him of his failure. Of the sacrifice Jacques made, perhaps the ultimate sacrifice for their pack. Once more he cursed the lack of a landline phone. He'd use it in a heartbeat and pay Tara back for the call later. Hell, he'd call collect. Yet, that wasn't even an option.

Revved up with left over adrenaline, Max stood and surveyed the room. He focused on the present. Tara. And her absence.

Worry returned in spades.

Max paced the house in restless agitation. Tara opted to leave him at home for the day after he laid around and refused to hop into the car with her as had been the usual over the past few days. Not a bad thing, as Max missed his long soaks in the tub, the abundance of food waiting to be thawed and cooked, and the almost rare pleasure of walking around on two legs. Yet, he found the house quiet—too quiet—without her there.

He'd had his bath, dressed in yet another towel, made himself a couple of hamburger patties, and cleaned up the mess.

Whoever thought I'd end up with dishwater hands? He smirked at the thought. In truth, he'd worked hard to feed his growling stomach and leave no evidence behind. Obviously, Tara had already noticed the missing casserole. In due time, she'd detect her freezer emptying out at an alarming rate and start to ask questions. Before that happened, he had to be gone.

His inner beast growled at the idea of leaving.

I know. I know. I couldn't do it before so what makes me think I can do it now?

He blew out his breath and plopped down on the couch in order to rest his face in his hands. Her cries broke his heart when he'd tried to leave. He'd have to be one hell of a bastard to do that to her. Which left only one option—tell her the truth.

And she'll shoot me thinking I'm some sort of perverted ax murderer waiting to ambush her when she comes home from work.

If only she knew about shifters, that would help a huge amount. He couldn't be that lucky. Judging by Rose's whispers to him and the lack of conversation between her and Tara concerning him as a man, Max picked up on the truth. Rose and her pack kept the secret tight lipped. Fine and dandy. Except that left him up a creek without a proverbial paddle when it came to telling Tara.

"What the hell am I supposed to do? Be in wolf form when she shows up, then change? Hi, Tara, before you take me out on a leash to pee, let me tell you something." He snorted. "Yeah, right. She'll fall over in a dead faint."

He stood and made another pass around the couch. "I'm a werewolf. Friendly werewolf. Not prone to biting or fits of aggression." *That's even worse.* He sighed. "How do I tell her what I am without freaking her totally out?"

No answers came.

He paused in front of the big front window and peered outside. For a split second he considered shifting and taking off. Just as quickly, he discarded it. He'd tried and failed. Thus, that option was off the table. Besides, his best chances to get back on his feet lay with Tara.

Not everyone would have been so understanding and compassionate to take a wounded dog in and care for him as a treasured pet. Most would have driven on, leaving him on the road to his fate. At that moment in time, he truly didn't care what the outcome would be. Exhausted and hurt, he'd long since accepted his inevitable demise. Now, he had a full stomach, complete healing, warmth, and a grasp on the future—all thanks to Tara.

Not for the first time he wondered about her. Why she lived on the edge of the wilderness, drove a car of all things, in northern Minnesota, and owned a bookstore. She looked like a bookworm, a pretty one at that. Intelligence flashed in her eyes. She carried herself with confidence and determination. He noted the lines of stress on her face and understood the financial burdens were weighing her down. She spoke of it. Apprehension carried in her voice as she contemplated what happened if she threw in the towel on her struggling business. He hated to see her sorrow, and remorse ate at him knowing that he put an additional load on her.

He could and would pay her back, though. Unfortunately, he couldn't say when that might be. Potentially too late to save her store.

She'd be devastated, no doubt. What she would do for a job after that, he didn't know. Doubted if she did, either. Times were hard, at least from what he'd heard before taking off and living off the land for a few months.

Tara didn't deserve the daily struggle. Her kindness and caring attitude were superior to what he'd seen in another person, especially a woman. Though there were a few exceptions, the majority of the women in his pack gave him a poor example of how ladies behaved. Unfortunately, he seemed to only have dealings with the troublemakers and they had soured his perception. He saw that now. Tara showed him there were angels on earth.

Why she didn't have a man, he didn't have a clue, just thanked his fortune that she was single. Because way too easily, he could imagine making her his and keeping her for all time.

Hunted prey doesn't have the luxury of a love life.

Reality returned with the shock of an ice bath.

His presence endangered Tara.

He sighed. *Can Garrison's thugs track me this far? Would they? Can Garrison ever just write me off as gone and give up?* Max didn't think Garrison would forget any slight, let alone outright disobedience and assisting the enemy. Still, for all Garrison knew, Max could be anywhere by now. Months of travel, even in wolf form, could cover many miles and several states or territories.

What's the chances he can find me? Slim? Too bad it's not none.

Antsy, he glanced around the room, finding everything orderly and neat. He'd love to spend the free time on the laptop computer or calling to check on Jacques but was totally out of luck as she took both items with her that morning. So, he walked around nearly in the buff, with only the television, a radio, and an empty house for entertainment.

If only I could access my accounts. Money wouldn't be an issue once he could get his identity cards replaced and transfer some funds around.

That's one thing he knew for certain couldn't be taken or destroyed by Garrison. Max worked hard to hide his income, to stash it away, far from Oregon and the pack. He understood Garrison would likely challenge Jacques—the bastard rumbled enough about it during the months that Jacques ruled. Max also knew the guy well enough to prepare. Garrison, once crossed, would never forgive or forget. By throwing himself in with Jacques, Max forfeited everything—his house, his standing in the pack, his very existence.

Except he'd made allowances for this scenario. The funds were untouchable. Even to him. Until he found a way to access them.

He tapped his fingers on his leg and kicked his sluggish brain into action. *How can I get cash?*

Certainly, there were no local branches of his bank. No. The amount he stashed required some big names in the banking field. They were also the most protected from hacking and willing to bend over backward for his business. That meant, he had to show up in person in order to make a withdrawal. Online banking he had, but that didn't put real money in his hands.

Unless...

He could transfer funds to Tara's account. She could withdraw that amount from her bank, and hand over the cash.

The more he considered the option, the more he

found it sound.

There was just one big problem—she thought of him as her dog.

Ugh. He blew out a breath in frustration. *And I'm back to square one.*

"It would help if I had more than this stupid towel to wear. She's going to walk in, see me in my birthday suit, declare me a rapist, and kick my ass." Sure, he could put the blanket back on, but decided he appeared more like a grim reaper with it draped over most of his body. Not the image he wanted to portray. At least the towel offered basic coverage with a smidgen less creepiness. Since the clothing option wasn't anything he could fix, he moved on. "Start as a man or as my wolf? Decisions, decisions."

****

Tara pulled into the garage, happy to be done with the day of work. Business had picked up only marginally, not enough to celebrate, certainly, but she'd take what she could get. A trifle was better than nothing. After parking her car, she shut the garage door again, shivering as she stepped out of the driver's seat. While the snow had mostly melted, another arctic front took the temperatures well down below zero. Too cold for anything to be outside for long.

She stepped into the kitchen, pausing to close the door behind her. "Hey, Cotton. I'm home."

Three observations hit her at the same time. The whole kitchen smelled of delicious hot food. Secondly, Cotton didn't come greet her. And third, a strange man stood at the stove stirring a pot. Not only didn't she recognize him, but he happened to only be wearing a large blue towel around his waist, the rest of his body bare. He turned toward her and offered up a small smile, as if he welcomed her home every day.

Fear stole her breath. She reached for the gun stowed in her purse only to find she'd left it in the car.

He was tall, muscular, and built. Any other time she'd drool over the picture he presented. Right now, she could only think about his intentions. The possibilities running through her head didn't evoke happy feelings in the least.

"Who are you? What are you doing here?" She realized the questions, though relevant, were ridiculous. "Never mind. Just get out. Leave. Now." She tried to add firm authority in her voice but heard the small tremor of fright anyway.

"Hello, Tara."

He knows my name. That didn't bode well. She swallowed the lump in her throat and backed toward the door. *Is he a stalker? A nude burglar? Something worse?*

"I'm not going to hurt you. Never could I do that." His low, quiet voice came across as soothing but she wasn't buying it. Men didn't run around naked in winter in this part of the country. Why he chose to break into her house, she didn't have a clue. The only thing that mattered was getting him out and fast.

Quickly, she searched all around, finding nothing amiss. Except Cotton. He was nowhere in sight. Dread made her stomach clench. A wave of nausea followed. "Where's my dog? What did you do to him? If you so much as hurt a single hair on his body…" She trailed off, leaving the threat open-ended.

The man set down the spoon he'd been using to stir with and took a step in her direction. She moved slightly away but noticed his relaxed stance, the lack of tension or rushing in his motions.

"I'm your dog, Cotton."

Oh, my god. A lunatic has broken into my house and done something to my dog. "What did you do to him?" She fought panic as Cotton still didn't appear. The thought of what could have happened sickened her further.

Spying a nearby skillet on the counter, she lunged, took it in hand, and held it up like a baseball bat. "Tell me where my dog is, then get the hell out of my house." As much as she'd like to run, she wasn't about to leave without Cotton.

He held his hands out to his sides. "Tara. Calm down. I'm not going to hurt you. I'll explain, if you'll just sit down and listen." The cajoling voice didn't lessen her trepidation in the least.

"I said now, buster." She waved the pan then swung at him.

He ducked just in the nick of time to avoid being smacked in the head. Standing, he yanked it from her fingers in a move so fast she wasn't sure she saw it. One second she aimed the impromptu weapon at him, the next it was back on the counter. "Tara."

He came closer. She retreated, searching for any opening to escape.

"Just give me a second to explain." He approached slowly, cutting off her exit back into the garage.

"I don't want explanations. I want answers. Where's my dog?"

"I *am* your dog. I'm Cotton."

In the next moment, Cotton stood before her, the towel having fallen to the floor at his feet. He stared up at her with those familiar brown eyes, wagged his tail, then nosed her leg.

She plunked down on the couch, too stunned to remain upright. "I'm seeing things." She reached out and touched Cotton's head, felt the familiar soft fur, and began to stroke him. The action gave her a semblance of balance and control. Not much, but better than when she stood staring at a man wearing only a towel. "You're my dog." She wasn't sure she hadn't lost her mind but the evidence was right in front of her.

Belatedly, she realized he knew the dog's name though she hadn't spoken it aloud. That allowed reality to sink in a bit further.

The man took the place of the dog, sitting on the floor, though he grabbed the towel and pulled it across his lap. "Sort of." He tilted his head and smiled slightly. "My name is Max. Max Jameson. I'm a wolf shifter. A werewolf if you prefer."

"Those only exist in fairy tales." The soft words slipped out.

He shook his head. "You see me, hear me. You were just touching my fur. Believe, Tara. Shifters exist. More so than you could know."

He changed forms again, this time remaining as Cotton for a couple of minutes. His eyes, those piercing, beautiful chocolate eyes, locked onto her. Those same ones that existed in the man's face when he transformed to human once again. She saw the intelligence, the truth. Never would she have guessed such a creature existed.

"I'm a shifter, Tara. Able to take either wolf or human form at will."

"How does one become a shifter?"

He smiled again, that crooked little grin that spoke of lazy amusement. "We're born that way, Tara. I can't bite you and turn you into a werewolf. That's only a myth."

"Like werewolves are?"

He inclined his head.

I can't believe I'm sitting here talking to a nude man in my house—one who just happened to be my pet. Or was. Is. Something like that. She shook her head trying to clear the fog and wrap her mind around this latest development.

"You have a family. A pack." She tried to work through some more information, filling in the pieces to the newfound puzzle that was Cotton—err, Max.

"That's a long story. To make it short, I've been on my own for a while now." He lowered his head slightly. "You were right when you said I wasn't doing well. It was a struggle. Then you picked me up from a snow-covered road. Rescued me."

She drew in air, her gaze never leaving his face. There was a story there, a big one. She'd learn it eventually.

"Cotton...Max." She tried out the new name, finding it fitting. "I thought you were a dog." Her face heated as she recalled her *faux pas*.

He gently patted her knee. "Thank God you did." He grinned sheepishly. "Although I won't say having to do my business at the end of a leash was my favorite part of the whole deal." A small chuckle followed.

"I'm so sorry." Embarrassment crashed through her as she realized what she'd done. "I didn't know." She covered her mouth with one hand, mortified that she'd done such a thing to him.

"I know. It's okay." He sat up a little straighter. "You opened your home, cared for me, fed me. Offered companionship without anything asked in return. That's a rare kindness, Tara. Don't regret a moment of it." He grabbed the towel and held it over himself. "I fixed some soup. Why don't we sit down, eat, and I'll answer more of your questions?"

She nodded, still in semi-shock. Curiosity and amazement replaced fear, although she still felt a little uncomfortable. If he'd put some clothes on, it would help. Belatedly, she realized he didn't have any. Certainly, she didn't have a single garment that would fit—not with his size. Tall and muscular, he'd likely not be able to wear even her socks, let alone anything else. Her heart went out to him, knowing he came with nothing, not even a pair of shoes. To be so absolutely helpless. To be so alone.

She didn't know him but she knew Cotton. He was quiet, respectful, and tender. Surely, the man wouldn't be any different? Weren't they one and the same? "Are you alike in both forms?" She couldn't imagine what it would be like to transform into an animal.

He walked over to the kitchen, opened a cabinet, and pulled out a couple of bowls before gesturing to the table.

A little hesitant, she stood up and took one of the chairs.

"Yes and no. I'm still me, just more instinctual in wolf form." He filled the two bowls, then carried them over.

She smiled up at him in thanks, then realized he must have done this before. "The missing food…"

Max returned with two glasses filled with iced tea,

setting them next to the plates. Silverware followed. "Too delicious to pass up. I didn't want to steal but I was hungry. So hungry." He sat and lifted his glass in a small toast.

Tara picked up the spoon and dipped it into the steaming food.

His words sank in. She remembered the way he came to her. Thin, dirty, and gaunt. So he'd rummaged through her freezer and ate part of her stash of meals. She couldn't blame him at all. She'd bathed him. That particular thought sent a wave of interest through her. Sure, he'd been in dog—err, wolf form, but she'd ran her hands over his body. That toned, primed, manly body.

She lightly tested a spoonful, finding the meal both hot and tasty.

Then she recalled something else. He'd seen her in the buff, in the tub and out. Her spoon clanked to the table. "Oh, my God. You saw me naked."

"Well…" He paused with his spoon in midair.

"You *saw* me naked," she reiterated. Her cheeks warmed in a big way.

"It wasn't bad."

"Not bad?" She arched an eyebrow at him.

He held up both hands. "You're beautiful. Inside and out."

"Uh, huh." Sarcasm entered her tone.

He smiled slightly. "It's true."

The sincere quality to his voice warmed her. She opened her mouth to protest flattery, then shut it right back. Something told her that he wasn't lying just to keep her good graces. "Thank you."

"You're welcome." He took another spoonful of

soup.

She watched the way he handled the utensil, the grace in his movements, the sure grip. As he opened, she noted his full lips, the way they gently closed down on the spoon. The flash of straight white teeth. No large fangs to be seen. Her stomach flip-flopped.

Oh, good grief. I'm turned on just watching the guy eat. That's a new level of desperation.

Now that her faculties started to work again, she appraised him thoroughly. His deep brown eyes reminded her of delicious, melted sweet chocolate. Right now they emanated contentment and curiosity. Not a bad combination. Black hair appeared a little shaggy, as if it had been a few weeks since his last trim. The slightly curly locks hung past his shoulders. That, along with the stubble on his cheek gave him a rakish appeal that worked for him. Wide shoulders flowed into powerful arms, the muscles snapping and extending with the simple act of eating. His chest sported no hair but appeared solid and definitely snuggle-able. She peered over the edge of the table, noting the well-toned six pack abs, the strong thighs, and a side view of his rear through the gap in the towel presently sitting on the wooden chair. A man in his prime, sculpted by hard work and hard living, she was certain. He carried strength and confidence, along with a small grin that drew out a dimple in his cheek when he caught her checking him out.

"Like what you see?"

She shrugged, pretending to be more unaffected than she really was. "Not bad."

Max chuckled.

Tara decided she liked the sound.

"Touché."

Tara took a drink then cleared her throat. "Can you tell me how you ended up being my dog?" That had to be quite the story and she couldn't wait to hear it.

Max finished his bite and swallowed. "Are you sure? It's not a pleasant tale."

She paused. What did she really know about the guy? Nothing, except as her pet, he was sweet, attentive, and could have mauled her at any point in time. Instead, he stuck it out and now trusted her with his secret. That had to count for something. "Yes." She picked up her spoon again and resumed her meal.

"I'm from the Throwback Wolf Pack from Oregon. Let's just say they're not the nicest shifters to be raised with. Old school, fight it out, meanest wolf wins."

"That's horrible." Tara easily read between the lines. "Survival of the fittest."

"Pretty much." Max took another spoonful. "Jacques, the alpha I aligned myself with, lost his position in less than seven months. The one who took the throne, Garrison, left him for dead."

Tara swallowed hard. She couldn't imagine such a harsh existence. Didn't want to think of Max in that situation. "How could he be so cruel?"

"It's winner take all in that pack. The loser is considered weak and forfeits his life because of it." Max took a drink of tea. "Jacques was trying to change that, to bring the group to the modern age. When Jacques fell, the rest of the new philosophy went with him." Max's fingers tightened on the utensil, hard enough to whiten his knuckles.

"What happened to Jacques?" She had to know upon seeing the hurt cross Max's face. Max cared for his friend. She could see that easily.

"I disobeyed orders, found him in the woods, and took him to a safe place where he could get medical care." The flatness of Max's tone told her he didn't regret his actions but felt guilty that he didn't do more. "I hurriedly returned to the Throwback Pack to cover my tracks and afford Jacques some protection with the ruse. Too late. Garrison and his thugs were waiting for me when I arrived."

"They hurt you." She knew they had. If they were brutal enough to nearly kill another wolf, they would make mincemeat out of Max for defying them.

Max shrugged. "I survived." He scooped up more of the soup.

She considered his tale. The sacrifice he made for his friend. The punishment his former family dished out. "Did Jacques make it?"

Max's lips thinned. "I don't know."

She pursed her lips. Max had been in wolf form all this time. No pockets to carry anything like a cell phone. No wallet for money. Not even the clothes on his back. Reality sank in. *Max truly had nothing.*

Her heart bled for what he must have endured.

She lifted her head. "Be right back." A quick dash out to the garage, she retrieved her purse from the car, and brought it inside. She dug her cell phone out and handed it over. "Call. Right now."

He met her gaze, reached out, and slowly accepted the phone. "I have to tell you I tried to call the other night when you were in the bath. No one answered."

She nodded. "Thank you for being honest. I appreciate that." Her mind whirled with puzzle pieces clicking into place. "You weren't chasing a rabbit that evening?"

"No."

"You were running away." She made it a statement, though it hurt.

"Yes."

"Why?"

His face scrunched for a few seconds. "I'm a hunted man, Tara. Yes, it's been months, but I can't believe that Garrison has given up finding me. His pride was hurt. Others in the pack were bound to find out. All that leaves a blemish on his reputation." He shook his head. "No. Garrison won't stop coming. I protected Jacques the best I could. Now, I must protect you."

Emotions welled up inside Tara. "No more running. We can face this challenge together."

Max opened his mouth, then shut it again. He lifted the phone in the air. "I need to call."

Tara nodded.

Standing, he made his way to the back bedroom, seemingly for a little privacy.

She watched him go with so much more enlightenment than before. Shame for what she'd put him through warred with sympathy. Max had been through the wringer. It was time for things to change. After all, nothing she'd seen to this point told her that he deserved a lick of it. Sure, she could be wrong, but she prided herself on the ability to read people. Maybe not from first impressions. Given time, though, she figured out what made them tick. Oftentimes, that made for an ugly picture. *Which is probably the reason I'm single and can't find a boyfriend.*

She replayed his words, finding them shocking, disturbing, and surreal. She hadn't quite wrapped her mind around the fact that shifters existed in the first place, let alone a family unit that took status levels to the extreme. The rigors Max must have faced before and after leaving the pack. She couldn't imagine such perils and cruelty.

I'm a sucker for sad cases.

If he's lying to me then I'm doomed. For she'd already made her mind up to help him in every way possible. It was the right thing to do.

Certainly, everything she knew about him meshed well with his story. His sorry condition when he showed up on the road. The gauntness, the hunger. The intelligence she saw in his eyes and the determination to survive. His seeming dislike of the game of fetch and the haughty snorts she heard now and again when she took him to the bathroom. She'd found them amusing before. Never would she have imagined the indignity he must have felt. How many times had he wanted to change to human form? To get his stomach completely filled? To stop eating off a platter on the floor?

Her shoulders sank as she realized what she's unknowingly put him through. The degradation when he was obviously a powerful, proud man.

A werewolf. The fact still amazed her as she struggled with disbelief. If he hadn't changed forms twice before her eyes, she would've called him a liar. Now, she simply tried to put the picture together, along with his story. He might be playing her, but she doubted it. Why else would he hang around and put up with such humiliation from her credence that he was an unfortunate, homeless dog?

This certainly changes things. Big time. Questions ran through her head, all without answers until Max returned and hashed more details out.

She focused on eating her supper, once again thankful that Max had been considerate enough to cook. No one had done so since her grandparents were alive.

A few minutes later, he strode back into the kitchen and placed her cell phone on the table next to her. "Thank you."

Tara searched his face, finding a serious expression, though he appeared a little more relaxed. "How is he?"

Max sat back down. "He's alive. Still healing and getting his strength back but he pulled through." Relief carried through in his voice.

Sympathy prodded her to do something to make it better. "Whatever we need to do, that's just what'll happen. I can close the shop for a few days. We can drive down to see him."

"No need."

"Why not?"

Max offered up a lopsided grin. "I'm a pilot and can fly."

She processed that little gem. "But you'd need a plane."

He nodded. "Yes. I don't personally own one, just grew up following in my father's footsteps as the pilot for the pack."

She blinked at the level of wealth that a group of people must have in order to afford their own plane. "Perhaps you can rent one?"

"Maybe. I can check into it but won't be able to do anything until I get copies of my identification and pilot's license." The corners of his mouth turned down.

"Where do we get that done? I'll take you

wherever you need to go." She found herself offering to drive him all over creation in order to obtain what he needed to get back on his feet and back to his friend. He belonged with those of his own kind, his friends and family, not out in the back forty of Minnesota with a woman who couldn't even keep her small business afloat.

"I'm not sure but we can probably look it up on the computer." He scratched his chin where a few days' growth gave him a more rugged appearance. "We used to have a pack member take care of all that stuff—getting licenses renewed and such." He snorted. "Not like I can go back and ask him."

"No, you can't." She thought for a moment. "Are you sure your wallet is forever gone?"

Max shrugged. "It was in my back pocket when I shifted, shook out of my clothes, and ran for my life. Even if it's still laying on my bedroom floor, I'm not sure stepping back into Throwback territory to retrieve it is a great plan."

"Yeah, I can see that. So, we're back to doing it the human way. Probably slow and through lots of red tape, too." She hopped up, made her way back to the car once again, pulled out her laptop, and carried it into the house. After setting it down next to Max, she pushed the power button, unraveled the cords, and plugged it into the wall. "You can search for whatever you need." She stepped back over to her side of the table, a little uneasy at the closeness.

"Thanks." Max adjusted the towel around his waist.

Which brought up another dilemma. "If you'll let me know what size clothes and shoes you wear, I'll leave you here tomorrow and do some shopping."

Max frowned. "You don't need to do that."

She tilted her head. "Well, you can't run around in the nude, especially not outside this time of year. In order to show up to get your identification, you will need to wear something. Since you presently have nothing and my stuff is too small, how else do you propose you get clothes to wear?"

Max sighed. "I was going to steal some from one of those big clothing donation boxes." He lowered his head as if ashamed to admit the truth.

She couldn't fault his thinking. After all, if there was anyone truly desperate, it was Max. "Now you don't have to do that. Just tell me what you need and I'll get them tomorrow."

"Look." Max ran his hand through his hair. "I know you don't have money to spare. The last thing you need to do is spend what little you have on me."

Tara lifted her chin. "I may not be rich but I *can* and *will* get you some clothes."

"Tara…"

She raised one hand. "Don't argue. Unless you're going to show up to the DMV wrapped in a towel, then you don't have much choice but to go along with it."

His lips tightened, then his shoulders dropped. "I'll pay you back. Every cent."

She waved her hand. "We'll discuss that down the road. Right now, we have to prioritize. You need to find out how to get copies of your identification and find a way to get to your friend."

He met her gaze steadily. "I'm not a low life freeloader."

She blinked at him. "I didn't say you were." When

he remained mute, she continued on. "There's no other option right now, Max. It's okay." She patted his hand gently. "Let me do this for you."

His gaze flicked from her face down to her hand and back again. Finally, he let out air. "Okay."

She smiled at him and put optimism into her voice. "It'll be all right, just you wait and see."

"Don't make those kinds of promises, Tara." Max picked up his spoon and began eating once more. "My life hasn't been a great example of that sentiment."

Tara heard the remorse in his tone, which pulled at her own heartstrings. She could fall hook, line, and sinker for him way too easily. Leeriness forced her to rein in her trust levels until she had more time to observe Max. Opting for cautiousness, she went with an olive twig. "Your path brought you here, turned things around. That's something."

He inclined his head. "That's more than something. It's a damn miracle." He stared at her a long moment, respect and appreciation lighting up his brown eyes.

Tara's breath caught. Never before had a man looked at her like that—as if she were an angel from the heavens come to bestow blessings on him.

A little uncomfortable with the praise, she cleared her throat. "Yeah, well, don't start putting my application in for sainthood yet. I did ask the vet about neutering you."

Max's lips hitched upward in a crooked smile. "There's that."

"Good thing he recommended to hold off for a while." She rambled on.

"Yeah, kind of him." Max went back to eating.

Queries bounced around her mind. "Are there

were-elephants?"

Max paused with the spoon halfway to his mouth. "Not that I know of." He took a bite of soup and swallowed before saying more. "Probably some were-cats. Other than that, I don't really know."

"Were-snakes." Tara shuddered. "I'm sorry. I don't care how gorgeous the guy might be, I couldn't live with a snake, not even a part time one."

Max chuckled. "Don't blame you there."

She finished her soup, then drank the rest of her iced tea. Full, she stood and placed her dishes in the sink.

Max did the same before turning her to face him. "Why are you doing all this for me?"

Tara considered the question for a long moment. "Because you need and deserve a break. Because you showed me unconditional love as Cotton. Because I believe you're a good guy that can do positive things if only given the chance." Truth carried in her voice.

You're sexy as sin too and I seem to have a craving for some werewolf lately. Uh, huh. Not like gorgeous men can't be serial killers. Seen enough horror movies to know.

She mentally shook her head to rid the topic from her mind and stared into Max's eyes, finding awe and something else she couldn't quite name reflected in his gaze.

He reached up, cupped her cheek, and lightly rubbed his thumb across the skin. "You're too trusting."

She swallowed, soaking up the gentle affection. "Maybe so, but I have to go with my gut on this one."

Max drew in a breath. The sight of his chest expanding touched her deep, leaving a hint of pleasure mixed with an abundance of desire. She maintained the stare, unable to break away.

Slowly, ever so slowly, Max tilted his head, then lowered.

Without hesitation, Tara lifted up to meet him, closing her eyes as she did.

His lips brushed across hers so lightly, she wasn't sure they'd actually made contact. She rested her hands on his shoulders and waited for the next pass—which didn't come. Opening her eyes, she looked at Max, trying to decipher the myriad of emotions flickering across his face. He didn't release her or budge an inch, only lifted his head and peered down at her.

Maybe he's waiting for permission? She didn't think Max could be called shy but a little positive feedback might help. "That was nice. Very nice. Maybe you should do it again."

"Tara..." The way he said her name, whispery and a little groan mixed in snapped her libido out of dormancy and into full swing.

She lightly bit her bottom lip as she paused for him to make a decision.

He searched her face, then pulled her against his chest in a hug.

Not as good, but this works.

His bare skin over thick muscles made for a nice pillow. She snuggled in, soaking up the warmth.

He rested his chin on top of her head. "I'll protect you."

The promise came out quietly but no less fierce. She didn't bother asking what prompted the declaration, just went with the flow. Cautiousness flew out the window as she realized she was already in too deep with Max. He'd break her heart, certainly. Until then, she'd enjoy every moment.

Seconds passed before he stepped back, releasing her. His troubled gaze once again found hers. "Why don't you go take a long, hot bath? It's been an eventful day for you."

The pile of dishes caught her eye. "I'll just do the dishes first."

He nudged her toward the hallway. "I've got it. You go ahead."

She blinked up at him as more puzzle pieces fell into place. "You were doing the dishes all along, cleaning up after yourself. That's why I never noticed the food situation."

Max grinned. "I'm nothing if not thorough."

Wonder if he's that thorough in bed.

She ignored the wayward, lust-filled query. Granted, she stood in the kitchen with the hunkiest man she'd ever seen, with only the towel covering his assets. Even a nun would be hard pressed to not get turned on.

And if I stay here much longer, I'm going to do something really embarrassing like yank that towel off and commence taste testing.

"If you're sure?"

He nodded and waved his hand. "Yep. Go enjoy your bath."

Tara didn't argue, instead seeing the favor for what it was—a gesture of niceness. Max didn't have anything to give but he did what he could. The effort didn't go unnoticed.

She headed to the bathroom, locking the door behind her for the first time ever. Self-preservation nudged her to take some precautions, for a little while, anyway.

A few minutes later, she slid into the hot water and began soaping up, her thoughts on Max.

Who knew werewolves existed? She'd read countless stories of shifters but never expected them to have any inkling of truth. If Max hadn't proved the point with a couple of transformations from wolf to human, she'd still argue it was all a myth. That brought up enough questions in her mind without a plethora of others bombarding her. Not just the specifics of how he can turn from one species to another, but how he could stay in such horrendous conditions, even go back to that knowing what could possibly happen. The fact that the group had enough money to own their own plane ranked at the bottom of the list of queries, but was still counted.

Still slightly nervous, she couldn't find a single piece of evidence that Max had lied or was up to nefarious purposes. For all intents and purposes, he was a man, a shifter, down on his luck through no fault of his own. *Well, okay, maybe his own fault but for all the right reasons.*

Am I just fooling myself? Buying a sob story and letting him screw me over?

The flash of realism made her stop and think hard. She had no proof except for what she saw with her own eyes. He'd had ample time to do her harm or steal her blind. She'd had Cotton for a while; plenty of opportunities existed for him. Yet, no evidence sprang forth that he'd done more than eat out of her freezer and clean up after himself afterward. She couldn't hold that against him. Heck, she'd given him dog food to eat. Who could blame him for chowing down on a casserole or two when he'd been half starved?

He needed clothes. That would give him greater freedom to walk away. Steal her car, too. Yet, her gut told her that wasn't his plan. He'd taken advantage of her hospitality, that was it. Nothing more, nothing less.

Which left her back to where she started, with a dozen questions begging for explanations.

Unable to still her whirling mind, Tara hurried through her bath, pulled the plug on the tub, gathered her towel, and stepped out. She quickly dried off and brushed her hair and teeth, then wrapped the terry cloth around her body, to hurry back to her bedroom. After closing the door, she pulled on loose sweats and socks. Content in her wardrobe, she returned to the living area, curious what Max had been up to.

He glanced up and offered up a small smile as he scrubbed dishes in the sink. "You weren't in there long."

Tara shrugged and approached closer. "I had a few things on my mind."

"You're concerned about me being here." Max didn't break eye contact. Instead, he paused in the middle of doing the dishes, picked up a kitchen towel, and wiped his hands off. "You're safe with me. I don't know how to prove it or make you believe that."

Tara nodded. "I believe you. After all, you've had plenty of chances to steal or kill me. You didn't do that."

"And I never will. I meant what I said about protecting you. Someone with such a kind heart doesn't deserve the worries and fears that I bring to your front door." He sighed. "I'll be moving on. It'll make things easier."

"No." Tara closed the distance between them and rested her hand on his forearm. "Really. I want you to stay. I'm going to get you clothes tomorrow. The rest we'll work out. Find a way to get your identification reissued, and a way to get you to your friend, too." She lifted her chin and went with her gut. "Maybe I should be scared and run for my life. But, I have to go with how I feel on this one. You've been dealt a lousy hand. I think you're a good man and deserving of a break." She trailed her fingers over the coarse hair on his arm. "One day at a time, okay?"

Max stared down at her for a few seconds before slowly inclining his head. "Okay. But, I don't want you to be frightened in your own home. If you have second thoughts, just say the word and I'll be out of your hair immediately."

Tara dropped her hand. "Fair enough." She glanced over at the couch. "I can take the sofa if you want the bed. I'm afraid you're a bit too tall to fit on it comfortably."

The corners of Max's lips curled up. "I'll fit just fine. You keep your bed, but thank you for the offer."

She knew he easily read her mind on the matter. After all, the bedroom door also had a lock. Not that it would keep him out if he truly wanted in. Still, it afforded her some peace of mind. "Okay." She picked up the drying cloth and took a place next to him. "If you'll wash, I'll dry."

He dipped his hands back in the sudsy water. "Talked me into it."

Tara grinned. "I have some more questions, if you don't mind?"

"I figured you would. Fire away." He cleaned a

bowl, then rinsed it under the faucet before handing it over.

She accepted it and started drying. "Are you going to go see your friend and stay with him?"

Max rinsed a handful of utensils. "I would have stayed before but really thought I could return to Throwback and pull off the ruse. A bit optimistic, I know." He turned off the water and dipped his hands back into the sink. "I didn't want to bring Garrison and his death squad to that pack's front door. They're small and don't have as much political power or money as most of the others. I couldn't become another drain on them. Still can't."

Tara considered his answer. While she appreciated his sentiment, she didn't have a clue where that put Max in the long term. "So, what are you going to do?"

Max finished, washed his hands, then dried them off using the bottom of his towel. "I haven't gotten that far."

She completed her task and quickly replaced the dishes in their respective places, then moved to the couch. Max followed suit, sitting down on the opposite end.

What a burden to carry. She couldn't fathom what it would be like to be totally alone in the world, with nowhere to go, and knowing that someone evil could show up at any point in time to finish what he started. She mentally grimaced at the proverbial between a rock and a hard place scenario.

She recalled he spoke of his father being a pilot for the pack but didn't elaborate further. "Do you have family?"

Sadness flashed in Max's eyes. "My mother passed

when I was small. An aggressive form of cancer. I don't remember her hardly at all." He rested his hands on his lap. "My father was killed during a takeover bid, protecting the alpha."

Tara's heart sank even as her mouth dropped open. "I'm so sorry." The whispered words were so small compared to his tragic losses. "Then you just about met the same fate trying to help your friend." She processed that for a second. "I don't care that those shifters are your family, but they stink."

He smiled softly. "That's putting it nicely."

"It's not right that people have to endure such turmoil and violence. To live under such threats and dictatorship." Anger flared at the very idea of what those people had to experience, especially the kids, growing up knowing that they'd be brutally torn to pieces if they didn't toe the line.

Tara saw Max in a new light. He'd seen what had happened to his father, yet stayed by his friend's side, even putting his own life in jeopardy by getting the old alpha medical attention and covering their tracks. That wasn't a man running from fear. That was a man who put everything on the line and barely made it out alive.

A couple of pink scars on his thigh drew her attention. She hadn't noticed them before, but in the light and close up, she easily made them out. Easily guessing what happened, she needed confirmation. "Is that from the fight?" She gestured to his leg.

Max nodded without looking at the area. "Shifters rarely scar because we heal so fast. Something to do with the genetics that allow us to take different forms causes us to patch ourselves up in quick fashion. Only the deepest and worst wounds scar."

Tara couldn't imagine what it must have been like, suffering such bite wounds, fighting to live another day, then running for miles on that leg. For all she knew there was more. Yet, Max had done just that. And for months on his own, hunting for food, and living as a wolf as he crossed miles and miles. The pain. The hunger. The desperation.

Her heart tugged.

"Stay as long as you like. Really."

"I didn't tell you that as a ploy for sympathy." He frowned.

She squeezed his hand. "I know. You're a brave man. One of integrity. I just wanted you to understand that you don't have to run off. I'd like it if you'd stay."

He stared at her for a couple of beats. "One day at a time."

She nodded. "That'll work."

Chapter 7

"Why aren't you married with half a dozen kids?"

Tara blinked at the question that came out of the blue. She finished folding the towel and grabbed another from the basket, sparing Max a quick glance. "Men suck."

She'd slept remarkably well the night before considering she had a strange man crashing on her couch. He hadn't snored that she'd heard and only visited the bathroom once. The flush of the toilet startled her out of sleep for a second before she realized it was just Max, the werewolf, using her bathroom.

The facts sank in, though she still saw them as a little surreal. As if she'd just fallen down a rabbit hole. Just in case, she'd pinched herself more than once, only to discover this wasn't some odd dream.

Max sat down in a nearby chair and watched her work. "Care to elaborate?"

Tara shrugged. "I keep searching for a prince. End up finding toads. Simple as that." She paused for a second and met his gaze. "I was driving home from a lousy date when I hit you with the car. Online date. He took one look at me, turned his attention to scanning the room, and strolled right up to the bar to chat with another woman."

"Ouch." Max shook his head. "His loss."

Tara absorbed the compliment. "Thanks. But, I'm

pretty sure since I'm long in the tooth, lack wealth, and don't have the body of a runway model, my value as a potential wife is marginal."

"That's not true." Emotion entered Max's voice. "You've got more class than most."

"That's sweet of you to say." Tara finished, grabbed the stack of towels, and carried them to the bathroom. She placed them in the cabinet. Afterward, she collected the clothes basket and returned it to the utility room.

Max followed. "It's true. You shouldn't discount yourself like that."

She stood up and met his gaze. "It's okay. I've accepted the fact that I'm not great dating material. No biggie." She waved her hand, then grinned ruefully. "I decided dog ownership was much more up my alley and immensely more rewarding."

Max's lips twitched. "You can still get a dog."

"True." She stepped around him and headed to the living area to sit down for a minute.

"You're all alone. You need someone."

Tara bristled despite trying not to. She'd heard the same argument before from others. Each time they stomped on her independent nerve. "I have all I need." She waved her arm in a sweeping motion in front of her. "This house belongs to me. My grandparents left it to me when they passed. How I loved spending the summers here with them. Getting back to nature. The peace and quiet of it all." She recalled the happy times, many of them, with her favorite people in the world.

"What about your parents?"

"They live in New York. Always trying to impress others with their social class and pretend money. They aren't rich but want everyone to think they are. Endless parties, kissing butt in the office. The rat race that never ends." How many times had she cussed living in the city and begged to live year-round with her grandparents? Probably as many times as she put on her shoes in order to go to school each day.

"Sounds like you're not really close to them."

"No. Not really. They call now and again. Badger me about my meager living. And remind me that there's nothing here that's worth staying." They also lectured her on the lack of a husband and children but she opted to leave that part unsaid.

"To each their own." Max held her gaze steadily.

"Yep." Tara peered over at the clock on the wall, stood up, and made her way to the kitchen where her purse waited. "On that note, I better get going. I'll catch up with you when I get back." She collected her purse and started for the door. "Oh, and I set out a clean, spare toothbrush you can use. I'll pick up another today. Can't have you getting cavities, after all." She'd thought of that late last night while brushing her teeth. Mentally, she'd added it to the ever-growing shopping list.

"Wait up. I'll go with you." Max hurried over.

Tara paused with her hand on the door knob to the garage. "I'm pretty sure I can handle this."

Max walked over. "I'm going with you. Just in case you have any trouble."

"What kind of trouble do you expect I'll find? This isn't the wrong side of Chicago after dark." *Speaking of stomping on my independent nerve.* Tara forced herself to not overreact and remain placid, but it was dang hard.

"You never know. Besides, those bags will be heavy."

Tara arched an eyebrow. "I hate to break this to you, buddy, but I'm pretty sure streaking will get you arrested."

Max scowled. "I'm not totally dense. I can go as your dog."

"Since you're not going to pass as a Seeing Eye dog or service animal of any other sort, I don't think that's going to happen." She shook her head and contemplated his reaction. "Why the sudden worry?"

"I'm being hunted, remember? One of my old pack stumbles across you, picks up my scent, and they'll tear you apart in order to get information out of you."

That sounds pleasant. Not. Tara straightened her spine. "I left you here before, when you were just getting back on your feet. What's the difference between then and now?"

Max rubbed his forehead. "There just is."

"Uh, huh." Tara wasn't buying it. She didn't mind his overprotective gesture. Another change since Cotton had turned up in her life. Before, she'd smack a man on the head for being so stubborn. Now, she embraced the sentiment, though she had no intention of backing down. "I'm not totally powerless. Living alone out here, a girl has to be prepared to take care of herself." She'd learned how to shoot at an early age, obtained her conceal carry permit, and had a .45 revolver stashed in her purse. She was far from defenseless.

Max blew out his breath and planted his hands on his hips, drawing attention to the knot holding the towel in place. More than once Tara wondered what would happen if that little tie came undone, letting the terry cloth fall to the floor.

"Look. I doubt they're that close but I can't be too sure. I've covered my tracks as best as I could but there's always a chance."

Tara nodded. "I understand but I'll be fine. I was before. I'll be again." She paused to offer up a reassuring grin. "I've been taking care of myself for a while now. That includes lugging around heavy boxes of books, groceries, and whatever else needs to be done."

"You're not taking this seriously. Shifters, especially males, are bigger and stronger than human men. Meaner, too. They'll kill in the blink of an eye just because they can."

Tara weighed his words. "You haven't." She said the statement with conviction. He'd had numerous chances to do her harm and never lifted a finger in aggression. Instead, he'd picked up some of the slack and pampered her in the form of a ready cooked meal when she got home. He also cleaned up and helped with the laundry while she soaked in the tub. Not a bad deal at all.

Max pinned her with his stare. "No. But, I'm perfectly capable of doing so." His voice lowered and carried a threatening tone. She recognized the feral-ness in his gaze.

Tara's nerves zinged at the ominous tone and words. She refused to look away, watching his face instead. She read the concern in his expressive eyes, and the truth. The sudden apprehension calmed rapidly. "So is the rest of the world. Face the facts, Max. Anyone can and will kill if it meant protecting their loved ones."

"No. Not everyone." His voice turned hollow.

She got the feeling she'd struck a nerve. "I'm sorry. I'd like to think that people are good and would stand up to defend their family. I guess that's too farfetched."

Max dropped his hands. "Go. Just be careful."

"Max…" She hated leaving him on such a bad note.

"Just go, Tara. Watch your back. Keep your gun with you."

She blinked. "How did you know I'm carrying?"

A little grin crept onto his lips. "I looked around that first night." He shrugged as if he'd done the same thing every night of his life. "Never hurts to be cautious."

For some reason that came across as humorous to Tara. She smiled back at him. "I'm glad to know I passed the test."

"Oh, you did more than pass. You aced it."

She paused for a second to absorb what he'd said. "Good to hear." She smiled at him. "Feel free to use the laptop while I'm gone. It's in my bedroom charging, where I keep it. Check up on your friend. Use the chat function if you want. The program is on the computer, though I've never used it."

"Okay. Thanks."

Tara waved. "Be back soon." With that said, she shut the door behind her, and climbed into the car.

****

"I'm living with a werewolf."

Never in her life had she expected to utter those words. *Never.*

Yet, here she stood, in the men's clothing section

of the largest department store in the county, searching for the basics in Max's sizes. She'd managed to find four pairs of jeans, a set of work boots, and another of running shoes, some sweats, and a handful of shirts. A thick black sweater topped the growing pile. Nothing particularly fancy, but they'd work.

She made her way further through the aisles, stopping in the underwear department.

Now this is a new experience for me. Wonder what Max would prefer, boxers or briefs?

She double checked her list, realizing that underwear had been left off.

Wonderful. Now what do I do?

She thumbed through the boxers on hangers, until she found a section of silk. A myriad of colors gleamed in the light—blues, black, reds. Even some grays and whites. All were luxurious and something she could easily see Max choosing. A quick glance at the price tag made her cringe. Pricey. She glanced over at the packages of white briefs in plastic then back to the boxers. Before she could change her mind, she picked out four, each of a different color, and dropped them into the growing pile of garments.

The thought of him modeling his new undies sped her heart, especially as she mentally pictured him tugging them down, exposing his glorious body completely for her viewing pleasure.

Good grief. In a mere day I've turned into a puddle of hormones.

She'd dated, but never came across a man she'd wanted so badly from the get-go. She'd loved Cotton. Then he'd turned into Max. All solid, hunky, powerful Max with the same sweetness inside. As far as she'd seen anyway.

The problem was all that running around in a towel. Boy howdy did she envy that towel. To wrap around his body, to feel his skin, to glimpse what he sported underneath.

Tara fanned herself at the sudden flush of warmth rushing through her body. Her stomach somersaulted in delicious fashion, testament to her body enjoying the thought of removing that towel and taking its place just as much as her mind.

Whoa, Nelly. I'm done with men. Remember? Besides she had more than enough on her plate with the quickly failing business, the decisions that had to be made as to the next step in her life. She'd have to find a job elsewhere. Perhaps move. While none of those tasks filled her with joy, they were pretty much inevitable. She had to sustain herself, and the small town had a decided lack of open positions. She'd looked. That left her with a couple of options—either pull up stakes and move elsewhere or drive a long distance to work.

The house had belonged to her grandparents. She'd grown up there, taking over after they'd passed. Her mother cared for her in her own way. The same with her father. But, Tara always seemed to be lower on the totem pole than their forever obsession with climbing the social ladder. She had to dress and act the perfect princess when meeting her parents' friends, something that she loathed. Still, she never rebelled because to do so would have earned their anger. Not that they ever hit her. No. Their frustration came with severe checks and harsh words. Her childhood was put on hold under the summers she spent with her grandparents. Those were the times she could finally be free, enjoy her days, and simply play.

A pretty sucky childhood but it could have been worse. She had her supportive grandparents who loved her for her, not for her ability to earn favorable brownie points with well-off families. Her grandparents' rural home had become a sanctuary for her. And it had again—this time for Max.

Which led her to here—the men's department, a decidedly unfamiliar territory.

Maybe it was time to concede and move on to greener pastures. Surely, Max would find his friend and settle down with other werewolves. The worry and need to be with his friend came across easily the evening before. She understood. They were his only family and he longed to be with them, to ensure his friend healed.

"I'll make sure it happens." It was the least she could do. After all, Cotton had given her hope and love, for that short period of time. Enough to leave his mark. Max would as well but she couldn't stand in the way of his happiness or his safety.

She wandered around a corner to the coat section. Spying a thick black one that appeared more than capable of turning back the bitter wind, she added it to her basket. The price didn't matter, only the size did. She kept her feet moving as she checked items off the list.

After a quick stop at the socks, she made her way to the checkout desk.

The total amount placed a hard dent into her already strained budget but she paid it anyway. Well, technically, charged it to her card to be paid later. What choice was there? Max couldn't run around in the nude. Not if she was to keep her sanity and her hands to herself. All that bare flesh proved way too tempting. Besides, he deserved some dignity, even though he seemed unconcerned about the lack of garments or self-conscious about his nakedness. He had his life to return to, documents to obtain, and a friend to reunite with. Each step of the way demanded the very essentials she'd obtained. Nothing more, nothing less.

An odd mixture of downtrodden and fulfillment washed over her as she placed the purchases into the trunk of her car. Max now had what he needed. Where they led him, she didn't know.

Tara closed the trunk, slid into the driver's seat, and buckled her seat belt. She had one more stop to make before heading for home—the grocery store. That would stick another large chunk of debt onto her credit card. There wasn't much choice. They had to eat, and Max needed some personal hygiene stuff. He had a big appetite, understandably so after all the meals he'd missed along the way. Not to mention, this time of year winter storms came around fairly often. She always made sure to be prepared in case another one closed the roads for a couple of days, forcing her to stay at home. The bookstore would work in a pinch but the lack of amenities, including a shower and a bed, left much to be desired.

She'd suck it up, shell out the money for the good products, then return home.

That particular thought cheered her. After all, Max would be there.

Max. Any other woman in her shoes would be petrified that a strange, nude man showed up in her kitchen, showcased his talents to turn into a wolf, and told a harrowing story about escape from a whole pack of the beasts. Not Tara. For some cockamamie reason, she didn't fear Max. Perhaps it was because she saw so much of Cotton in him—the gentleness, the kindness. Maybe she was too blinded by his perfect body and overwhelmed with the abundance of sex appeal that she couldn't see the forest for the trees. Either way, she found herself stepping up to the plate and struggling with her newfound libido to practice hands off.

The idea that he'd stay lingered but didn't hold much weight. After all, he had a best friend to check on and reunite with. Not to mention, the inevitable antsyness he'd experience wondering when those who hunted him would finally strike pay dirt. All that told of Max picking up and moving on at some point in time.

Next, she had to consider her own dismal situation. She couldn't make next month's rent. Not unless a flurry of new interest showed up and purchased all the books in the store. The additional burden of the clothing and extra food would take its toll as well. In the end, she'd have to close the shop for good and search for another job just to try to make ends meet. All well and good, except the death of her dream broke her heart and the lack of employment opportunities made her stomach sink.

That's tomorrow's worries. One day at a time. The reminder didn't cheer her in the least.

Tara pulled into the parking lot of the grocery store, found an empty space, and cut the engine. For a few seconds, she battled tears before pulling herself together. Hope existed, however tiny the flame. She'd pray for a miracle while updating her resume and searching the local ads for places that might be hiring within driving distance from her home. She'd sell the house as a last resort, but even that wouldn't net her enough to live on for long.

Overwhelmed, Tara stoically pushed the worries aside. *Tomorrow will just have to take care of itself because I have more than enough on my plate for today.* She lifted her chin, collected her purse, opened the door, and locked the car as she stepped out. *No sense crying over spilled milk or for falling on hard times.*

Besides, first things first. Food, then return home to a small happiness in life—having an intriguing, unusual, and hunky man waiting for her to get home. A novel experience but one she was quickly becoming accustomed to.

Two hours later, she made her way into the kitchen, with Max pulling up the rear carrying the rest of the bags.

"You bought too much stuff," Max softly scolded.

Tara sat her load on the kitchen counter and started unloading the food. "I got the basics."

He pulled out the jeans first, followed by shoes, shirts, and the rest of the clothes.

Out of the corner of her eye, Tara caught a glimpse of him lifting the boxers out and running the material over his hands. "Tara…"

She pasted on an innocent smile. "Oh, you found them. I knew you'd love them. Soft, luxurious, and definitely sexy. I saw them and knew they were perfect for you."

Culpability and appreciation clashed on his features as he set aside the boxers and pulled out the rest of the garments. "You really did get too much. I could have gotten by just fine with less than half of this.

It's too much money. It should go back." His tone reflected guilt and a little shame.

Tara's heart ached. She placed a bunch of bananas on the counter, walked over, and rested her hand on his forearm. "Max. You needed clothes. I can help with that." She considered what she could say to make him feel better. "As much as I like to see you running around in a towel, it's probably safer if you have real things to wear."

He arched an eyebrow at her.

She shrugged. "No point in denying the fact that you're sex on a stick. Even dressed you'll make for eye candy." Leaning in, she whispered loud enough for him to easily hear. "You can't imagine how many times I've been tempted to take a peek at what's under that towel."

A slow smile appeared on Max's lips.

"Since men are toads, it's best that I refrain from such things. Much better to get you in regular clothes where I can probably manage to keep my hands to myself." *Unfortunately.* She'd miss the towel wardrobe. Big time.

"I can handle a few more days in this." He gestured toward the terry cloth he presently sported. "Or, maybe you're prefer that peek right now?" His hands went to the knot.

She retreated quickly before she gave into her curiosity and growing desires. "Umm. That's okay. I'm good."

"Uh, huh." He grinned knowingly.

Tara enjoyed the bantering, much preferring it to the sullen mood prior. "I'll start dinner if you want to try on your new clothes." She watched him dig through the rest of the bags, noting the muscles coil and relax with every movement.

"I'll model them for you." A mischievous twinkle sparked in his eyes.

"Umm." Tara tried to pry her gaze off his magnificent body but failed.

Max gathered up the armful of clothes, stood up, giving her a wonderful view of his towel clad rear, and walked over to stand just behind her. "Thank you." He nuzzled her cheek, paused, then walked toward the bedroom.

Tara's heart sped at the small act of affection. The view of his bare back and the shimmy in his walk added to the flutter. *Oh, good grief. I'm turned into one large overactive hormone.*

She lectured herself on the reasons why she needed to practice hands off. All of them sounded weak. Sure, her heart would likely end up shattered, but that's the price she was willing to pay for this chance of a lifetime. Tara read somewhere that the key to happiness was living in the moment. She'd never understood it until then.

Dinner's not going to cook itself.

With that thought, she headed to the kitchen. Deciding on hamburgers, she plucked the meat out of the bag and started forming it into thick patties. By the time she had them cooking and the potatoes in the microwave, Max strode back into the living room modeling a pair of jeans and a sweatshirt. While she preferred just the towel, the addition of clothes didn't take his sexual yumminess away. Not in the least. "Very nice."

Max grinned. "Thanks. You did well. They fit perfectly."

She considered the smile and the meaning behind it. More than likely due to him finally feeling human again rather than anything sensual. "How long has it been since you wore clothes?"

"A few months." Max glanced down at his feet as if checking the length on the jeans, then back up at her. "It's a nice feeling being properly dressed again."

"I bet." She swallowed as a lump formed in her throat at the reminder of what he'd been through. Recalling his words about the loss of his parents, she couldn't contain the question on the tip of her tongue. "Why didn't you leave the pack after your father died?"

Max's eyes turned from happiness to stormy.

She kicked herself for spoiling the mood. "I'm sorry. I shouldn't have asked."

"All I had left was Jacques. We were teens. His sister, Becky, was several years older. By the time of the uprising, she and her mother had moved off. I guess they couldn't stand the politics any longer. Jacques's father stayed." He paused a second. "I'm a wolf shifter, yes, but a mixture—timber and arctic wolf. The pack didn't care for half breeds or crossbreeds. They're considered lower than dirt. Except Jacques and Becky. They accepted me fully."

The pieces of the puzzle started to fill in. The fact that Max was a product of two different varieties of wolves wasn't a surprise. Not really. "And Jacques's father?"

"Dead."

She processed that, deciding that way too many people experienced short lives in that pack. Another thought struck. "No one interfered when Jacques defended his position? When he stood for something

128

besides cold-blooded murder?" The shock came in that others wouldn't back their alpha, a kind one to boot, who was getting mauled in a coup. "Why didn't anyone else step in and help while he was getting the tar beat out of him?"

Max's lips thinned. "They were too afraid to defy Garrison."

Tara gasped. "Too afraid? Even you?" She whispered the last words.

Max grimaced. "They were afraid. I bided my time. Throwback Pack rules are inflexible, solid, and set in stone. The battle is between the present alpha and his usurper. That's it. No one else can interfere, no matter what." He sighed. "Garrison and his family are brutal and not above punishing disobedience by hurting others a person cares about. He's ruthless. It's the one trait that seems to pass down through the generations and actually worsens with time."

"Yet, you and Jacques had the courage to try to change things."

"Yes." The word fell flat.

"I'm sorry. I can't imagine." Tara reached out and cupped Max's cheek. "No wonder you were so dedicated to Jacques. You were all each other had." She stared into his eyes, saw the sorrow, the loss, along with a small flicker of hope. That part she vowed to fan into full flames. Somehow, someway, she'd help him get back on track. Even if that track took him away from her. "You need to be with him. Soon."

He rubbed against her hand. "I'm communicating with him. That's working well."

"Still, we need to get you those documents in order for you to be free again."

He sighed. "I'll never be free, Tara. Not as long as Garrison rules Throwback." With that said, he turned and walked down the hall, presumably to take the clothes off and toss them into the washer. He paused midway. "You've given me reason to fight, Tara. Reason and the ability to get some of my life back. I can never repay you." With one final intense, heart-tugging look, he continued down the hall.

Tara blew out air. The beeping of the microwave drew her attention. She grabbed a spatula out of the drawer, checked the burgers, and wondered how an exiled shifter could reclaim happiness with a posse on his tail.

Chapter 8

Max peered out the window, noting the brilliant sunshine which bathed the once frozen land while heating up the glass window at the same time. Clouds had moved out, leaving a warm, dry day in their wake. Too nice to stay inside after such a cold spell.

He glimpsed Tara as she returned from the laundry room, pausing to move abreast of him. "Wow. What a difference the sun makes."

"Yep." He smiled down at her. "Feel up to a little walk?"

The corners of her lips curled upward. "Sure. I'll show you some of my favorite trails." She hurried back to the kitchen, removed her coat from hanging on a chair, and tugged it on. Max did the same with the brand new black heavy jacket she'd purchased the day before, not bothering to zip it up. Anticipation and eagerness nudged him to hurry up and get back into nature. Ordinarily, he'd change forms and go as his wolf, enjoying the whole experience with heightened senses. With Tara accompanying him, he opted to remain in human form. To talk to her, to walk beside her, to enjoy the moment as a man, not as her pet.

She stepped out the door and drew in a deep breath. "It's marvelous out here. Like a spring day." Pulling a scrunchie from around her wrist, she collected her thick hair, and secured it in a ponytail.

He agreed. The temperatures felt to be in the mid to high fifties. An uncommon treat in late February in Minnesota. Warmth soaked through to his whole body, granting him energy and uplifting his spirit. Tara joining him made the outing that much more pleasant.

She spun around in a circle, closed her eyes, and seemed to enjoy the same experience. He read the pleasure easily in her body language. He felt the same way. After all the snow, ice, and cold, this day could only be called picture perfect.

"You mentioned trails?" he asked.

"Yep." She latched onto his hand and tugged him to the left. "I spent many hours wandering through these woods. Found all kinds of interesting, amazing things." She looked over at him. "No wolf shifters, though." Her lips twitched in amusement.

He found the telltale sign endearing. "Imagine that."

"You're not going to change? Bound around after bunnies?"

He shook his head. "No. I prefer to stay as I am. Walking and talking to you. Can't really do that with fur."

"There's that." She gestured toward a small hump. "Just over that is a deer trail. Goes through the woods and back to a creek."

Max picked up on the well-worn path, his excellent vision detecting the trampled leaf litter, the absence of bushes. His nose told him deer still used it. Recently, if he had to guess. "You like hiking?"

"Yeah, it was something I could do way back when. No other kids around. Just my grandparents and I." Tara pushed a tree limb aside. "My grandfather took

me out pretty often. Showed me all kinds of things."
She smiled wistfully. "I loved those times."

"Where were your parents?"

Her smile turned upside down. "In New York, living up a lifestyle they couldn't afford. I think I briefly mentioned their obsession with perceptions. They're still that way. All about status and being considered one of the 'in crowd'. They never cared for the country or the simple life."

He noticed the tension that gripped her when she spoke of her parents, remembered the same last night when she spoke of them. Obviously, they weren't a big part of her life even back then or a happy one either. He worked to put the gladness back on her face. "Your grandparents raised you?"

"I spent a lot of time with them. The only place I could really be myself and run free." She slowed her steps. "I don't know how to explain it. Just that the wilderness called to me. Made me feel content. Peaceful. As if I belonged here."

"You do. Belong here, that is." He ducked under a limb and sidestepped a large rock. "You're happy here." He could sense it all the way to his bones. She simply went with this land.

Tara met his gaze and smiled. "I think you're right." She took a few more steps, leading the way into a wider clearing at the top of a fairly steep hill. "Every time I walk this property, I remember my grandparents. How poor, yet happy, they were."

"Money isn't the answer." Max considered the affluence of the Throwback Pack. Private plane, a fleet of specially painted vehicles. A mansion for the alpha. They weren't lacking in that category but they sure came up short in most other ones—namely family bonding, faith, support, community, and a simple enjoyment for life. Brutal takeovers and bullying to keep people bonded in their roles took a toll, a very high toll at that.

She chuckled. "Maybe not, but it does come in handy at times."

He paused, taking in the rugged beauty of the land. Sure enough below them an open area stretched out from the numerous trees. Water trickled along a shallow groove splitting the flatland in two. An oasis of dormant meadow grass lined both sides all the way to the tree line where pine and a few oaks picked up.

Two deer, both does, warily checked out the area before stepping out from cover. They made their way to the stream and took a drink. Each took turns sensing the area between swallows.

"How pretty. So refined." She sighed. "Do they sense you? Or us?"

"We're upwind. I think it's just their natural cautiousness." Weeks ago, he would have stalked them, gathering his quickly waning strength in a bid to end his relentless hunger. Now, he stood at the top of the rise, peering down at the beautiful sight.

All because of Tara.

He noticed the expression on her face. Joy. Relaxation. Sheer pleasure in the beauty of nature.

She turned his way but the sparkle of happiness didn't wane. Not in the least. Instead, it morphed into a brilliant shade of green filled with appreciation and more than a little want.

His heart skipped a beat.

All his life, he'd wanted a woman to see him as

more than a quick lay. To value him as a man.

The way Tara looked at him made him feel like a giant amongst mankind. The guy responsible for hanging the moon in the sky every night. A man who was worthy. Of living. Of loving. Of her.

He lost himself in her eyes.

She twined her fingers with his and squeezed. He savored the small act of affection, bent over just enough to nuzzle her cheek, then blew air into her ear.

Tara softly laughed.

The sound carried straight to his soul. Enticed him. Made him crave it all the more.

He cupped her cheek with his free hand. She leaned into it and peeked up at him from under her lashes. Unable to resist, he lowered his head and brushed his lips over hers.

She responded in kind. Soft. Gentle. A fleeting caress.

He straightened and offered a lopsided smile.

She tilted her head, nibbled her lower lip, then nipped his finger.

"Hey." The small sting barely registered. Still, he thought it best to protest—even just a token one.

A playful smile appeared. "As part wolf, I thought you'd actually like biting."

He groaned at the sexy imagine of doing just that to her naked flesh. Love bites. Here. There. And all over. Making her cry out with blazing passion as he finally covered her.

And you wanted to leave this? His inner wolf chastised.

No one said I was the smartest shifter on the block.

A snort echoed through his head.

Okay. I deserved that.

The voice went silent again.

"Max? Oh, Max? Don't tell me you mentally ventured off on some kinky wild sex fantasy."

He blinked at her and shrugged. "Well…"

She rolled her eyes. "Every six seconds, my foot. More like every two. Horny toad, I swear."

"Wolf here."

"Yeah, yeah. I know. You can lick yourself, too. Big deal."

Her sassiness amused him all the more. His appearance and the resulting shocks of what he was hadn't rattled her too much. Instead, she'd seemingly taken things in stride. After some precautions, understandably. Her personality and spirit appeared perfectly intact. Just as he'd noticed during the first bath as Cotton. "It kind of is a big deal." He waggled his eyebrows.

"I'm so not going there." She shook her head, swiveled and started walking, dragging Max along with her as he still claimed possession of her hand.

He let the banter slide to the back burner. For now. "Tell me more about your grandparents. They seem like good people."

"They were the best." She stared straight ahead as if watching a memory replay in front of her. "I remember one Christmas. I was maybe ten. Things were really hard that year. My grandmother was a teacher, didn't make much money. My grandfather worked as a mechanic, but had been laid off. Times were lean. Still, my grandfather took me out to find the perfect Christmas tree." A ghost of a grin settled on her lips. "I didn't want to chop down a tree and kill it. So I found a small one and Grandpa dug it up, put it in a pot, and pampered it all through the holiday. We wrapped a blanket around it, made some paper decorations, and a perfect construction paper star. After the day, we took it back outside and planted it. That's the big spruce in the front yard." A few seconds ticked by before she spoke again. "We didn't have any presents and no big feast. But, I didn't mind." She looked over at him. "I think that was my favorite time. When I knew the real meaning of family."

He sensed the love and devotion she felt for her grandparents. How much they meant to her. How they largely influenced her life.

"How about you? Did your family have a large Christmas celebration each year?" She glanced up at him, then focused on the uneven trail, pushing a branch aside as she went.

"No. My mother died when I was really young, leaving just my father and I. We were too busy just trying to survive in the tumultuous pack politics. My mixed genetics added to the pressure. No real time or much to celebrate."

She stopped and met his gaze. "How sad. I'm so sorry."

He shrugged. "No big deal. You can't miss what you've never had, right?" He smiled with little humor trying to play down the seriousness of his years with the pack. Her concern and sympathy touched him deeply, making him wish for those days to come. With her.

Tara looped her arm in his. "Next Christmas I'm showing you how to have a good old-fashioned celebration. Making decorations. Stringing popcorn. All kinds of fun stuff. Just like when I came here every holiday break from school to spend with my grandparents. We had the best time."

"Next Christmas?" They didn't know what was just around the corner, let alone months away.

"Yep." She nodded. "It's about time you enjoyed some holidays. I'll be there to make sure it happens."

Her vow flushed warmth through his body. "Tell me more about growing up here. I like your stories."

She pushed her ponytail to her back and thought for a moment. "I remember another time, Grandma insisted on going ice skating. There's a good-sized pond about a mile from here. She dug out her old skates, then borrowed some for me. Grandpa had his own, a pair of old worn leather ones from way back when. Anyway, we drove over to the pond. It was dang cold, but Grandma said that was the only way to skate—freezing your butt off in the cold. She was so graceful. Just glided over the ice. Grandpa too. I tried shuffling, hit a slick spot, spun around, and did a belly flop. When I tried to stand up, I overbalanced and went flying straight into a snow bank." Laughter bubbled over. "It was funny. Not so much at the time, but looking back, it was hilarious. My grandparents laughed about it for years afterward."

He could picture her trying to make her way across the slick ice. "Ever go ice skating again?"

"A few times. My career as an Olympic figure skater began and ended on that pond." She tittered.

A few steps later, she squeezed his hand. "Don't you have any special holiday memories?"

Max pondered the question. "Nothing as sweet as yours."

"Surely there was something," she persisted.

"We had money. Presents on birthdays. One each on Christmas. Sometimes my father would take me on the plane and we'd go on a trip. One summer, we flew to the Florida Keys. Another, we took a charter to Brazil."

"Wow. How neat. To get to travel the world and see so many things."

He recalled the excitement with rare alone time with his father. Pack responsibilities snared his father's attention nearly 24/7. Still, his father made sure to take him away from time to time. To see the world. And to get away from the constant barrage of backstabbing politics surrounding them. Never once had his father considered pulling up stakes and leaving. Max often wondered why.

Now, he had his answer. Throwback Pack, with all their troubles and stymied culture, was still his family. He could no more turn his back on them than he could leap off the nearest cliff. He and Jacques could help them, had helped them, and perhaps would again. Until he had no other recourse, Max promised to do anything he could to change things for the better. In his father's name and honor.

"You're frowning."

Her observation pulled him back to the present. "Just thinking."

"About your father? Missing him?"

"Yeah, I guess."

"And?" She stopped moving.

"Just hoping he didn't die in vain."

For a long moment, only the natural sounds of the woods broke the silence.

"He was proud of you," she said.

He quirked an eyebrow. "How do you know that?"

She kicked at a loose rock. "Who wouldn't be? You're a pilot. That's a big deal. And you were loyal to your friend. That counts, too."

The comment took him back. The expression of absolute satisfaction and delight on his father's face when Max finished his first solo flight without any assistance. The pat on the back. The happiness. "Yeah, I think he was proud of me."

"And would be still today, if he were here," Tara affirmed. "You survived and got your friend to safety. You succeeded. That's more than most would have done." Her tone brooked no argument. "Against the odds, you prevailed."

He shook his head at her optimism and perception through rose colored glasses. "You're making me into a knight in shining armor. I'm far from that."

She just smiled. "Who needs a suit of heavy armor that clangs with every step when you can turn into a furry beast who truly dislikes the game of fetch and finds dog food totally disgusting?"

He chuckled. "I guess you've got a point."

Leaning in, she stage-whispered. "If you ask me, wolves are cool. Knights, ehh."

He tucked their joined hands into his pocket, surveyed the land, and took notice of the sweet remembrances they were creating.

Because soon, really soon, this would be just that—a distant memory.

Chapter 9

The next day at work, Tara spent her downtime pondering the situation, all to no avail. For hours, she researched how to get Max's documents replaced. All that revolved around getting his birth certificate or a passport. She didn't know diddly squat about shifters, but kind of doubted they filed birth certificates with the state. She'd have to ask Max when she got home. Since she only had her cell and no landline, she couldn't really call him and ask.

Her thoughts returned to the night before. She'd stuck her nose into his business and took away the joy in his new garments. He'd been somber the rest of the night, obviously weighed down with the burden pressing on his shoulders. She'd do anything to take that from him. The only problem was how.

No matter how many websites she visited, that particular answer never appeared.

At least she had the luxury of knowing that Max would be there when she arrived home. He'd tried to leave before and ended up changing his mind. She didn't think he'd do it again. Not without saying goodbye at least.

The little chime above her door sounded gleefully. Tara glanced up to see Rose entering. The visit put a sincere smile on her face. "Hello, Rose."

Rose grinned back before scanning the room.

"Where's that pretty dog of yours?"

"Ummm…I left him at home today." That much was the truth.

"Oh?" Rose walked slowly to the front counter.

"Yep. He didn't seem to want to hang out." Tara nodded. "So I let him stay home."

Never would Tara divulge Max's secret. She guarded it closely, even from her only real friend in this town. While she trusted Rose completely, she also understood Max's being a shifter was his tale to tell, not hers.

"I see." Rose eyed her for a long moment. "So, anything new with you? I haven't seen you for a few days. You could have found a new man by now."

Tara nearly choked on her spit. "Nope. No new man." She managed to get the words out in a rush. A tad bit nervous about the subject, she took charge of the conversation. "Were you looking for a particular book today or just stopping by for a visit?"

"Just wanted to see how things were going with you, dear." Rose's grin appeared a little wolfish.

"Oh. Would you like some coffee?"

"No, thank you. I have an appointment with Dr. Silas. If I don't arrive on time, that old coot will hunt me down and tie me into his chair. Something about being overdue for my eye exam."

Tara relaxed. "You don't even wear glasses, Rose. I'd say your eyes are good."

Rose inclined her head. "I'll let you in on a little secret." She leaned toward Tara as if going to whisper a confidence. "He put me in glasses a decade ago. I never wore them."

"Uh, oh." Tara grinned. "Aren't you the rebel?"

Rose snorted. "I can see just fine. It's not my fault that furniture gets in my way sometimes."

Tara chuckled. "There's that."

"Well, I guess I shouldn't make Dr. Silas wait any longer." Rose sighed.

"Yeah. Thanks for stopping by, though. It's been quiet today. Kind of lonely, too," Tara admitted.

Rose eyed her for a second. "Bring Cotton next time. He'll keep you entertained."

"I'll think about it."

"Do."

Rose gave a little wave then walked through the door, turned left, and disappeared.

"I don't think Cotton will be returning to the store." Tara glanced at the food and water bowls that sat on a table in the back room.

She missed Max. Cotton. Both of them. Wondered what he'd been doing all day. Would have checked in except she had no landline phone at home.

He needs a phone of his own. How else would he be able to get in touch with someone if he needed to?

She glanced at the clock, then to the front door. No one passed by her shop, hadn't in the last three hours. No sense standing around bored in her store when she had a purchase to make and the thoughts of Max occupied her mind.

Might as well close up and go buy him one. It's not like a huge crowd is waiting to get in.

With that thought, she flipped the sign to Closed, locked the front door, grabbed her laptop and purse, then left through the back door.

An hour later, with a new phone in hand, she headed toward home. "I have a man waiting for me when I get there."

The thought made the day, oddly enough, crawl by. She always felt at home in the bookstore. The scent and peace carried through the small place. Never had boredom crept in or the eagerness to flip the Closed sign around been so strong. Today, she'd experienced both. All because she wondered what Max did to pass the time. What he was wearing. If he soaked in the tub or took a long, hot shower. Did he run around in the buff while she was gone?

What an argument for getting cameras placed in her house just so she could get a glimpse of Max in such a state. Not that his wandering around in a towel left much to the imagination. She enjoyed every inch of what she'd seen and longed for more.

A slap and a tickle wasn't her style, though. Max's future was up in the air but as soon as he got back on track, he'd be off again. That meant that long term romance was about as likely to come about as for an alien spaceship to land in Times Square.

The question became did she jump on board the Max train and ride it while she could? Or was protecting her heart more important?

Heck, it's too late on that front. Her heart was already involved.

Noticing a car stuck in the ditch ahead, Tara slowed down to appraise the situation. Sure enough, a woman sat in the driver's seat, her windows mostly up, and talking to a big burly man who stood next to her driver's side door. He appeared frustrated, judging by the scowl and waving arms. Something about the woman conveyed fear and struck a chord with Tara. She pulled over right behind the car, dropped the keys into the purse, pulled the strap over her shoulder, and climbed out. As she shut and locked her door, she kept an eye on the man while sliding her hand into the special compartment inside the purse which held her pistol.

Being a woman alone in the world, traveling back roads after dark, and working by herself, she had to be prepared for anything. Thus, the handgun and a conceal carry license both stashed away in her purse.

"For the last time, lady. Get out of that car and get into my truck. No one is going to come get you and I'm your only chance to avoid freezing to death."

"No thank you. I've already called my ride. They're on the way." The woman argued back, a small tremor evident in her tone.

She was definitely scared. Rightfully so. Stuck on an isolated road, unable to travel farther, with an overly zealous man demanding she leave the safety of her car and get into his. Tara's nerves drew taut as she warily approached the situation, knowing she might have to shoot her way out of an abduction. *Reality sucked some days.*

"I can scent you. No way am I letting the opportunity of taking another wolf's mate pass me by. Finders' keepers and all that. Now, get out of there before I get really pissed." He jerked at the door handle and banged on the glass.

The woman inside stifled a scream.

Tara stiffened her spine and lifted her chin, preparing to address the man. She didn't pause to ponder his odd statement. Instead, she simply chalked them up to a deranged lunatic trying to kidnap a frightened vulnerable woman. Reasoning with the moron probably wouldn't work, but Tara opted to give it a try. She wasn't about to leave the poor woman to the scary fate with the monster. "As you can see, her ride is here now. Thank you for trying to help, but I assure you she doesn't need it." Making sure to keep a reasonable distance between her and the man, she braced herself for his reaction.

He glared at her and frowned. "I've got this taken care of. She doesn't need you."

"Wrong, mister. I've got her. Now, I'd say it's time for you to get on along and leave us alone."

The man's dark eyes snapped with cruel promise, reminding her of a rabid wolf right before he tore into human flesh.

She drew in a deep breath, bracing herself for what she might have to do in order to protect herself and the other woman. She tightened her grip on the gun. "The police are on their way and I really don't think you want to explain why you're out here harassing a couple of women for no damn reason."

He spit on the ground and stepped back from the door. "You don't know who you're messing with." His hands fisted as he took a menacing stride in her direction. "She's mine for the taking. We can make it two to join the party now."

"Looks like you'll have to have that party all by yourself."

Fear lanced through her at his approach and the ominous promise in his eyes. *Time to put up or shut up.* She gathered her courage and stilled her trembling hands. Trying to remove the gun from the small special compartment would take time and potentially be a little clumsy. If things went to hell in a handbasket, she'd just have to make do with the gun in place. "Yeah, I do. A prick that can't take 'no' for an answer."

Long strides carried him in her direction. "You fucking bitch. You had your chance, now you'll pay for crossing me."

Tara stood her ground, cocked the small revolver, and pulled the trigger, sending a shot right between his legs. While it made a hole in her purse, she really didn't give a damn at the present time. Because it was the only thing standing between her and the overly aggressive asshole intent upon causing her harm.

He jumped and cussed fluently.

"Like I said, time to move on. The next one is going a little higher, and you'll be finding new ways to pee for the rest of your life." Tara added threat to her voice, emphasizing the fact that she wouldn't hesitate to do whatever it took in order to send the guy on his way—somewhere else or straight to hell if he pushed the issue.

"You're going to regret this." He glared at her once more, sniffed, then froze. His face furrowed then he sneered. Evil satisfaction flared in his dark eyes. "Where the hell is he?"

"I believe you were just leaving." Tara reinforced before cocking the gun again.

The man paused for a long moment before cussing fluently, turning, and retracing his steps. "No woman tells me no. Shifter mate or not." He stopped at the door of his truck and glared at Tara. "You're going to regret hiding him."

Tara didn't have a clue who the man was talking about and truthfully didn't care. She just wanted him gone and fast. She un-cocked the gun while she quickly memorized the make, model, and license plate, knowing the police would need that information to track him down, when he jammed on the gas and fishtailed before speeding down the road. While he might not have technically committed a crime, she had a feeling he'd done this before. To the detriment of the poor woman.

She held her ground until he spun his tires, then sped off. Only then did she hurry over to the driver's window. "Are you okay?"

The blonde inside nodded. "Yes, thanks to you." She shuddered. "He's evil. I could see it in his face."

"I agree. Do you have a piece of paper to write down the details to give to the police?"

"Already did." The woman held up a notebook with a page filled with notes. "Also got a video of it all on my phone. Words and actions both."

"Smart girl." Tara found the woman holding up quite well despite the near miss. "I'm not sure he won't come back. Personally, I'd rather be gone when he does. I'll gladly give you a lift wherever you need to go."

"If you don't mind. I don't think I can sit here any longer just waiting for the next creep to show up." She stuffed the notebook into a large bag and opened the door.

When she stood, Tara noticed her rounded stomach. Pregnant to boot. *Poor woman.* Well, she didn't have to worry any longer. Tara would gladly get her home safe and sound.

A stiff wind picked up, sending a chill through Tara. She'd forgotten the frigid temperatures well below zero and the thick covering of snow in all the excitement. "Brrr. Let's get back to my car. It's old but the heater works well."

"I agree. I'm so cold I can barely move my fingers."

"Need some help carrying things?" Tara offered.

"Nope. All I have is this." The woman double checked inside, then clicked the lock button, and shut the door soundly.

Tara led the way to the car, keeping an eye out for the guy to return. When no other vehicles appeared, she blew air in relief, climbed inside the driver's seat, dug out her keys, and placed her purse in the center of the console.

"Thank you so much for getting involved. I couldn't get any bars on my cell phone out here and was terrified he'd tear the car apart to drag me out."

"He was damn determined." Tara placed the key in the ignition, cranked the engine, and turned up the heater before placing the car in gear and driving back onto the road. "I'm Tara, by the way."

"Abby."

"Do you know that guy?"

"Nope. He was at the station where I filled up with gas. Hit on me then. I turned him down flat. Next thing I know, my tire's flat, and he's driving up trying to be my knight in shining armor."

Tara shuddered. "How much do you want to bet he messed with your car? Set you up."

Abby nodded and stared straight ahead. "I figured that out already. One reason I got all the information written down to give to the police. If he's doing that to a pregnant woman, he'll do that to any woman."

"Scary. Really scary." Tara mentally shook off the

chill. "I didn't ask. Where do you want me to take you? I'll go anywhere you like. Home. A friend's house. Some safe place." She pulled out her phone and checked. "No reception for me either."

"I'd like to go somewhere that I can make a call. My husband will be beside himself with worry if I don't arrive home or check in soon." She held her cell phone up and peered at the screen. "No service."

Tara commiserated. "Yeah. These woods are notorious for not allowing any cell tower signals through." She paused only a second. "How about you come to my house? It's just a couple of minutes away. I always have reception there. You can use my phone if yours still can't get a signal."

Abby seemed to think it over. "That would be nice. If you don't mind. I really need to call him and go to the bathroom. For some reason, squatting in the snow doesn't sound too appealing."

Tara chuckled. "I bet not. Don't worry. My house might be more of a cottage but it's far from icy."

"Sounds like heaven right now." Abby sat back in the seat with a sigh.

It is. Tara's thoughts turned to Max. She'd brought him clothes yesterday. Hopefully, he'd opted to wear them instead of meeting her at the door in the nude. It was a toss-up either way. "I just hope Max deems to wear clothes today," Tara muttered.

Abby blinked at her. "Max?"

Tara realized she'd spoken the thought aloud. Well, crap. "He's my…" *Roommate? If I say that she's going to think we're refugees from a nudist colony.* "Boyfriend."

Boyfriend? Did I just call Max my boyfriend? Oh,

geez. I still haven't completely wrapped my mind around his being part animal and now I'm going all out hussy on wanting his drop-dead gorgeous body.

"Ah. I see." Abby smiled. "A boyfriend with an aversion to clothes?"

Tara swallowed, trying to avoid fidgeting at the uncomfortable subject. "Nah. More like, 'if you have it, you might as well flaunt it'." *And, boy howdy, did he have it.*

For the first time since they met, Abby giggled. "Yeah. I know how that is. Have one of those at home, myself."

"Good. Then you won't faint at the sight of a man in his birthday suit." Tara glanced over at Abby's belly. "Considering how you got in that state, I'd say a naked man doesn't bother you in the least."

"Granted, I'd prefer my own man. But I'm not opposed to a bit of eye candy now and again." Abby grinned.

"I think I like you," Tara replied sincerely as she pulled into her driveway, crunching over the gravel where the snow had melted all the way through.

She hit the button and pulled into the garage. After shutting off the engine, she closed the door behind her. "Let's go inside where it's warm."

"I'm ready. And, if it's okay, I'd like to use the bathroom."

"Of course." Tara got out of the car, grabbing her purse as she did. She waited for Abby to make her way around to her before opening the door to the kitchen. "Max. We have company."

She stepped into the kitchen, ushered Abby inside, then closed that door as well.

Max stepped into the room, wearing denim jeans and a black t-shirt. White socks covered his feet. His hair had been combed and he looked rested, clean, and simply lickable.

"Who do you have here?" He appraised Abby, looking her over from head to toe.

"Max. This is Abby. Abby, Max. Her car was stuck in a ditch and she couldn't get her cell phone to work. I didn't have any bars either, so brought her here so she can call her husband to pick her up."

Abby smiled at Max. "Nice to meet you."

Max inclined his head in acknowledgement.

Abby glanced back to Tara. "The restroom?"

"Oh, yes. Right this way." Tara stepped in front of Abby and led the way. "First door on your right."

"Thanks." Abby shut the door behind her.

Tara caught Max's eyebrows furrowing. "What's wrong?"

He met her gaze. "Nothing."

Tara wasn't buying it. "Abby's not a threat."

Max didn't say anything, just went to a counter and opened a cabinet. "Hot tea or hot chocolate?"

Tara blinked. "What?"

Max turned to peer over at her. "I figure you ladies would like something hot to warm you up. I have a pot pie in the oven but it won't be done for a few more minutes."

"Maybe tea." Tara set her purse on the end table by the couch and pulled out the new phone. "I have something for you."

Max filled a teapot with water, then added the tea bags, the strings hanging out the sides. Only after placing it on the stove, did he look in her direction.

"You've already done too much."

Tara waved her hand. "Here. You need this." She placed the cell phone in his hand. "To call friends or simply touch base."

Max stared at the device, then met Tara's eyes. "I don't know what to say."

Tara smiled. "Try thank you." Impulsively, she kissed his cheek.

Max caught her around the middle with one arm, pulled her against his body, and sealed his lips over hers. Ever so softly, he kissed her. Coaxing, exploring, then more aggressively when she responded in kind.

Passion flared so intensely, Tara wondered if she was having a hot flash. She opened her mouth, nipped at Max's lower lip, then nearly groaned when he thrust his tongue inside, sweeping the area in a thorough plundering.

The clearing of a throat startled Tara. She pulled back as far as Max's hold would allow and peered over at Abby. Abby's smile made Tara's cheeks warm.

"Sorry to intrude, but I wondered if you could give me the address so I can tell my husband. My phone is picking up a signal now." She held up her phone covered in a bright blue case.

"Oh, sure." Tara rambled it off, already regretting the loss of Max's embrace and the feel of his lips under hers. If Abby hadn't interrupted they'd probably be stripping down and doing some naughty things on the kitchen table by now.

"Thanks."

"Would you like some hot tea? It'll be ready in just a couple of minutes," Max asked.

Abby smiled softly. "That would be wonderful.

Thank you."

"You're welcome." Max swiveled, opened a cabinet door, and pulled out three mugs. He set them on the counter. "Hot tea coming right up. There's turkey pot pie in the oven. You might as well stay for dinner."

Tara beamed at Max. "That's a great idea."

Abby slowly nodded. "All right. Talked me into it."

****

Max eyed Tara, who sat on the couch next to Abby. The girls chatted away as if they'd been friends for decades. He saw the gift in Tara, the way she had with people, the kindness that she carried. She'd waved his praise off before but he truly meant his words. After all, he'd never met another woman like Tara. Someone that put others before herself. Rare, indeed.

Abby laughed, drawing his attention. Something about Abby bugged Max from the start. Her scent. It was…different. Not bad. Just enough to nag at him. But, no matter how much he studied her, he couldn't put his finger on it.

Shrugging it off as a non-issue, Max turned his endeavors to making the woman feel at home. After Tara's explanation that she'd found Abby's car in the ditch, with the temperatures well into the frigid category, and Abby unable to call for help, his protective instincts flared. More so for Tara but Abby was definitely included as well.

He stared at Abby's rounded stomach and wondered how Tara would look in the same situation, carrying his child. Her beautiful dark hair cascading over her shoulders, green eyes sparkling and matching the smile on her lips, as she rubbed her belly and looked at him.

What the hell? He hadn't thought of having his own family in years. Now, with his life up in the air, why did that oddball idea pop into his head?

Before he could delve into the causes, a potent scent carried to his nose. "Wolf." Max spun to face the front door and growled low in his chest. *How did they find me? Why here? Why now?*

He glanced back at the women. The questions didn't matter. Only getting them to safety did. "Listen to me. Take the car and run. I'll hold them off."

Tara blinked at him. "What in the world are you talking about? Hold who off? Why?"

"There's no time. Just do as I say."

Abby stood and strode over to Max. "You're one of them, aren't you? A shifter."

He stared at her with a hint of surprise along with the answer to the question that bugged him since Tara brought her home. The reason her scent reminded him of something. Someone. The fleeting trace didn't click before. Now it did. "You're mated to a wolf." The words slipped out before he could bite them back.

Abby nodded. "Yes. That's who's at the door now, about to lose his mind with impatience." She smiled and pushed past Max. "I guess we shouldn't keep him waiting."

Max jumped in front of her. "No. He's furious right now. I can sense it. He'll hurt you."

"No, he won't." Abby's expression softened. "He might grumble and complain but he'd never hurt me, not even a tiny pinch. Will you, Brighton?" She raised her voice and directed her query to the door.

"As if. But, if this door isn't opened in the next

155

three seconds, I'm afraid it will be pretty useless in keeping the cold out."

"Wait." Tara hurried to the door. Or tried to. Max snagged her as she zipped past. She struggled, he held snug with one arm around her middle, his protective instincts in overdrive with another shifter, especially a wolf, so close.

Taking advantage of his distraction, Abby calmly walked over, flipped the lock, and opened it.

Max turned to face the enemy, shoving Tara behind him in the process. He snarled at the sight and strong scent of a dominant wolf shifter filling the doorway. Brighton stood about the same height with dark hair, muscular body under casual clothes, and a primal, almost haughty carriage that came from an abundance of self-confidence.

This wasn't an omega to turn his belly up at any wolf that came along. Max knew status and power when he saw it.

The man pulled Abby into his arms, then met Max's gaze with curiosity. "There's no need to go all beastly berserker. I'm only here to collect my mate. And to thank you for assisting her. That's all." The deep voice carried calmness and a soothing quality.

Max's mouth fell open as he processed the lack of aggression from the other man. His concerns ebbed a little. "Whatever you do, leave Tara out of this. She's innocent."

"Max?" Abby lifted her head from her mate's chest and spun in his embrace to face Max. "Why are you so threatened? I promise you Brighton isn't some killer here to maul you both."

Brighton tilted his head, lifted his nose, and

sniffed. "Hybrid."

Max tensed. He couldn't help it. That word always preceded a thrashing and a run for his life. His mixed heritage was the bane of his existence until he'd befriended Jacques in their young teens, who hadn't minded in the least. Jacques went on to become alpha by seizing the coveted throne, knocking out Garrison's cousin in the process. For that time, his declarations ruled and Max's life turned around for the better—until Jacques's reign fell after a mere seven months. The days of acceptance were certainly gone along with the few good changes Jacques implemented. Max had barely begun to settle into an optimistic view when Garrison rose to power in a flurry and pretty much sentenced the tumultuous pack to another decade or so in the Dark Ages.

Max had learned what sacrifice felt like in the snap of a pissed off alpha's jaws on his rear legs as he sprinted for safety in an effort to survive the hunt.

Tara stepped around him and rested one hand on his shoulder. "No more running. Whatever happens I'm here to fight by your side."

"No…"

She placed her finger over his lips. "Yes."

"There's no need to worry about fighting or running." Brighton's low voice carried easily through the room. "A shifter is a shifter, no matter the unique DNA make up. We have to stick together and help one another out in order to survive hiding under the noses of millions of humans."

Max's attention centered on Brighton. He flashed a fang. "Yeah, right. Where I came from, hybrids were considered worse than sewer rats. Not to mention I sided with the wrong alpha and now have a bounty on my head for defying orders and helping him."

Brighton's dark eyes flared. "That's not a pack. That's a cult whose abuses can't continue any longer."

"What are you going to do about it? Declare war? Sacrifice yourself and your pack for a matter that has nothing to do with you?" Sarcasm dripped from every word.

"Yes. If that's the only way." Brighton pinned his gaze. "If no one stands up for others, then we're one lousy molehill of a society."

Max heard the truth in Brighton's words and voice, but years of hard lessons kept him from believing.

"How about we all sit down and have some dinner. We can discuss some things. Get to know one another better." Tara tugged at Max's restraining arm. "Please?"

He peeked down at her, saw the pleading in her gaze, and gave in. He still was uncertain about their new visitor but he could be civil. *For now.* "Okay."

"That sounds delightful. I'm starved." Abby tugged Brighton inside and shut the door behind him. "He'll eat just about anything as long as he doesn't have to cook." She rolled her eyes and dodged her husband's grasp. "Big bad wolf is afraid of pots, pans, and a little stove. I swear."

"Abby…" He grumbled and shook his head but Max could see the genuine affection he felt for his mate.

Abby grinned over her shoulder at Brighton, then took a place next to the oven. "It's turkey pot pie. I mean, who doesn't like turkey pot pie?"

"Exactly." Tara hastened over to pull some utensils

and plates from the cabinets. She cut Max a small smile of encouragement.

He relented. "Fine." Still not thrilled or comfortable with a wolf shifter in such close proximity, Max kept an eye on the man while filling glasses with ice.

Once the food was on the table and everyone sat down, Brighton glanced over at Tara. "Thank you for helping Abby."

Tara smiled. "No problem. I would have done it for any woman, especially with such a creepy man trying to forcefully get her out of the car."

Brighton's eyes flashed anger.

Max read the fury on the other man's face. His own temper ignited even as a foreboding of dread washed over him. "What do you mean, force?"

Abby took a bite of food, chewed, then swallowed. "I ran across him at the gas station. He hit on me. I turned him down." She snorted. "Can you imagine? Hitting on me? I'm as big as a whale."

"You're beautiful." Brighton wrapped an arm around her shoulders and kissed her temple. "Now tell me more about this man."

Abby nervously looked at her mate. "You'll go bananas."

Brighton shook his head. "Tell me."

Abby sighed. "He's a wolf shifter, talked about the ruse of stealing another wolf's mate. Not one of our pack but definitely a shifter. He was strong, demanding. Very aggressive."

"Are there lots of werewolves around here?" Tara asked.

Brighton spared her a glance. "You're smack dab

in the Glacier Pack territory. The closest pack to ours is quite a distance away and peaceful. We've been allies for generations." He frowned as he lightly massaged Abby's nape.

"A rogue?" Abby asked.

"Could be. One we're not aware of," Brighton answered.

"We can track him. I got his plate number," Abby offered helpfully. She paused for a second. "The truck was a dually but what caught my attention the most was the odd color, solid black with dark red trim, like an old blood red."

Max's gut clenched all the more. He swallowed with difficulty, washed it down with water, then set the glass back down.

"With Oregon plates," Tara added.

"Black and a red wolf silhouette on the bumper?" Max gritted out.

Tara's face furrowed. "Yes, how did you know?"

He didn't answer, couldn't as a lump lodged in his throat.

"We can run the plates."

"Don't bother," Max spit out. He ranted inside his mind, seeing the truth written clearly in their statements. It had to be Garrison's death squad. Other male shifters would rise up to the occasion and protect the mate of another. The death squad probably sensed who Abby was and decided to screw with her and her mate. Bullying was their pastime and they'd perfected the art, always ensuring they got what they wanted. They were nothing if not bastards.

Besides, all the pack vehicles carried the same paint job. Solid black with blood red trim—the devil's own colors. He'd once had one of his own.

How many times had he'd been the recipient of that same treatment? How many times had he been beaten down? Harassed? He'd learned to fight back, developed a keen edge, and an ability to survive. The hope for the future brightened when he'd joined forces with Jacques, then shattered into darkness the moment Jacques went down. He'd finally broke out of hell only to find the hounds were still on his trail.

Hardly able to exchange oxygen and carbon dioxide, Max focused on containing his hot fury mixed with an equally large dose of trepidation.

Brighton peered across the table, his gaze locked on Max.

Max met him unflinchingly, refusing to break contact.

Brighton stared at Max for a long moment, searching his face. "What do you know?"

Max glanced over at Tara, then made a decision. He had to trust someone, for Tara's sake. The bastard wasn't going to forget she backed him down anytime soon. He'd be looking for revenge and Tara would suffer. Max would protect her with his life but he needed backup. After all, those assholes of Garrison's tended to disperse in small packs. "It's Garrison's death squad. They're trailing me and causing havoc along the way."

"How can you be sure?"

"The attitude. The aggressiveness. The relentless bullying in order to get what he wants. That's the Throwback motto in a nutshell. Not to mention the pack is from Oregon, all their vehicles sport the same black color with blood red trim along with that special seal.

They've all been that way as long as I can remember and I grew up in that hellhole called a pack." Max rotated his shoulders trying to loosen the tightness to no avail.

"The Throwback Pack? Are you shitting me?" Disgust coated Brighton's face. "The sorriest bastards ever created. No wonder you're on the run."

Max flinched but didn't disagree. After all, it was the truth.

"Who's the alpha you're loyal to?" The bite left Brighton's voice.

"Jacques."

Brighton nodded. "Heard of him. He tried to make radical changes, then was taken out in a duel to the death."

"He's not dead." Max bit his tongue, annoyed that he'd let that precious little piece of information slip out in front of another shifter he barely knew.

The room went silent as Brighton slowly nodded. "No wonder that new prick wants your hide. You stole his victory by saving Jacques."

Max shrugged.

"That took some balls." Brighton didn't mince words. Instead, he picked up his spoon and sampled his meal.

"I did what I had to do." Max left it at that. He didn't need praise from the other shifter, not in the least.

Respect gleamed in Brighton's eyes. "You're a good man to have at a friend's back." Brighton's body relaxed.

Max tilted his head in an offer of peace and acknowledgement. "We have to do something." He saw the love between Abby and Brighton and hated the fact that he'd brought his problems to their door. "I'll figure out how to draw them away. Far from your pack and people."

Brighton shook his head. "Not happening. You're not doing this alone."

"It's my problem," Max insisted.

"Until he threatened Abby. Then it became mine and the rest of Glacier Pack's." The firm rebuttal told Max that Brighton wasn't about to back down from this. "We'll figure out a way to join ranks and to protect the women while ridding the earth of such vile rogues."

"It's not that easy. That's all these men have done their entire lives—track and kill."

"I have it on video. Maybe that'll help." Abby pulled out her phone. Max stood up and peered over her shoulder. The instant he saw and heard the man's voice, his inner wolf started growling with intensity.

There was no question about it. He easily recognized Tagart, Garrison's right-hand man. "Shit. It's them all right."

Max's gut clenched as he returned to his seat. His fears had come true. Somehow those bastards had found him. A vast nation and Tagart stumbles across him in BFE.

Tara sat up straight. "Oh, my God."

Max glanced at her. "What?"

"That man, when he got close to me, he lifted his head as if sniffing the air. Then he said, 'Where is he?' " Tara's eyes became stormy as she met Max's gaze. "He had to be talking about you."

Tension pulled Max's shoulders so tight he could barely move without fear of shattering. He exhaled and centered himself by peering at the others and finally focusing on Tara. Tagart had caught his scent from Tara. *Damn my luck.* "They will trail you until they come across me. I won't let them have you."

"No one is getting their hands on Tara or Abby or anyone else," Brighton stated firmly. "We'll figure out how to deal with this threat, but first, we need to eat before this wonderful food gets cold. He drew in a breath, then picked up his spoon. "I say we dig in before all that hard work that went into this meal goes to waste." He sampled a bite then grinned at Tara. "Delicious. My compliments to the cook."

Tara smiled back. "Thanks. I had help, though. Max has a talent for cooking, it seems."

Relieved with the change of topic, Max took another mouthful. "I'm better at eating than cooking." He rubbed his nose against Tara's ear, unable to refrain from touching her. She scared him to death with the knowledge she'd stood up to one of Garrison's assholes. Yet, her courage impressed him all the more. He'd do whatever in his power to protect her, even if that meant leaving. But, since one of Garrison's thugs could recognize her, Max didn't dare leave her side.

He'd learned to fight at a young age, and those lessons would come in handy now.

Because no one was getting within arms' reach of Tara. Not on his watch.

Max could hardly eat with the knot in his stomach. Antsy, he forced himself to take a few mouthfuls even as his mind whirled with questions and a struggle to come up with a sound plan in order to protect the ladies while ridding the rest of them of the deadly nuisance of Garrison's right-hand men.

Thirty minutes later, Max still came up short as they cleaned the dishes and escorted Brighton and Abby to the door. He'd accepted Brighton somewhat, knowing that he needed friends in order to protect Tara. The thought of taking her away fleetingly visited his mind, only for him to quickly discard it. While she might be struggling with her bookstore and have to close it soon, that didn't mean she'd appreciate being uprooted from her grandparents' home, filled with happy memories, and placed into a violent game of catch me if you can.

"I need to get Abby home. And put out word to the rest of the pack." Brighton paused to whisper so the girls wouldn't hear. "We'll close ranks. You and Tara can come stay with us if you'd like."

Max glanced over at Tara who spoke with Abby as she helped her into her coat. Abby's baby bump was more pronounced with the movement. "I'll ask but I can pretty much promise she won't leave her home, and I'm not leaving her."

Brighton frowned. "You're too far out from the pack."

"I'm not about to cower with my tail between my legs. I'm tired of running. I have something to fight for, so I will."

Brighton nodded in acknowledgement. "We'll exchange phone numbers. I'll keep you in the loop."

"Sounds good." Max hooked a finger in his jeans pocket, debating confessing his lack of resources to Brighton, then mentally shrugged. Brighton already knew of his plight. Not like telling him more would make any difference. "Tara just got me a new phone this evening. I'll give you that number and hers. While I can talk to people, I still can't access my accounts. All my ID was left behind at my house when Garrison confronted me. For all I know he's burned it to the ground."

"We have a guy that takes care of all that for us. I'm sure he can set you up, get you new copies."

Max perked up. *That'll solve one large issue.* "I'd appreciate that."

"I can vouch for him. He does all our stuff. Aging slower than the general population has its drawbacks when it comes to documentation."

"We had someone do that for us, too. But, I doubt he'll take a chance on me." Max found a piece of paper and a pen, handing both over to Brighton.

"No worries. Chip's reputation is solid. I'll give him a heads up that you'll be in contact." Brighton jotted down some numbers, then gave the items back.

"Thanks. That means a great deal."

"No problem." Brighton pulled out his phone and entered in the number Max rattled off for both his phone and Tara's. Max did the same, making a mental note to add Brighton's number to Tara's that evening.

Task done, Brighton stepped toward Abby. "Just so you know, we look out for one another here."

Max saw the truth in Brighton's eyes. Envy flashed through him. What would it have been like to grow up in such a pack? To know there were others to help? To support and teach? He couldn't imagine the joy of such a life.

"Stick around. You'll see what I'm talking about."

Surprised at Brighton's statement, Max blinked at him.

Brighton chuckled, then leaned close. "It's written

clearly on your face, Max. That and the way you feel for Tara."

Max turned his attention to Tara, found her smiling at Abby. His heart buoyed as did his determination to ensure she remained unharmed. "Just keep her safe. If things go to hell in a handbasket…"

"We take care of our own. That includes you two, now."

"I don't need charity and I can take care of myself." The boast sounded flimsy to his own ears. He'd tried it alone and failed.

"You were lucky before." Brighton cut him a stern glare. "Don't let stubbornness get in the way of common sense."

Max bristled, then gave in. Brighton was right. He couldn't take care of Tara alone, especially against two or three of the hoodlums. *Hell, I couldn't even defeat Garrison one-on-one.* Failure forced his shoulders down.

Brighton patted him on the shoulder. "We'll figure something out. They'll be watched over."

"Thanks." Max appreciated the offer, more than he could have expected when Brighton showed up at the door.

Brighton put on his coat, rested his hand on Abby's back, and escorted her out the front door and to his waiting truck.

"They seem nice." Tara turned back to him after locking the front door. She offered up a lop-sided grin. "I'm just glad you had clothes on. I'll admit I was a little concerned you like running around in the buff just a wee too much."

The off-the-wall statement eased Max's tension

and replaced it with languid humor and a healthy dash of desire. He'd been thinking of Tara all day long. How he'd love to run his hands through her hair, kiss every inch of her body, to send her over the edge into climax so hard that she'd never want to let him go. The thought of how close she came to getting hurt by Tagart only stirred his possessiveness and increase his want and need of her. Time might be short for them, and he intended to enjoy whatever he had left with her. He wanted to treasure her, cherish her, and show her the beautiful angel she truly was. "I thought you liked looking at my nude body. Hell, I caught you doing it enough."

Color blossomed on Tara's cheeks. "Well, okay. You got me there."

"Thought so." He smiled, enjoying the teasing. "You were wondering what that towel hid."

Tara's mouth fell open and her eyes widened. "Well…" She crossed her arms over her chest but the gleam in her eyes told the story.

He laughed. "I don't need to read minds, honey. Not when you're staring at my crotch, undressing me with your eyes, and licking your lips like you're a thirsty lady and I'm an extra-large glass of water."

"Ummm."

He closed the distance between them. "No use denying it. I can smell your arousal."

If possible, her eyes grew bigger. "You're lying."

"Nope. Wolf-shifter here. I've got a damn good nose." He trailed his finger along her jaw. "Want me to tell you what scents you're putting off?"

"No. Yes. No." She blinked and waved her hands. "No." The word came across as less than confident.

He grinned, thoroughly enjoying the banter. "Well, which is it? Yes or no?"

Tara lifted her chin and met his gaze. "Fine. My body wants you. I won't deny it. But, it's not in charge."

"Ah. I see." He combed his fingers through her hair. "What might it take for your mind to throw in with your body?"

"I'll tell you when I know." She stepped around him, pausing to pat his rear. "Firm. Just as I knew it would be."

He chuckled at her antics even as his cock began to ache in need. The cramped space of the jeans didn't help in the least, either. "Was there any question?"

Tara smirked up at him. "Not really. I know a good rump roast when I see one." Her eyes twinkled in happy humor before she walked away.

He blew out a breath and grappled with the urge to follow her, pull her into his arms, and kiss her until she couldn't see straight.

Rump roast indeed.

The only monkey wrench in the evening kept him at bay and a serious issue on his mind—Tagart and all that he represented. Max shuddered as he realized what the bastard could and would have done to Tara if she hadn't been able to defend herself. He'd always be thankful for her courage and her foresight to be armed. Still, he'd have nightmares of the encounter for years to come.

And what bugged him the most is how Tagart found him. After all this time and in the rural areas, hundreds of miles from home. Dumb luck couldn't stand up to the odds. There had to be another explanation. One that would be his downfall if he didn't get his head on straight and fast.

"So, what do you want to do tonight?"

Tara's voice broke into his thoughts. He turned to find the same worry he felt plastered on her face. *Damn Garrison and his men for taking away Tara's brightness and happiness.* He vowed to stay on guard and prayed for a day or three in order to come up with a foolproof plan before Tagart and whoever else he called closed in for the kill. That wouldn't likely happen tonight.

Time to stop and smell the roses.

Max forced a smile and worked to return to the teasing banter they'd left behind. "Well, there's always strip poker."

Tara snorted but seemed to perk up. "Can't wait to get naked, huh?"

Max grinned wolfishly. "Maybe…"

"I guess I could give Cotton another bath." Tara waggled her eyebrows.

Max groaned. "Talk about torture." He stepped toward her, noticing she held her ground and crossed her arms. Defensive, for sure, but her playfulness and scent told him something more. She wanted to tease and wasn't immune to him. Not in the least.

With doomsday right around the corner, he threw his hat into the ring with enthusiasm. Tara wanted to play. Far be it for him to dissuade her. Especially since he found the friskiness contagious. "You sure checked out my assets during bath time." He grinned wickedly, enjoying the sight of color blossoming across her face. "And you've been checking them out since."

"Bad. Very bad." She shook her finger at him.

"You're so full of yourself."

He chuckled. "You like that too."

She rolled her eyes, then peered up at him from under her eyelashes. "You're good looking. I'll give you that. A hunk if I've ever seen one."

The compliment went straight to his already hardening cock. "And?"

"And, you were pretty cute running around in that towel." She trailed one finger down his shirt covered chest.

"Cute?" He arched an eyebrow. "I thought I was sex on a stick."

She grinned. "I plead the fifth."

"Uh, huh. I have a perfect memory when it comes to that." He edged closer and reached out to play with the hem of her shirt. The pheromones emanating from her stirred his passions to a fevered pitch. She wanted him, he was absolutely sure. "You think I'm one hell of a man and can't wait to see what that towel was hiding. You even admitted it."

She arched an eyebrow, crossed her arms, then tapped her bottom lip with a finger. "Hmm. Did I?"

Max nodded. "Yep, you did."

"Moment of insanity."

"Uh, huh." He grinned at the playful banter. The other women he'd been with never had more on their mind than getting their just due, to put it bluntly. They cared less about him and certainly never would be amusing. Demanding and teasing, yes. Happy and fun, absolutely not. Just another way Tara was refreshingly different. He didn't care that she was human. She possessed all the traits he wanted in a lady and then some. He'd hit the jackpot with her and intended to hold fast to his treasure for as long as she would have him.

He wanted her more than he wanted his next meal. Yet, he had to make sure she was on the same page. Sex with her would be binding in his mind and he needed her to crave him for himself, not because she was rattled, worried, and wanted comfort. He'd give her that certainly, in the form of holding her, reassuring her. But, intimacy in the physical sense would be a big step and she had to be onboard one hundred percent.

"So, Tara. Ready to see what that towel hid?" He lowered his voice and watched for her reaction.

Her lips parted and eyes sparked.

Anticipation swept through him, making a beeline for his cock. An aching fullness quickly followed. The throbbing increased. He'd never been this hard for a woman.

A gust of wind slapped a tree limb against the far window. Max caught a glimpse of the movement from over Tara's shoulder.

Tara startled, jumped, and gasped. She spun, stared at the offending branch, then slowly turned back.

"It's just a limb. Nothing to fret about," Max reassured. Never before had she been this jumpy. He bore responsibility for the change. Her once safe haven sat in the crosshairs of vengeance.

She sobered, deep lines appearing on her face. The brightness dulled into an expression of apprehension, of fear. "They're coming to kill you." A shudder quaked her body.

His light mood vanished in an instant. Other emotions took over, namely worry and concern. The fevered excitement quickly faded in the wake of reality.

He nodded. As much as he wanted to shield her from the truth, he couldn't. "Yes."

"And they won't stop until you're dead."

"No." He much preferred the bantering than this gut-wrenching topic. Still, he couldn't deny her questions or the severity of the situation.

She looked down at the floor for a long moment then blew out a breath. Lifting her chin, she met his eyes. "Make love to me."

"I'll protect you. You don't have to be afraid."

She shook her head. "I know what I want."

"Comfort. Reassurance." He stared at her. "You don't have to sleep with me in order to get those things."

She ran her hands over his chest as if ensuring that he was indeed solid. "*I know what I want.*" She added emphasis to the words this time.

He narrowed his eyes. "Sex is a big step... Maybe we should take a minute. Think about it. Revisit it when you aren't scared out of your mind."

Her face scrunched in annoyance. "I'm not scared out of my mind. I'm a big girl and I know what I want. So, enough chit-chat. *Make love to me already, damn it.*"

Max hesitated. He needed her to understand. To be absolutely certain. He'd gladly take her to bed in a heartbeat, but only for the right reasons and with her full consent and knowledge. "I can't promise you tomorrow."

Tara bobbed her head once, slowly, her gaze locked on his. "I'm not asking for tomorrow. I'm just asking for tonight."

He'd have to be made of stone to turn her down.

The beseeching in her eyes, the explicit trust, the need. All of it called to him on a deep level. And matched his own. "I'll protect you. No matter what I'll—"

Tara placed her fingers over his lips, silencing him. "Shhh. Just make love to me. Please."

He kissed her fingertips. "Are you sure?"

"Yes."

The softly whispered confirmation sent a fiery jolt through him, lashing his temporarily decreasing libido into a frenzy. Unable to wait a second more, he drew her into his embrace, slanted his lips over hers, then lightly caressed. Her mouth opened on a gasp. He took immediate advantage by slipping his tongue inside for a grand exploration, teasing her with licks to her lips in between.

He trailed his hands down her back, along her sides, and cupped her ass, just like he'd been wanting to do for ages. He patted the area, groaned, and pulled her flush against his chest, needing her touch, her presence more than he needed anything before.

She responded in kind, wrapping her arms around his neck and rubbing her breasts against his still clothed chest, increasing the ache in his already hard cock tenfold. No longer passive, Tara took an offensive role, peppering kisses along his neck and jaw, before sealing her lips over his and aggressively plundering inside. She clung to him, roamed his body with her eager touch, and rallied him to greater levels of hunger.

And if they didn't slow down, he'd take her right then and there, hard. Fast. In a violent joining that had little romance or control. Not what he wanted for their first time together.

In one of the hardest tasks he'd ever faced, Max

pulled away, clenching his teeth against the nearly overwhelming need to rip her clothes off, pick her up, settle her against the wall, and commence taking her with all the gusto and hunger burning in his veins..

Confusion covered her face.

He took her hand in his and kissed her fingers. "Don't you think the bedroom might be a little more comfortable?"

A sage smile covered her lips. "That's a great idea." She used his hold to lead him down the hall, paused just inside the door, and turned. "You have way too many clothes on."

"Gonna do something about it?" he challenged.

"Oh, yeah." She reached for his shirt and lifted.

Max bent, allowing her to pull the unwanted garment from his body.

She dropped it on the floor, then traced his exposed flesh with her hands. She rubbed, she caressed, she drew out a map that made him moan with ever increasing need.

Taking the hint, she dropped her hands to the zipper on his jeans. Slowly, way too slowly, she pushed it down, then released the single button at the top. His heavy cock sprang free.

Relief was short lived as she started petting his sensitive flesh. Hot fire rapidly replaced uncomfortable tightness from the cramped space of his clothing.

He closed his eyes, drew in a steadying breath, then nudged her hands away. He opened his lids and peered at her. "Your turn."

She pouted. "I wasn't done playing."

He grinned wolfishly. "I'm not done either. But, what's good for the goose..." He trailed off, gripped her shirt, and tugged it off. Carelessly, he tossed it aside, unfastened her pants, and shoved them down. While he stepped out of his own shackles of jeans, she did the same.

"So beautiful. Perfect." He couldn't take his eyes off her. The pretty white lace bra only accentuated her modest breasts, adding a romantic, sexy dimension to the already sizzling picture she presented. He molded one breast, gently plumping, then used his thumbs to unhook the latch. The bra opened, exposing her naked flesh.

He narrowed his eyes as his cock began to throb. Absently, he brushed the material aside and totally off, lowered his head, and feasted on a pebbled raspberry tip. He lapped and ever so carefully ran his teeth over the area, both feeling and hearing her intake of breath at the intimacy.

She grasped onto his shoulders, ran her hands upward and into his hair, then tugged him closer in a wordless request for more.

He lifted his head, saw the light red hue and dampness from his rapt attention, then flicked his focus to her face. Arousal, bright and total, lit up her pretty eyes. Her chest expanded with a breath, drawing his attention back down to her cleavage. With a sexy grin, he bestowed the same treatment to the other side.

"Oh, Max." The breathless calling of his name told Max all he needed to know. Tara was on fire for him.

He ran his free hand over her stomach and further south, cupping the junction between her thighs. Dampness met him.

She shimmied in response, widening her stance just a bit.

"You're wet. Soaking those panties." He could barely form coherent thoughts as he lifted enough to study her face as he dipped his fingers under the material. "So hot."

She whimpered as he pushed the crotch of her panties aside in order to run his fingers through the cleft.

"Tell me you want me."

She arched her back and extended her neck, closing her eyes in the process. Her lips opened but no sound emerged.

"Tara." He waited until she once again met his gaze. "Tell me."

She swallowed hard. "I want nothing more." She placed her hand on the back of his neck and drew him down for a kiss.

A fiery tempest erupted in his blood. He plundered her mouth, jerked hard on her panties, and heard the resulting rip. Nothing separated him from his prize. The fact sent him into another dimension.

"Condom," she whispered.

He paused, then smiled a little sheepishly. "No wallet. And no pockets in my fur coat."

She chuckled. "I have some in the bedside table."

That admission surprised him.

Finding the drawer, he plucked one out, tore open the package, and rolled the rubber on, wincing a little at the snugness. Obviously one size didn't fit all. Another interesting fact drew his attention. "Umm. Why do you have red and white striped condoms?" The rubber made his cock look like a giant peppermint stick.

Tara blushed brightly. "You don't want to know."

"Actually, I do."

"Too bad. I'm not opening that can of worms. No way."

Max grinned. *That had to be one hell of a story.*

Shifters didn't normally use condoms. He'd worn them before, especially with human females that didn't understand that shifters didn't carry any diseases and the likelihood of pregnancy was slim. But, never such a brightly colored one as this.

A twinge of jealousy struck. "Bring your dates home often?"

"Never. Only you."

The words lashed his libido to greater heights. He had no idea if the condom would last, especially if his knot swelled, but he wasn't about to bring that up right now. Shifter reproduction had a few tweaks. That discussion would have to occur later. Much later. Right now, she was safe, condom or no. But, if it made her feel more comfortable, he'd wear it, no matter how silly he felt in such a get up.

With iron control, he lifted her in his arms, carried her to the bed, and placed her in the center. "I'm going make you scream with pleasure."

Her eyes brightened. She bit her lip. "Do it."

The order made him grin. He nudged her legs apart making room for himself. Stretching out, he slowly pressed his index finger inside while using his thumb to brush over her clit.

She bucked and cried out.

"That's it. I need a taste. Just a little taste." He replaced his thumb with his lips, then ever so slowly ran his tongue over the hard button.

She moaned and gripped the sheets tightly with her fists.

"Like that?" He knew she did, but couldn't help asking. Everything had to be perfect for her. Absolutely perfect.

"Yes, oh God, yes." She lifted her head and stared at him.

He dipped back in and went to work. As he licked and sucked, he moved his finger in and out. After a minute, he added a second one, needing to ease the tightness in order to prepare her for his full shaft. She was dripping wet, so hot, and snug. He couldn't wait to slip his cock inside and soak up the moment.

She writhed. Sexy little sounds escaped her lips.

He reveled in her responses. Each little cry added more demand to his need, yet he wasn't about to rush. This was for her. Nothing less would do.

Suddenly, tension gripped her body. She clamped her thighs on either side of his head, trapping him in between. Her breathing caught.

Rapidly, Max flicked her clit with his tongue, then sucked with tender care. He pushed two fingers inside her slit as far as they would go.

For a second, nothing happened. Silent, immense tightness prevailed.

Then, with a jerk, Tara's body flew into orgasm. Strong contractions alternately gripped and released his digits in a rhythmic dance as old as time.

He quickly covered her, careful to keep his weight from her supine body, took his shaft in hand, and pressed inside. The ripples drew him in as well as licked at him with searing intensity. He groaned at the sensation.

Tara lifted her legs, wrapping them around his hips.

The new angle allowed him to venture deep and destroyed his control. He pulled back and set forth a quick pace. Thrust after thrust, he slid in and out, watching her face the entire time. Her eyes lost focus as her lips parted. Breaths came out nearly as grunts. Still, he pushed her harder. "Again, Tara. Come for me. Again." He punctuated the command with a sharp nip to her breast.

Tingling in his balls alerted him to his upcoming release.

He growled, grasping for a tiny bit of control to hold off, just for a bit longer, in order to send Tara into a frenzy of rapture once more. Wedging his hand between their bodies, he found the nub he searched for and strummed.

Tara cried out, her nails digging into his back as she hit the pinnacle.

Max followed suit, surging into her once more. Her tight walls massaged his buried cock with fervor.

The swelling in his shaft grew in pressure, then in extreme ecstasy as it locked them together.

Tara whimpered and wiggled.

"Shh." He kissed her lips, then stared down into her face, noting the wonderment mixed in with sheer sexual bliss. "It's okay. I've got you."

"You're…"

He grinned then groaned as another wave of pleasure shot through his body. "All part of the benefit package when dating a shifter."

She smiled then tossed her head back. Her expression of delight told him all he needed to know.

She'd found satisfaction in his arms. And a whole lot of it.

Pride and happiness added another element to his present state of paradise. He pressed up and forward ever so slightly, unable to move more than a smidge, but it was enough to allow him to rub against her clit.

She bit her lip and sucked in air.

Oh, yeah. This was so worth playing fetch. And then some.

****

A long time later, he held her against his body, lazily running his fingers through her hair. She'd relaxed in his arms, seeming as content to share the quiet moment as he was. Never before had he enjoyed the luxury of cuddling afterward. Hell, the pack females that had searched him out normally demanded more. No rest, no stopping until their needs were sated. As soon as that happened, they were all too happy to kick a man out of their bed. At least with him. Other men, to hear them talk, seemed to have a much better experience. Max didn't doubt his mixed genetics played a part. After all, the women liked his style and were attracted to his looks and big cock. But, as soon as they were finished, they pointed to the door. Bedding him was one thing, being seen in public with him was another. He grimaced at how superficial the ones who chose him were.

But, not Tara.

He pressed his lips against her nape. Her long hair had fallen to the side, but a few strands still tickled his nose. Not that he'd minded in the least. In his mind, nothing could darken the moment. It had been perfection. Emotions cascaded through him—sensitive, powerful feelings that he'd never felt for another woman. New and novel, he questioned if they truly existed or if he'd conjured them up.

He opted not to analyze them. Doing so would only make him crazy. Until then, he'd simply enjoy. Pressing matters called but he'd attend to them later. His time was growing short and he intended to spend every moment with Tara that he could.

Bathing in the aftermath of the best sex he'd ever had, Max had no urge to get up anytime soon. Tara felt way too good. Warm. She fit his body like a lock for his key. He'd test that theory again and very soon.

She sighed and partially turned to look up at him. A happy smile covered her lips. "Care to explain that whole thing at the end?"

He nuzzled her shoulder. "The knot?"

"Is that what you call it?"

"Yes." He decided that the event was so much easier to experience than to discuss. "We share some of the same gifts as our wild cousins." He thought about the intact condom he'd removed. As much as he hated the awful color, it had held up. The knot didn't stress it past what it could handle. Pretty impressive.

She pursed her lips. "Big hands. Big feet. Big…parts. And a knot to make for a big bang at the end?"

He chuckled. "Something like that." He squeezed her lightly.

"Interesting." She rested her hands on his arm. "I might have to do some personal research on the matter."

"Anytime you want. I'm all yours."

She smiled. Teasing fulfillment sparkled in her eyes. "Very kind of you to offer."

"It's the least I can do. After all you've done for

me."

She froze and her lips flattened out. "Meaning?"

Shit. I just stepped into it. Max averted his eyes. His brain blanked when it came to a proper, acceptable response.

She sat up, holding the sheet against her chest.

He hated the loss of the sight of her pretty breasts, but didn't think she'd appreciate him ogling her at the moment. He went on the defensive. "I said I couldn't promise you tomorrow."

"Yes, and I understand that completely." She frowned. "What I don't understand is how this," she waved her hand, "is considered a payment for helping you out."

Max scrubbed his face. "It's not."

"Then what did you mean, 'it was the least you could do'?" Her tone carried a definite bite and one that warned of impending explosion and not in a good way.

"I…" He bit his lip, trying valiantly to come up with an explanation that wouldn't send her running for the skillet. Or worse, her gun.

"Forget it," she snapped. "Just consider your debt paid in full." Tossing the covers aside, she climbed out of bed, her motions jerky as she pawed through her drawers, pulled out underwear, and started dressing.

"No. Wait. Tara." He stood up, found his discarded jeans and tugged them on, not bothering with the boxer shorts. "Just wait."

"Nice to know I work in a pinch when you have an itch to be scratched," she flung back at him, anger apparent in every movement. "I'm nothing more than a pity fuck to you." The crass language, so unlike her, shocked him. It also told of her immense upset.

"Tara." He tried again, growling as he threw up his arms. How they got from sated and happy to outright arguing, he didn't have a clue. *Because of your less than tactful mouth*, he reminded himself in frustration.

She shook her head, marched to the closet, snagged a shirt, and put it on. A pair of stretchy workout pants followed.

"That's not what I meant at all."

"It doesn't matter," she insisted.

"*Yes. It does.*" He grappled with the self-loathing his careless words caused, however unintentional and innocent they were.

He recalled her confessions to Cotton about how men overlooked her or chose others right in front of her. Realization struck in the form of his heart breaking for the pain he'd unwittingly laid on her, just like the other men she'd spoken of. Unknowingly, he'd tapped into her self-esteem issues when it came to dating and lowered himself to the level of slime mold like the others. The fact bothered him greatly. For in his eyes, she stood out like the brightest star in the night sky.

"Save it." She spared him a cutting look, then headed for the kitchen.

He followed, cussing at his lack of a filter from his brain to his mouth. His inner beast growled in aggravation with his loose tongue as well.

I know. I know. He ran his hands through his hair and followed her. "Tara. You have to listen."

She opened a cabinet in the kitchen and started digging out pots and pans, setting them on the counter—loudly. "Nope. I'm good. Don't need to hear anything else. *Really.*"

He grabbed her gently, spun her around, and caged

her against the counter. "Yes, you do." He pinned her gaze and refused to relinquish it. "This isn't about payment or settling a debt. This is about you."

She opened her mouth to speak.

He shook his head. "Just listen." When she remained silent, he continued. "I'm bad news. Even if we deal with Garrison and the bastards that follow him, that doesn't mean the threat is over. He has distant cousins. Hell, his blood line has ruled with an iron fist for nearly my whole life. Every time another alpha steps in to try to change things, one of Garrison's family members takes them down. Not to mention someone else might covet that position." He saw the anger leaving her face and blew out a breath. "There's still the potential they will want revenge on what was done to Garrison. If we make it through this, there's likely more to come." He steeled his gaze and willed her to understand. "I want nothing more than to stay here, with you, and see where whatever is between us can go. You're amazing. A true woman like no other. I've never known a woman could be so kind and caring. So gentle and sweet. You've given me everything and I've only brought danger to your doorstep. You're a rare treasure that I can't risk. The longer I stay, the harder it is to leave. But by staying here, I'm jeopardizing your life and your happiness. That is something I can't allow."

She worried her bottom lip. "What about what I want?"

"Your life *is* priority," he affirmed.

"I'm stronger than you think and willing to fight for what we have. Even if it's just for a day." She cupped his cheek and ran her thumb across his lips.

He kissed the tip. "I've never made love like that before. So complete, so wonderful. You're the reason. I wanted to please you, to show you how special you are. To show you…" He couldn't admit those emotions. To do so would bind him to her even more than she was now. And that was damn strong.

Admitting his feelings would only worsen her pain later. His, too, though he already knew the cost of leaving her. He'd felt it once before when he'd tried to leave. The next time it would be more than devastating—it would be soul wrenching.

Tara gazed at him, then the tension left her face. She offered up a slight smile. "It's okay, Max. I get the picture."

"You do?" He blinked at her.

She grinned toothily. "Yep."

His inner warning system beeped loudly in his mind. "What is that picture exactly?" He waited eagerly for the reply.

She tilted her head and crossed her arms. "You think great sex is the answer. It is, but I think it's a cover up for another very important issue."

"What's that?" He stood up straight, putting a couple of feet between them.

"I'll let you figure that out for yourself." She ducked to the side and commenced pulling out cooking pots.

Well, hell.

Chapter 10

Max's gut ate at him. All morning he'd scoured his mind trying to figure out how Garrison trailed him to this very place—to no avail. As far as he knew Garrison had never met Becky or knew about where she'd gone even if he did. While it would be a consideration if he recalled Jacques's only sibling, Garrison had no way of knowing where she lived. No one did—except Max.

Which left him back where he started—with no answer to the question of how Garrison found him. He knew it would mean something important if he could just come up with a rational way they discovered his whereabouts. Something. Anything. A single clue. His and Tara's life depended on it.

Tara exited the bathroom and walked into the kitchen. Her still wet hair curled slightly at the ends, dampening the light blue sweatshirt she wore. Black leggings and white socks completed the outfit. Even though the clothing lacked finesse or fineness, they didn't detract a single inch from Tara's beauty. She could walk around in a gunny sack and still be gorgeous.

He cringed when he thought of their argument the evening before. How he'd hurt her with his words. Not on purpose, certainly, but she'd taken the statement and twisted it all different ways—none of them good.

They'd shared the bed last night, just to sleep. He'd

reached for her half a dozen times before changing his mind. As much as he wanted her, he knew she had to make the first move. She was right in one respect—great sex cured some things. Only he wasn't so sure this was one of them. He'd unintentionally cut her to the core and now sought ways to make up for it. Fixing breakfast was the first step.

He dropped bread into the toaster. "I'm sorry about last night," he offered up in a soft tone.

She glanced up at him. "I'm sorry, too. I did some thinking. It's my fault for trying to force too much into what happened."

He shook his head, opened his arms, and breathed a huge sigh of relief when she stepped into his embrace. Holding her snug, he kissed her crown and rested his cheek on the top of her head. "You sell yourself way short."

She snorted, but didn't try to break free. "I know the truth, dealt with it for a long time. It's okay." She lifted her head and met his gaze. "Life is too short to spend bickering over such things."

"I'd never in a million years hurt you." The truth slipped out. "I care for you too much for that." He bolstered his courage and went with his gut. "The women I've been with, members of the pack, they only took. Manipulated. They'd be with a man when it suited them and kick them out of the bed the moment they were appeased. I didn't know any better until you bundled up a hurt wolf, took him home, and treated him like a beloved pet. I didn't know what to think or do."

She smiled slightly. "That's better."

He grinned in return. "You knocked me off balance, woman." He sobered. "But, the thought of anything happening to you gives me nightmares." He hugged her close.

She returned the affection with just as much gusto.

The chiming of a timer interrupted the moment.

Reluctantly, he pulled back, brushing her hair out of her face in the process. He bracketed her cheeks and brushed his lips against hers. "No matter what, I'll protect you with my life."

Tara arched an eyebrow. "If I said those words back to you, does that earn me a scowl?"

He grunted, heading for the oven and turning it off. "Yes." The scent of fresh baked goods hit him long before he opened the door.

"How about a growl?"

"Maybe." He collected the hot pads, took the pan out, and set it on top of the stove.

"A spanking?"

The question surprised him. He spun around and blinked at her. "You want to be spanked?"

Saucily, she shrugged, her eyes alight with mischief. "I hear it's titillating."

"Titillating?" He shook his head. "You've been reading some of those erotic bondage romances in your store, haven't you?"

She giggled. "Who, me?"

"Uh, huh." He smiled happily. Her playful side was back and he found it too tempting to pass up. Besides, it sure beat arguing. "Bring one home for me to look over. I might need to do a little research."

She shook her finger at him. "What's good for the goose is good for the gander."

He blinked at her. "You want to spank me?"

"Hmmm." She tapped her lip with her finger.

He rolled his eyes. "Can't we just play fetch instead?"

"Ehh. How about hide and seek?"

Arousal flared. He found it escalating rapidly inside his body, making a beeline for his dick. Even better, he scented it in the air, emanating from them both.

Seems Tara has a naughty side. I like it.

"What are we hiding?" He waggled his eyebrows.

She burst out laughing. "After breakfast, perhaps I'll let you find out."

"The muffins will wait," he suggested with more than a hint of longing in his voice.

"So they will." She closed the distance between them, grabbed the zipper on his jeans, and shoved it down. A second later, she undid the top button, and pulled the material aside. Lovingly, she stroked his shaft that jutted out the second she released it. "I'm hungry this morning."

He inclined his head to the treat he'd just baked.

She stared under her lashes at his cock she gently teased. "I think this is what I'm craving." With that said, she lowered to her knees, tugged his pants down further, and flicked her tongue over the mushroom head of his dick.

The instant pleasure was so powerful it threatened to take his knees out from under him. Something he refused to allow to happen. Especially when Tara seemed quite intent on driving him nearly mad with her affections. He grabbed onto the nearby counter to steady himself. "Damn."

She grinned wickedly. "There's plenty more where that came from." Maintaining eye contact, she opened wide and drew the tip of his shaft into her mouth, laving it with her talented tongue like an ice cream cone. One hand grasped the base of his cock, the other she lowered to take his balls in hand, lightly rolling them in her palm.

White heat soared through his veins.

Immediately, he considered and just as quickly forgot how ridiculous he must look, standing in the kitchen with his jeans around his knees, and the oven mitts still on his hands. He needed to touch, to give back, to make this gift of hers better. Quickly, he removed the mitts and dropped them on the counter so he could hold Tara's head, gently guide her motions.

She took more into her mouth and began to suck. At the same time her hand started a slow, steady rhythm on the lower section of his shaft.

"Just like that. Oh, shit. Just like that." He threw his head back and gulped in air. Excitement ratcheted up at a rapid pace, sending him close to the top in just a matter of seconds. He struggled to slow his reaction down, to savor the moment, to draw it out.

She leaned back, then reversed course, only this time, she dragged her tongue the length of his aching cock all the way to the tip. Teasingly, she winked at him, then greedily lapped at his slit. Over and over, she worked the area, as if asking for a reward for her efforts.

He groaned, let one hand fall to his side, keeping the other on the back of her head. The urge to take over and control her arose and just as quickly, was squashed. This was her gift and he'd be damned if he ruined it. Instead, he focused on a soft touch, steadily. Intimate. A link to her as she unselfishly gave.

Tara engulfed his shaft once again, took him deep into her throat, then moaned.

The vibrations carried all the way through him before setting off a chain reaction in all the nerve cells in his body, but especially his cock and balls. He shot up to the precipice and held there by absolute sheer will alone. "You're going to make me come if you do that again." He gritted out the warning. Already his knot had begun to swell, a sure signal of impending climax.

Tara, sweet Tara. She eyed him mischievously, bobbed her head, and repeated the action.

Riveting hard rapture slammed through him. Pulse after pulse of fiery passion followed, his release powerful, full, and total. He wasn't sure, but thought he'd even howled as she continued to lick and lightly nibble on his shaft while exploring the swollen knot. She brushed her fingers over the area, sending him to another massive spike in rapture.

A tremor quaked his body as he slowly came down from the unbelievable orgasm. He petted her head, encouraging her to ease off as his body had become too sensitive to tolerate more than the lightest caress.

Tara smiled up at him and licked her lips.

He laughed in sheer delight. Warmth enveloped his heart. Insight flared. His pride meant pittance compared to Tara's wellbeing. He'd do anything and everything to ensure her safety. If throwing in with Brighton helped keep Tara safe, he'd jump on board wholeheartedly. He'd face the Devil himself if he had to.

One thing is for sure—no matter what happens, I'm going to have the time of my life with this woman for as long as I can.

The vow came out of nowhere but stuck solid. He didn't know the first thing about love, but knew that if he hung around for much longer, she'd teach him all about it.

****

"Why did you want to be a pilot?" Tara took a large bite out of a blueberry muffin she'd just slathered margarine onto a few seconds before. "These are wonderful, by the way. Thank you."

He inclined his head. "Boxed goods are this chef's greatest asset." He chuckled, then turned to her original question. "Because my father was. I idolized him as a kid. Always wanted to follow in his footsteps." Max finished his first muffin and grabbed another from the plate. They'd cooled considerably due to the previous distraction of her excellent blow job. No matter. A few seconds in the microwave worked just fine.

"That must have been something, getting to travel all over the place."

"Yeah. I started taking the controls at age ten. Flew an entire trip by myself with my father as co-pilot at age twelve. Went solo at sixteen."

"Wow. Talk about a prodigy."

Memories came to the fore. "That was the best time with my father. We could speak openly about anything when alone. In the pack, there were always ears around. He told me about his vision for the future and how he and the alpha he aligned with wanted to wrestle control away and change things for the better." *Fat lot it did, though.*

"I take it that didn't happen?"

"No." Max took another bite, chewed, and swallowed. "He was killed during an uprising, along with the man he followed. Garrison's family retained control."

Sympathy coated Tara's face. "I'm sorry. I can't imagine what that must have been like, living in such a violent society. Awful."

Max shrugged and focused on eating. The images rushing through his mind only reminded him the high cost others had paid for attempting to make things better for all.

And it will happen again if I don't figure out how in the hell Garrison found me.

"Nowhere will be safe from Garrison. He found me here. How, I still don't have a clue." Stress tightened his shoulders once again. The burden returned with a vengeance.

"Phone?"

"I destroyed both mine and Jacques's before returning home. I knew they could track us and didn't want to take a single chance. I had already memorized Becky's phone number, so didn't dare write it down on anything, either."

Tara took another mouthful, seemingly deep in thought. "Didn't Garrison already know about Becky and figure you'd take Jacques there?"

He'd thought of that hundreds of times over the past few weeks. "She left the pack when Jacques and I were around thirteen. Garrison is a couple of years younger. I doubt he remembers her. She was always shy and not one to stick out."

"Family records? The library? Birth certificates?" Tara asked.

"We have one guy that takes care of all the birth and death certificates as well as licenses. Since we

194

prefer to stay out of the public's eyes most of the time, we have to have someone else handle the legal stuff." Max considered the possibilities. "Even if Garrison discovered or recalled that Jacques had a sister, he wouldn't know where she went. Since she and her mother left the group years ago, there's no marriage certificate or any forwarding address. Her mother divorced her father, then, last I heard, remarried and became part of her husband's pack a while after she vanished from Oregon. Becky found her husband and went to live with him. Their father passed later, leaving Jacques and me as the only people who know where Becky lived. With him on death's door..." Max trailed off, finding the thought a dead end.

Tara took a drink of her milk, then tapped her fingers on the kitchen table. "Don't planes have GPS?"

The internal light bulb in Max's head clicked on. After all this time, he finally had the answer. Eagerness and relief coursed through him. Along with the certainty that he'd screwed up big time and put not only Becky at risk, but Jacques and her entire family pack. "That's it."

"What's it?" Tara tilted her head.

"Most planes don't use GPS as tracking tools, only for navigation to help the pilots. But the pack plane was newly purchased and includes an ADS-B system— Automatic Dependent Surveillance Broadcast. Not only can a plane be tracked on radar, but using this system, certain websites let people follow the path of planes equipped with this new technology." Puzzle pieces flew into place. "I forgot all about it. They were able to trace my location, could see where I landed. Date, time, everything." He raked one hand through his hair.

"Which means, they realized where I was, put two and two together, and came up with Becky, Jacques's sister. It wouldn't take a rocket scientist to pull some strings and tap her phone." He cussed at his own stupidity.

"You didn't know."

Max met her eyes, filled with compassion and sympathy. "I knew but was in too big a hurry to think about it." Worry washed through him. "I have to warn Jacques. They know where he is." Without another word, Max stood up, grabbed his phone, walked into the garage for a little privacy, and punched in the number. Purposely, he'd memorized it and not added it to the contact list. Phones fell into the wrong hands at times, and he didn't want any links to Becky and Jacques. *Too fucking late.*

Jacques answered on the first ring.

Max didn't bother with formalities. "You need to know that they tracked my flight and tapped Becky's phone. Garrison knows where you are."

A moment of stillness passed. "And traced your location through it, too." Jacques made it a statement.

"Yes." Max swallowed hard. "Tagart showed up harassing a woman stranded in her car. The lady I've been staying with intervened, but Tagart picked up my scent from her."

"They'll close ranks, then come in force."

"I can handle it."

"How? One against two or three isn't any kind of odds, even if they stick to the rules and only attack one at a time."

Tell me something I don't know. Max bit back the sarcasm. "I have help."

"The woman you mentioned?"

Max heard the curiosity in Jacques's voice. "Well, yes. But, more importantly, from the local shifter wolf pack, particularly the alpha. It was his mate that Tara helped out."

"Damn. You're flying under the right star."

Max snorted at that idea. His luck had been running nothing but bad for so long, he didn't know how to react to something good falling into his lap.

"Now, tell me more about this woman," Jacques insisted.

"Her name is Tara. She owns a local used bookstore."

"Uh, huh. Smart, considerate, and pretty, too," Jacques added.

Max grinned. "How did you know she was pretty?"

"Never knew you to get all excited about one that wasn't." Jacques chuckled. "Hell, don't remember you getting excited about the pretty ones, either."

"She's different. A human. But, she took me in, cared for me." Max recalled that first day as she pampered him, giving him the first meal in ages. How comfortable he felt. The way she spoke to him, soothed him, gave him a reason to believe.

"And she didn't faint when you told her you were a shifter?"

Max bit back a laugh. "She tried to smack me upside the head with a skillet."

Full blown snickers carried through the phone line. "Sounds feisty."

"That she is. With the heart of an angel."

"Sounds like you two are close. Involved." A pregnant pause followed. "Is she your mate?"

Max blew out a slow breath. "Things are too up in

the air to make that kind of commitment. Garrison won't stop hunting me. I've already put her in enough danger. I have to take care of that now then I need to move on."

"That won't protect her. They'll just use her as leverage," Jacques pointed out.

"Maybe if I…"

"You know how Garrison's mind works as well as I do. All perceived threats are hunted down and killed. If that means harming innocents in the process, then so be it. If he can't do it someone else will. As long as his family is in power."

Max's gut knotted. He already understood the risks, but hated to hear them spoken out loud. They became somehow more real that way.

"I'll do what I have to do to protect her."

"You do that. Mates are hard to come by." Jacques's wit came through loud and clear with an edge of humor.

The tone of Jacques's voice keyed Max in that something was up in the guy's social life. "Don't tell me you've found yours."

"I'll get back with you on that."

"You better." Max grinned as he considered the woman that might be able to wrap Jacques around her little finger. His friend deserved some female torment now and again along with someone to love him for the man he was.

Just like Tara did for him.

"Watch your back." The last thing he wanted was for Garrison's men to rain down on Jacques, especially while he was still healing.

"No worries. I can hold my own." Self-confidence

carried through, just like the old Jacques that Max remembered.

"They have to go through me first." Max straightened his back. "I'll update the local alpha. Brighton will want to be kept abreast. It's his territory after all."

"And his mate they messed with. That makes a man pretty damn pissed off," Jacques added.

"Sounds like you know from personal experience." Max caught the unsaid attitude coming through loud and clear. Jacques had a special woman. There was no doubt. Most likely one of Becky's pack and possibly one of the reasons Jacques pulled through. If he ever met the lady, Max would thank her greatly.

"You too, bro. You, too." Jacques grew silent for a few beats. "Where are you?"

Max saw through his plans easily. "Not happening. We've got it covered. You need to stay put, warn Becky's pack, and be prepared. If we don't pull through this, you'll be the last stand against Garrison."

"Max…"

"I mean it Jacques. You might be an alpha, but I'm laying down the law." Max grew serious and put command in his voice. "You hold the hope of a better future for Throwback. If Garrison gets to you…" Max couldn't finish the statement.

"Not going to happen."

"Better not."

Jacques chuckled. "I think you've picked up a few alpha tendencies on your own."

Max couldn't help but grin. "Maybe just a few. Nothing for you to worry about. I'm not the least interested in playing judge, jury, and dealing with whiny females when they don't get their way."

"The joys of leadership." Jacques snorted. "Listen. Be careful. Garrison has a grudge and he'll likely hit you when you least expect it. He'll use whatever leverage he can, too."

"Already ahead of you," Max assured.

"Take care of yourself and keep me updated."

"Will do." Max hung up then turned right around and called Brighton. It rolled over to voicemail so he left a quick message, then disconnected. Chore done, he returned to the kitchen.

Tara glanced up at his arrival, conveying concern by chewing on one nail and playing with the muffin wrapper now and again. "Well?"

"I told him what we know. He wanted to know where we are so he could come join in the fun."

Tara's eyes widened. "Did you tell him?"

Max shook his head. "He's still healing. This is no place for him to be right now."

"Good." She pursed her lips. "And Brighton?"

"Left a message. I'm sure he'll call back when he gets it." Max wasn't worried on that front. Brighton seemed like a man true to his word. And, he had a score to settle with the guy who terrorized his mate. That alone put Brighton firmly on their side in the impending battle.

She glanced at her watch. "I better get to work. I'm already late as it is."

Max frowned. He knew she'd have to go back but hated the idea of her at the bookstore like a sitting duck. "I'm going with you."

Tara's eyebrows furrowed. "There's no need. I'm perfectly safe at the shop."

"Bullshit." He eyed her sternly. "No offense, but your place isn't a hubbub of people at any point in the day. Even if it was, there's no telling when Garrison or his men will appear, drag you off, and use you as bait." The thought alone sent chills down Max's spine and ramped up his protective instincts like nothing else. "Not happening. Just call me your shadow from now on."

She opened her mouth then shut it again. "You're going to be bored out of your mind."

He grinned wolfishly at her. "Not as long as you have all those good erotic bondage books just waiting on the shelf."

Brilliant color blossomed across Tara's cheeks. "Well…"

"Oh, no, lady. You're not backing out now. You've got the goods and you're going to hand them over."

She sighed as if in resignation. "Fine. But just so you know, there's no way I can hope to explain howls coming from the bathroom to customers. So, if you feel the urge to say…take matters into your own hand, take something to bite on with you." She grinned slyly. "I still have that old chew bone from your time as Cotton. I'm sure that'll work just fine."

Max rolled his eyes but couldn't hold back the chuckle.

Chew bone my ass. He'd just flip the Closed sign around and take her with him. As much as he'd enjoyed the superb blow job this morning, he wasn't about to shoot off again without her joining him.

Chapter 11

Tara finished dusting the final shelf and returned her supplies to the back room. The brand-new brackets complete with a board across the back door drew her attention. Max had insisted they stop by the hardware store this morning to pick up those items, then spent over an hour installing them. Stout, they appeared more than capable of withstanding an invasion. The fact only eased her anxiety a teeny bit.

After placing the furniture spray under the bathroom cabinet and dropping the dirty cloth on the back table to take home, Tara returned to the front of the store.

"Lemon-y." Max glanced over at her with a crooked grin.

She matched his smile. "Yep." Despite the seriousness of the situation, she couldn't help but add a little teasing to the conversation. "Don't tell me you find it arousing?"

Max chuckled. "The scent of the cleaning stuff, not so much. Your scent…"

Her heartrate kicked up as her stomach did a flip-flop.

The chime of a bell drew her attention before she could delve deeper into the sexy bantering. She turned to see Rose entering, carrying her cane rather than using it as she should. Tara shook her head and hurried over to greet her friend. "Good afternoon, Rose."

"Hello, dear." Her attention turned to Max. "And, who is this?"

"Oh, where are my manners? Rose, this is Max. Max this is Rose." Tara stepped back when Max stood, took Rose's hand, and brushed a kiss across her knuckles.

"My pleasure." He smiled up at her.

Rose beamed. "Aren't you a charmer?"

The front door opened again. Tara's nerves jumped, then she recognized the middle-aged lady as a good customer. Hurriedly, she excused herself to help the woman.

"Hi, Mae. Can I help you find something today?"

Mae shook her head. "Just browsing."

"Very good." Tara turned her attention back to Rose, finding her in a quiet conversation with Max. They seemed to click, as if they were old friends, chummy to be exact. She recalled Rose's way with Cotton and her sage advice. The older lady hadn't asked about Cotton lately. As much as she seemed to enjoy the visits with Cotton, surely Rose would have asked about him. Something started to click. Tara went on a hunch and decided Rose knew exactly who Max was. How she knew, Tara couldn't say, but since Rose was sharper than a tack, it wasn't a total surprise.

She walked over to them. "Did I miss anything?"

"No." Rose grinned ruefully, as if she had a secret and wasn't going to share. "We've just been chatting." She patted Tara's hand. "Take my advice and hang onto this one. He's a looker." She winked.

Max coughed and Tara chuckled. *Leave it to Rose to come right out and say what she thought.*

"Well…"

Another person entered the store, the little bell busier than it had been in a while. Tara swiveled, caught a glimpse of Brighton, and felt her insides knot. She studied his face, found no signs of impending doom, and relaxed marginally.

She glimpsed Mae leaving, sneaking behind Brighton and slipping out the door. Tara grimaced at the loss of another sale.

"Brighton, come over here. I'd like you to meet some people." Rose gestured with her cane.

Brighton strode over, kissed Rose on the cheek, then grinned. "I've already met Tara and Max."

She blinked up at him. "You have?"

"Yep. Comes with being a smart man and keeping my eyes and ears open," he added with a tone of playful pride.

Rose snorted. "Always the last to know."

Brighton chuckled. "I'll make it up to you. If you're finished here, your chariot awaits."

Rose peered up at him. "Are we going by the coffee shop?"

"If you wish," he answered.

Satisfaction crossed Rose's face. She focused on Tara. "He's a good grandson." With a final pat of Tara's arm, Rose tottered back toward the front door.

Brighton stayed behind. "No news, yet?"

"Nothing." Max answered. "Revenge is best served cold. It might be a while."

"True. I've got people watching this place, just in case."

"Thank you." Tara clasped her hands together. "I don't know if I want this to happen sooner and be done with or later."

"Sooner," Max replied.

She cut him a look.

"The longer we have to wait, the more likely we are to lose our vigilance. Boredom and the constant stress will take a toll. That's when we'll get sloppy."

She understood what he was saying but still couldn't bring herself to wish for an end today. They had so little time left and she had so much more to enjoy.

Brighton looked at them both. "Call if anything changes."

"Okay." Tara gave a small wave, then watched as Brighton held the door open for Rose, offered his arm, and escorted her down the sidewalk.

"Brighton is her grandson." Trying to make the connection in her brain, Tara pursed her lips. "Does that mean…?"

"She's a wolf shifter, too. Yes. And the matriarch of the pack," Max replied.

"I never knew."

"We exist alongside and within human society. But, don't get me wrong, we're far from human."

She looked into his dark eyes and saw the wildness, the primal side of him lurking just beneath the surface. Oddly enough, that didn't scare her in the least. Excitement, yes. Fear, no.

Tara pulled up what she knew about wild wolves. "Do you mate for life?"

Max shook his head then shrugged. "In that way, we're much more human. We can enjoy many partners, but if we happen to find that one special woman, our mate, nothing can drag us away."

A sudden memory came to the fore. "So, Jacques's parents weren't mates?"

"No. Sometimes shifters pair up for other reasons, including love. Just like human relationships, they can fall apart. True mates, though, have something more. A glue that holds them together."

Curious, Tara tilted her head. "How do you know when you find your mate?"

"We just know."

She frowned. "That's vague."

"Tell me about it. It'd be so much easier if all the women came with a sticky note on their forehead."

Tara chuckled. "Oh, yeah. Same for human men. Jerk. Idiot. Cheater. Yep, that would be *so* much easier and save a lot of time."

She plopped down in one of the overstuffed chairs, appraising Max as he walked over to the other one and sat down. His movements, always fluid, reminded her of a great jungle cat with enormous power just waiting to explode at a moment's notice. Amused, Tara opted to keep the kitty comparison to herself. For now.

"Not much business today." Max appraised her.

She sighed. "As you probably already know, my business is drying up like a mud puddle in the desert. The downturn in the economy hit everyone hard. Books are a commodity that most people gave up, especially since they can borrow the same ones from the library. A few people still want to hold onto their best liked books, but a sale now and again doesn't bring in much money." Tara scanned the room with her gaze. "At this rate, I can't make next month's rent. When that happens Nora will shut me down." She clasped her hands together and rested them on her lap. The truth hung over her head like a dark cloud for a while now. She'd come to terms with it a while back. Losing the business would certainly hurt but she tried to look at the positives. Instead of working six days a week, she could find a job that would only insist on five. She'd be out under the heavy weight of business ownership. No worries about the store's expenses, insurance, taxes, rent, trying to come up with plans to keep the doors open. When she changed gears and became an employee to another company, many of those headaches disappeared.

"Have you thought of selling out?"

Tara gave a brief nod and lifted her eyes to Max. He broadcast sadness and concern. Along with a definite impression of mentally going through steps in his mind to save the shop.

He was wasting his time. She'd been through everything and still nothing. Doomed seemed appropriate at the moment. "I made subtle inquiries. No one wants a failing business in the middle of nowhere. The potential just isn't there."

"How do you feel about closing the store?" he asked softly.

Whether he considered doing it now to allow them to focus on her home for an impending attack or if he meant down the road, she wasn't sure. Not that it really mattered in the end. "I'd be sad to see this dream die. But, I think, I'd be a little relieved too. All the pressure would be gone. That's a plus."

He gave a slow nod. "Thought about what else to do for a job?"

"Actually, I have. Been watching the want ads and such." She turned in her seat in order to avoid the strain on her neck from having to keep it turned. "The truth is, this area has been hit hard by the recession. Not a lot of business to begin with and nothing new moving in. People drive long distances from here to their work. That's a challenge in the dead of winter."

"Tell me about it," he growled. "You need a four-wheel drive. That car will try, but when the snow gets deep you'll be stuck."

"Been there, done that." She waved her hand as if blowing it off.

He wasn't telling her anything she didn't already know. However, a new vehicle cost money, something she didn't have at the moment. She snorted to herself. *At the moment? Who am I kidding? I've never had it.*

"You want to keep the house." He made the comment a statement.

"Yes. It was my grandparents'. They passed it down to me." She bit her lip and stared at her hands. "It's really all I have left of them." She glanced over at him again. "Besides, it's paid for."

"There's that." Max tapped his fingers on the arm of the chair. "I'm not an economics guru or an entrepreneur, but I don't have a clue how to bring in more customers."

Tara smiled sadly. "That's okay. Neither do I."

****

Max dropped his silverware in the sink filled with soapy bubbles and water. Takeout pasta alfredo had been delicious but sat in the pit of his stomach. He didn't blame the meal as much as he put the responsibility on the constant tension riding him hard.

All day he'd watched the front door of Tara's bookstore, waiting for his enemies to appear. Nothing.

That didn't help anyone's nerves, especially Tara's. She flitted around for hours, rearranging, cleaning, and staying busy. He understood her antsy-ness revolved directly from the situation upon them—sitting around like a staked goat, waiting for Garrison's men to reappear and attack.

He knew two things for a fact—the bastards would show up when least expected and he had his guard down, and Tara was going to lose her business. It didn't take a financial wizard to see that selling less than five books per day wasn't going to pay the bills. She'd done everything she could but the economy and location were too much to overcome. A shame. He saw her hard work and dedicated efforts in that store. All of it would go to waste.

Damn it. He stood at the sink and stared out the window at the woods. *If I only could tap into my accounts.* A couple of days ago, he'd called Brighton's man, gave him the information. The guy seemed professional enough. Still, he'd warned Max it would take a week or two before he could secure all the documents necessary to get Max not only back on his feet but in the cockpit of an airplane and access to his money. Not that it mattered. He was certain she'd refuse his offer of a financial input, as certain as snow would come to northern Minnesota in the winter. If she declined, he didn't have much hope of assisting her. Even if he bought the store for her, she'd still be upset. Tara had a huge independent streak, and no way would he squash that. Unfortunately, her stubbornness levels were just as high. All that spelled out one thing—she'd thank him for his help and just as quickly reject it.

Which left her in the same boat she was now—

finding another job or moving.

For a second, he considered plucking her from this place and taking her away. Somewhere safe. Somewhere she could start over. Somewhere *they* could start over.

Running isn't the answer. Look how well that turned out before.

Max admitted that his inner wolf was right. Garrison's thugs had his scent and wouldn't stop until he was dead on the ground. He and Tara had taken precautions, checked everything three times, added locks to the doors, and kept the curtains closed after dark. He'd installed security cameras which would alarm if someone approached from the front or back of the house. They'd done everything in their power to prepare. Max made sure Tara kept her gun within reach. He didn't need one. The thugs would battle him the old-fashioned way—in a wolf fight to the end. That he knew for certain. Honor code amongst killers, so to speak. Not to mention the shifter way of things. Shooting was the easy way out and shameful. The way to prove oneself as top dog was to rip and tear through another's hide. The satisfaction alone was worth the effort. While slime mold, Tagart and his cohorts would fight it out in the same way Throwback had always done things—in animal form. Max had not a single doubt.

His heart pinched, not for himself, but for Tara. No one growing up in Throwback Pack expected a great longevity. Too much violence existed to live a peaceful existence. He'd accepted that long ago. Now, after all these years, he'd found a true angel, a woman who made him smile, laugh, and turned up the heat in the sack like no other. Now, he might only have hours left to enjoy such paradise. The sheer thought stole his breath.

Turning, he spied her wiping down the kitchen table with a cloth. The fluid motions and stretched-out position called to him. She caught his look and offered up a crooked smile, filled with playfulness.

His heart skipped a beat.

Fuck them. They're not taking me down. I have too much to fight for. I will win.

With that vow, he walked over, took Tara's hand, removed the rag, and left it on the table.

She blinked up at him, her pretty eyes flashing as she read his face.

"I need you."

A slow smile appeared on her lips. "About time you asked."

Despite the seriousness of the situation, humor washed over Max. "Sassy."

"Yep." She grinned ruefully up at him. "Besides, we might as well use those new condoms that you bought today."

He'd made a quick pit stop on the way home. Food and condoms, though not in that order. "Yeah, well, somehow candy cane stripes just aren't my color." He shook his head at the memory of those silly things.

"You were cute."

"Uh, huh. Cute wasn't what I was aiming for." He loved the playful banter with her. Foreplay. Definitely foreplay. It affected her just as much as it did him, judging by the spicy aroma of arousal radiating from both of them.

"What? You want tiger stripes instead?"

He couldn't believe they were having this conversation. "Hell, no." He rolled his eyes. "How about something more studly?"

"Well…" She tapped her lip with her finger.

He narrowed his eyes and pinned her with his gaze.

She squealed and dashed off.

In hot pursuit, Max followed her straight to the bedroom. "Don't you know wolves love to chase?" he asked languidly, already feeling the burners on his libido heat up.

She faced him at the edge of the bed, her eyes lit with excitement. "Do they?"

"Yes."

"What else do they love to do?" She nearly purred the question.

His cock took notice in a big way, hardening to granite in a split second. "All kinds of things. Namely getting you naked and worshipping your body."

Her eyes sparked. "I like the sound of that."

The heady scent of arousal filled the air.

"You're wearing too many clothes."

She grinned wickedly. "I could say the same for you."

Languidly, Max stripped off his pants and stood before her, his shaft at full attention. His shirt soon followed. He stepped out of the shackling hold of his pants and tossed his shirt to the floor. All the time he watched Tara's face. Saw the appreciation in her eyes. And knew how a real man felt when his woman looked at him with desire, longing, need, and something more. He knew she saw the entire person as she seemed to delve into his very soul.

His hunger escalated as she seemed unable to take

her eyes off him.

She stripped quickly, letting the garments fall to the ground. Standing up straight, she presented her nude body for his viewing pleasure.

He took in the glorious sight, noticing that Tara's gaze dropped down to his dick and stayed there.

Recalling a detail, he plucked a condom out of the top drawer of the bedside stand where he'd stashed the new box, tossed the foil aside, and rolled on the condom, thankful it wasn't one of the silly red and white striped ones. He had his pride after all.

Tara stared for a long moment. Her lips turned up into a wide smile. Her lips twitched. A giggle escaped. Then another. Followed by full blown laughter. She fell back on the bed, still rolling with amusement.

Now, he wasn't the least bit shy and knew he had been gifted in the endowment department. His ego could withstand quite a bit, but a woman looking at his naked body then rolling on the bed guffawing made a big dent. "What's so funny?"

Tara breathed, then chuckled some more. Finally, she sat up to face him.

He looked down. Nothing out of the ordinary caught his eye. Sure, his full erection jutted out and curved slightly downward at the tip. Nothing unusual about that. She'd seen it before, certainly. He was clean, fit, and free of lint. *So what the hell?*

He docked his hands on his hips and waited.

"I'm...I'm sorry. It's just that..."

"What?" he demanded, his patience wearing thin. Men were sensitive about their dicks. *Didn't she get that?* Annoyance grew along with a hint of concern.

Tara finally managed to tamp her reaction down to

a wide grin. "It's just that I remembered something."

"Like what?" The drawn-out explanation was sapping his wavering self-confidence in a hurry.

"Like the fact that I was going to take you to the vet to be neutered." She fell over on her back once more in a fit of giggles.

Neutered?

His mind flashed back to when she first brought him home, in his wolf form, and bathed him. Not only did she tug on his cock while washing him, but she rambled all the while. A vet visit was mentioned along with a small, minor surgery. She'd brought it up once more when she did usher him off to the vet. Thankfully, the guy offered him a reprieve. That whole experience had been humiliating enough, but if the vet even had a thought of cutting off his balls, Max would have made sure to chew off his leg first.

He shuddered at the thought, then watched as she crossed her arms over herself, still giggling away.

Her humor proved contagious. He rolled his eyes and relaxed. *Two could play at this game.*

Climbing into the bed, he draped his body over hers, lowering just enough so their skin brushed with each breath. "Now that would have been a very bad thing."

"Uh, huh. A tragedy." She beamed up at him, then her lips twitched again.

He locked his lips over hers, sealing her comments for the moment.

Her fingers ran down the center of his chest, then wrapped her hand around his shaft. He lifted his head on a low moan at the sparkling sensations the simple touch provoked. "A waste of some remarkable, prime manhood."

"Absolutely. A huge tragedy indeed." He growled in her ear before nipping her ear lobe. "So, no more talk of neutering me."

"Nope." She stroked him, building the fire back up to where it had once been and then some.

Pleasure shot through his veins.

Needing her at the same level of need, he peppered kisses down her neck and over her chest. Taking one nipple into his mouth, he sucked, then laved. He released that breast in order to treat the other to the same affections.

Tara ran her hands down his back, arched her back, and wrapped her legs around him. The change in angle placed his cock right at her entrance. He could feel the heat and dampness as he rubbed himself along her folds.

Her breathing caught and she nipped his shoulder. "Now."

He shushed her with a brushing of his lips over hers. "Patience."

She growled. The sound would have done any wild wolf proud. "Now."

He chuckled. "Bossy."

"Yes." She pushed at him. "Turn over."

Wrapping her in his arms, Max rolled them, settling with his back on the bed and her on top.

Tara sat up, took his cock in her hands, and stroked.

He groaned.

She grinned wolfishly. "My turn to play."

He bit back another moan, this one mixed with frustration and excitement. Knowing Tara, she'd torture him until he pleaded for mercy in the form of her impaling herself on his throbbing shaft. How soon that would happen became a challenge and a goal to find out.

She continued to rain pleasure down on him with her confident touches, the way she handled his swollen flesh, and the light caress to his balls.

He widened his legs in order to give her easy access. "You like this way too much."

She grinned. "What woman wouldn't? I get to sit here and play with the sexiest man alive. A dream come true."

Her words sent another zing of heat through his veins. He drew in a breath and pulled on his iron control to keep from rocketing to the edge.

"Two can play at this game." He lightly pinched her nipple, then dropped his hand to the junction of her thighs. Tunneling, he found her clit, firm and prominent. He lightly strummed across it, smiling when she gasped and closed her eyes.

She trembled.

He bracketed her hips. "Ride me, Tara."

Her eyes flew open, pupils dilated, and lips opened at his command. He assisted her to scoot forward, to the right spot.

She lined up his cock, then lowered her body, taking his shaft an inch at a time.

The snug heat seared him, welcomed him, and promised a spectacular trip straight to ecstasy. He had no doubt. His only concern was holding on long enough to take that trip with her.

After only a brief pause, she began to move. Tentative and slow at first, then the pace picked up. She bounced and gyrated, rocked and surged.

Max kept one hand on her hip, keeping them joined, but otherwise settled back for the amazing event. Idly he teased her clit, all the while watching her face. Her breathing escalated, she threw her head back, then leaned forward, planting her hands on his chest.

The small bite of nails digging into his pecs spurred him quickly up the ladder.

"Take what's yours. Everything you need. Take it from me." He rubbed more firmly on the hard nub.

She whimpered, tightened, then held her breath.

He lifted to meet her, pounding into her depths with each frantic thrust.

Just as a tingling in his balls warned him of impending climax, he felt the powerful contractions of her inner muscles squeezing his cock, milking him for every drop he could give. Throttling over the edge, he soared with a muted shout, and lodged himself deep. The knot expanded, sealing them together.

Tara cried out, lowered her head, and jerked with each ripple.

Seconds later, she lay across his chest.

He wrapped her in his embrace, kissed her head, and made a silent vow to keep her safe. To protect the most beautiful thing on the planet. The one who'd left a soft, wonderful mark on his black heart.

****

He slid out of bed, careful not to wake her. Tara curled up on her side, facing him. He tugged the blankets over her to ensure her warmth and comfort before quietly leaving the room, snagging his jeans on the way. He paused for a moment in the hallway to slip them on before continuing on.

Leaving the lights off, he made his way to the kitchen window and looked out. Only the evening breeze stirred and the usual night sounds carried through to his advanced hearing. Satisfied, Max checked out the front. When he knew for sure nothing was amiss, only then did he sit down on the couch and drop his head into his hands.

He'd picked up some early alarm motion detectors and placed them around the outside of the house just after he realized how close Tagart had come. If anything broke the plane where the eyes were aimed, a beeping inside the house would follow. The enhanced security allowed him to sleep at night and to turn his full attention on Tara. However, while he trusted the technology, he still couldn't let his guard down too much. Things had a way of failing, and Garrison's bastards weren't stupid.

How long he sat there, he didn't know. Just that his problems and a definite lack of solutions pounded at him. Worry, above all else, took a front row seat.

He'd just found Tara and now his past threatened to take her away. He believed in himself and his promise to protect her but couldn't get the results of his last encounter with Garrison out of his mind. He had a powerful reason to fight but would it be enough?

Light footfalls drew his attention. Glancing up, he found Tara approaching him, wrapped in a blanket from the bed. If she wore anything underneath, he didn't know, but was damn curious.

"Hi."

"Hi," he answered softly.

She sat next to him, then reclined back against his chest.

"Wait a second." Max turned, snagged a couple of pillows, and placed them behind him. He stretched one leg along the back of the cushions, making a spot for her between his thighs. Leaning back against the pillows, he let the arm rest support him. Comfortable, he patted the cushion. "Sit here." As soon as she did, he slid his arms under her wrap, pulled her flush against his chest, and rested his cheek on her head. Bare skin met his touch. He smiled softly, resisting the urge to pet her. Instead, he caught the concern in her actions, wrapped his arms around her middle, and sought to soothe her the best he could.

"You look pensive," she whispered as she rested her hands on top of his. "And you're not sleeping."

"I could say the same about you."

She wiggled her rear into the V of his legs. The contact made his randy shaft take notice. "I missed you in bed."

He kissed her shoulder. "I just wanted to check things out."

She arched her neck, exposing more flesh for him to attend to.

Not about to disappoint, he pressed his lips gently to her nape and then again behind her ear.

"What are your dreams in life?"

The question surprised him. "What kind of dreams?"

She shrugged. "You know. Bucket list. Things you've always wanted to see or do since you were a kid."

He thought about it for a moment. "Since I was a kid, I wanted to follow in my father's footsteps. Not only as a pilot, but to be on part of the team that turned

Throwback around. I wanted peace, support. Caring. When Jacques defeated Garrison's cousin, I thought our dream of a new beginning had finally come true. A few months later, we lost it all."

"Is that still your dream?" She drew small circles softly on his arm. The light touch helped settle his restlessness.

"Yeah. It's all I've ever lived for. In that moment of victory…it all fell into place. I want that again. For the pack. For the people that are bullied and coerced. Jacques wants that too." He nuzzled her cheek, enjoying the sweet aftermath of sex with cuddling. "Our people deserve better. My father tried to make that happen. I can do no less."

Silence fell, then Tara rubbed her cheek over his bare chest. "After everything you've been through, you'd still go back?"

"With Jacques, yes. Don't get me wrong—it's a huge load to take on. I wasn't their favorite member due to my mixed genetics."

"You mentioned that before. Two kinds of wolves, right?"

"I'm part timber wolf and part arctic wolf."

"Ah, so that's where Cotton got his beautiful white coat."

He grinned at her words. "Yeah. The pack wasn't thrilled with any mixes, but could forgive such things when I ascended to a status position as Jacques's beta. I suspect that will be the case again. *If* we get another chance."

"Is that what you and Jacques want?"

Max pressed his lips to the back of her head. "I haven't spoken to him about it, but knowing him, he's not going to let a near-death battle stop him. He's pretty intent upon making those changes happen. So the deaths before us weren't in vain."

"And, you, Max. Is that what you want?" She whispered the question as if a little hesitant to find out the answer.

He paused, torn by her inquiry. "I want to be with you. To protect you. To wipe out those killing monsters for once and for all."

"And the pack?" she persisted.

"I owe my loyalty to Jacques." He left it at that. Right now, he didn't want to be anywhere but on the couch, snuggling with Tara. The future hinged on so many things. None of them he wanted to analyze too deeply tonight. He had more important things to do, like hold Tara and show her how much she meant to him. Maybe not in words that always seemed to lodge in his throat, but in his actions.

He didn't know much about love or tender feelings. Sure, he understood loyalty and dedication, obedience and hard work, but that paled in comparison to what he really did feel for Tara. At first, he thought it could be compassion or sympathy or perhaps appreciation for all that she'd done for him. That didn't quite make the grade either. What he did know was that he wanted Tara. Even his inner beast agreed wholeheartedly. She was the one for him. No other woman would match her in personality, spunk, sexiness, and inner strength.

But how can I make promises when I might be dead by morning?

Conflict caused his gut to clench and sent an icy chill to his heart.

He held her close, felt and heard her steady

breathing, and set this moment to memory.

Too many questions remained to spend time going through each one. Priorities were in place. Survival before exploring his emotional tie to the woman presently wrapped in his arms.

All he knew was that she felt good there. Right. Comfortable. Perfect.

"You're worried." Her whispered voice carried easily through the silence.

He didn't bother to lie. "It's not *if* they will come but *when*."

"You lost once before. Feel you're lucky to have gotten away, and now believe that history will repeat itself."

She was far too perceptive for her own good.

"Yes. It's a definite possibility." He wiggled a little to remove the poking sensation from his back. "Do I think they will bomb the store or the house? No. Do I think they will ambush us? Possibly. Do I think they will do anything in their power to cause me pain, including stealing you right from under my nose? Absolutely."

She twisted around so that she could look into his face. "So we shoot them on the spot."

He grinned at the suggestion. "No honor in that."

She snorted. "When it comes to life and death, honor is important, despite the fact that they are murderers?"

"Actually, yes. The pack rules are written in stone. To kill off an enemy by shooting them doesn't count. Only a wolf to wolf combat win does."

"How odd."

He petted her hair, enjoying the softness and silky

texture. "It's been that way for centuries. Just another reason trying to bring the pack into the modern age is an uphill battle. Change is hard. Even change for the good."

"Are you afraid?"

He trailed the tips of his fingers along her jawline. "For myself? No. I came to accept my fate a while back."

Her lips parted and real fear entered her face.

He continued before she could speak. "Don't get me wrong. I'm not ready to throw in the towel. I'll fight with every ounce of energy in my body. And I'll win. Because I have something very important to live for."

"What's that?" Her gaze locked on his.

"You."

She sighed softly and tucked her head under his chin. "Just call me Red Riding Hood."

Max laughed. "I thought she ran for help and got some woods men to kill the big bad wolf."

"Oh. We can't have that." She grinned up at him. "No getting killed on my watch." She kissed his chest, then rubbed her nose over his nipple.

The sweet fire, formerly dormant, fanned into flames.

"I think you're too delicious to take a chance on losing."

He swooped down and meshed his lips over hers. Sweet tenderness ruled the day. He intended to savor her. For as long as he could.

Chapter 12

Three days later

Another day of pins and needles had arrived. Tara found herself jumpy, edgy, and irritable just waiting for the shoe to drop. Every noise cranked up her anxiety. Worry became a constant companion, as did wondering when Max's old pack mates would make a move. She kept her gun close, mentally and physically prepared to fire if they showed up and decided to pick up where they left off the last time they'd seen Max.

He'd vowed to protect her above all else. While she believed him, she also felt it unnecessary. She'd taken care of herself for too long. Independent and capable, she was fully prepared to carry her own weight should Armageddon land on her doorstep. She'd take care of herself and Max, too. But, Max didn't need to know that little secret. Not yet. Let him flex his masculine chivalry muscle and beat his chest like a caveman. He amused her when he did. If things went south, screw male pride. She'd take matters into her own hands. Gladly.

Because what she had with Max was truly worth fighting for.

The comment that he'd had sex with her the first time because it was owed to her still stung. She'd let it roll off her back by the next morning, at least for the most part. After all, she might only have a very short time left with Max and didn't want to spend it fighting. He hadn't meant it the way she took it, that she knew for a fact. Her sensitivity when it came to men and her lack of a social life just went haywire as soon as he'd uttered the words. He'd apologized. So had she. That was the end of it.

Now, she could focus on something much brighter and pleasant, namely Max sitting in one of the comfy chairs, one leg crossed over the other, as he read probably the juiciest and naughtiest erotic book she had in the entire store. She gave him kudos for not having to use the facilities. Yet. She didn't doubt if he made it to the end of the tale, he'd be hard pressed not to try to find relief. *Really hard. Granite hard. Steel post hard.* She smirked at her own pun.

Truth be told, Max was driving her absolutely nuts. Following her around like a lost puppy. Hell, she couldn't hardly go to the bathroom by herself without him standing at the door. As if another portal would open and she'd fall in. She mentally rolled her eyes. He watched her almost constantly making her feel like a lab rat in a psych experiment. *Well, maybe not quite that bad.* Other times, he looked at her as if he was a thirsty man and she was a long, cold glass of ice tea. Those, she didn't mind so much except they proved to be damn distracting. More than once, she considered locking the front door, heading to the back, and hopping on board the Max train for a quickie.

One thing was for sure. Max knew what he was doing in bed. Big time. Her panties still dampened every time she replayed the events through her mind. Never had it been like that for her. Explosive. Searing.

Primal. So hot, she feared they'd burn the house down. And, that whole knotting thing. She couldn't get it out of her mind and intended to do some more personal research as soon as possible. Boy howdy did she. Because somewhere along the line, Max had turned her into a cat in heat. Who only had the hots for a certain canine shifter. Not for the first time, she wondered if his horniness was actually contagious.

Ugh. And we're back to naughty thoughts again. She mentally rolled her eyes at her seemingly one-track mind. *Just great. When I'm not scared out of my wits, I'm horny. Nice combo.*

Over and over again, she had to remind herself that her dream bubble was bound to burst, sooner rather than later. Max belonged with his pack, and with Jacques, working together to form a new pathway for those under their charge. He'd pretty much said so already. Yes, there was another alternative, but it didn't bear considering. Death wasn't something she'd think about. He said he'd win and she believed in him. Totally. Completely.

Time grew short and she knew it. As much as she'd trade her entire store for another few days, she knew things didn't work that way. She found herself eagerly anticipating the evenings, where they shared cooking and cleaning chores. Then, he'd lead her to the bedroom and show her how a real man treated a lady. Afterward, he held her tight, as if he too felt their wondrous time winding to an end.

The cheery little bell over her door chimed, announcing a visitor. Automatically, tension gripped her until she recognized the person. Relief quickly followed. She was keyed up and jumpy, that was a fact.

Over and over again, she repeated the circle of anxiety then easement. Ironically enough, the event used to bring optimistic happiness. Now, it brought her acid reflux.

Brighton strolled in, his steps confident and with a hint of swagger. She supposed that if one was alpha and looked that scrumptious, he'd earned the right to strut.

His gaze flicked to Max before a wide grin appeared on his face. "Nice reading material."

Max held up the book. "Yep. I'm learning all kinds of things about women's fantasies." His eyes flashed with sensual promise.

Tara's stomach somersaulted in response. *Good grief. The bad guys could appear any second and commit a massacre. Yet, all I can think of is Max and that silly book.*

"Really?" Brighton eyed the cover a little more. "Maybe I need to take a peek at that when you're finished."

"Might be a while," Max replied.

"No problem."

"I believe you're going to have to find another woman to tie up. Not happening with me." She grinned ruefully. "Unless you want to be the tie-e?"

Max smirked but remained mute.

Brighton grinned wide for a fleeting second, then sobered as he approached Tara.

Max left his book on the chair and took a position at her side.

"Still no word?" Brighton asked.

Max shook his head. "Not a peep but I don't expect anything. Garrison is ballsy but he's not stupid. He fully understands the element of surprise."

Brighton nodded. "I have my men on watch here and around your house." He looked over at Tara. "Don't shoot anyone you don't know."

She snorted and crossed her arms over her chest. "No worries there."

His lips twitched but the amusement didn't quite reach his eyes. Concern coated his face.

She had an inkling he kept Abby under lock and key at all times under the circumstances. Probably already had been trying to due to her advancing pregnancy. "How's Abby?"

"Doing well. Chafing at the forced containment." A ghost of a smile hovered over his lips. The love he felt for his wife could clearly be seen in his eyes.

"Has she threatened you with a frying pan yet?"

Brighton cocked his head. "No, and don't you be giving her any ideas." The slight scolding sounded a little forced as if he tried hard to joke but just couldn't summon the proper mood.

She hated that she'd brought this to his doorstep. He should be enjoying his wife and the upcoming arrival of their first child. Instead, he'd circled the wagons and prepared for a mighty charge from some overaggressive, too-big-for-their-britches, werewolves. The regret sat heavily on her shoulders, along with the other heavy burdens she carried. Some days she wasn't sure she could continue under such weight.

Thick tension filled the room. She hated that, too. Always before the store had been her haven. Now, it felt more like a jail cell.

She needed something to lighten the room. Anything to ease the nearly crackling electricity coming from the two men. Herself, as well. "So, Brighton?"

"Yes?"

"How do you know if a woman is your mate?"

He stared at her, then cut a look at Max.

Max just shrugged.

Stubborn mule.

Brighton turned back to her. "Let me guess. He's not telling."

"Nope."

Brighton sighed. "It's a feeling, I guess. A man just knows. He will do anything for her. Her happiness is foremost." He leveled his gaze at her. "But, not above her safety."

"I see." That didn't really answer anything in her mind. She decided to go with the other question that Max had so easily side-stepped in the past. "About that knot…"

Brighton blinked, checked his watch, then started for the door. "Sorry. I've got to be somewhere." With that, he was gone.

Tara frowned, then caught the grin on Max's face. Inspiration flared. "If you won't fess up, then I'll just find someone who will."

"Uh, huh." He didn't appear the least bit worried.

"Just wait until Rose comes in."

Max groaned dramatically. "You wouldn't."

She smirked with victory. "Oh, I will."

"Well, hell."

She crossed her arms over her chest and tapped her toe. "I'm waiting."

Max set his book aside, pushed one hand through his hair, and then stood. "Like I said, it's just like our wild cousins."

"I get that part. Why do I get the impression it's

important?"

Max approached her slowly, gracefully gliding across the floor with long powerful strides. "It's just part of who we are."

Tara absorbed the information. "So, the knot is needed for pregnancy?"

"Since it always happens, I can't really say."

"Oh. Kind of disappointing."

He tilted his head. "Why do you say that?"

"Oh, I don't know. I just thought maybe it would only appear with the right woman. Kind of make it special or such."

A slow smile hovered over his lips. "I don't need the knot to tell me that I'm with a special woman."

She waited for more explanation, but it didn't come. "And?"

"And what?"

She blew out a breath, hanging onto her patience by a thread. "And how special does that person have to be to become a mate?"

Max opened his mouth.

The chime of the bell interrupted.

Tara's heart pounded as she lifted her gaze to the door. An unfamiliar man entered. He didn't appear the book-ish type. No glasses, no suit. Just jeans and a casual long-sleeved shirt with a light jacket on top. Brown hair matched his eyes. She'd never seen him before. That fact along with his large frame and robust body, had her reaching for her purse.

Max stepped between her and the newcomer. He appeared more curious and perhaps a little annoyed rather than concerned. "Brighton sent you?"

The guy grinned as if he knew they'd perceived

him as a threat and found the idea amusing. "Yep."

Tara relaxed by increments. "I've never seen you before."

He shrugged. "Don't get much time to read. But, I think I might be picking up a new hobby." He winked at Tara.

She smiled in return, relieved but still a little leery. His playfulness eased her nerves but warned her of a well-practiced charmer in her presence. Something about his carriage and demeanor reminded her of Brighton. The angle of his eyes and the strong chin solidified the observation.

Max didn't budge. Just stood his ground, staring at the guy. Tara could almost feel the protectiveness emanating from Max. She wouldn't be surprised if he growled or offered to take the shifter outside for a brief butt kicking.

"Well, welcome to my store…"

"Xavier."

"Xavier. Nice to meet you." Tara tried to step around Max in order to greet Xavier with a handshake, but Max moved to block her path.

The man smiled knowingly at Max. "Boss said you were a little touchy. Too early in the day for a pissing contest, don't you think?"

Max snorted. "Let me guess. He's ready to throttle you and decided to torment us with your presence instead?"

Xavier shrugged with one shoulder. "Boss ain't got no sense of humor."

"Uh, huh." Max crossed his arms. "What did you do?"

For a split second, the man's expression turned

sheepish. Just as quickly, he replaced it with a cocky grin. "I might have given Abby a pair of handcuffs and a dog collar to use on her mate."

Max whistled low. "And he didn't kill you?"

"Nah. Boss likes me." Xavier smiled wolfishly. "Besides, he can't kill his baby brother. Grandma would take him over her knee. I'm her favorite," he added with much self-assurance.

Tara decided she liked the outgoing younger brother of the local alpha. "I bet Abby liked the present."

"Yeah. Made her smile. Poor thing has had so little to be laughing about lately. After that attack." He sobered. "I wanted to thank you, ma'am, for helping our little Abby."

Tara nodded. "No thanks necessary. She's a nice lady. So's Brighton. I would have done it for anyone."

"Still, we owe you and we're gonna make sure those mother...err, bastards don't get their hands on you." His dark eyes filled with determination.

No one in their right mind would cross him. Tara could easily see the predator underneath the playboy facade he put forth. "Perhaps you'd like to pick out a book? There's a lot of options. First one free, for all that you're doing for me." She offered up a friendly grin. "Brighton has dibs on the bondage erotica Max is presently reading."

Xavier's eyebrows shot up.

Tara laughed. "Far wall, back corner."

Xavier strode off to take a peek.

Max watched him go then turned back to her. "Hell, get the word out that you've got sex books and the place will be humming."

"With horny men?" she asked tongue-in-cheek.

He smiled wickedly. "Probably."

Xavier reappeared, an old paperback book in hand. "Find one?"

"Yep." He started to pull out his wallet.

Tara shook her head. "On the house. Remember?"

He paused then gave a quick nod. "Thanks."

"No, thank you."

He left through the front door and hooked a left. Tara didn't think he'd go far.

Max snickered.

"What?"

"Did you see what he picked out?"

"No." She didn't pay much attention to which particular novels customers chose, just happy that they'd done so.

"A biography on Lincoln."

Tara blinked. "No sex? No erotica? No action?"

"Guess he's a history buff."

"Well, well." Tara found the tidbit interesting. "He seems like a different kind of person altogether."

Max's eyes hardened with knowledge. "Don't believe what you see."

"I got the feeling he's the more dangerous between him and Brighton."

Max pondered the statement for a few seconds then pursed his lips. "With Brighton, what you see is what you get. Xavier is sly. Sneaky. You won't see him coming."

Enlightenment came to Tara, along with tendrils of trepidation. She'd been seeing all of them as men. The knowledge that these men, all of them, could shift into wolves and tear a person apart finally clicked.

Comprehension and truly realizing the facts were entirely different things. "Good grief. What have I gotten into?"

Max walked over and took her hand, warming it between his. "Finally scared?"

She lifted her chin and fought to find her previous bravery. Still, she couldn't lie. "Yes."

He met her gaze, then brought her hand up to his lips in a gentle kiss. "I've been with other women before, both humans and shifters. None of them can hold a candle to you. Even my inner beast agrees. For once."

The confession stole Tara's breath. "He doesn't always?"

"No. He didn't care too much for the others. You, he likes."

She absorbed that information. Nice to know a shifter has a dual personality. The fact wasn't quite shocking. Compelling, certainly. "Then how do you know which is the right woman for you?"

"I go with my gut. And my heart." He waited a beat before continuing. "Wolves mate for life."

"And shifters?" she asked on a whisper.

"Do the same."

Butterflies took flight as did a healthy case of nerves. For Max there could only be one. And, she'd bet her next rent payment that her human genes kept her from making par.

She thought of Abby. The lady was definitely human, judging by her comment about Max being 'one of them'. Tara's spirits lifted on a ray of hope.

Max lowered his lips, meshing with hers.

She shelved the internal debate, too busy savoring

the exquisite taste of the man she'd fallen for, head over heels, for as long as he was there.

Chapter 13

Tara plopped down in a chair, leaned over, and rested her elbows on her thighs. "I should just have a huge sale and get it over with."

Max retained his position leaning against a wall, but flicked his gaze over to her. His heart ached seeing her suffering like this. Watching her dream slowly deflate and die. Tara was proud, probably too proud, yet she seemed intent to go down with the sinking ship.

Not for the first time he cussed his lack of access to his funds. He'd give her everything he had in a heartbeat.

Tara scrubbed her face, lifted her head, and sighed. He spied the twinkling of unshed tears in her eyes.

His gut clenched at the sight.

If the situation hadn't been critical, Max would have herded Tara into the back room and kissed her senseless, anything to distract her from the constant worry of a death squad appearing on her doorstep and the reality of the failing economy which was snuffing out her business. He wanted to wrap her in his arms, promise her everything would be just fine, and shower her with all the emotions he couldn't quite speak aloud.

He'd tell her. If they lived through this ordeal.

Brighton, good to his word, had sentries watching the place, and he'd stopped by just now to check on the status of things. One of those sentries happened to be

Xavier. He'd swung by that morning, helped himself to come coffee, winked at Tara, and headed out—presumably to his watching spot for the day. Max shook his head at the youngster. Xavier no doubt tried Brighton's patience. He had to. But the potential that young wolf carried was immense. Only a fool would taunt or cross him. It probably took Brighton and their grandmother combined to keep Xavier in check. For now. Something told Max that Xavier would break free one day.

Max considered Tara's fading business once more. "Settle this, then I can get access to my bank accounts. Brighton's man is working on it right now. He'll have it in a few days. I intend to pay you back, every red cent. Chip in to cover your costs, rent. Whatever else you need to keep this dream alive for you."

She looked up at him, hope flashing in her eyes for a split second before she quickly shut it down. "No."

He sighed, knowing that would be her answer, but hating to hear it all the same. "Why not? You need the income."

"I'm not going to take from you."

He stood up straight. "But it was okay for me to take from you?" Her stubbornness frustrated him and prodded at the guilt he still felt for the additional drain he'd placed on her already too tightly stretched budget.

She jerked her head up. "Yes. You had nothing. *Nothing.*" She narrowed her eyes. "And don't argue. You paid me back in every way possible. Still are."

He snorted. His inner wolf snarled, irritated with the whole conversation. He wanted Tara close, safe, and happy, not tearing him a new one. Max agreed. Unfortunately, that particular situation didn't seem possible at the moment.

"Like I said before, we're even."

He shook his head. "Not even close."

Tara's eyes spit fire. "Don't go there again."

He'd noticed the tension steadily increase with each passing day. Tara was on edge, plain and simple. Rightfully so. Even as they clung to one another at night, they both knew time drew short. The waiting was wearing on them both.

He tried everything to shoulder the anxiety, to take it from Tara. To soothe and reassure her. No such luck. She grew tighter wound until he feared she'd snap. Like today. Normally, she was slow to rile. But not now. Now, she flung answers back at him as if they were too vile to consider.

Just another sin on Garrison's growing list.

Max silently cussed the man for it.

He collected himself and tried to avoid taking the bait Tara tossed out there. Irritated, he turned his attention to the door. "No chance of that. However, this is a whole different matter. I *will* pay you back. And cover your rent."

"Like hell."

A looming figure appeared in front of the door. He tugged it open easily, stepped inside, then lifted an eyebrow as his gaze landed on Max first then to Tara. "Problem?"

"Nope. Things are just hunky-dory. Thank you for asking." Tara barked, stood up, and disappeared into the back room.

"Nerves or otherwise?" Brighton asked.

Max closed the distance between them. "Both."

Brighton grimaced. "This waiting isn't doing

anyone any favors."

"No shit." Max found Tara's prickly mood contagious this morning. He opened his senses, trying to check on Tara from afar. If he wasn't careful, she might take her gun out and shoot him. Not that he'd blame her.

Brighton shook his head. "Going off half-cocked isn't going to help."

Hearing the subtle reminder for what it was, Max checked his attitude and encouraged his inner beast to stand down. Brighton wasn't his alpha, but he was alpha of the territory and the only one that had Max's back right now in his bid to protect Tara. Respect was due the man. Max inclined his head in acknowledgement.

"I'm afraid she's going to break before this is over," Max quietly confessed to Brighton. "I'm doing everything in my power to take the stress off, but it's not doing one damn bit of good."

Brighton stilled as if pondering Max's words. "She's strong. She'll make it."

Max briefly glanced toward the back of the store where Tara had disappeared. "I wish I was so sure."

"You'll help her. So will we."

"Thank you." Max found the words inadequate for all that Brighton had stepped up to do.

"There's one thing I can't figure out. Why didn't you just stay with Jacques and the other pack? You would've been safe there." Brighton glanced toward the front door of the bookstore then back to Max.

Max had ridden in to the store with Tara only to find the day too damn quiet for his liking. No customers. No Garrison and his thugs. Just him and

Tara all morning and half the afternoon. While he didn't mind spending time with her, he couldn't enjoy it. His gut told him something was up and it had never been wrong before. Too much rode on him being alert and hypervigilant. Tagart and the other squad members would take what advantage that they could, especially against Tara. The continued wait had taken its toll, leaving them all on edge. Sleep hadn't come, though he spent those normally restful hours in other activities— namely reaffirming life in Tara's arms.

Max met his gaze. "I had to keep his location secret. Didn't want anyone snooping around, figuring out where I flew him to." He took a breath. "Besides, I needed to return to Throwback and see if I could band anyone together, to take back the leadership."

Brighton's mouth fell open. "You went back to incite a coup." The words came out whispered but filled with incredulity.

"Someone has to stand up to the lowlife bastard."

"Why you?" Brighton persisted.

"Following in my father's footsteps, I guess. He was killed during a takeover trying to protect me and others from the cruelty of Garrison's relative. I couldn't let him die in vain."

Brighton shook his head. "That's one majorly fucked up pack."

Max grinned without humor. "Tell me something I don't know."

Silence reigned for a short period of time as Max glanced around the store, his senses tuned in for the slightest hint of trouble.

The cheerful bell on the door announced another visitor, this one a woman. Tara emerged from the back room, greeted her warmly, and assisted her in search of a book.

"Who would have thought of GPS on that fucking plane? You could have pulled it off if not for that." Brighton scratched at his chest.

Max sighed; frustration at his own oversight ate at him. "I know. I'd forgotten about it in my haste. They knew where I took Jacques. After they discovered that clue, it didn't take a rocket scientist to figure out he was staying with his sister and tap her phone. They figured I would check in at some point." *And they were right.*

"Surprised they didn't go after your friend first." Brighton turned his attention from Tara back to Max.

"Guess going up against a whole pack, no matter the number, is a lot of trouble for Garrison." Max shrugged. The rotten bastard was a coward at heart, at least in Max's opinion. Garrison talked big and walked around with a huge chip on his shoulder. But, when the chips were down, Garrison couldn't be counted on. That was the angle Max planned to exploit in order to change the pack's culture. *Not that it did any good.* "I just wish he'd hurry up and make a move."

"Revenge is a dish best served cold," Brighton reminded. "Complacency is his advantage."

He wasn't saying anything Max hadn't already thought of. He alternated between wanting to hurry up Garrison's move and putting it off in order to prepare, to share more time with Tara, and to simply enjoy his newfound life. "I just wish I knew what he had in mind."

Brighton nodded. "If he's smart, he'll go for your weakness."

"Tara." Max figured that part out already, which

was why he stuck to her like glue.

"That's what I think. He'll make his move on her. If you're there or not doesn't matter." Brighton tilted his head. "She's the link to you. They'll converge on her, knowing you'll be nearby."

Max watched as Tara rang up a customer, smiling at the lady who'd purchased a couple of books. "She worries they'll hit here. Burn it down. Or even attack when there's customers here. She's debating on closing up shop until they make their move."

Tara turned, met Max's gaze, and offered up a small smile.

Max's heart kicked against his chest. "Her business can't withstand any of those things."

Brighton nodded. "Rose told me things were pretty slow."

Looking at Brighton, Max detected similar features as to Rose. The nose, the sharpness of eyes. Even the fluid movement. He hadn't paid that much attention before but now he easily saw the similarities.

Wouldn't it be nice to live in that kind of stable world? Lineage of power passed down from generation to generation. Not fought over tooth and nail like his psychotic pack.

Max shoved aside the thought and focused on the conversation at hand. "She's one amazing woman. Stubborn and powerful, too."

"That would be my grandmother. She doesn't have issues with speaking her mind, popular opinion or not." Brighton sobered. "She really likes Tara. While she's glad Tara has you, she worries that Tara will lose everything and walk away from it all."

"It's a strong possibility." Max understood the

score. Memories, her grandparents' home, and the store kept Tara grounded here. Without those, she'd have no reason to stay. From what he saw of the small town, jobs weren't thick on the ground, leaving a person pretty much between a rock and a hard place whether to stay or go.

"If the bastards decide to hit at her house, she could lose it as well."

Max nodded. "Yeah, I know. I've been patrolling, keeping an eye out. Got mechanical eyes on the place to give me a heads up there's someone snooping around both day and night. They'll try to catch me at a bad time and make their move. Anywhere from the house to the store and everywhere in between." He scrubbed his face. "Waiting sucks."

"Yeah. It's just a matter of time before they show up, maybe with reinforcements," Brighton pointed out.

"That's what I'm afraid of." Max blew out a breath. "You and your pack shouldn't be in the middle of this. If it's all-out war, then it's my war. Not yours. No need for your people to be hurt all because of me."

Brighton appraised Max for a long moment. "We're not cowards. Besides, if no one stands up to them, they'll only think our lands are free for the taking." Brighton paused for a second. "Don't forget he threatened Abby. If he did that to her, he'll do it to others. No, we have to take a stand. To eradicate them once and for all."

Max swallowed. He'd never killed before. Sure, he'd been in fights—plenty of them, saw more than his fair share, but never had he snuffed out a life.

He glanced over at Tara who presently pecked at the laptop computer. She stared at the screen, her eyebrows furrowing a she concentrated on reading.

Tara. Sweet, kind Tara. For her, he could kill. To keep those motherfuckers away from her, to protect her, he'd do what he had to do. Including some shovel work after a battle if needed. His inner beast barked softly in agreement.

Chapter 14

The instant Tara turned off the road and onto her long driveway, Max went on full alert. The hairs at the back of his neck stood on end and his inner beast began to growl. He understood why a couple of seconds later when a black truck with deep red trim came into view. They pulled in behind Tara's car, blocking her in on the narrow lane. If that wasn't warning enough, two men stepped out of the vehicle, one from each side. Max's stomach clenched as he recognized Tagart and Conley.

Both were of good size. Powerful. Definitely wolf shifters. They took their job seriously and had a reputation to uphold. Punishment was a given. Death became a good possibility.

"That's the guy who tried to kidnap Abby," Tara whispered as she looked in the rearview mirror.

Max glanced over at her, saw the worry and fear written clearly on her now pale face. "When I get out, find a spot to turn around. Drive through the ditch if you have to, but get out of here. Then I want you to head straight back to town."

Tara turned and stared at him, her lips parting. "You aren't thinking what I think you're thinking?"

Max smiled without humor. "That didn't even make sense."

Tara appraised him with a frown. "You're going to take them both on. A fight. One where you can be killed, especially because of the odds."

He didn't bother to lie. No point when the facts were clear as day. "Those are Garrison's right-hand men. The ones who rein in those who disobey."

"By killing."

Max shrugged. She didn't need to hear the gory, graphic details. He didn't want to think about it much, either.

His enhanced hearing picked up the sound of her racing heart. Her terror nearly consumed him, bringing out his protective instincts like never before. He studied her face, saw the determination and bravery, and absorbed the emotions. Each one he fed into his growing fury. How dare they show up now, just when he found Tara, and threaten his and her very existence.

Movement drew his attention. The men strode over to stand in front of the car, crossed their arms, and watched.

Max understood the gesture. They would only wait so long. When their patience wore thin, they'd make a move—one that would put Tara in the middle of a bloody battle. Something that he couldn't allow to happen.

He sighed, cupped Tara's face, then brushed his lips against hers. "Don't argue. Just do what I told you." With one final look, he opened the passenger's seat door, and shut it behind him.

Ever so slowly, he walked in front of Tara's car, putting himself between her and the other men. When he heard the car engine cut off, he scowled but didn't take his eyes off his opponents. There was no backing down or fleeing this time. No. Max knew the situation and stood his ground. He'd tear the death squad apart if he had to, even if it meant his untimely death. Garrison wasn't there but his lackeys were. They'd pay the price for hunting him and threatening Tara and Abby.

"Garrison sends his regards." Tagart spit on the ground.

"He can go straight to hell." Max narrowed his eyes and frantically tried to come up with a plan on how to take on both men and come out the victor. Nothing came to mind.

"You know we're going to rip you apart. No one disobeys and lives to tell the tale," Tagart tossed out.

"Liar. I did." Max threw the truth back at them, not about to appear intimidated or weak. "You had your chance and blew it."

"Well, ain't it too bad that we found you and that pretty lady? Can't wait to get me a taste of her once I'm through with you." Conley sneered.

Max's inner wolf leapt at the threat. *Easy boy. Patience. Once we have a plan, he's all yours.*

Come on. Think of something. Anything.

The answer appeared in the form of Brighton walking up and stopping at Max's side.

Max glanced over, surprised to see the alpha. "That was fast. Didn't know you were around."

"I figured they'd be sneaky. Easier to ambush somewhere besides the store in broad daylight. Sentries were posted just in case they decided to show up here. They saw them arrive, called me on the cell phone, and reported in. They had your back while I hurried over."

"Thanks. I appreciate the forethought." Max gave a nod of acknowledgement to the men he'd never seen before and turned his attention back straight ahead.

"I suggest you stand down," Brighton ordered.

"Who says?" Conley fired back.

"I'm the alpha of Glacier Pack. You're in my territory." Brighton's voice carried authority.

Tagart sneered. "We don't fucking answer to you. So, why don't you move along before you find yourself minus a couple of limbs?"

Brighton bristled.

Max could feel the restrained anger emanating from Brighton and knew the alpha prepared for a vicious battle to come. One that he had no business sticking his nose in. "This isn't your fight."

Brighton spared him a glance. "He threatened my mate."

"My pack, my problem," Max insisted. He hated the thought of Brighton getting injured or worse because he involved himself in Max's situation. Blame weighed heavily enough on his shoulders. He'd stood back and watched Jacques take a beating and did nothing, all because of centuries old rules of the pack. He'd almost lost his best friend in the process. Now, he'd dragged Tara and Brighton into the mess. Innocent people that didn't deserve any of this.

Max stood straight, ready to die for the people he'd come to respect and care for. "I can handle them."

Brighton shook his head. "Like it or not, you're no longer alone. You want the other guy, have at it. But the one that scared the shit out of Abby is mine." He glared at the men. "One of you terrorized my woman. For that, you'll pay."

Tagart sneered. "You mean that ugly, pregnant bitch? I was trying to do you a favor."

In the blink of an eye, Brighton shifted and launched himself at Tagart. The two rolled around in the dirt before Tagart managed to transform into his wolf form. They squared off with plenty of raised hackles and threatening growls.

Max focused on Conley. The man glared and made a come-hither motion.

Without further delay, Max shifted form, shook off his clothes, and faced Conley who'd already done the same. Absently, Max noticed Tara slip around them and into the garage she'd just opened. He silently ordered her to shut the door and stay inside.

Conley pounced, pulling Max's attention away from Tara and completely onto the struggle to survive.

Max absorbed his charge, rolled, then jerked away as Conley snapped onto his leg, the teeth brushing just deep enough to draw blood. The burning sensation motivated Max to get moving. He dashed in, aimed for Conley's throat, only to be knocked back down by a brutal sideswipe from Conley.

Before Max could hardly take a breath, Conley was on top of him.

Max growled and bit at Conley's front legs, scratched with his back, and tried to protect his tender stomach. All to no avail. Conley had him pinned and the bastard knew it.

Max glimpsed Tara over Conley's shoulder, holding a shovel. He struggled again, with the same results.

"Oh, no you don't." Tara swung the shovel, landing a hard blow on Conley's back. Immediately, Conley released Max and turned on the new threat.

Tara made another swipe only for Conley to jump aside, lunge, and catch the wooden part with his teeth. A tug-of-war ensued until Tara lost her grip. Conley tossed the object aside and bared his teeth at her. Tara backed up slowly.

Where the hell was her gun? That would be a fucking better weapon than a shitty shovel. He'd lecture her. Later.

Max darted to place himself between her and the stalking Conley, just in time for Conley to leap. Max met him, took the brunt of the hit, and fell back into Tara, knocking her to the ground, hard.

With no time to check on her, Max went on the offensive, lashing out and coming away with a mouthful of fur in the process. He dove and retreated, unable to land a decent blow or catch more than air in his jaws.

Conley charged, hitting Max square in the ribs and sending him toppling over. Max gained his feet, side-stepped the next assault, then latched onto Conley's rear leg as he tried to spin around. Max clamped down with all the power in his jaws. The loud crack echoed through the trees.

Conley howled, jerked, and furiously snapped at Max.

Carefully Max held on, dodging those sharp teeth as he shook his head and yanked with all his strength. Conley went down and stayed there.

Tired and panting for air, Max turned away from Conley's beaten body. He'd let the bastard slink back to Garrison and face the devil's wrath.

A cry from Tara was his only warning.

Max spun just in time to avoid razor sharp teeth aimed at his jugular. Conley's aim took him too low and past Max. Conley didn't stop. Instead, he hurried on three legs, making a lunge for Tara.

Max jumped on top of the other wolf, bit down on the back of his neck, and shook. A loud snap sounded before Conley went limp. Max spat him out and met Tara's gaze.

Shock conveyed in her wide eyes and parted lips. She lifted her hand to her mouth and stared at Max.

Well, shit.

The one thing he tried to avoid had come to pass. Not only had he killed, he'd done so in a brutal, violent way right in front of her. Sure, he'd done it to save her, but that seemed a little trivial at the moment.

Movement caught his eye. He lifted his nose to the air, drew in the scent, and froze. *It can't be.*

Sure enough, Garrison himself stepped forward from the east side of the house, making a beeline for Max. He stopped a few feet away. "Time to finish this once and for all."

A strong bolt of trepidation rolled through Max. He ached from the numerous wounds Conley committed on his body. Worn out from the intense struggle, Max knew he'd been dealt a particularly nasty hand. His confidence waned even as his determination hardened.

Steeling himself, Max faced Garrison and glared at the bastard who carried responsibility for so much misery and so many deaths. Not just him, but his father and grandfather before him. Generations of that sadistic family tree ruled. It was past time for their power to come to an abrupt end.

"I believe this is my fight."

Garrison swung around.

Max blinked as he recognized Jacques approaching through the small group of bystanders.

Jacques inclined his head to Max then turned his

full attention to Garrison. "We have some unfinished business."

Garrison sneered. "You couldn't defeat me the first time. What makes you think you can do it now?"

Jacques unbuttoned his shirt, letting the garment fall to the ground. "I might bear a few scars but I've learned a thing or two as well."

Fearing for Jacques, Max rushed Garrison.

"No." Jacques's voice cut through the silence and put the brakes on Max's intentions to take advantage of Garrison's distraction.

Max stood and stared at Jacques in bafflement. Together they could take down Garrison. Alone, the odds were hugely against them. Garrison had been born to fight, to dominate, to rule with an iron fist. Those lessons had paid off in a major way.

Jacques shook his head at Max before removing his shoes. "Throwback rules. No one else intervenes."

Unable to speak in this form, Max quickly shifted, ignoring the fact that he stood nude in front of a small gathering of people. "Are you insane? You've barely had time to heal." He addressed Jacques in an effort to talk so sense into him.

Jacques offered up a small, carefree grin. "It's been long enough. Besides, I have a score to settle." He focused on Garrison. "I challenge you for alpha rights to the Throwback Pack. Winner takes all. Battle to the death."

Garrison snorted. "Your death."

Max strode over to Jacques. "Don't do this. Let me."

Jacques met his gaze and held steady. He placed his hand on Max's shoulder. "You're a good friend.

The best. But, I have to finish this once and for all."
With that, Jacques shifted into his wolf form. He didn't
waste a second, simply lunged for Garrison, hit him in
the chest, and rolled him. Aggressively, Jacques
growled, bit, and clawed, relentless in his attack on
Garrison.

Max stood in a mixture of amazement at Jacques
and fear of a repeat from before. He sent up a little
prayer, hoping someone in power would listen.

"Here."

Max tore his attention from the action for just a
moment to see Tara standing next to him holding his
clothes. "Thanks." He took them and quickly pulled on
his jeans. He didn't bother with the rest despite the
cold, prepared to jump back into the ring if Jacques
faltered. Too keyed up, he didn't notice the chill in the
least despite the lack of garments.

The fierce battle once more captured and held his
focus.

Fur and leaves flew as both wolves slid, jumped,
and ran through patches of snow. The hollow echoed
with the growls, yelps, and snapping of jaws. Brush
rustled when one or the other landed hard against the
dormant branches. Red stains dotted the formerly
pristine coating, leaving a trail even a pup could follow.
As Max tracked, he noted the amount of blood
increased dramatically. Small puddles replaced
droplets. No doubt one or both wolves had been gravely
injured and were slowly bleeding out.

Worry hastened Max's steps. Visions of the first
battle between Jacques and Garrison filled Max's mind.
His gut tightened as he recalled the critical state of
Jacques's body as Garrison touted his victory. *Not*

again. Please, not again.

Suddenly, the land went quiet. No more signs of movement or even a single bark. Nothing. The silence pushed down Max's shoulders.

Picking up the pace, he easily followed the crimson path. The sight before his eyes had him freezing in place. Jacques, still in wolf form, hovered over the body of Garrison. Jacques released the death grip on Garrison's throat, exposing his bloody muzzle, and leveled his gaze at Max.

Max released a long breath. "You okay?"

Jacques limped around the body, stopping a few feet from Max. He shifted despite the below freezing temperatures. Blood streaked his body and a couple of bite wounds on his shoulder and right arm oozed. His eyes were sharp, clear, and filled with victory and retribution. "That will be the last fight to the death ever in Throwback Pack." Authority filled Jacques's voice.

Max nodded. "It's good to have you back." Uncaring of the smeared stains spotting Jacques's body, Max hugged him tight. "Damn good to have you back."

Jacques pulled away after a few moments. He raked Max from head to toe. "Looks like you came through with flying colors."

"A few scrapes is all. Not bad if I do say so myself. Definitely better than before. You should have seen me a while back. Just about met the end of the road. Would have if I hadn't been nearly run over by a car."

"Fate works in mysterious ways." Jacques brushed some dirt and leaves off his skin.

"You can say that again." Max inclined his head. "Shall we return to the house? We both need a shower. I've got some clean clothes you can wear afterward."

"Thanks." Jacques moved abreast of Max as they headed back the way they came.

"How did you find us, anyway? I told you not to come. Deliberately kept the address from you."

"I took a page from Garrison's book. Traced the cell phone." He didn't look one bit repentant.

Max shook his head. "And just happened to show up when Garrison did?"

"Yep. Had a gut feeling and followed it."

Not about to argue with Jacques's instincts, Max recalled the situation at hand. "What do you want to do with his body?"

Jacques didn't bother to look at it. "Burn it. Bury it. Leave it for the buzzards. I don't give a shit. Just take a picture for the disbelievers that'll demand proof that the leadership has changed."

Max scanned the area, seeing nothing but trees, brush, and forest floor. Digging a hole with all those roots would be a definite pain in the ass, especially as deep as they would need to go in order to bury the body well. Burning would be a risk with all the old leaf litter. As much as he wanted to just let the body be, he couldn't forget this was Tara's backyard. To leave her with such wouldn't be fair. "I'll think of something."

As they approached the edge of the woods, Max spied a couple of people waiting on them, namely Brighton and Tara. Less than a handful of other shifters, one of them Xavier, leaned up against the black truck belonging to the Throwback Pack.

Xavier gave him a thumbs up. Max gave him a nod.

Tara swiveled, locked gazes, and hurried over. "Are you all right?" Her voice told of her rattled state quickly regaining composure.

Max gave her a quick squeeze. "I'm fine. Just in need of a shower as does Jacques." He paused as Jacques's steps slowed.

"We've never formally met. I'm Jacques." He held out his hand, obviously not the least bit self-conscious of his naked state.

Tara shook it then smiled when Jacques pressed his lips against the back of it. "Tara."

"Nice to finally meet you. Max told me about you. You have my gratitude for taking him in and saving his hide." Jacques halfway grinned at Max.

Max rolled his eyes, not only at the charm Jacques lavished on Tara but on the small josh about Max's plight of getting nearly ran over by her car. He didn't care for Jacques's lazy flirting but consoled himself that it would take more than such grand overtures to win Tara over. She had a good head on her shoulders and a tough attitude when it came to men. He'd heard it all as her pet dog.

His inner wolf growled at him as he watched Jacques flirt while standing there the buff. The only thing that kept Max from grabbing a coat and slapping it over Jacques's groin was the fact that Tara kept her focus on the guy's face, not his cock.

"It was my pleasure," Tara answered quietly. She dropped her hand and rubbed her arms if trying to banish the chill.

Max wasn't sure if it was the brisk temperatures or the aftermath of horrors that held the fault. He wanted to kick his own ass for giving her plenty of fodder for nightmares that might last the rest of her life. He'd gladly take it back if he could. *Damn Conley and his unwillingness to let it go.*

Brighton approached. Max quickly did the introductions.

Jacques shook Brighton's hand. "Thanks for the assist."

"Least I could do." Brighton met Jacques's gaze steadily. "Pretty damn ballsy of you to come back here and take that nuisance down,"—he gestured to the pink scars riddling Jacques's body—"especially when you're still healing."

"Wasn't about to let Garrison win a second time." The firm tone carried truth.

"Can't believe you guys still fight to the death. Talk about archaic." Sarcasm dripped from Brighton's words.

Jacques tilted his head. "As I told Max, this is the very last battle to the death Throwback will ever see."

"If you're smart it will be." Brighton straightened.

Max tensed, waiting for Jacques to snap back at such a comment. Normally easy-going, Jacques still possessed a temper and the whole 'bite me' attitude all alphas seemed to carry.

Jacques bristled, then gave in with a small smile. "I'm too damn tired to take you on. Besides, you're right."

"Always," Brighton replied with a grin of his own.

"Oh, hell. Don't be telling him that. His head is plenty big already." Xavier nudged his brother with his elbow.

Brighton rolled his eyes. "One day…"

"Bring it on, big brother." Xavier's lips curled up at the end for a fleeting second.

"Thank you, Brighton. Xavier. Please tell the

others how much I appreciate their efforts." Tara smiled at them as she sincerely expressed her gratitude to them. "Free books and coffee anytime you want."

"You don't have to do that," Brighton protested.

"I want to. And I expect you for supper one evening. All of you," Tara added.

"Boy howdy. Count me in." Xavier rubbed his hands together.

Brighton smacked him on the arm. Hard.

"Ow. Hey. That was uncalled for." Xavier rubbed the spot.

Max didn't miss the apparent affection between the two brothers. He and Jacques used to be the same. He hoped they'd return to that level of camaraderie. As soon as they returned to Throwback and set their plans back into motion.

"What are we going to do with these bodies?" Xavier asked the obvious question.

Max saw Tara flinch.

He moved to her side, drawing her against him.

She leaned into him despite the blood, mud, and muck he wore on his skin compliments of the skirmish. He wanted to take her straight to the shower, to wash her, to hold her, and to make love to her until they were both too tired to move.

Unfortunately, they had guests.

Still, the moment didn't go unnoticed. Max looked at the people standing around and knew deep down, he'd found a surrogate family.

And, he was finally free.

Free to pursue Tara. Free to return to the pack with Jacques and set things right. Free to reach for the stars and get those dreams to come true.

Excitement and anticipation coursed through him until he felt the tremor that wracked Tara's body. Reality returned like an ice-cold bath. He'd done what he had to do in stopping Conley but whether Tara could ever forgive him became the most important question. One he couldn't ask. Not yet.

"We'll haul them off. Got a good idea on where to bury them," Brighton answered.

"You can do it in the woods here, if you want," Tara offered. "Dragging them around is too much work."

The men shared a look.

Max bit his tongue. He knew the spot would always be a reminder to her of what had happened.

"Bixby's Hollow is just over the rise. We'll go there." Brighton started toward the vehicles.

Tara grabbed his arm. "Thank you."

He peered down at her with a half-grin of bemusement. "I didn't do anything."

"Yes. You do. All of you. I mean it. Give me a couple of days and I want the whole crew here for dinner."

"Okay. If you insist." He gave her a quick hug, then walked off.

The others followed, leaving Max, Jacques, and Tara standing in the cold.

They'd pick up two of the bodies first, saving Conley for last. To spare Tara. Max understood their thinking because it was his as well. "Maybe we should get cleaned up?" he prodded.

Tara nodded. "If you'll follow me, I'll show you to the shower while Max finds you some clothes."

Her voice lacked energy. She appeared worn, tired,

and resigned. He could guess as to what because his gut clenched at the thought of what the next hour would bring. Decisions. Hard decisions.

****

"Nice boxers." Jacques grinned as he emerged from the bathroom wearing Max's clothing. They were a tad bit snug but made for a decent fit.

Max inclined his head toward Tara. "She has good taste." He'd taken his turn after Jacques and cleaned up fast. Tara had tossed their dirty clothes in the wash and even wiped up the tracks on the floor. In all that time, she hadn't said a word. Just threw some burgers on to cook and went about her chores.

Her silence weighed upon him.

"I'd say so."

Tara scooped up the last hamburger from the broiler in the oven, then shut it off. "I hope you don't mind hamburgers. It was fast and easy."

Jacques smiled. "Not in the least." He sat, pulled a bun out of the package, and added condiments to it. "Thank you for being so considerate."

Max took the chair next to him and dropped a couple of bags of chips next to Jacques as Tara brought the meat over. He took a long drink of the lemonade he'd hastily made and used to fill each of their glasses.

Tara placed the rounded plate of patties on the table, then sat. "It was no problem. I figure you two will be hungry after..." Her face pinched.

"We're always hungry," Jacques reassured her, then shared a knowing look with Max.

"You're safe now. Always will be." Max took her hand in his and squeezed lightly.

She offered up a small smile. "I know. Thanks to

you. Both of you." She included Jacques in her appreciation with a quick glance.

Jacques forked a thick chunk of meat onto his bread, put the top bun on, then took a large bite. He ate with gusto as if he'd missed a few meals.

Max understood completely. His belly growled with hunger, reminding him of those awful days on his own.

"So, you found this furry beast on the road?" Jacques asked.

Tara nodded, finished putting together her meal, and sipped her drink. "Kind of a funny story. I was out on a blind date. The creep took one look at me and started chatting up a skinny redhead at the bar. Insulted and angry, I left for home in the snow. Vowed to be done with men for good because no way would I be able to find one unless fate dropped him right in my path." She grinned. "I guess that part came true. I ran into Max. The rest, as they say, is history."

Jacques shook his head. "Living on the edge, bro. Lucky she didn't flatten you."

Max cringed. "At that time, it wouldn't have been the worst thing ever." He took another bite, chewed, then swallowed. "She put me in the backseat, dragged me into the house and straight for the bathtub. Now that was an experience." He smiled over at Tara.

She rolled her eyes. "Please. You were covered in filth and half-frozen. Starved and weak. Don't tell me under those conditions you got all hot and bothered."

"Okay. I won't tell you."

Jacques smirked. "You're a brat. I think Tara is one strong and patient woman to put up with you."

"Hey, I wasn't entirely horrible. I even played

fetch," Max defended lightly.

"For all of thirty seconds," Tara added.

The put-upon quality to her voice told of her loosening up, pushing past the horrible scene she'd just witnessed. He much preferred her sassy to the wide-eyed badly shaken woman she'd been just a few minutes earlier.

"Then he decided to show me the truth one day. After moping around at the bookstore, avoiding all the customers that just wanted to pet him. About gave me heart failure when I walked in to find a naked man in my kitchen."

Jacques shook his head. "No couth."

Max snorted. "I had a towel on. Not like I could wear any of her stuff. And, yes, I tried."

Jacques broke into a wide, wolfish grin.

Tara's mouth fell open. "You didn't."

"Not your underwear. Jeez." He took another drink. "Your robe didn't fit worth crap. That's why I ended up in a towel that day."

"Oh." She blinked at him, but the little twitch to her lips gave her away.

Much better, lady. We're finally getting somewhere.

"I might like your undies just fine, but not well enough to try them on. They're damn sexy on you. On me, they'd show off my chicken legs and not even come close to covering the essentials." He punctuated the statement with another large bite into the sandwich.

Tara giggled.

Jacques burst out in laughter.

Max congratulated himself on breaking the icy tension. To hear beautiful sounds of Tara's happiness, he'd do silly any day of the week.

"So, you were going to tell me about this lady of yours," Max prodded Jacques while he ate.

"Ah, Carmen." Jacques's eyes brightened at the sheer mention of her name.

Oh, yeah. He has it bad. Max was thrilled for his alpha. True mates were hard to come by. *If anyone deserves a loving woman at his side, it's Jacques.*

"Is she a shifter, too?" Tara asked.

"Yes. Part of Becky's pack." Jacques crunched on a chip. "Beautiful. Sweet. And full of enough stubborn fortitude to whip all the whiny pack females into line."

Judging by the quirky smile on Jacques's face, Max decided Jacques didn't mind that particular trait in the least. "That's exactly what they need, too."

"Is she your mate?" Tara asked.

Jacques tilted his head, then grinned. "Yes."

"How did you know she's the one?" Tara leaned forward.

Max groaned to himself. Tara was too nosey for her own good.

"I just know. She fits me. It's more than caring. More than dating. It's…" He shrugged and looked to Max. "Help me out, here."

Max held up his hands. "You're asking the wrong guy."

Tara pursed her lips and grasped her glass. A brief flash of disappointment crossed her face, disappearing as quickly as it had appeared.

Max's gut clenched as he put two and two together. *Damn my loose lips.* He'd smooth it over. Later. Right now, he wasn't sure of a lot of things. Too many life changes in too short a time. One thing he knew for a fact was that he wanted Tara at his side. Was she his mate? He couldn't say for certain, but the idea of being with another turned him sour. They just needed time together to feel things out and see where their relationship could lead.

"Is she going to join you there?" Tara took a drink, her attention locked on Jacques as if he held the answers to all the world's problems.

"Yeah. I needed to take care of business first. I'll send for her in a couple of days, just as soon as I get the pack straightened out on the new leadership and what's expected."

"Why do I have a feeling she's going to keep you on your toes?" Max smirked at the thought.

"Probably because she already does," Jacques answered. He finished his meal and drank down the rest of his lemonade. "Speaking of the pack, I should be getting back. I've got a lot to do in a short amount of time."

Max swallowed the last bite. "You mean 'we'."

"Then let's go home. We'll pick up where we left off." Jacques inclined his head toward the door.

Max's heart sped as he realized their dream could finally come true. Together, they could reset the clock and lead Throwback into the present. Change the violent culture into one of acceptance and togetherness. He wasn't naïve enough to believe it would happen immediately, but with time, things would slowly take hold. Optimism flared for the first time in months.

"We'll make it happen this time," Jacques added with conviction.

"Yeah. The pack will support us this time, with Garrison and his thugs out of the picture." He believed the reason most of the group hesitated to rally behind Jacques before was because they were always looking over their shoulder for Garrison. Now, with the notorious bully gone, they no longer had to live in fear. "Finally, we can make a difference."

"Absolutely." Jacques grinned at Max. "Brothers in arms to the end." He held out his hand.

Max took it, stood up, then pulled Jacques into a hug. "Brothers to the end." The whispered words filled with emotion and steadfast confidence in his friend.

Glancing over, Max found Tara studying him with concern and a bit of regret written on her face.

Unsure what to say or do, Max stood and started clearing the table. Now that the time had come, nerves and uncertainty leashed his tongue.

Jacques followed suit, adding his dirty dishes to the sink. Once deposited, he strode toward the door, obviously having left everything in the SUV. He'd been nude when he'd entered her house, but now wore Max's clothes almost proudly. Clothes that she had purchased for Max. Insisted on providing, even though she didn't have a dollar to spare.

Remorse ate at Max once again. He opened his mouth, then shut it again. Words of wisdom failed him.

Tara joined him, her plate still containing uneaten food.

"You didn't finish." Max gestured toward her half-eaten burger.

"I wasn't as hungry as I thought." She set it aside and turned back to Max, her expressive eyes dulling with sadness. A lump formed in his throat. Stepping over, he took her hands in his. "Come with me."

Her mouth fell open. "The house…the store…"

"Keep them. Sell them. It's up to you, and you don't have to decide this instant. We have plenty of time. Just come back with me."

Jacques returned, phone in hand. He glanced at them both, but said nothing.

She gazed at Jacques then back to Max. "I'm human."

Max caught the gist of her concern. "A beautiful, thoughtful, and wonderful human. One that I want to spend the rest of my days with."

"You're welcome to join us. Really," Jacques reassured. "Whatever issues we come across, we can fix." He gave a quick nod before striding out of the kitchen presumably to give them some privacy.

A flash of hope appeared then just as quickly fled from her face only to be replaced with deep worry lines. "You said your pack was unsettled. Violent. Brutal. Even cruel." She motioned toward the woods. "I've seen it for myself and don't know that I can live in that kind of environment."

Max's gut clenched. He hated seeing the trepidation and uncertainty on her face. "Jacques and I are changing that, starting today. We're bringing the pack into the present. Making it better. No more battle to the death to claim the alpha position."

Tara blew out a breath. "I know that's what your goal is. But, it will take time. Rome wasn't built in a day, and your family unit won't go from vicious to easygoing in that amount of time, either."

"We laid some groundwork last time. It won't take that long." He brought her hand to his mouth and brushed his lips across her fingertips. "I *will* protect you, that I promise. You have no reason to fear."

"This is bigger than me, Max. It's your people. They need attention, support, and reassurance. They need Jacques and you both." She blew out a breath, then met his eyes. "They come first as well as they should."

"Damn it, Tara. I'm not just walking out and leaving you." He fought to control the extreme frustration at being caught between a rock and a hard place.

She searched his face.

"Max? Ready to hit the road?" Jacques asked from his position at the front door, his hand gripping the knob.

Max cussed under his breath at Jacques's rush and Tara's unbending resolve.

Tears pooled in Tara's eyes.

Max's gut clenched in dread. "Come with me," he coaxed.

Tara blinked, glanced down, then met his gaze again. "Your pack needs you. Jacques needs you. Go."

"Tara." A lump formed in his throat. The day he'd been dreading had arrived in more ways than one.

She lifted up on tiptoe and softly kissed his lips. "If you love something, set it free." She stepped back and lightly tugged her hand free. "Go, Max. You have a family to look after. To set things right. You have a big job ahead of you and don't need the distraction I'd make. Besides, you'll have enough trouble getting the pack to fall into line. I'm certain bringing a human into the mix will only complicate matters all the more."

"I won't let it."

Tara softly grinned. "There are things out of your control, big guy."

"No. I won't leave you. Come with me or I'll stay." Torn, he pulled out all the stops, needing to convince her that she had a place in his life, too. An important one, right at his side.

Sadness and determination reflected in Tara's face. "I didn't ask for tomorrow, Max. I understood. You belong with Jacques and the pack. With your own kind." She lowered her chin and a humorless smile appeared. "What a surprise you were. A flash of brightness in my life." She looked at him again. "But that's all it could ever be—just a flash. Goodbye, Max."

Choked up, Max held out his hand. His spirit plummeted when she glanced at it, then turned and walked away.

He watched her disappear down the hallway toward the bedroom. His heart cracked a little more with every tiny squeak of her footfalls.

He wanted to rant at the heavens, to scoop her up, carry her to the couch, and hold her until she listened to reason. One last glance at her stiffened spine told him she wasn't about to be swayed. Nothing he could say or do would make a difference at the moment.

I'll work my ass off with the pack. Give it a few days. Get Jacques securely established. Then I'll be back. If he had to choose, he'd do so. But not right now.

With nothing more to do or say, Max grabbed his phone where he'd left it on the counter after retrieving it from the car earlier and followed Jacques outside, shutting the front door soundly in his wake. A lump formed in his throat and in his stomach. Even his inner wolf whined with dejection.

"I'm sorry." Jacques wrapped his arm around Max's shoulder. "I really thought she'd come with us."

"I did, too." The words tumbled out. Still hurting, Max pulled on his inner strength and stood up straight. "Let's get moving. The sooner we hit the road, the sooner we'll be home." *Home.* The idea lacked conviction or inspiration. He'd learned a lesson in his straying days. Home wasn't about a place. It was about people.

Chapter 15

One month later

"If you love him, set him free." Tara muttered to herself as she packed the supplies she'd purchased for Cotton into the same box as the last of her belongings from the store. The collar, she pulled back out, touched it with reverence, then carefully placed it inside one of the bowls.

She'd debated on what to do with the stuff. Since she didn't have a dog, they were of no use, yet she couldn't quite bring herself to donate them to the local animal shelter, either. Too many memories were attached to those items, however short of a time they'd been used.

"And that saying officially sucks." With that statement, she closed the lid on the box, taped it shut, then carried it out the back door to her car. She set it in the trunk with the rest of the containers, and closed the lid.

"It was good while it lasted." As she walked back to finish packing and lock up the store for the last time, she pondered if she meant the business or the relationship with Max. Both dreams had fired hot only to fizzle at the end. "Some people didn't even get that much." The thought didn't cheer her in the least as she stepped inside, surveyed the empty shelves, and did a final look over.

With a shake of her head, she blew out a long sigh. The facts were written clearly on the wall. Max was a different species entirely. A man with potential, with hopes and dreams, all in a far-off place with others of his own kind. All along she knew nothing could come of their relationship—too many obstacles stood in their way.

That didn't stop her from falling head over heels and ending up with a badly broken heart.

She glanced at the box of books she'd salvaged from the closing sale. All erotica, including the one Max read a couple of weeks ago. She'd gifted Brighton with a couple but kept the rest. Deep inside, she hoped he'd return and claim the unusual present. Though, the more time passed, the less that particular scenario seemed likely.

Setting the tape close by, she shut the top on the last box. Sadness and resignation washed through her.

The ringing of her cell phone drew her attention. She checked the caller ID, winced, then forced a smile onto her face. "Hello."

"Hey beautiful."

"Max." Tara held the phone up against her ear with her shoulder as she closed the laptop and stashed it on the top of the books in the final box. Her heart picked up speed just hearing his voice. He'd called twice before. Each time a flare of excitement, longing, and happiness clashed with regret and loneliness. No matter how many times she'd questioned her decision, she always came to the same conclusion—she'd done the right thing. "How's it going?"

"Busy. We've got things rolling again with the

pack. A few hiccups, but everyone seems relieved that Jacques is back in charge."

"I bet. That's wonderful." Tara found pride and joy when it came to Max's accomplishments. He'd been through hell and worked hard to achieve them. Any reward he garnered, he'd certainly earned.

Purposely, she'd avoided calling him, not wanting to come across as pushy, needy, or interfering in his busy schedule. How many times had she stopped herself from hitting his number on her contact list? Dozens. Each time she chided herself that the more contact she had with the guy, the more she craved. In order to heal her broken heart, she needed to let him go. Except he kept calling and she didn't have the will to deny him that small bit. Part of it was a selfish attachment and reminder of the past. Part of it was the realization that his friend list was majorly limited. And, yet another part was fear he'd show up on her doorstep if she didn't answer or return his message.

That, she certainly didn't want. Not when she'd just sold out everything she could, pulled the banners from the walls, and was presently packing the last of the items from the store as they spoke.

She refused to discuss shutting the bookstore's doors for good. Each time he asked about the shop, she answered with a vague 'fine', and moved on. If he knew about the crisis and her final decision, he'd insist on doing something. Showing up unannounced. Giving her money. Hell, she wouldn't put it past him to track down Nora and buy the place. While chivalrous and touching, she couldn't let him do that. She had to make it on her own or not. End of story.

"How's the store? Is business picking up?"

"It's okay. One day at a time." She injected happiness into her voice and reminded herself she wasn't really lying. Just not divulging the whole truth. A topic switch was definitely in order. "Did you meet Carmen? Jacques seemed smitten when he spoke of her."

"Smitten is underrating those two. He dotes on her." Max chuckled. "Lights up every time she comes near. I swear he's like a lightning bug around a lantern."

Tara smiled. "Sounds like they are right for one another." *Unlike us.*

"Oh, yeah. The other females were snippy at first, but Carmen put them in their place. No way would one try to trespass, even if Jacques would let them in the first place."

And what about you?

Tara bit her tongue to keep the question from tumbling out. No answer was better than the one she feared. After all, Max was a gorgeous, smart man in his prime. Of course, the women around would take notice. *She sure did.*

Her upbeat attitude began to tire under the relentless reminder of what had been and could never be.

Needing an excuse, Tara strode over to the front door, opened it, let it close again. The cheery bell, something she decided to leave behind, sounded loudly. "Oops. I need to go."

"Okay. Umm. Tara?"

"Yes?"

"Just give me a chance. One single chance to prove that I can make you happy."

A lump formed in Tara's throat and tears sprang to her eyes. "Max. I...I have to go." Before she could give in, she hurriedly disconnected.

Sitting down in one of the overstuffed chairs, she lowered her head and simply cried for what she'd lost, for what could have been. For the cruel twist of fate that first gave her Max then took him away.

Watching him drive off had been the hardest thing she'd ever endured. She'd wept all night long, missing his presence, his prowess in bed. His love.

"No sense crying over spilled milk, Tara." She spoke to herself now because there was no one else to listen and wiped at her tears. *He's a shifter, I'm not. He's part of a pack revolution. Jacques needs him right now so much more than I do.* She thought about that sentiment for a moment, wondering if it was indeed true.

Finding a tissue, she blew her nose. "When one door closes, another opens." *Not sure I believe that right now, but what the heck.*

She stood up and searched every nook and cranny of the store, finding it bare and completely empty.

With nothing else to keep her there, she tucked her phone in her purse, quickly taped up the final box, and stuffed the roll in her pocket. Task done, she carried the special box out to her car and placed it in the back seat. The same back seat she'd wrangled Cotton into that one night under a full moon during a snow storm.

Her eyes began to water. Fighting for composure, she hurried back inside, locked both doors, and returned to her car. After a quick stop by Nora's house to drop off the keys, she headed home to unpack and ponder what could have been. After that pity party concluded, she'd have to face reality and start looking for a new job. Fast.

The drive home was uneventful. Unloading the car proved to be a little more difficult. She stored a couple of boxes in the spare bedroom, then carried in the one containing the last book Max had read. The laptop she placed on the kitchen table, knowing she'd need it for an employment hunt. The other books, she stared at for a long moment, unsure what to do.

Glancing up, she scanned the house. Memories of the love she'd shared surrounded her. From her grandparents who took her in and taught her the joys of being an important member of their family. From Max, who'd started out on the couch in his wolf form and ended up sharing her double bed as a man. "That's all I have left. Memories." No prospects, no career opportunities, no doors opening. No potential. At some point those same recollections stymied her, leashing her to the place. She visualized her dreams over the years only for them to mostly remain unfulfilled.

"Would it be so bad to take a chance? To see another part of the world?" The house and land would wait for her, of that she was positive.

Unfortunately, the place couldn't rekindle hope or promise. It could only sit in silent testimony to what had occurred. The same with the woods. Tree leaves might rustle in the wind during most of the year, but they didn't offer any answers or constructive advice. Only a living, breathing person could do that.

She sighed heavily. The familiar surroundings offered both comfort and discontent. Isolation and tranquility. Too quiet, the house wasn't the same without Cotton or Max.

She hadn't slept well and nightmares visited her almost nightly. Horrific scenes of Max fighting for his life and losing while she was paralyzed to help. That trauma would never go away. Still, she knew of only one way to drive the demons out—to be with Max. In his arms, her fears would dissipate. She trusted him as she trusted no other.

But, to call him up, to go to him, put her smack dab in the middle of a wolf shifter turf war.

Sure, she could move forward, find another man to date. While it hadn't worked out before, that wasn't to say she couldn't hit the jackpot on the next try.

But, the thought of dating left a bad taste in her mouth.

She wanted only one man. And, he had an immensely important agenda in Oregon. Far away from her quaint little house and town.

"What am I going to do?" Tara pulled out one of the kitchen chairs, sat down, and rested her face in her hands.

Life had just given her a wagonload of lemons and she hadn't a clue how to make lemonade.

****

"There you are. I've been looking all over for you."

Max glanced up to find Brooke, one of the more aggressive pack females, standing at his door.

Brooke leaned back against the door jamb of his office. Her mini skirt barely covered the essentials and her boobs pretty much spilled out of the cut off t-shirt she wore. Lipstick painted her full lips and her long blonde hair hung in bouncy ringlets. Ordinarily, her long legs, curvy body, and sultry expression would make his cock leap to attention and his mouth to dry up.

Today, as it had been since he'd returned, his only reaction bordered on disgust. Certainly annoyance. Definitely anger as well. He'd told them all he wasn't interested. That hadn't slowed them down a bit. They tracked him down day and night, always teasing, pleading, and pouting when he turned them down flat. He'd give them credit for perseverance if he wasn't so damn pissed with them for their senseless flirting wasting his time.

Even worse, those same women previously sneered at him in disgust or walked well out of their way to avoid him. Now, they couldn't get close enough and practically rubbed all over him like a cat in heat every time they could. *Cat in heat? Shit. More like wolves in season and looking for a power boost to their status in the pack.* They tolerated his mixed DNA because he was in a position of power, nothing more. He'd refused every single one of them and cringed every time they set their sights on him.

They ambushed him. He'd be worried if he wasn't positive they had sex on the mind.

"Max. I ache for you. Burn for you." She trailed her finger down the middle of her ample cleavage. "I want you to take me." She nearly purred the request as she thrust her chest out, drawing attention to the straining material. "Take me."

Max scowled. "Forget it, Brooke. Not happening. How many times do I have to tell you and the other women that I'm not interested?"

Her mouth dropped open. "But…"

"No buts, damn it. I'm. Not. Interested." He bit off each and every word. "Get it through your thick skull. I'm not taking any of you to my bed. Ever." He glared at her, willing her to get the picture before he had to do something rash like throw ice water on her every time she appeared claiming to be hot and bothered.

The thought held some appeal, at least.

She huffed, spun around, and stormed off. *Thank God.*

Too bad I'm not a forget-and-forgive kind of guy. Besides, I found the woman I want.

Everything boiled down to the fact that the women weren't what he was looking for. They didn't have the right hair color, the spunk, nor the beauty he sought. Only one woman did—Tara. No one else would do.

She might still be in Minnesota and stubbornly refusing to give in but he wasn't daunted. Not yet. He had too much to fight for in getting Tara to believe in him again.

"Damn ridiculous." Max grumbled under his breath as he watched Brooke turn out of view. He'd had more than his limit of dealing with women lately and Brooke took the prize.

"Break another heart?"

Max turned to see Jacques approaching with a wicked grin on his face.

Max snorted. "More like crushed her power hungry, gold-digging intentions."

"That'll make you popular with the ladies. Not."

"I don't want to be popular with them. They're all out for one thing." He fisted his hands in aggravation. The only woman that ever wanted him for him was hundreds of miles away.

Tara. She'd cared for him, perhaps even loved him, despite his wild story, his lack of a single penny or clothing, and all the trouble he brought to her door.

Jacques studied Max for a long moment. "Can't get the human off your mind?"

"No." Max ran his hand through his hair. "I can't sleep at night wondering how she's doing. Worrying about if she has the funds to pay the rent on her shop."

"Send her the money," Jacques advised.

"I did. As far as I can tell she hasn't cashed the check. Hell, I'd transfer it directly to her bank account if I had the number."

"Ask Tos. He does wonders with computer stuff. I'm sure he can track that number down and transfer the funds for you."

Max shook his head. "No. That's too sneaky, not to mention illegal. I don't want to pry or push on Tara. She has to make up her own mind." He sighed. "I just wish I knew what she was thinking."

"Call her."

"I have, trust me. She's always civil and upbeat but I can hear it in her voice. She's not happy."

Jacques rubbed his chin. "Wonder why not."

Max waved his hands in the air. "I don't know. Maybe because she's damn broke, her business is on its last leg, and she has one whole friend in the town." Brighton had promised to watch out for Tara, so that sort of made him a friend, Max conceded. Add in Abby and that made three whole people that possibly cared about Tara in that small area. "Then I came along, introduced her to brutal pack politics. She witnessed the killings herself." He'd have spared her that if there was any way. Unfortunately, the bastards opted for a showdown at her home, forcing the issue. Angry and frustrated at the whole situation and himself, he glared at his alpha. "Besides all that shit, I can't think of a single, fucking reason." Sarcasm rolled easily off his tongue.

Jacques shook his head and grinned even wider.

Max narrowed his eyes.

Jacques held up his hands. "Don't get all pissed off. At least not until you hear me out."

Max stood down, for the moment. Just because Jacques was his alpha and his best friend didn't mean he'd bow to him. No way. Under the circumstances, Max was fully prepared to tackle Jacques, sending them both into the dirt for a knockdown drag out. He'd end up with his butt kicked but right now that didn't matter.

"You don't see it."

"See what?" Max bit out.

"You miss her."

"Hell, yes, I miss her. She's sweet and kind and understanding. She had the guts to take in a stray wolf and pamper him as her pet." The animosity left his voice. "She saved my life."

Jacques shook his head. "Blind as a bat, I swear. You love her. That's why the pack females turn you off. That's why you're tossing and turning at night. That's why you're biting at people and about to get your ass handed to you by a collective few."

"She deserves better." The small admission came straight from the heart.

"The way I see it, she's getting the best—in you."

Max wasn't buying it. He had a lot of sins on his plate. "She's human. There's no way she could understand shifter roles and takeovers. Not that I fucking understand it, either." He scrubbed his face. He would just have to protect her from such violence. *Like I did before?* He cussed at himself for exposing her to such a horrendous event.

"Hey. That's in the past. We're moving forward. Already made some big leaps." Jacques rested his hand on Max's shoulder. "You're the best friend a guy could ask for. My right hand man. But, you can't keep tearing yourself up like this."

"I'm—"

"Go to her. Talk to her. Work it out." Jacques squeezed lightly. "She's good for you. If you can't get her to come back, then I'll understand why you're staying with her."

Max's mouth dropped open but no words came forth.

Jacques met his eyes and slowly nodded. "Go to her."

"I'm not sure this is the time. We have so much left to do…"

"I can make it an order," Jacques threatened.

Max knew when to bow out. He held up his hands. "Okay. Okay. I'll take the plane, stop in, and check on her. What can it hurt?"

Chapter 16

Three days later

Max's stomach tied in knots as he pulled into a parking space in front of the bookstore. No other cars were close. Although not a total surprise due to the lack of customers in the recent past, his gut told him this time was different.

The entire trip, he'd rehearsed what to say. His answers to the litany of questions to come. The explanations of why she should come back with him— at least for a glimpse into his world. How could she decide if she didn't walk around the pack lands, hang out with him for a few days, and give him a chance? The words were sound. He only hoped Tara would be receptive to reason.

Stepping out of the car, he shut the door of his rental behind him, then stepped up to the entrance. Previous excitement at seeing Tara again plummeted to fear as he found the door locked, the room empty, and a "For Rent" sign posted in the front window.

Regret washed over him.

Shit. I'm too late.

She'd lost the business. Closed intentionally or forced didn't matter. It all had the same ending.

Where is she?

With a thousand possibilities, he whipped out his

phone and pulled up Brighton's number. Calling Tara wouldn't do any good. If she didn't tell him of the impending closing, she probably wouldn't be happy that he swung by unannounced, either. The last thing he wanted to do was piss her off before even saying 'hi'.

"Max. How's it going?" Brighton asked.

Max reminded himself to be civil. Just because Brighton promised to watch over Tara didn't mean he held responsibility for reporting every time she stubbed her toe. Although losing her shop ranked much higher than a bruise. "It's going. I'm standing outside the bookstore right now. It's closed."

"Been like that for a few days."

"Damn. I knew she was teetering. If she'd only have let me help."

"I know. I offered. Rose offered. She refused us all. Had a big sale, locked the doors, and handed the keys back to her landlady."

And you didn't think to let me know? Max bit back his frustration with Brighton and the whole situation. "Where is she now?" Max rocked his weight from one side to the next awaiting the answer.

"She took a job at Dr. Kendall's office."

Max wracked his brain. "Dr. Kendall?"

"The local vet. Chelsea, the receptionist, is on vacation. Tara is filling in for her."

That's something. Max blew out a long breath in relief. She hadn't run. Though, if she did, he'd track her down. He had the knack and the nose for doing just that.

Unable to recall the exact location, he simply asked. "Okay. Where's the office?"

"Harris and Timberline."

283

"Thanks, buddy."

"No problem. Oh, Max?"

"Yeah?"

Brighton paused a second. "Tell me I don't have to worry about any more potential Throwback trash turning up to traumatize my mate."

A small grin appeared out of the blue. "No worries on that. Jacques has the pack firmly in hand. No more thugs or death squads."

"Better not be," Brighton grumbled. "And, Max?"

"Yeah?"

"She's vulnerable right now. Go easy on her," Brighton warned.

"It never occurred to me to do anything else," Max answered truthfully.

"Play nice with the pretty lady," Brighton instructed with a definite flare of amusement in his tone, then disconnected.

Such an alpha. Max shook his head, then jumped back into his rental car, entered the information into the GPS, and headed out.

A few minutes later, he entered the veterinary office, spied Tara sitting at the front desk, and paused.

Her beautiful brunette locks had been pulled back into a ponytail, contrasting well with the solid deep green oxford shirt she wore. She looked more radiant than he recalled. Perfection—except for one thing. A small frown creased her forehead and pushed her lips slightly downward.

He didn't have to wait long to figure out the reason.

"Callie. Let me have the pen."

A tubby calico cat stretched out across the large

desk calendar directly in front of Tara. Patches of black and orange stood out against a white blanket of fur. The black cap of the pen could barely be seen sticking up from under the cat's chest. Yellow eyes glared at Tara when she tried to tug the pen loose.

"Please?"

Tara almost touched the elusive object only for the cat to pin her ears and cuff Tara's hand—hard. No claws, no marks, and no blood. But the rebuff made no bones about it—Callie considered the pen her personal toy.

Tara scowled. "Listen here. That's the third pen you've stolen today. These aren't Easter eggs, I swear."

Callie appeared totally unconcerned with the obvious lack of writing implements remaining. Her lightly slapping tail warned of further action should Tara try to confiscate her prize.

Tension eased from Max as he watched the two rivals square off. He couldn't help but grin in amusement at Tara's patient manner as she lightly reproached the feline. A feline that most likely ruled the roost and didn't give a fig what Tara wanted.

So was the way with cats. At least in his experience.

"I don't think you're going to win. Might be easier to find another pen than to try to steal hers back. Safer, too."

Tara lifted her head, spied him, and recognition blossomed across her features. Her mouth dropped open as her eyes widened. "Max?"

"The one and only."

She beamed, peered over her shoulder, then hurried over to give him an enthusiastic hug.

He wrapped his arms around her, relishing the feel of holding her close once again. His heart kicked against his ribs and his world felt right.

Before he could do more than press a kiss to her crown, she stepped back.

"I can't believe you're here. How's things with the pack? Are you and Jacques getting things back on track? Are you okay? Any more fights?" She raked him with her gaze as if searching for injury.

"Whoa. Slow down." He wasn't sure what his reception might be but couldn't have written a better script. Her reaction was genuine. His senses collaborated and agreed. She felt as happy to see him as she appeared. Perhaps more so. Definitely matching him in excitement. "Everything is fine. The pack is on track and beginning to relax and thrive under Jacques's changes. I'm okay and no, I haven't had to fight to the death recently. Neither has anyone else."

"Excellent." Her smile remained, even as she dropped contact.

"I went by the store…"

Her grin evaporated and she grimaced.

He wanted to kick himself for ruining the good mood. "I'm sorry. I wish you'd have let me help."

She shook her head. "My business. My problem." She shrugged and pushed a wayward strand of hair out of her face. "Dr. Kendall was kind enough to let me fill in for Chelsea while she's on vacation." Relief carried in her tone.

He could imagine. As far as he knew, Tara didn't have any financial reserves. She'd put everything into the store and lost. His heart broke for her. Dreams made for excellent times but only if they succeeded.

Otherwise, they ushered in some serious emotional pain. A hint of that flashed into her pretty eyes.

"What time do you get off work?"

She blinked at him as if the change of topic took her off guard. "Five-ish."

He gave a quick nod. "I'll be back then."

Furrows of puzzlement appeared on her face. "What are you going to do?"

"For starters, take you out to dinner." He grinned at her.

Her shoulders lowered as if the tension abated. "You don't have to do that. Maybe it's not the best idea. You have your own life—"

"I want to." He shushed her before she could start on the litany of excuses why they couldn't be together. He meant to prove each and every one wrong. Later. First, he had to get her to agree to spend some time with her. Max flashed her a grin. "I *really* want to. Let me take you out. Please say yes?"

He waited with bated breath for her answer.

Emotions crossed her face before she smiled softly. "Well, okay, then. I'd like to have dinner with you."

Relief washed through him. "Excellent. Five it is."

****

Why did he have to come back? Tara blew out a breath as Max exited the front door. She couldn't contain her enthusiasm at seeing him again. Or, keep herself from studying his fine rear as he sauntered out. Yet, at the same time, she knew she was in for another bad heart break. How could she not? She loved the guy and he belonged elsewhere. Hard to get over such a thing when he appeared on her doorstep with a smile that launched butterflies in her stomach. She couldn't decline the sweet dinner invitation. While it might have been for the better, she just couldn't say no.

Just call me a glutton for punishment. Or a fool. Maybe both.

Seeing him made her day. Heck, her week. It had been the best thing to happen since he'd walked out after that horrible bloody battle at her house. His calls brightened her life but left her feeling hollow. Like she was standing outside a looking glass at a particularly beautiful and compelling perfection that remained untouchable.

How many times had she wanted to tell him the truth? To admit her feelings? Every single time, she reminded herself of the big picture. A picture she didn't fit into no matter how hard she'd try.

So, why is he here? She didn't delude herself to think she'd managed to slip her upended life past him. Forcing herself to sound happy might have worked, if he wasn't who and what he was. Still, she had to try.

Now, he appeared out of the blue, seemed thrilled to find her, and immediately asked her out. A dream come true, one of hers to be exact, except happily ever after didn't exist. Not in her world.

"Oh, God. What have I gotten myself into this time?"

"What? Having second thoughts about dinner with your one-time pet?" Dr. Kendall strode over.

Tara's mouth fell open. *Dang, he's light on his feet.* "Well…"

He shook his head. "You're smart. Brave, too. Not every human woman could handle a wolf shifter male. But, *you* can."

She swallowed at his complimentary words. "How

do you know for sure?"

"Let's see. You dragged an injured wolf into your car in the middle of a snowstorm and cared for him like a loved child. You brought him here, refused to leave his side, and watched over him with a protective glare that would do any momma grizzly proud." He smiled. "Love knows no bounds."

"Uh, huh. So far those old sayings are batting zero for me."

"Then take an old man's advice. Give him a chance. He came all the way from Oregon just to see you. Talk to him. Spend some time with him. Let him show you how it can be between a shifter and his woman."

"How do I know if it's right?"

His eyes twinkled with amusement. "No little bird learned how to fly by sitting in the safety of the nest." Dr. Kendall spun around and walked off, only to stop a few feet later. "The bird that doesn't leave the nest doesn't find food, water, or a mate." With those words he disappeared through the door to the back.

"What if she's afraid of heights?" she mumbled to herself.

When no answer came, she focused back on her work. Or tried to. Every little bit she lifted her gaze to the front door as if expecting Max to reappear, though the clock hadn't come close to five.

Just admit it. The heart wants what the heart wants. And mine wants Max.

Before she could extrapolate further, a client walked in, pulling her attention away from the upcoming evening.

Two hours later, she took the first bite of her

alfredo, closed her eyes, and sighed in bliss.
.s wonderful." She opened her eyes again to find
. staring at her with a bemused expression on his
.e and a spark in his eyes.

"You said it was good," he reminded her.

Tara nodded. "Everything here has always been delicious. I haven't been in a long time, but it's never disappointed me yet." She forked another bite. "Thank you again for bringing me here."

"My pleasure." He took a mouthful of steak, chewed, and grinned. "Excellent."

"Yep." She took a drink. "So, you said things were going well back home?" She dared not say 'in the pack' and risk someone eavesdropping and catching onto the secret.

"Very well. People were ready for a change. Embraced it. Welcomed us back with open arms. Already they seem happier and optimistic. Some are still leery, but they'll come around."

"That's great. Just what they've needed all along. And, they have you and Jacques to thank for it."

Max continued eating in silence.

She got the impression he was through talking about the subject—whether because they were in public or because he didn't care for the praise, she didn't quite know. No matter. She could always take a hint.

"They're calling for another snowstorm starting Sunday. Feet of snow this time." Over the years, she'd been through more than one blizzard. Her little car couldn't make it until the roads were plowed. Sometimes that took a few days.

At least this time I don't have anywhere pressing to go. The sad thought dampened her spirits.

Max met her eyes, his eyebrows furrowed. "How long do you have to fill in for the receptionist?"

"Just until tomorrow. Dr. Kendall only works every other Saturday. This coming one is his scheduled one off."

"Then what are you planning to do?"

She chased a noodle around her plate. "I haven't gotten that far, yet."

He opened his mouth, then closed it as the waitress appeared at their side. "Would you two like anything else? Dessert perhaps?"

Tara shook her head. "No thanks."

Max glanced at the display in the center of the table, advertising the specials for the week. "How about the chocolate cake to go?"

The waitress nodded and smiled. "I'll get that right out to you."

"I thought chocolate was toxic to canines?" she asked in a hushed whisper, unable to keep the silly question contained.

He shoveled in the last of his meal and swallowed. "There are a few important differences."

"Do tell."

"How about I show you instead?"

Tara's breath caught. The sultry sparks in his eyes and the flaring of his nostrils gave her all the clues she needed to pick up on his train of thought. Ordinarily, she'd be offended if a date wanted to hurry back to her house for a romp in the hay. Max was different. She'd missed him and everything he brought to the table. Including the best sex of her life.

Not smart, Tara. He's just going to rush off again. Sleeping with him now will only hurt more later.

The logic had her joining in the play but determined to not cross into the line of nudity. No way could she resist the temptation a naked Max offered. Better to keep the clothes on and focus on friendship. Companionship. And brace herself for the parting sure to come.

"Too much, too fast, huh?"

She took a long drink before answering with the absolute truth. "I'm a little off-balance right now. No need to murky the waters any further."

"Fair enough." He wiped his hand on the napkin, then took her hand in his. "No pressure. I'm here if you want me. If you don't, you only have to say so."

If only she had the courage to do just that it might prove easier in the end. Instead, she found herself holding tight to his hand, lest he stand and walk out of her life forever. "Don't go. Not yet."

A relieved smile appeared on his lips. "You'll have to chase me away with a broom."

"Or a dog collar and leash?" she asked.

He chuckled. "That I can probably handle. It's the dog food that would do it." He shuddered dramatically.

She giggled. "Good thing I donated it to the animal shelter, then."

"Nice of you."

"I try to be now and again."

"You're the kindest person I've ever known." He stared over at her with a look of appreciation and wonder, sweetness and longing.

Her heart melted.

How can I let him go away again?
I can't. Not without a fight.

Chapter 17

Max placed the cake on the countertop, noticing the cardboard box on the table as he did so. "What's this?"

"The clothes you forgot to take with you." Tara draped her jacket over the back of one of the chairs.

Max whooshed out air as if he'd been kicked by a mule. Felt like it, too.

"In the bottom of the box are the books I kept for you. From the erotica section." Tara grinned wickedly at him.

Relieved, he drew in a deep breath. She wasn't trying to erase him from her life after all. Just collecting his things for when he returned. Not the best news, but not the worst, either. A pile of mail caught his eye. Her credit card bill sat on the top of the stack—unopened. He'd get her to open it, declare the amount, and pay her. After all, he'd promised. She didn't need to bear the burden of his expenses. Not when he had his identity cards and accounts back.

"Thank you. I didn't quite finish that one. Must say, it did hold my interest."

She snorted. "I could tell." She made her way to the bedroom presumably to change out of her work clothes.

He scented the air, finding only her particular aroma. His lingered faintly. *I'll have to change that.* At least she hadn't had any male suitors over. Though, if she did, he had no grounds for protest. They hadn't really discussed plans or feelings before he left. Just gave in to their desires in the heat of the moment. Words didn't seem important then. They sure did now.

Speaking of having men over... "Ever going to tell me the story about those candy striped condoms?"

Tara returned dressed in jeans and a sweatshirt. White socks covered her feet. She smirked. "Probably not."

He rolled his eyes. "Tease."

"Yep." She plopped down on the couch and patted the cushion next to her. "To be honest, it's not that exciting of a story."

"So, tell me already." He sat next to her, swiveling to be able to watch her as she spoke.

"I won a door prize at a New Year's Eve party. Those were it."

He grinned. "Nice gift."

She snorted. "I would rather have won the big screen TV."

"Hey, free is always good."

"True." She pulled the scrunchie from her hair, letting the locks fall free. They kept a little waviness as they hung down past her shoulders.

He picked up the scent of her floral shampoo even as he enjoyed the light illuminating the deep color of her brunette hair. As much as he wanted to run his hands through the richness, he resisted. They had some things to discuss and he didn't want to get sidetracked just yet.

"I was meaning to ask, was your home still standing?" She peered over at him.

"Surprisingly, yes. My wallet was still on the floor, in my jeans pocket, where I'd left it, too."

"Wow. You have some honest and trustworthy people in that pack. Around here, I doubt that wallet would have lasted more than a day or two."

He nodded. *Another notch in the favor of her coming back with me.* "I called Brighton's man and told him not to bother, that I'd recovered everything. I was pretty damn relieved to see it."

"I bet. Your life literally back in your hands." She bent one knee and turned to face him. "I'm so glad for you. After everything you've been through, it sounds like things have not only come full circle but they're working out as they should have."

"Except for one thing."

She tilted her head. "What's that?"

"You."

Tara picked at her jeans and found the couch enthralling. "Max…"

"Why didn't you let me know that you were closing the bookstore?" He knew her pride bore responsibility. Still, that wasn't reason enough in his opinion.

She crossed her arms over her chest and lifted her gaze. "I lost my business. It's not like I broke my leg."

"Either one is reason to call," he insisted. When she said nothing, he continued. "I'd gladly buy that strip mall, give you the rent money. Hell, I still intend pay you back for all that you spent on me. That would have made a difference. Whatever it takes you to get your shop back, I'm up for."

"I don't want charity." Her voice carried steely determination.

"Damn it, it's not charity." He waited a beat, reined in his frustration, and started again. "Tara. You said it yourself that place was your dream. I've got the means to give it to you. Why won't you let me help?"

She regained her feet and started pacing the living room. "I need to do it myself. To prove that I can or can't. Turns out I can't. Not here. Not with this economy. It's okay. Really. I've come to terms with it." Pausing, she met his eyes. "Besides, there are other things I want out of life. This isn't the end all."

He considered her words and her antsy state. "What other things?"

She halted and blew out a breath. "I…" She threw her arms up in the air. "I don't…"

Max stood and walked over to her, taking her hands in his. He willed her to look at him. "Where's the courageous woman who took a shovel to a ferocious wolf shifter in the middle of battle to try and save me?"

"She turned into an ostrich and stuck her head in the sand," she sassed as she peeked up at him from under her lashes.

He chuckled. "I don't believe that. Hiding for the moment, maybe, but you can't deny what's underneath." Leaning in, he nuzzled her cheek. "Come on, Tara. Tell me what you want."

She blew out a breath. "If you…"

"Yes?" he prodded.

"Maybe you could take me back with you. Just for a day or so. To see what it's like." She blurted out the request as if she'd lose her nerve if she didn't.

He smiled down at her, thrilled she'd asked. "It would be my pleasure."

She searched his face. "I can't promise anything."

"I know." He nodded, then kissed the tip of her nose. "You can't promise tomorrow, and that's okay. So, we'll take this one day at a time."

The tension ebbed from her body. "Thank you for understanding."

"Thank you for giving me a chance." He hugged her close, then meshed their lips, kissing her with gentleness. "I missed you."

She grinned. "I missed you more." She licked his bottom lip, then drew it in to suck on.

He found the caress erotically stimulating. "Mmm." Just when he started to take over and deepen the kiss, she put a little space between them. Curious, he tried to read the emotions in her expression, then recalled what had happened back at the vet's office. *Too much, too soon.* They'd both been on a rollercoaster ride lately and needed some time to settle back down to whatever the new normal would be. "Ready for some cake?"

She nodded. "I think that's a great idea."

"Yep. We can talk about when you want to visit. I know you have to finish your job at the clinic tomorrow. If there's a storm coming in on Sunday, then we have a day or so to work with." He pulled the covering from the treat while she grabbed bowls and utensils. "Or, if you want to wait until after the storm, that's fine too."

She handed him a butter knife, then placed the bowls next to him before getting out the milk and setting it and the forks on the table. "I think Friday night or Saturday morning would be fine. I'm sure you're eager to get back."

He sliced two big pieces, sliding them into the

bowls, then carried them over. After sitting, he watched as Tara collected two glasses from the cabinet, filled them with milk, and took her seat. "There's no rush. Jacques has things well in hand." He took a bite and pondered the topic at hand. "He ordered me to come back."

Her eyebrows shot up. "Ordered? Were you really bad?"

He chuckled. "Not at all. Just moping around and cranky. Seems I missed a certain person and became a bear to deal with because of it."

"Interesting." Her eyes lit up as she tasted the dessert. "So, tell me about the pack. Everything I need to know before I visit. Who's who and all that."

"You already know Jacques. Carmen is there now. You'll love her. She's a mischief maker in the nicest way."

"A couple of allies. Always a good thing."

He caught the glimpse of concern flash through her eyes and recalled the last time she ran into members of the Throwback Pack. "We're not like that. Blood, guts, and violence. Not anymore. Things are stabilized. People are more upbeat. Happier. We're getting the infrastructure and services up and going again. No more dictatorship. Not ever."

Her face scrunched. "What about all that alpha business? I thought he ruled?"

Max shook his head. "Yes and no. In Jacques's mind, he's like a president or chief. He's the voice of the people and represents them. Protects them. But, he depends on others to be his advisors, to work together for the good of the pack." He took another bite and swallowed. "The plan is to lead the pack toward a democracy and give them reason to believe. To want Jacques to continue as the leader."

"Big happenings in a short amount of time." She took a long drink.

"It was time. Like I said before, we'd set the ground work last time. When we returned, it was easier to refer back to that. Much easier. Honestly, I think they were relieved. Garrison was a prick to pretty much everyone. People lived in fear. With that cloud gone, they see the possibilities." Max finished his cake all the while keeping an eye on Tara. She'd gathered up enough gumption to ask about going to visit his pack but that didn't mean her worries were over. They wouldn't go completely away until she could see for herself what the people were like. To experience the good that shifters could do and be.

She'll see and learn. I'll make it happen.

Because his heart hung in the balance.

"What happens if I can't...?" She bit her lower lip.

He took her hand in his, warming her chilled fingers. "We'll figure it out. Your happiness is important. Very important." He squeezed her hand. "Just keep an open mind and give me the chance to prove things to you. That's all I ask."

She nodded. "I'll do my best."

He leaned over enough to nuzzle her cheek, then lick her earlobe. She squealed and giggled.

His heart sang at the musical sound.

It'll work out. It just has to. Even if I have to resign my post and move back here with her. No way am I leaving her behind ever again.

Chapter 18

"Max? I'm home." Tara called as she entered the house through the garage door. Her final day at the vet clinic sped by due to the sheer busyness of the day. She didn't complain, not when it netted her a decent paycheck which would go a long way in helping pay her bills. Besides, it kept her too busy to fret about her upcoming visit to the pack and what that meant for her and Max in the long run.

The aroma of delicious food caught her attention. Curious, she walked into the kitchen and peeked into the oven. A cobbler bubbled inside. On the stove she found a hearty stew, also hot and ready to eat, with big chunks of beef, potatoes, tomatoes, peas, and green beans. It all smelled heavenly.

"Hey there. Welcome home." Max strode down the hall wearing his typical jeans and a loose sweatshirt. White socks covered his feet.

She smiled at the sight. Never would she tire of seeing the man coming to her, with a grin on his face.

He closed the distance, pulled her in his arms, and kissed her like there was no tomorrow.

Tara met him with enthusiasm. They'd shared the bed last night but hadn't done more than hold one another. She was still uncertain about everything with his sudden appearance and her tumultuous feelings on the matter. Snuggling fit the mood and felt pretty darn good.

He slowly pulled back, rubbing her back as he did so.

Her stomach flip-flopped. "This is a really nice thing to come home to."

"Plenty more where that came from." His smile carried up to his eyes. "After you eat. I know you must be starved."

"I am actually." She gestured toward the food. "Thank you for all this."

"I wanted to treat you. Figured you'd be hungry when you got home." He picked up a spoon and stirred the stew, then turned down the heat. A timer went off. After turning the oven off, he slipped on some mitts, then collected the cobbler, placing it on the unused burners to cool.

"Wow." Impressed, Tara lifted up in order to kiss him on the cheek. "Thank you."

He smiled softly. "You're very welcome." He glanced down at her clothes. "Want to take a shower before dinner? Looks like you've got some serious hair issues going on."

"What? Oh, yeah. It was a crazy day and all kinds of furry things wanted to get up close and personal." She started to wipe at her shirt, then decided not to. After all, it would be easier to toss it in the washer rather than try to sweep it up. "I think I might take that shower after all."

He nudged her along. "Go ahead. I'll keep things hot for you."

"Hot? Even you?" The teasing words slipped out.

"Go." He patted her on the behind with a bark of laughter.

She giggled, made her way down the hall, and into the bathroom. There, she hurriedly stripped down, and jumped in the shower. As the warm water ran over her, she couldn't rein in her wayward thoughts, all revolving around Max, particularly of him nude and covering her for a long, delightful trip to ecstasy.

Not about to linger, Tara quickly finished washing, including her hair, toweled down, then slipped into some sweats and a matching shirt. Her hair left damp spots on the gray shirt but she didn't care. It would dry soon enough. Until then, she had a delicious looking meal waiting for her. And, Max, too.

Time to live in the moment, Tara girl. Enjoy the present. Let the future take care of itself. With those words of wisdom in hand, she left the bathroom and returned to the kitchen.

Max glanced up from dishing up healthy portions of stew into two bowls. "That didn't take long."

She shrugged and grinned. "All that nonsense about women taking forever in the shower doesn't take into account when there's a wonderful meal on the table waiting for her."

"I'll have to remember that." Max set the bowls on the table, and filled her glass with tea, then his, before taking his seat.

Tara picked up her spoon and dug in, blowing on the bite before placing it in her mouth. The slightly spicy taste complemented the fare completely. She swallowed, amazed that a simple stew could be so delicious. "There's something different."

"You like it?"

"Very much so. What is it?"

Max blew on his food. "Chef's secret."

She grinned. "Not going to tell me?"

"Nope."

She pursed her lips. "Even if I torture it out of you?"

His eyes lit up and his chest expanded. "Do your worst."

She laughed, feeling more carefree than she had in a while. *Maybe I should have focused on the present before, saved myself a lot of worry and grief.* While unrealistic, it served as a reminder that sometimes she had to let things go—even if just for a few hours.

Tara stopped thinking and started eating in earnest. Indeed, she was hungry and couldn't get enough of the delicious food.

A few minutes later, she finished her meal and carried her dishes to the sink. "I think I'll go ahead and pack."

Max looked over at her. "If you want to. But, like I said, we can stay here longer if you like. I'm in no hurry."

Tara shook her head. "I think with this big storm coming, it's better to get out while the getting is good. If not, it might be a while before we can dig out enough to leave."

"Okay." He placed his dirty dishes in with hers. "Need some help?"

She grinned. "Nah. I think I can handle it." Heading back to the bedroom, she dug out the old suitcase that she hadn't used in years, wiped off the dust, placed it on the foot of the bed, and unzipped the top. Starting with underwear, she began to load it.

"How long are you planning on being gone?" Max asked from the doorway.

Tara filtered through her closet, trying to decide which shirts to take with her. "I don't know. A few days, I guess." She hadn't really thought that far. The whole trip was one of those play-it-by-ear things in her opinion.

"My cabin is modern enough to have a washer and dryer," Max said tongue-in-cheek. "In case you need to clean things you won't have to put them through a wringer or hang them outside to dry."

She glanced over at him and grinned. "Never would I accuse you of being less than modern."

"Uh, huh."

"Sexy and mischievous, yes. Backwoods, no. Despite being a part-time wolf."

"I'll take it." Max smiled playfully.

Settling on some sweatshirts and a sweater or two, she tugged them off the hangers and folded them. After placing them in the carrier, she moved to the dresser across the room in search of jeans.

She deposited three pairs in the suitcase, then headed toward the laundry room for a couple more.

They were clean and folded, just hadn't been put away just yet. With those in hand, she returned to the bedroom, passing by Max standing in the doorway just as he was before.

She dropped the jeans on top of the others, then started to make more room when she noticed something out of place. In the spot she'd left for them sat a box. "What's this?" She pulled it out and held it up, quickly realizing what she held in her hands—the box of condoms Max had purchased before he'd left.

Max glanced over from across the room, spied what she held up, and grinned wickedly. "Let's just say

I'm prepared for anything."

She rolled her eyes and stood. Max was sex on a stick and seemingly horny day in and day out. Not that she minded. Most of the time she was right there with him. "Uh, huh." Like now, she could almost hear the humming of the electricity in the room between them. It made her heart pick up speed and caused a needy ache down below.

He stalked her. "I'll let you in on a little shifter secret."

Curiosity was piqued as she watched him draw near, his graceful power evident in every small movement. She knew what those clothes hid and couldn't help but wish them away. "What's that?"

"Our DNA gives us some major advantages in some ways. We don't get diseases, especially sexually transmitted ones."

Her mouth fell open. "Nothing? Not even…" She trailed off as she searched for the right terminology.

He shook his head. "Nope. Nothing." Stopping directly in front of her, he snagged the box from her loose grip. If he took a deep breath, their chests would touch.

She could feel his body heat from the closeness. Sexual tension escalated, tempting her to reach out and touch, to strip off his clothes, to run her hands over his primed body, and hop on board for a hard ride.

"We don't need condoms."

Her rational brain kicked in despite the grand distraction he created. "What about pregnancy? As much as you guys seem to like sex, I'm sure that happens fairly often."

Max grinned. "Wolf shifter here, of course we like

sex, and lots of it. But overall, we're not a fertile bunch. Randy, yes. Prolific, no. We don't carry disease, so you don't have to worry about that. The chances of pregnancy exist, certainly, but they aren't great odds."

"Interesting." She bit her lower lip. The urge became almost unbearable. She clenched and released her hands a couple of times, then went with a little playfulness. Who said foreplay was a lost art? Max had it down to a science—even if they happened to be having a pretty serious discussion at the same time.

"Meaning?"

Do I trust him? Believe him? Absolutely. Tara tilted her head and peeked up coyly from under her eyelashes. *Time to take a big step.* "I have a little surprise, too." She gestured to the inside of her upper arm. A small scar served as proof along with a tiny bump. "I've got the pregnancy part covered. Got the hormone implant a couple of years ago. I thought I'd found the guy that I wanted to be with. It fell apart, but I didn't see the need to get it removed."

Max's nostrils flared as he took in the information.

She could have sworn his body temperature cranked up a few notches judging by the flares of sensual desire in his dark eyes.

"How long does it last?"

"Five years or so."

Max beamed. "So…?"

Tara grabbed the box of condoms out of his hand and tossed them over her shoulder. Then, she wrapped her arms around his neck. "I'd say we're good to go. For about another three years."

Max laughed, then sealed his lips over hers. He picked her up, swung her around, and held her up in a cradle position.

She looped her arms around his neck. "Why, sir, what big teeth you have."

Max snorted. "I've got something else that's big, too. Really big. Something that you'll like."

She blinked innocently. "Your hands?"

"Nope. Try again."

"Your feet?" She barely contained her laughter, thoroughly enjoying their teasing.

"Technically, yes, but that's not what I'm talking about." He set her on her feet, took her hand in his, and pressed it against the bulge in his jeans.

Her eyes widened. "*Oh*. You mean that."

He bent down, found her earlobe with his mouth, and laved the area.

She giggled.

"Yes, silly woman. I mean there. That's what you do to me. Make me hard. Really hard. And so turned on that I can't think of anything else other than the amazing feeling of you coming under me."

Those words certainly did the trick. She sucked in much needed air, felt her stomach somersault, and decided she'd never wanted anything as much as she wanted him in that very moment. "I'm all yours."

With a low growl, he started undressing her, first by tugging her shirt over her head. He lowered his head and kissed a path from her neck down to her breasts. After unsnapping her bra, he feasted on first one side then the other. She held his head in place, needing more of the blissful sensations he created from his attentions.

Needing to touch, she tugged at his shirt. He lifted his head long enough for her to pull it off and cast it aside. She focused on his jeans next, managing to get the zipper down, then finally the button undone. She shoved at the unwanted denim.

Max hooked his fingers in her waistline, and pushed. She did the rest, stepping out of the puddle as he did the same.

Her gaze locked on his gorgeous manhood, jutting out, with a small bead of moisture leaking from the tip. She licked her lips, excited, as she witnessed the evidence of his desire for her. Forcing her attention higher, her gaze raked his body. Roped muscles snapped and extended with every motion of his large frame from his shoulders downward to his six-pack abs. The man could put a fitness model to shame.

Never would she tire of seeing him naked.

His eyes drew her attention. The darkness which sparkled with immense need. The way he stared at her as if she alone could set his blood afire and send them both soaring to the heavens. "I want you."

"And I need to taste you." The deep, gravelly sound of his voice and that sexy admission added more to her already heightened state.

He grabbed the suitcase and dropped it onto the floor, the packed clothing unruffled in the least.

Heat rushed over her. "Only if I can do the same."

"My turn first." His wolfish grin stole another chunk of her heart. "Up you go." He lifted her off her feet then deposited her near the center of the bed.

She watched as he crawled toward her, settling himself between her thighs. "Spread for me."

Without hesitation she did so.

He reached out, ran his hand over her abdomen, then lower, dipping between her folds before centering on the entrance. "So wet." He pressed a finger inside.

"Wet. Hot. And tight." Stretching out, he lowered himself to the mattress. "Now, I'm going to feast on you."

Tara held her breath, felt the first brush of his tongue over her sensitive nub, and jerked. Like a small bolt of lightning hit her square. No one had ever done such a thing to her before and she reveled in the brilliant pleasure Max bestowed on her.

He lapped, long caresses while adding another finger to join the first.

Pressure and searing sensations combined to ratchet her up on a fast track to the pinnacle. She grasped the bedsheets and writhed, a willing captive under his gentle plundering. "Oh, yes. Max. Oh."

He drew the nub with his lips, adding light suction.

Tara saw stars. Her body tightened and she could barely catch her breath.

"Almost there. You're soaking my hand, honey. So responsive. So beautiful. Let me watch you come." His warm breath on her sensitive areas added another dimension to his teasing.

His encouragement pushed her that much closer.

Max flicked her clit with his tongue. Over and over, a gentle rain tapping where she needed his caress the most. Still, his fingers worked inside her, spreading, thrusting, pressing on a spot that made her absolutely wild.

Her muscles drew even tighter—so tight she feared she'd break. That is, if she could have thought of anything but the way Max played her body like a finely tuned instrument and reaching the top before freefalling. "Max." She gritted out his name as she sat on the very precipice.

"That's it, Tara. Come for me." The near growl of his command added another element of spice.

He latched onto her nub, laved and sipped.

With a cry, Tara hit the crest on a headlong rush.

The next instant, Max covered her, sinking fully into her.

The exquisite feeling drove Tara higher and extended the bliss.

"Damn, you feel good."

Tara managed to open her eyes, meet Max's gaze, and wrap her hands around his neck. "You, sir, make me wanton."

He grinned wide. "Then I'm doing something right." He lowered his lips to hers, kissing her with leashed passion, rocking their bodies together as he eased her down from the intense climax.

She sighed, trailed her fingers down his back, then squeezed his rear.

He groaned and pressed his lips against her neck. "Can you take more?"

"Yes, oh, yes." She had no doubt. Anything less would be a disappointment.

He lifted enough to stare down at her. "It might get rough."

She smiled with feminine confidence and knowledge. "Bring it on."

His jaw tightened, nostrils flared, and eyes narrowed.

Whether from trying to regain his control or from the immense delight of her challenge, she couldn't say. Just that in the next moment, he pulled out, flipped her over, and helped her onto her knees. The new position, highly erotic and primal, sent another white hot bolt through her.

He rubbed her bottom, ran his fingers along her slit, then pressed the tip of his shaft to her opening. "Show me you want me."

Tara rocked back against him. "Take me, Max. Please. Take me."

Without hesitation, he sank deep.

She grunted at the fullness.

He kept going. Deeper and deeper yet. Finally, he stopped and began to brush her sides and press his lips against her spine. "Okay?"

"Yes." She drew in air and adjusted her stance. The small movements added a saucy zing to where they connected.

"If I get too rough, tell me."

Those words added a hint of danger and a whole lot of hunger to Tara. As turned on as she was, she knew she wouldn't deter him. Encourage? Yes. Demand? Probably. Tell him no? Not happening.

Languidly, he began to move. Long, sure strokes that brushed up against her walls, leaving sizzling pleasure in their wake.

Tara bowed her back, pressing her pelvis toward him in an effort to get closer, to take more. She widened her stance and braced herself as Max picked up the intensity with shorter, deep jabs which rocked her world in the most delightful ways.

He reached under her, molded a breast, and lightly tweaked the nipple.

Tara bit back a moan at the dual sensations. When his fingers found her aching clit, she could no longer hold back the sounds of her excitement.

"Damn, Tara. Those sweet cries are so hot. So

damn hot."

And his words were doing the same for her.

He fluttered over the area, jacking up Tara's arousal by leaps and bounds. Between his talented fingers and his hard cock, she could only try to keep her balance and revel in the glory of Max. An eager recipient of his hardcore lovemaking that seared her to her very bones.

Every so lightly, he pinched her nub.

Tara jerked at the slightly rough caress. She threw her head back and gasped.

Max poured more power into his movements. Mixing up the speed and depth of his strokes.

"Oh my god." The variety shook Tara, driving her further and higher. She lowered her upper body, needing the stability of the cool linen against the fiery pleasure racing through her.

Max wrapped an arm around her middle, using the other to brace himself. His chest rubbed her back, then he thrust at a new angle. One that took her breath away.

She whimpered and cried out, shoved back and met each and every thrust. Hunger didn't begin to describe the incredible need he'd created in her. She had to have more. Anything. Everything. Nothing was enough. "More. Max, please."

He obligated with a grunt, an increased paced, then a low moan. The slapping of their bodies and loudness of their breathing filled the room. The unmistakable scent of sex carried in the air, a testament to the wildness he brought out in her.

She heard a near wail, belatedly realizing it was her. She couldn't help the sounds which tumbled out on their own accord. Primal. Erotic. The words were pale in comparison to the way she gyrated under him, stole every ounce of pleasure, and gave it back in spades.

Each growl and every groan from Max, every single touch edged her that much closer. Her world narrowed down to the place where their bodies met and Max's near frantic thrusts. She whimpered with a need so great it consumed her.

Still he maintained the pace, stroking in and out. Over and over again.

"Tara. Come with me. Just let go and come with me." The command came across as more of a growl than anything.

Yet, she understood perfectly.

Everything she had, she let loose. Forgot inhibitions, forgot insecurities. Nothing mattered more in that moment than fulfilling Max's request.

The knot began to swell, scraping on her inner walls as Max stroked in, out, then in again. Pressure followed, then a flare of heat so powerful Tara cried out. Locked together, she rode the tides, with Max covering her back, directing their course. Wave after wave rolled over her, sustaining her ecstasy at previously unreached levels. She gasped for breath, clutched the linens, and simply held on, trusting Max to hold her through it all as she launched into a soaring freefall.

The climax had faded to small tremors when Max, using the strong band of his arm around her middle, gently and carefully eased her onto her side, their bodies still joined.

He rained kisses over her back and shoulders, still holding her close. "You okay?"

"Mmm." She didn't have the strength to do more

than exchange oxygen and carbon dioxide.

"Tara?" Concern laced his voice.

She cracked her eyes open and wiggled her rear against him. "If that's what shifter sex is all about, sign me up."

Max chuckled. He wrapped her in his embrace and pulled the covers over them. "Rest, sweetheart. I've got you."

She didn't need more encouragement than that. Closing her eyes, she drifted into a doze, thoroughly happy with her man.

Chapter 19

"Welcome to Throwback Pack." Max took Tara's hand and led her from the vehicle to his back patio. "And to my house."

I can't believe I'm on the grounds belonging to a shifter wolf pack. The setting seemed similar to some of the fiction works she used to carry in her store. The heroine traipsing along and finding herself surrounded by strange creatures.

Strange creatures, indeed. Sexy ones, too. At least Max.

She looked away from him and took in the sight of a good-sized wooden cabin sitting on the edge of the woods. It reminded her of home. Except her home wasn't made out of expensive logs or happened to be part of a whole complex of houses that seemed to spring up from clearings. While the two places were approximately the same size, this one had a whole natural feel. Blending in with nature, so to speak. The overhanging roof allowed for a shady spot to sit, eat, read, or just enjoy the beautiful day. She could only imagine how nice the inside looked.

The entire area was clean, without overgrown brush, and several trails took off through the trees in different directions. Even the temperatures were nice. Much better than the frigidness of Minnesota right now.

The long, winding road that brought them here

promised special things to come, if one had the gumption and permission to venture through to the center. She'd glimpsed other houses along the side road, each with a driveway attaching to the blacktop. The setup, from what she could tell, took a commonplace route. Cabins, nicely spaced for privacy, lined both sides of a large clearing. What appeared to be businesses were downhill from those. Trails led in all directions—some simple dirt paths, others elaborate brick sidewalks. To the left, trees dotted the landscape, mostly evergreens, but with plenty of deciduous trees, now just starting to blossom, thrown in. The natural screen prevented her from seeing much, only a peek, but enough to allude to other homes up and around.

No huge mansions or strip malls existed, at least in her line of vision. Instead, tidy, well cared for homes and a couple of stores stood proudly against the forest background. They spoke of pride and community without greed or lordship over others.

Considering the horrible men that showed up at her house and tried to snuff out Max and Jacques's lives, Tara was surprised. She'd expected a castle with peasants living all around. Instead, she'd stumbled across a nice little refuge where equality seemed to be the norm.

Tara looked around some more before deciding the center of the village lay below the surrounding residential areas where she stood on the far edge. Max's house sat just beyond the outskirts of those, more solitary and off to the side. Like a middle ground before the rural section began.

The pack lands were everything she pictured a rustic resort in the mountains would look like. Blending into the landscape, serene, and still with a modern edge to make roughing it easy. All she needed was a hot tub and an ice cream shop and she'd be in heaven.

"Well? What do you think?"

Okay. Who needs the tub and ice cream when Max was around? He makes for a fine dessert. She knew that from personal experience.

Good grief. I'm back to being a walking hormone. Belatedly, she wondered if hanging around shifters made her go into heat. If so, she was going to bean him with a frying pan and soon.

"Tara?"

Her name being called joggled her back to his question. "Wow. This is nice." Her nerves had been on edge since she exited the plane about an hour ago and climbed into the black SUV with blood red trim pack vehicle. She easily recognized it from the one that carried the threat of violence and death to her very doorstep. Yet, once she had a chance to stretch her legs, her antsy-ness seemed to ease. For the moment. She had no illusions about facing the other shifters. Call it a survival instinct. A human amongst wolf shifters felt all too like Little Red Riding Hood. And she had no intention of becoming anyone's dinner.

The trip had been incredible, thus far. Max flew the small plane like a pro, even taking a longer route to show her some sights like the Great Lakes and Rocky Mountains. The leisurely diversions were something she'd never had a chance to do—at least from the air— and made for a wonderful morning. Even better, she sat in the co-pilot's seat and experienced them with Max. Now, she'd arrived at his beautiful homeland and couldn't be more excited to start the next leg of this particular adventure.

Max smiled warmly at her. "Let's drop off your bag first then I'll give you a big tour of the grounds."

"Okay." Tara retraced her steps, taking her luggage in hand as Max shouldered the cardboard box filled with his books and clothes from her house. She'd noticed the odd expression on his face when he'd seen everything so tidily packed for him and realized he thought he'd been kicked out. Just the opposite. But, confessions were never her strong suit. She battled with the need to admit her love and sentence herself to a life filled with anxiety and dread, fearing when the next up and coming male would dethrone Jacques and banish the pack back to the Dark Ages. Sure, she could insist on staying back in Minnesota. Max might even agree. However, he'd never be happy. Too much of his life and dreams revolved around his home and the community there. To take him away would be like parting branches from the tree they grew from. The resulting tree couldn't live and thrive under such conditions. Neither could Max.

So, here I am. Spreading my wings and seeing if I can fly.

Her gut churned with anxiousness.

"Come on in." Max opened the back door and ushered her in. He placed his box on top of the kitchen counter.

Tara took a few steps inside, marveling at the vaulted ceiling with bare wooden beams darkly stained, which gave the front room an open and airy quality. Furniture, in the form of a couch, and a couple of recliners faced a large screen television resting on the far wall. Natural hardwood floors held a glossy shine and went on as far as she could see. The kitchen had the usual appliances, all appeared fairly new, in black, which matched well with the dark wood theme of the cabinets. The lighter-colored granite counter caught her eye, as did the island with its own sink. "Amazing. Fancy." The kitchen drew her, promising ease of baking and plenty of options to experiment with tools she'd seen but never had the chance to test.

"Thanks. Since my cooking consists of boxed meals, I don't use it to its full capabilities. Not like a person who loves to cook or bake would."

She lowered her suitcase to the floor and traced the cool granite with her fingers. "It's beautiful."

Pride covered Max's face. "Ready to check out the rest of the house?"

"Yes." She followed him as he walked down a hall, pointing out bedrooms, bathrooms, laundry rooms, and storage areas as he went. Each one boasted of tasty décor and cleanliness. His bedroom, in particular, caught her interest. Definitely masculine, the color scheme worked with all hues of browns, from deepest dark chocolate to light tan. The bed, the comforter, the desk, and closet door all fit perfectly into the relaxing feel and warmth of the nature theme. "You have one talented decorator." Even the artwork on the wall lent itself to the overall subject with grand paintings of trees, prairies, and mountains, all in wooden frames. Each one appeared to be crafted from the mind and hand of a master.

"I didn't do too bad, if I do say so myself."

She swung around to stare at him. "You did all this?" She waved her hand to encompass more than just the room.

"Yep. Well, I didn't build the place. I just picked the floor plan I liked best, then found what I liked to go inside."

"You've definitely got an eye." The small tidbit impressed her. Just another piece of Max she didn't have a clue about. There were bound to be more and she couldn't wait to discover each and every one of them.

"Thanks. Jacques teases me that if I ever grew tired of politics, I could make a career out of interior design." His sheepish grin pulled on her heartstrings.

"I agree. Impressive." She smiled up at him. "You're full of surprises."

He inclined his head. "All good, I hope."

"Well..." She tapped her hand on her thigh. "I'll admit that you scared the crap out of me when you turned up nude in my kitchen and with Cotton gone missing." She cracked a smile. "But, that turned out just fine."

"If you miss Cotton, I can bring him back." He waggled his eyebrows.

"For a game of fetch? Sure."

He groaned dramatically.

She laughed. "Okay. Maybe not." Feeling more at home, she closed the distance between them and brushed a kiss across his chin. "What other surprises do you have in store for me?"

He grinned wickedly. "All kinds of things."

"Uh, huh." Her body heated with the spark of desire in his eyes. "I meant outside the bedroom. For now."

"That, too." He offered his arm. "If you're ready?"

"Ready as I'll ever be." She tried to breathe

through the increasing tension.

"Don't worry. It's going to be all right." His soothing tone quieted some of her anxiety as did his body heat emanating from his close proximity. "Just give them a chance. Give *me* a chance. If you aren't comfortable, just say something, and we'll go back to your place." Truth and promise carried in his words and tone.

She held onto that with firm conviction.

He led her down a path, through a nicely landscaped park area, and down the hill to a brick and mortar building. The light breeze played with her hair and added a slight chill. Nothing like she'd been having back home, though.

She glimpsed people here and there. Even a couple playing with their young son. Yet, none of them approached, waved, or anything. The fact didn't bode well. Still, she intended to give her best effort. Max deserved that.

Max opened the door of the building and ushered her in. "This is the main office. The administration building, if you will."

Tara's eyes adjusted pretty quickly, allowing her to see three smaller rooms, two facing one another, the third in the center and a bit farther back. Jacques presently occupied that one, staring at a computer screen.

He glanced over at their arrival. "Tara. So we meet again."

She returned his welcoming smile. "Jacques. I hear you've been quite busy since you left. Something about getting people in line and a democracy in place?"

He chuckled. "In a nutshell. Max has been a great

driving force of that. He's a people person, convincing everyone to give it a shot."

"A people person?" She glanced up at Max. "Really?"

Max shrugged.

"You're full of all kinds of wonders today." She recalled a time not too long ago where Cotton hid in the back of the bookstore, unwilling to mingle with the few customers that had appeared that day.

"He won't toot his own horn but he's just as responsible for this as I am." Jacques stood up and walked over. "I'm glad you decided to come. He's been moping around and getting on everyone's nerves with his bad attitude lately. I'm afraid more than one person has threatened to kick his ass. Good thing I'm smart, realized the issue, and sent him back." Jacques grinned ruefully at Max. "I'd just about had to see how high I can kick."

Max snorted.

Tara chuckled. "Sounds like a brotherly thing to do."

"Indeed." Jacques gestured toward the door. "Since you're here, would you like to meet Carmen?"

"Absolutely." Tara, in the company of Max and Jacques, began to relax a little more. The kidding around and bantering of the two large men helped alleviate some of her stress. She hoped the more she saw, the better off she'd be.

They didn't have to go far before Jacques held up his hand. His attention focused solely on a woman standing in an open area, staring at an old building. She turned her head this way and that as if trying to picture something special in the dilapidated wood.

Jacques silently moved forward.

"Jacques. If you think you're going to sneak up on me, think again."

"You take all the fun out of things." Jacques didn't sound the least bit upset. Instead, he wrapped the woman in his embrace, gave her a squeeze, then turned back to them. "Carmen, this is Tara."

Tara appraised the lady who stood about a head shorter than Jacques. Her short chestnut hair tended toward more reddish hues than brown, giving her a youthful and mischievous appearance. The twinkle in her brown eyes solidified the thought, at least in Tara's mind. Carmen wore jeans and a bright pink sweatshirt, nothing fancy, with an open heavy jacket to keep out the chill of the mid-afternoon air.

Carmen moved closer, a welcoming grin on her face. "It's so nice to finally meet you." She extended her hand.

Tara shook it firmly. "You, too. From what I gather you're keeping Jacques on his toes."

Carmen eyed the man in question. "A woman's gotta do what a woman's gotta do."

Tara laughed, immediately liking the petite Carmen. "You're not intimidated by him? Or any of them?"

Carmen shook her head. "I was raised in a pack. And, I'm a shifter, too."

"She rules the roost," Max stage whispered.

Jacques snorted.

Carmen elbowed him in the ribs.

Jacques grunted, rubbed the spot, then wrapped an arm around her middle. "You say that, but, truth be told, you can't get enough of me."

Carmen rolled her eyes. "We don't need to be giving these men any bigger heads than they already have." Carmen stepped forward, latched onto Tara's arm, and tugged her along. "Let's go for a short tour. Away from these troublesome guys. I'll show you the important things. Like the beauty salon and the best place to hang out and watch the moon rise."

Moon rise?

Tara glanced back, saw Max's grin, then willingly traipsed along. Not like she had much choice with the other woman's firm hold. "Ummm. You do know I'm human, right?" Tara thought she'd better set things straight from the get go.

"Yep. No mistaking your scent."

"I smell? Great."

Carmen tittered. "Not stink. You have your own unique aroma, but it's definitely human."

Tara sighed and confessed one of her fears. "I'm afraid that very thing will be a strike against me."

Carmen slowed her steps. "I imagine there's a lot of concerns on your mind. I had some of them when Jacques first brought me here. A pack in upheaval, with generations of former alphas slain in a bloody battle to the death. The new leadership trying to change the culture and bring the pack up to modern times. The instability of constant turmoil. Oh, yeah. I had my doubts."

Tara listened closely, understanding Carmen's words, for they echoed a few of the questions racing through her head. "What did you do?"

Carmen spared her a glance. "I believed in Jacques."

When no other explanation came, Tara frowned.

"That's it? You just believed in him?"

Carmen nodded. "He brought me here, promised to show me the good, and he did. Sure, I've had to stand up for myself, but that was nothing new. Even though shifters tend to be more human than animals most of the time, status is still important."

Tara swallowed, not sure how Carmen had to stand up for herself and too afraid to ask.

"I love Jacques. Wouldn't want to be anywhere else. This,"—she waved her hand—"pack and territory is in his blood. He's fought for it. Shed blood for it. Bet his life on it. How could I take that from him?"

"Max feels the same way. He's determined to help his people."

"And, they're succeeding. Every day they make another step forward." Carmen released her arm to pat her shoulder. "You love Max."

Tara opened her mouth, then shut it again.

Carmen shook her head. "I can see it in the way you look at that man." She pursed her lips then smiled softly. "They aren't the easiest to live with."

"Tell me about it." Tara recalled the first time she spied Max in human form and how he pretty much took over her life. He'd done so as Cotton but grew worse as Max.

"But, when a shifter loves his mate, he will do anything in his power to give you happiness," Carmen softly added.

"I just don't know that I have what it takes to do this."

"You just might surprise yourself." Carmen dipped her head and started forward once again. "The beauty shop. Britta does excellent haircuts and nails. She has a knack for seeing what really works on a girl."

"Good to know." Tara only paid half attention to Carmen's words, too absorbed with her thoughts. *Can it be that simple? Just trust Max?* Nothing in her life had been that easy. She truly doubted this would be, either.

"Let's stick our heads inside and introduce you."

Tara balked.

Carmen gave her a not-so-gentle nudge toward the door. "Confidence, Tara. Put a smile on your face and be sociable."

Tara opened the door and stepped inside. She found a handful of women in various stages of getting their hair done. One other sat at a desk while a lady worked on her nails. All of them stared at her.

"Ladies, this is Tara. Tara, this is Clair, Zoe, Tasha, Mary, Elizabeth, Nala, Alicia, and Allison." Carmen pointed out each one in turn.

"Hello." Tara put on her friendliest smile. "Nice to meet all of you."

"Tara's here visiting. With Max." She added a little emphasis to his name.

"Oh," a few said in unison. Astonishment on their faces quickly turned to curiosity.

"You and Max?" the nail technologist asked.

"It's a long story." Tara cleared her throat. She wasn't about to spill the beans to anyone she'd known for a whole two seconds. Besides, she had a sneaky suspicion they'd all know the details by nightfall, anyway.

"We're just touring and can't stay long, but I wanted to introduce you all." Carmen backtracked to the door.

"Come back again soon," Clair waved.

"Thank you." Tara inclined her head and headed out. "Please tell me there won't be a quiz on names any time soon."

Carmen chuckled. "No, but once you get to know the ladies, you'll find they're good people."

"I've always heard people are the same no matter where you go. Have the same wants and needs. The same goals."

"I imagine that's true."

Tara wondered if the same idea carried over to shifters. Or if they fit outside the bubble because of their particular animal DNA. With so many extra gifts, surely they had other interests than the same old goals regular people announced right after New Year's Day for their annual resolutions.

Carmen pointed out a few more locations then circled back without any more stops. Thankfully.

"Once you get settled in, I'll take you to the local spa. For a girls' day out."

"You have a spa here?" Tara couldn't believe the amenities. She saw half a dozen places of business all along what could be called a small main street, perhaps half a mile from where they stood on the backside of a park and a mile or so from where Max lived. Little traffic flowed. Instead, people walked. A couple older kids rode bicycles. Little noise carried to her ears. Mainly the breeze and the rustling of the trees.

"Yep. There's another strip to the east. If you follow this street down, hang a sharp right, you'll run right into it."

"Aha. So, there's more to this village than the walking area we're on?"

"Oh, yeah. This is part of the newer section. From

what I understand the lower levels are the old part. As the pack has grown, they've expanded, not only the shopping areas but built more homes." Carmen waved her hands as she talked. "This part is in good shape. The other…it's a work in progress. Those before Jacques didn't put much stock in infrastructure and services. They much preferred keeping people in line through brute force. A lot of buildings suffered. The guys are trying to get them back up and going. Creating jobs in the process."

"That's a great idea." The plan reminded Tara of her history lessons and the Great Depression. It had worked then and probably would do so again, if they had strong leaders to guide the way. She didn't doubt Jacques and Max fit into those shoes well.

Up ahead, Tara noted Jacques and Max standing where they'd left them, having a seemingly light-hearted conversation. Max laughed, then scowled when a beautiful young woman approached. She grinned up at him, ran her finger down his chest, then rubbed up and down his side like Tara imagined a cat in heat would do. *Or a wolf shifter.* With her extra-large breasts barely bound in a tight shirt and wide hips accented by black tights, she didn't have to do much to get her point across. Jealousy hit Tara—hard. "Who's that?"

"Brooke. One of the pack females eager to buy fame and fortune from selling herself and capturing a man in the process." Carmen crossed her arms over her chest. "She's not a horrible person, just not smart enough to go about it the right way.

Tara readily picked up on the tense undercurrents. "Tell me how you really feel."

Carmen scowled, then brightened. "Looks like Max is smarter than the average wolf shifter."

Tara watched Max peel Brooke off his body, put some distance between them, then rebuff her. She couldn't hear the words, but the expression on Brooke's face said it all. Rejection. And a harsh one at that. Ordinarily, she'd feel sorry for the girl. Not this time. Not when Brooke was too busy being a slut to take a hint.

Chastising herself for the petty thoughts, Tara rubbed her forehead, pushed some blowing hair out of her face, and reminded herself of the truth. She had nothing on the gorgeous Brooke. Not even the same species. What if Brooke kept throwing herself at Max and one day he accepted? And who could blame him for doing so? After all, the woman was drop dead gorgeous. *Something I'm not and never will be.*

Her earlier enthusiasm waned.

"I need to be getting back to work. Tara, good to see you again. Don't be a stranger." Jacques offered her a smile.

Carmen waved, took Jacques's arm, and sauntered off with him.

Max closed in to stand at her side. "What do you think of Carmen?"

Tara mentally pulled herself from the newfound fears and focused on the present. "She's fun, easy-going. Energetic. Smart, too. Seems to have a good head on her shoulders." Tara truly liked the lady. Respected her. Saw her as a definite friend potential should she decide to hang around more than a day or two.

"She is that. A nice match for Jacques." Max

scanned the area. "She didn't have it easy. Many of the Throwback females saw themselves in her shoes, taking the top female spot in the pack."

Tara caught an inkling of that from Carmen's words. "She didn't have to fight them, did she?"

Max shook his head. "Fighting is outlawed now. Not that Carmen wouldn't have wiped the others in the dirt for daring to try to take her man." He smiled ruefully. "She simply stated her position and held firm. Her sharp tongue and quick wit helped. Nothing and no one would budge her from Jacques's side. After a couple of tries, the women gave up."

Will that happen in your case as well? She bit her tongue to keep the question from popping out. More followed. *Will the women give up so easily once they recognize me as a human instead of another shifter? Could they ever respect me as such?* Worries returned to push her shoulders back down under their considerable weight.

"Ready to go back? Or push on ahead?" He took her hand in his.

She appreciated the affection more than he could know. "I'm good if you want to go farther."

He pulled her hand up and kissed it. "We'll take a short cut."

Stopping after a short distance more, he nudged her to the side and down an old dirt path in the woods which reminded Tara of home. "I know every woods is different but this feels quite familiar."

"Yeah. I thought that too, back at your place. Similar features despite the distance. Same roll to the land. Clearings. Even a creek. It's uncanny."

She walked along farther, letting her thoughts free

as they forged ahead. Soon, they emerged into another clearing and connected with a cement sidewalk. "Where did shifters come from originally?" Tara asked. The whole place seemed to be connected by walking paths. Good for exercise and avoiding getting lost. Bad in the fact that they seemed to cover miles and miles.

"No one knows for sure. The leading theory is that we evolved alongside humans. Perhaps as a direct extension of Neanderthals." Max surveyed the land, his gaze raking over seemingly every inch.

A predator checking out his territory for any signs of trouble. The similarities weren't missed on her.

Tara snorted. "Why does that sound entirely reasonable?"

Max's lips curled up at the corners. "I think I'll avoid going there. For the sake of mankind, of course."

"Of course." Tara smiled, the day too beautiful to ignore. The sun shone brightly and birds chirped. It was the middle of April, and it showed with the temperatures and cheeriness outdoors. A little chilly, but pleasant, especially compared to her home.

She recalled the timeline and was surprised when she did the math. Everything had been a whirlwind. Cotton showed up mid-January. Then she found out he was really a man named Max. The horrific battle followed on the heels of that shock. Add on a few weeks of separation and nearly a third of a year had flown by. Boy had her life turned from dull to dramatic and real quick-like, too. She didn't regret any of it.

"Let's go in here." Max tugged her to the right. He opened the door and waved his hand. "After you."

Tara entered, finding the building empty and the lights off.

Max flipped a switch, illuminating the area. Shelves upon shelves appeared. Some were filled with books. Others bare. Boxes were scattered everywhere—on the floor, on top of tables. Chairs sat helter-skelter through the exceptionally large room. For all intents and purposes, the place appeared abandoned and turned into a storage area for junk.

Despite the dust and mess, Tara felt the pull at once. "A library?"

"Yeah. Or what used to be. I'm afraid that it fell into disarray a while back. No one really had the time or motivation to get it up and going again. The kids wanted electronics. Tablets. Phones. Computer games. While they went to school, the teachers relied upon digital stuff. I'm afraid books are simply outdated."

Tara knew and understood the theory of modernization and technology, yet never figured out why people decided that books were suddenly null and void. Fascinating stories existed on those pages. Tons of little-known facts. Biographies of the rich and famous. Even fiction novels that allowed a reader to escape the real world for a few hours and share an adventure with a favorite character. The state of the library saddened her. At the same time, it gave her inspiration. Images and ideas rushed through her mind. Computer stations. Reading time for the kids. Research sections. Even a large corner filled with romance novels. With some manual labor, a little income, and a lot of heart, the place could once again stand proud and appealing to everyone in the pack—from the youngest members to the aged with tales of their own to share. Maybe even make recordings of their history, their memories, to tap into that knowledge before the chance was long gone.

Excitement rushed through her along with anticipation. "This place has so much potential." *This could be home.* A place to use her talents to right a wrong and help others—which was her dream all along. Provide an abode others liked to visit and get their questions answered and escape from the stress of everyday life. *I can be myself here.* The simple fact stuck in her mind.

"Yes, it does." Max agreed. "We're hoping to encourage culture in the pack. Art. Reading. To allow members to learn and express themselves. Without the constant threat of upheaval, we're hoping they can settle into normal lives and allow their inner talents to emerge." He stepped farther into the room. "For the kids to have a place to go. To learn. To have fun." He grinned. "I'll even nominate Jacques to do a weekly story reading for the little ones."

Bemused, Tara grinned. "Does he know about that yet?"

"Nope. Not telling him, either. Not until it's time."

"Evil."

His eyes twinkled. "All part of the package that's me. Besides, he needs to not come across as the big bad wolf to the little ones. An image problem he's trying to fix."

"Sitting down and reading to kindergarteners would certainly help in that department."

Tara blew out a breath, the last of her tension fading away. *Here I can do some good.*

Her stomach growled.

Max chuckled. "I'm negligent in getting you fed."

Tara grinned. "We sorta skipped lunch." She'd

even teased him about the lack of a meal on the plane ride. He'd tossed her some peanut butter crackers. They'd taken the edge off but had long since worn off.

"There's a nice little restaurant on the other side of pack lands."

"A restaurant? On pack lands?" For some reason she couldn't quite wrap her mind around that particular tidbit.

"Yep. For all intents and purposes, we're a village. As you've seen, all kinds of stores exist. Specialty ones, basic ones. We have to travel a ways to find bigger shopping venues. So, a number of pack members decided to open their own businesses. Food. Clothing. We even have a post office."

"Wow. Here I expected a small group of houses in the middle of the woods. The proverbial Little Red Riding Hood story, I guess. Boy, was I wrong."

Max smiled. "There's a lot more to us than you can imagine." He kissed her temple. "And I'm going to show each and every one of them to you."

Enjoying the show of affection, Tara hesitated to move onward. Only the insistent rumbling of her belly made her start moving again. "Please tell me they serve more than venison and rabbit."

He laughed. "No worries. I'm pretty sure you'll find something you'll like."

I already have.

Chapter 20

Tara bit back a yawn. It had been an eventful day filled with excitement, nerves, and some amazing revelations. The more she thought she understood, the less she actually knew. *Talk about the tip of the iceberg.*

They'd had an early dinner then returned to his cabin for some downtime. She'd checked the place out, found a huge television with all the stations a satellite dish could offer, and a few books too. She'd teased him about shelving his bondage erotica next to his others books. To her utter shock, he did just that.

Max. He'd definitely turned her life upside down. And still kept her off-balance. Though, in a good way.

Tara still found it hard to believe that shifters existed undetected right under the noses of humans. Certainly, with a few exceptions. If she didn't know better, she'd swear she wandered around a resort with humans. Granted, she'd just been there a few hours, but she had yet to see any furbearing creature cross her path.

Still, she couldn't quite wrap her mind around the whole part-time wolf issue. Even as she lay in one's arms, fearless and happy, she found herself with a myriad of queries since the whole matter compelled and intrigued her. The features of the species. How they changed forms, the body morphing into another being entirely. All those instincts that must remain from the olden days, leashed to the animal part of the DNA. It boggled her mind even as it tapped into her curiosity.

If she was going to live with a shifter, she probably needed to learn a few more details.

Snuggling against Max, dressed in her old pajamas, she pondered the ins and outs of the shifter universe. "Tell me more about shifters."

Max adjusted his position leaning against the arm rest of the oversized leather couch. Big, fluffy pillows supported his back, as he reclined with her resting on top of him. Lightly, he drew lines up and down her body, relaxing her into a comfortable, pleasurable mush of goo. "What do you want to know?" He kissed the top of her head.

Tara sighed in contentment. "Anything. Everything."

He chuckled. "That's a lot of stuff."

"Okay." She considered which of the endless questions to begin with. "How do you change forms? And doesn't it hurt?"

"It's programmed into us, I guess. At some point in life, usually around puberty, we simply figure out how to change. Think about the form we want to become, and poof, we're it."

"Poof?" She grinned. "That simple?"

"Pretty much. It hurts some, sure, but we get used to that pretty fast. The reward is much greater than the pain to get there."

That made sense. "It must be amazing the first time you change. To experience life as a wolf."

Max smirked. "Amazing. Scary. Fascinating. Learning to run, to hunt. Lots of new things, that's for sure."

A sudden thought hit Tara. "Will Brighton and Abby's baby be a shifter? I mean have the abilities?" She didn't know a huge amount about genetics, but diluting the blood seemed like it would also lessen the powers.

Max rubbed his chin on the top of her head. "It's a toss-up. While shifters don't mate with humans that often, a few have produced offspring that had the same abilities as their shifter parent. Others possessed some extras but were unable to change forms."

"That must do a job on their self-confidence. For their friends to be able to do it, to know they have some of the DNA, but not enough to attain their full gifts." She frowned as she realized that any children she had with Max would face the same issue.

Cross that bridge when and if we ever get there. First things first. Determine if she could fit into the shifter world and if Max even wanted to stay with her. He said so, but he might change his mind over time. That left a lot on her plate.

"They do just fine, from what I understand. Kids are resilient. So are shifters. Why fret over things you can't change?"

She smiled ruefully. Sometimes she'd swear he could read her mind. "True."

Memories of Brooke pawing at Max clouded Tara's contentment. "Have you been with Brooke?"

Max tensed under her, the rigidness turning her soft pillow into one of steel. "Does it matter?"

"I just wondered why she's so persistent now." Tara knew the subject proved uncomfortable, but couldn't seem to let it go.

Max sighed and wrapped her in his arms. "When I

was younger, I wanted acceptance more than anything. Being of mixed blood pretty much relegated me to the outskirts. Only Jacques really befriended me. The others saw me as inferior." He paused for a second. "The most aggressive females flirt and tease. That's their nature. They looked down their nose at me until I rose in the ranks as beta to Jacques. Then, they saw me as a man. Or so I thought. For a few days, I reveled in the attention. Then I wizened up. Grew tired of being used."

"All the women are like that?" She thought about those she met earlier. They seemed…normal.

"No. Of course not. But the only ones that seemed to want anything to do with me, sought me out because of my exoticness or my looks, my power, or my prowess. They never bothered to ask me what I liked to eat or what my hobbies are. Those are the women I have experience with."

Tara's heart broke for what he must have been through, just wanting to be a part of the group, even one as warped as Throwback. "And now?"

He petted her hair. "I'm not the callow youth I once was. Figured out a few things along the way."

She arched her neck in order to look up at his face. "What things?"

He leaned in and kissed her gently. "That a person's heart is much more important than the outside. That I don't need to waste my time trying to fit in. I'm who I am. They can accept it or not, I really don't care."

She held her breath. "And the pack females?"

"Can't hold a candle to you," he whispered.

"How do you know they never will?" She hated to

ask, but needed an answer.

"Because. I know you. I know what kind of person you are. They are superficial where you're deep."

Her spirit soared. "You're an amazing man."

He smiled softly. "You don't know how much that means to me."

Silence reigned for a few minutes.

"What do you think of the pack so far?"

Tara didn't have to think hard. "The grounds are gorgeous. The few people I've briefly met seem nice enough." *Barring one over-sexed shifter with a Max complex.* "But, I haven't seen anyone in wolf form."

Max chuckled. "Wolves take to the woods. Not much fun to trot down the cement walkway when you can bound through the leaves and stalk prey."

"Aha. So, I won't see many people in wolf form?"

"Not too likely. Most live their days as humans. The night is time for the animal side to come out." He went back to rubbing her back.

"Good to know. I won't have to worry about being ambushed by a feral animal then."

"Ambushed? Nah. Eaten, perhaps." The sultry tone made her toes curl.

Tara sat up. "Race you to the bed." She leapt to her feet and dashed back to his bedroom, hearing Max's footfalls right on her heels. Laughing, she jumped into the center and arched an eyebrow at him.

He slowly approached, shucking his clothes in the process.

She followed his lead, removing first her shirt, then the bottoms. Nude, she shivered. "Brrr." After pulling back the covers, she climbed in.

Max slid in next to her, pulling her against his

chest in spoon fashion. "Better?"

"Much." She tilted her head, allowing him access to her neck and shoulder. The kisses he placed were tender and sweet.

A deep howl broke through the quietness of the night. Tara startled.

Max wrapped an arm around her, holding her snug. "You're in the middle of Throwback territory. Howling is a given."

She listened as the single animal voice continued as if singing a slow, sad song. "It gives me goosebumps." She rubbed at her bare arms.

Max tugged the covers up over them and pressed his lips to her nape of her neck. "Want me to translate?"

She twisted in order to see his face with the help of a three-quarters moon casting a little illumination into the bedroom compliments of the large window. "You know what he's saying?"

"Yep." Max grinned wide, his dimples popping out. "All part of the shifter package. We learn to communicate in a variety of ways from early on."

"Neat." She trailed her finger along his jawline. "So, professor, tell me what the wolf is saying."

He kissed her digit. "That's Jacques, by the way."

Before she could ask, he clarified. "We recognize voices just like you do when talking to people."

Tara smiled. "What's he saying?"

"He's calling Carmen, his mate. Speaking of his undying love for her. How she makes his world brighter and him happy."

She blinked. "You got all that from the howls?"

"Yep." He brushed her lips with hers. "A male wolf shifter sings to his mate. The one female he chooses to be next to him for all time."

She processed the information. "Just the one?"

"Just the one woman that he loves above any other. He only sings for her. No one else."

"That's so romantic." She'd never considered how wolves might serenade their loved ones. Now, she knew. Her heart warmed at the realization.

She'd witnessed the rabid beasts they could become. She'd also seen the tender side. Parents caring for their children. Lovers holding hands and laughing. And, now, the alpha of the pack, telling the world how he felt about his lady.

"What are you thinking so hard about?"

Emotions flooded Tara. "Just how things aren't always black and white."

He lightly brushed his lips over hers. "They rarely are."

Chapter 21

Tara had slept restlessly, woke early, and climbed out of bed, careful not to disturb a still sleeping Max. She shivered at the loss of his body heat in the chilly air. *Clothes are good. Definitely a necessity.* She performed a quick clean up then drew on heavy clothes, preparing for another hike around the grounds. The place fascinated her, the small part she'd seen. With plenty more out there, she pulled on her heavy jacket and stepped outside.

The fresh air greeted her, filled with the scent of pine. A hardly noticeable breeze barely ruffled her ponytail. The sun peeked over the horizon, signifying another beautiful day in the village that reminded Tara of a neat mountain resort. The rays of the sun warmed everything, including Tara as she hooked a right and started down one of the many trails.

Her home would be covered in several inches of snow. A foot or more, even. Yet, here in Oregon, she enjoyed spring-like weather. Bright and cheerful. A far cry from the frozen tundra of Minnesota. Definitely a nice change.

Once again, she scanned the area, noting the cabins seemingly built into the forest and the endless well-maintained trails connecting them all. The side road pulled up along the backside, giving the view from the front window of nature at its best. At least that was the case with Max's cabin and those she could see along the trail. The developer obviously followed a plan, aiming for a community feel amidst the wilds. Tara found the arrangement unusual and pleasing.

She paused to study the landscape, deciding on which direction to take. Max's house resided about a mile from the business area. The distance wasn't an issue, certainly, but she wondered if there were more places she hadn't yet seen just waiting for her to explore.

A tendril of caution poked at her. She'd been on pack lands for less than a full day. Venturing around, especially in lesser populated areas, could be taking a chance. She had a feeling wolf shifters, like their wild cousins, didn't approve of strangers showing up and tromping through their territory. The consideration gave her pause and reminded her of the differences between her and Max. The hurdles they faced.

How do I stack up as a human in a pack of wolf shifters? The women are downright gorgeous. The men strong and handsome. It was almost easy to forget they were natural predators and end arguments by tearing one another apart with their sharp teeth.

She shuddered as the memory of Max's and Conley's fight flashed through her mind. The violence rattled her.

Sure, Max promised her those days are over. *But, how do I know for certain? How can I fit in? Where can I fit in?*

The library. The forgotten place bore potential, just as she supposed she did. There, she could blossom, show her strengths and her visions. Except, to take on such a job, she'd have to forsake her home in

Minnesota. The house she adored, filled with happy memories of her grandparents. The town she'd chosen to spend much of her time around.

But, to pick Minnesota meant that Max would either have to travel back and forth, give up his position as Jacques's right-hand man, or break off their relationship entirely. Each option sounded worse than the next, adding to the heavy burden she already carried.

Deep down, she knew she couldn't ask him to choose, to give up his dreams and wishes. That would kill his happiness as surely as a spear to the heart. Which left her as the one to bring about the change.

Can I give up what I've always known in order to be with Max? Can my love be strong enough for both of us?

"The bird that doesn't leave the nest doesn't find food, water, or a mate." Dr. Kendall's words replayed through her head.

Time to put on your big girl panties, Tara.

"What makes you think you're good enough for him?" a woman's voice asked.

Tara jerked her gaze up to find Brooke emerging from behind a tree. She collected herself, reminded herself to take the high road, and tried to slow her speeding heart after Brooke nearly scared her half to death.

"We respect one another."

Brooke sneered. "That's all you've got?"

"It's more than men have for you."

Brooke's mouth dropped open. "How dare you!"

Tara kept her arms relaxed at her sides. "Max isn't interested. I think he made that absolutely clear. Think about setting your sights on another guy, one who isn't attached."

"You know jack shit." She waved her hands in agitation. "He's just playing with you. A human. But, he'll tire soon enough and come back to me. A mere human can't keep his attention. He longs for one of his own kind. I'll be here when he throws you aside."

"Not going to happen." Tara appraised her rival and went with her gut. "I'm not perfect. Not as smart as some or as dumb as others. I've been through the dating game a time or two. Gave up on men because I preferred my own company rather than some dunce who was distracted by every long-legged woman he saw."

Brooke's face scrunched in confusion. The anger abating, gradually.

Tara didn't bother to pat herself on the back. Instead, she took the opportunity to make a strong statement. "I believe that a woman has to be herself before she can enter into a relationship. You don't suddenly lose your identity, your dreams, your likes, and dislikes. She simply learns all about give and take and how to compromise. Because the man they're with treats them right. I don't mean a good time in bed, though that's part of it. I mean every other minute of the day. Respect. Caring. Kindness. That's the sign of a true man."

"Ugly women have to make excuses."

Tara bit back her flaring temper. "No. Strong women stand up for themselves. Demand to be treated like a lady, not just chattel." She lifted her chin. "Max and I have something special. Something that you won't know about. Ever. Unless you love yourself first, learn to depend upon yourself, and then decide to allow a man into your life. For the right reasons."

"You're a pity fuck, that's all it is."

The barb stung, but Tara plowed ahead, keeping her anger in check. She'd said the same thing weeks ago. Now, she truly understood the difference. Saw how far she'd come. How far she and Max had progressed as a couple. With confidence, she lifted her chin. "Wrong again. Loose women are easy to discard and forget. Men want a woman who can hold their interest—in and out of bed. Right now, you've only got half the battle figured out."

"You bitch."

"No, you're the bitch. Where were you when this pack was struggling under Garrison's rule? Where were you when Jacques and Max fought to hold onto control and oust the dictator?"

Brooke's mouth fell open. "Women don't fight."

"The hell they don't." Tara's anger broke free. "This is your home, your community. You and the others couldn't raise a hand to help? To make your voices heard?"

"You don't have a fucking clue what it was like." Brooke glared at her, her hands fisting at her sides.

"Maybe I wasn't there, but I do know this. Jacques and Max risked their lives for this pack. They both *barely* survived. Not only that, but they came back. They fought to the death, ending Garrison's and his thugs' reign for good. They didn't have to do that. *At all.* They could have said 'screw you' and went about their own lives. But, they didn't. They cling to the dream of turning this place around." Tara lowered her voice and added sternness. "You'd think the rest of you would see their sacrifices for you and actually get up and help. Do something. Anything. Sitting around and waiting to see is bull crap. Be a part of the new. Have a voice in matters. For that matter, get out of men's beds and do something more productive."

"Yeah, advice from someone who doesn't know jack shit." Brooke sneered and waved her hand dismissively.

"Maybe, maybe not. Either way, I know one thing. A person fights for what and who they believe in." She paused for a second. "A real woman has no problem standing up when things are on the line. I can and will do just that."

Brooke growled low in her throat, then lunged.

Don't back down and don't look away. Tara stood her ground, narrowed her eyes, and fisted her hands. If she had to defend herself she would do so. *And probably get my butt kicked, too.* But, her instincts told her Brooke was all talk and no action. That gave her the courage to stand up straight, glare down haughtily, and dare the female shifter to do her worst.

Pulling up, Brooke glared at Tara for a few seconds, glanced around, then sauntered off, but not before spitting one last insult. "You're just a stupid human bitch."

"Yeah. I can live with that." Tara rubbed her hands together, trying to get the blood flowing again. She wasn't positive that her pants were still dry after that near charge. Only the absolute intuition that she had to stare down Brooke to earn her respect kept Tara rooted to her spot.

"Nice."

Tara swiveled to see the nail tech, Allison,

approaching. "Thanks. Allison, isn't it?"

"Very good." The woman flipped her long black hair behind her back and smiled softly. "I'm impressed. Didn't think you had the guts to go head-to-head with Brooke."

Tara shrugged. "A girl's gotta do what a girl's gotta do," she added a grin.

Allison chuckled. "You'll do, Tara."

The vote of confidence built back some of Tara's depleted confidence.

"You decide you need your nails or hair done, come by the salon. I'll be glad to do them for you."

Thrilled, Tara could only grin. "I will. Thank you." She gave a little wave. "If you can make my hair even close to how beautiful yours is, I'll be in your debt."

Allison tilted her head, sending the thick wave to the side. "You have your own beauty and I think your man sees it just fine." She lifted her chin. "Good morning, Max."

Tara spun around to find Max ambling toward her, dressed in a pair of jeans she'd purchased for him and one of the long-sleeved t-shirts. His coat hung open, showing off the wide expanse of his chest.

Oh my, that man knows how to make an appearance.

Her observation skills picked up a few other details aside from his hunky body and the strength contained in every stride. She noticed the firm set of his jaw and the checked fury in his gaze. *Oh, hell. This is the last thing I need or want right now.* Her own temper rose to the occasion.

She'd just stood toe-to-toe with a pissed off shifter female. Now, Max showed up prepared for battle. That fact pinged her last nerve. *I swear, if he goes all alpha male on me, then I really am going to kick his ass.*

****

Max searched Tara's face, needing to judge her mood and level of upset. He'd heard Brooke's words, as did several other members of the pack, and cussed Brooke for her aggressiveness and blatant attempt to hurt Tara and drive her away.

He'd also heard her stalwart words in his favor, lashing Brooke and, indirectly, others, for not doing more to direct their lives. People were slowly coming around, finally believing that the pack was stable. He understood. Knew Tara probably stomped on some toes. But, couldn't help the flare of pride in her for staring down a shifter and tasking her to be better.

A shifter that could have easily torn her apart.

His gut clenched again at the thought. Fear like he'd never experienced before slowly began to dissipate. Nightmares were sure to follow.

He saw the hint of hesitation in Tara and saw the slight tremble of her hands—adrenalin or suppressed anger or emotional distress, he wasn't sure. Probably a combination of all three. Still, he caught the spark of desire that lit up her eyes as he approached and the welcome smile that she saved for just him. Only this one seemed to bear more teeth than usual.

His inner wolf whined in warning. Max ignored him. "Everything okay?"

"Yeah. Just a…debate." Tara focused on her feet.

"Uh, huh." He didn't believe her for a second, not just because he knew the truth but because she was a terrible liar. Her averted gaze gave her away each and every time.

Damn Brooke and her viper tongue.

Max reined in his fury, slid an arm around Tara, and pulled her close. "You snuck out."

"I didn't want to wake you. Besides, I thought I'd have a little look around. Enjoy the morning."

And get waylaid by a jealous witch.

She sidestepped, putting a few inches between them.

He frowned at her actions. "Let's go back to the cabin. Have some breakfast." He nudged her to start moving, careful to keep from caging her in. Something told him if he tried to wrap her in a bubble, she'd go off on him. Instead, they walked along in silence, which unsettled him all the more.

She's got some major rage and it's about to blow.

He didn't argue with his inner beast, not when he could see the signs for himself. The problem was he didn't have a clue why she was in such a state. *And, I'm not dumb enough to ask.*

Once they were safely inside and the door shut, he took off his coat, tossing it over a nearby chair. Tara did the same, then entered the kitchen.

Max followed, grappling for the right words. "I'm sorry. Brooke has been a thorn in my side for a while. She sees you as a threat to getting what she wants."

"Ya think?" Sarcasm came through loud and clear.

Max grumbled under his breath at her volatile emotions. "I'll talk to her."

Tara shook her head. "Don't bother. Either she figured things out just now or she didn't."

"I don't think she's going to give up." Max vowed to keep a closer eye on Tara. Sure, the laws forbade fighting, but he wouldn't hold his breath that Brooke gave a damn if it came right down to it.

"She will. Shame and peer pressure will eventually sink into her thick skull." Tara pushed her hair out of her eyes.

"She's too stubborn to listen." He rubbed his forehead. "Listen, she's a shifter. Able to really cause some damage with those teeth. One bite and—"

Tara eyed him with anger. "I'm not defenseless."

Max held up one hand. "I know. It's just that—"

"That you don't think I'm good enough?" Tara lashed out.

Max's mouth fell open. He grappled to keep up with the quick turn of events. "What? No. That's not it at all."

"I can hold my own. Don't need anyone to fight my battles. Never have and never will." She huffed and crossed her arms over her chest.

Max easily recognized the defensive body language. "I'm not fighting your battles, but I'm sure as hell going to put my foot down before she hurts you."

"Why?" Tara fired back.

"Why what?" Confused, he stared at her, willing her to open up and spit out what was eating her.

"Why bother. That won't earn me any respect, even if it mattered." Tara's shoulders fell and her voice decreased in decibels. "I can't compete with Brooke and the other women. They're gorgeous. Models right off the magazine page. And, one of your own kind."

He frowned. "There's no competition. I don't want them. Never have." Max rested his finger under her chin and lifted until she met his eyes. "They only want me because of the status I hold. Before, I was scum under their feet. That hasn't changed and won't.

Besides, why would I want one of them when I can have you?"

Tara stilled. "But, I'm human."

"So?" He countered. The fact that they were finally hashing this out frustrated the hell out of him, but gave him a semblance of hope at the same time. He had to make her see things from his perception. In order to do so, she needed to spill her fears. "Look at Abby and Brighton. They are human and shifter. It works just fine."

Tara placed her hand on the countertop. "Max. I just don't think we're supposed to be together."

His next breath froze in his lungs. "Why, Tara? Tell me why." Fear fed his anger, his feeling of impending doom. She was pulling away and he felt helpless as how to stop her.

"You belong here at Throwback. With Jacques. The greater good," she reminded him. "Besides, you've already paid me back for all the help. And then some. You're free of any debt."

"You didn't cash the check."

She shrugged. "It's enough that you sent it. You paid me in so many other ways. I don't regret anything. But, the truth is Jacques needs you. The pack needs you. They give you so much that I can't."

"Bullshit." He was sick of hearing that lame excuse. No way would he let Throwback come between him and Tara. If he had to leave and return to Minnesota, then so be it. But, he wasn't letting Tara go.

She blinked at him, obviously surprised by his vulgar retort.

He fisted his hands, then blew out a breath, and gently latched onto her upper arms. "Tara. Listen to me.

It wasn't about returning a favor. It never was."

She stared up at him as if waiting for the shoe to drop.

"It's not even about Throwback."

"Max. This is your home. Where you belong. You said yourself that was your dream to come back and change things. Your dream is now."

"And it's not worth anything without you."

She blew out her breath. "I'm not good enough for you." Her tone carried resignation.

What will it take to make you understand? "How the hell can you say that?"

"Isn't it true?"

"Fuck, no, it's not true. Screw Brooke and the rest of the pack. I don't give a shit what they say. Their opinion doesn't count." Desperation washed over him as he fought to keep the only woman he'd ever cared for. The only woman who ever gave a damn about him. He found the words stuck in his throat. Determinedly, he forced them out. "Damn it. I love you."

Tara's eyes widened. "What did you say?"

"I said I love you. The complete you. Life isn't the same without you at my side. It's not about debts or bedmates. It's not about where we are or where we live. It's about the fact that I love you with my whole heart." He softened to a whisper, emotions nearly choking him up. "None of this means anything without you." He studied her face, frantically trying to read her reaction.

A slow smile appeared on her lips. "I thought I'd never hear those words from you."

Hope blossomed. "And?"

"About time," she sassed.

He persisted, not about to let her off the hook until

he knew exactly where she stood. "And?"

"And, I love you, too. Fur ball and all." She threw herself into his arms with a happy squeal.

Relief washed over him. He caught her against his chest, held her snug, then lifted his head enough to kiss her soundly. When he came up for air, he couldn't wipe the joyous grin off his face.

"I was so afraid our differences were too much. That the obstacles would be too high. That tomorrow would really not happen."

"Oh, honey. I'd move heaven and earth for you. Those weeks being away drove me nearly mad. I missed you, ached for you. I dreamt about you. It was then I realized that I didn't want to be without you. Ever again."

She sniffed and wiped at a stray tear. "I thought once you returned to your pack, you'd forget me. Find one of your kind to be with. That our time was over in the blink of an eye."

"Never. I might have been slow to figure some things out, but I have. I don't care where we have to go or what we have to do, I'm not leaving your side."

She smiled happily.

He continued on the same train of thought, needing to know her wishes. "Where do you want to live? I'll go anywhere you want."

She didn't hesitate a single beat. "Right here with you."

Surprise and excitement washed over him. "Are you sure?"

"Absolutely. I'm home wherever you are. As long as I have your love, I don't need anything else."

He laughed. "And I'll love you forever."

She didn't get a chance to respond as he sealed their lips together

Passion ignited, sending cascades of warmth, hope, and searing hunger through him. He'd savor them now and for years to come, if he had his way. For he knew one thing—life would be nothing without her. He'd handed over his heart into her keeping and didn't regret it for a single moment.

Chapter 22

Two days later

Tara wiped the back of her hand across her face, ignoring the smear of dust sure to be there. Stretching her back, she stared at the nearly overwhelming mess, trying not to focus on the big picture. *One section at a time. One task. One day.*

Max had a meeting with Jacques and some work to attend that morning. He'd frowned with the admission, but Tara understood. She'd told him so. Never once did she expect him to be a babysitter for her visit. Instead, she had the opportunity to do something productive— namely start with the clean-up job on the library.

He'd shaken his head, smiled with pride, then escorted her to the place. With a quick kiss and a promise to collect her for lunch, he left for the office with a reminder that he was just a phone call away if she needed anything.

I need something all right. A new body. After only two hours of stacking books in boxes and moving heavy shelves, she decided she was horribly out of shape. The promise of suffering later made her groan in dread but didn't deter her in the least. She had a mission, a project, and wasn't about to let a little overused muscles keep her from it.

"Rome wasn't built in a day, but they had to start

somewhere." She picked up a broken chair and set it to the side. Until she sorted through what could be salvaged and what couldn't, her visions of the place would never come to light.

The creak of the door opening drew her attention. She turned to find Carmen standing there. A couple more women Tara remembered from the salon stepped in behind her.

"I heard you might be in a spring cleaning mood." Carmen smiled and raked the area with her gaze.

Tara offered up a small smile. "I seem to have this obsession for books. Even lonely and dirty ones."

The ladies grinned.

"You remember Mary and Claire." Carmen gestured toward them.

"I do. Nice to see you again, ladies." Tara pushed a loose lock of hair from her face.

"What are you planning on doing with this place?" Mary asked.

"Return it to its former glory—as a library. A place children and adults alike can come to play, to lounge, to learn something. I loved my library growing up, thought of it as a getaway from everyday life. I want that for this place and for the pack."

"Garrison hated the library. Closed it down. Said it was stupid and people needed to spend their time elsewhere." Mary planted her hands on her hips.

"As history points out, the way to keep people under your thumb is to make sure they remain uneducated. If they don't know any better..." Tara shrugged. She'd read more than once about how those greedy, slimy people in power strove to keep the public from thinking for themselves or questioning. To do that, they discouraged and mocked learning. "After everything you guys have gone through, all the bad stuff, I thought it might be nice to create a space where the community can come together. To heal. To enjoy. To share."

The women looked at one another, then gave a quick nod.

"Count us in," Mary declared.

Shocked, Tara blinked at them. "It's messy work. Are you sure?"

Claire snorted. "Dirt washes off."

Tara beamed. "Oh, thank you." Excitement and a sense of accomplishment and acceptance hit her hard. She wanted to hug them all. "You don't know what this means."

Carmen smiled. "You don't know what it means for you to want to help."

"Or for what you told Brooke about Max," Claire added.

"You heard that?" Tara knew others were nearby and that Allison gave her a figurative thumbs up afterward.

"Good news travels fast." Carmen picked up some stacked boxes and set them next to others. "You flayed Brooke and shamed her at the same time. Hell, you got the rest of us to thinking as well. Expecting the top men to fight it out and decide what our lives will be might have been in the past. Now, we know better."

"Exactly. Who wants to go back to living like that? Waiting for a pin to drop? Wondering if Garrison and his men would show up at the door and throw us out for some concocted reason." Mary picked up some papers and torn up cardboard and placed it in a growing pile of trash.

"They'd throw you out of your own homes?" Tara's stomach churned in rage at the very idea.

"Not often. But, if anyone went against of them—"

"Just a tiny whispered rumor was all it took, too," Claire finished.

"That's horrible. Talk about a cruel dictatorship." Tara couldn't imagine living under such constant stress and strain.

"Ridiculous. Absolutely ridiculous." Carmen's face scrunched in outrage, her eyes snapping in fury. "Never happening again. If I have to take a pitch fork to the bastard myself."

Tara could just see feisty Carmen doing just that. "If it makes you feel any better, I clobbered Conley with a shovel."

The ladies gaped at her.

Tara shrugged. "He had Max down, trying to rip out his throat. I wasn't about to stand aside and do nothing."

"That took some guts," Carmen said.

"Choices. It's all about choices. I wasn't about to let some idiot take the only man I've ever loved away from me." Tara lifted her chin. If she had to do it again, she would. Even if it meant sacrificing her life in the process.

A slow smile appeared on Mary's face. "You'll do, Tara."

The compliment wrapped Tara in warmth like a favorite blanket.

"So, where do you want this stuff?" Carmen asked.

Tara gestured this way and that, pointing out stacks and piles that she'd started.

The ladies jumped right in, seemingly happy to make a difference in the once forgotten library.

Tara's heart buoyed. They came to help, showed their appreciation. It was a start. A really good one at that.

****

"Come on, girl. We don't want to be late." Carmen stood in the doorway fidgeting with her watch.

Tara fluffed her hair once more, frowned when it stayed flat, then blew out a breath. "Okay, okay. I don't know what the big hurry is anyway."

"You don't want to be late for Max's big surprise." Carmen waved in an obvious effort to hurry her along.

The last twenty-four hours had already been a big surprise. Max declaring his love. She did as well. A glorious celebration. Now this—whatever this was.

"Where is he anyway?" Tara hadn't seen hide nor hair of Max since supper. He'd helped her clean up, kissed her sweetly, and said he'd see her later. That was it. Not a single clue.

They'd discussed some arrangements and made a few calls earlier in the day before he'd wandered off. Tara couldn't bear to part with her house. Max understood. After a quick discussion with Brighton, she learned that Xavier had been looking for an out-of-the-way place to call his own. He was willing to rent it and keep up the repairs for her. With that problem solved, Tara embraced her new home. And Max. *Especially Max.*

Until now, when he'd disappeared and she felt like a human sacrifice being led to the volcano.

At least I'm not a virgin. And there's no volcano.

The mental quip settled her nerves only marginally.

Jacques led the way down a path she'd not seen before. Dimmed street lamps illuminated their way. Thankfully, for Tara feared she'd stumble and fall in the darkness due to the lack of exceptional night vision that the shifters most likely possessed. The light from the full moon helped, too, making the landscape bright enough for Tara's comfort.

Carmen kept pace at her side. As they passed a bench area, Tara noticed a small group of women gathering around. She recognized most of them as the ladies from the beauty shop. That didn't surprise her as much as the other woman standing at the far side of the gathering. Brooke.

Tara slowed her steps and stared. She didn't know what to expect and prepared herself for a confrontation to come.

Instead, Brooke inclined her head as if in acknowledgement and respect. Shocked, Tara blinked, not sure she hadn't made up the small movement.

"She's trying to tell you that she's backing off, that you've won," Carmen explained.

"Won what?"

A sly grin hovered over Carmen's lips. "You'll see soon enough."

Okay. This just gets odder and odder. Tara lifted her hand in greeting to the women then started walking again.

They continued on in silence until another open area appeared. This one had a rock wall, a bench, and three lawn chairs, presently empty. They all faced north, where a low rise could easily be seen with a backdrop of hills covered with evergreen trees. The full moon stood out huge, as if it set directly on the ground before her, well within touching distance.

The surreal scene touched Tara deep. She committed it to memory as she knew the beauty of the spot would be unsurpassed for the rest of her life.

"Have a seat." Jacques gestured toward the three lawn chairs lined up.

She started to take the end one, only for Carmen to nudge her over into the middle.

The excellent view allowed Tara to see the full scene of the moon, the rise, and the gracious backdrop. Yet, nowhere did she see Max.

Bracketed by both Carmen and Jacques, Tara began to seriously question the upcoming events.

Before she could ask, Carmen patted her hand. "Relax. Enjoy your surprise."

"I'm still not sure, if it's my surprise, why you guys are here."

"To translate," Jacques quietly answered.

In that moment, she glimpsed movement. Focusing in that direction, she saw a large white wolf emerge from the trees, take his place at the top of the small hill, and turn his attention to her. The huge moon, with its darker spots served as a background, silhouetting Max perfectly. A picture and moment worth more than a thousand words.

"Cotton?" The name slipped out. Hurriedly, she corrected herself. "Max?"

He stared at her for a long moment, lifted his muzzle to the sky, and began to howl. A beautiful, sweet solo melody which sent a cascade of warmth over her very soul. She couldn't take her eyes from the glorious sight. No matter that she didn't understand the words, she picked up on the emotions. For they matched hers.

"He says you're special. Precious. Kind," Carmen whispered. "You gave of yourself to him, teaching him what love is."

A few seconds passed as Max continued on with his serenade.

"He says you're the only one for him. He loves you. Fully. Completely." Jacques paused while Max continued his song. "And wishes with his whole heart for you to agree to be his mate." Jacques rubbed his nose as if needing a moment to collect himself.

"A mate for life," Carmen finished.

Max grew silent and waited.

Tara stood, her legs a little shaky, then started moving. At first a walk, then a jog. Before long she found herself running all out only to stop and kneel in front of Max. She ran her hands through his thick fur and kissed his nose. "Yes. Absolutely yes."

He shifted, sitting before her completely in the buff. "I love you, Tara."

She blinked back tears. "I love you more."

He laughed, pulled her into his arms, and sealed his lips over hers.

Tara matched him in enthusiasm. She held him tight. Joyous. Thrilled. And so in love with the man of her dreams—who just happened to be a part time wolf.

All around them, howls filled the night sky.

"They're congratulating us," Max said quietly between peppered kisses. "On our mating."

Tara laughed. "You make me the happiest woman in the world."

He beamed. "I promise to try to keep you that way for as long as we both shall live."

"That'll work." Tara wiped at the overflowing tears.

Max shivered. "Maybe we should take this celebration back to the cabin before I freeze my ass off."

Tara laughed. "If we don't get moving, I'm afraid Mother Nature will take care of my threat to have you neutered."

Max barked out in amused laughter. "We decided that would be a tragedy. So, get moving, woman." He helped her to her feet and strode next to her, seemingly uncaring of his nudity or the quite cold temperatures.

For me. The best present she could ever imagine receiving. All because of Max.

Epilogue

Six months later

"And the prince and princess lived happily ever after. The end." Jacques closed the book. The small gathering of youngsters clapped from their seated position at his feet. He grinned at them.

"Read another," one little girl hollered.

"Another!" a chorus followed.

Jacques held up his hands. "Okay. Okay. Just one more then I have to get back to work." He picked up another book on a nearby shelf, opened the cover, and began reading.

Tara smiled at the reception from her position near the book checkout counter across the room.

"He's loving the attention."

Tara swiveled around to see Max standing behind her. Once again he snuck up on her. At least, after this amount of time together, she'd become somewhat used to his stealth. "The children adore him."

Max wrapped his arms around her middle and kissed her neck. "Almost as much as they adore you."

She snorted. "Uh, huh." She closed her eyes and savored the affection.

Over the past few months, she'd worked full time to get the library in order. After that initial day, others began to trickle in. Before she knew it, many of the pack stopped by to help. They cleaned, rearranged, and created new artwork and signs. Lights were replaced and new computers, filled with children's games, arrived. Books appeared in large boxes, covering a wide array of topics. She developed a teen section devoted to their interests, another for younger children, and one more for adults. A research area sat to the rear, filled with old history books, biographies, and even a couple of laptops with genealogy software already installed.

Donations poured in as families began to take advantage of the free services the library offered. Tara added in comfortable chairs for adults to use while reading, bean bags for the kids, and more sturdy wooden chairs and matching tables for those wishing to focus on serious learning. She'd aimed to turn the place into a hangout, for young and old. Judging by the smiles all around and the numbers of members visiting, she'd hit the nail on the head.

"You've done a great job with this. With everything," Max praised as he hugged her from behind. "I'm so proud of you."

"I couldn't have done it without you." She rested her hands on top of his. "You encouraged people to give it try. Even talked Jacques into a weekly story hour. That's a huge draw."

Max chuckled. "I twisted his arm the first time. Now, he spends half a day lining up books for the next one. I think I've created a monster."

Tara chuckled. "A benevolent and well-liked one at that." She sighed happily. "I don't know how I got to be so lucky."

"To get to listen along with the kids?"

She grinned. "Well, not exactly." She turned

around and cupped Max's face. "I thought my life was falling apart. No successful dates. Not good enough for any man. My business going down the drain. Then, one fateful night, I about ran over a dog."

"Wolf," he corrected with a soft smile.

"Who changed my life forever." She glanced over her shoulder, then nudged Max back a few steps into the office area, away from prying eyes. "It's like a fairy tale come true. Some hard parts, some scary parts, but my knight came through in the end."

He wrapped his arms around her and tugged her close. "Do you miss your old life?"

"No. Not at all." She spoke the truth. "Since Xavier is renting my house, I don't worry about it falling apart or getting burglarized, or the mice taking over. That's a huge relief."

Max smirked. "I don't envy the person who would try to break in with Xavier there."

Tara shook her head. "He'd bite them."

"And then some."

She tilted her head. "Do you think he's turning it into a man cave or a shifter bungalow?"

Max laughed. "No telling."

"With the house in good hands, I had nothing else holding me back. Sure, I miss seeing Rose, but we talk by phone. I promised to visit soon. Abby and Brighton still touch base now and again, though they have their hands full with their little boy."

"Just tell me when and I'll fly you in for a visit," Max promised.

She stared up at the man who fate dropped into her world. He'd changed her, for the better. Taught her perseverance, inner strength, and battling through her fears. He also taught her about love. "How did I deserve you?"

"I ask myself that every day, but the other way around. An ostracized wolf shifter on the run. I brought danger to your doorstep. Yet, along the way, you showed such kindness, caring, and resilience. I couldn't imagine a woman—human or shifter—could ever possess those qualities." He lowered his head, pausing just before their lips met. "I'm the lucky one. Ready to give up, I found the woman of my dreams. My love. My wife. My mate."

"I love you more, mate."

He chuckled. "Not possible."

"Let's call it a tie."

"That's more like it."

Yes, it is. Tara lifted, meshing their lips into a kiss filled with emotion and the promise of a long life together. Sharing. Living. Loving.

They might have been from different worlds, but sometimes opposites do attract. Like with Max. When it came to love, nothing else mattered. Not their DNA nor their backgrounds. Only the intense feelings counted. And, she intended to work each and every day to keep that love burning bright. After all, Max pledged his life to her, in all ways possible. He still serenaded her, reminding her and the rest of the pack of his immense feelings for her. Each time brought tears to Tara's eyes. He treasured and cherished her. So much more than she ever thought possible.

A fitting life indeed for a woman who'd almost lost belief in happily ever after. Only for fate and one lone wolf shifter to prove to her that dreams really do come true.

A word about the author...

Cheyenne Meadows, while growing up in the Midwest, began reading romance novels in high school, immediately falling in love with the genre, to the point where she decided to write professionally for a career. However, that dream splattered against a brick wall, resulting in a quick death, in her first writing class in college when the professor told her bluntly that she wasn't any good at it. She shifted gears quickly and left her writing dreams behind, eventually settling on becoming a nurse.

A few years back, she stumbled across a fan-fiction writing site on a favorite author's webpage. She began to read stories others wrote, not only making some wonderful close friends from the experience, but also really learning to write for the very first time. Here she was able to share short stories, practice her writing skills, and truly develop into a writer. More than that, the experience allowed her to revitalize her dream, as she rediscovered joy in writing.

Now she spends her days off with her alpha-male characters, quick-witted heroines, and seeing how much trouble everyone can get into. When she's not working or writing, she enjoys playing in the garden, hanging out with her diva kitty, and using her backyard as a living canvas for her whimsical landscaping, and, of course, reading romance novels.

Facebook:
https://www.facebook.com/cheyenne.meadows.10
Blog: http://cheyennemeadows.blogspot.com/
E-mail: Cheyenne1.meadows@yahoo.com

www.ingramcontent.com/pod-product-compliance
Lightning Source LLC
Chambersburg PA
CBHW050028030726
47506CB00001B/176